BEFORE THE ANIMATION BEGINS

Gouache for Alice in Wonderland *by Mary Blair, 1951.*

Other Books by John Canemaker

The Animated Raggedy Ann and Andy (1977)

Winsor McCay—His Life and Art (1987)

Felix: The Twisted Tale of the World's Most Famous Cat (1991)

By John Canemaker and Robert E. Abrams: Treasures of Disney Animation Art (1982)

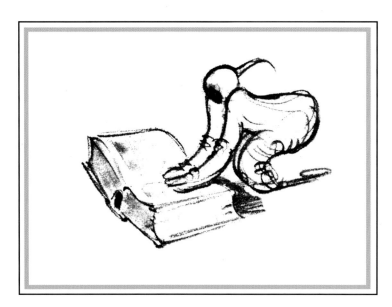

Line drawing by Albert Hurter.
OPPOSITE *Color pastel by Bianca Majolie.*

NEW YORK

BEFORE THE ANIMATION BEGINS

The Art and Lives of Disney Inspirational Sketch Artists

by JOHN CANEMAKER

Library of Congress Cataloging-In-Publication Data
Canemaker, John.
Before the animation begins : the art and lives of Disney inspirational sketch artists / John Canemaker. — 1st ed.
p.   cm.
Includes bibliographical references and index.
ISBN 0-7868-6152-5
1. Animators—United States—Psychology.   2. Creativity in art.   3. Walt Disney Company.   I. Title.
NC1766.U52D5317 1996
791.43'092'279493—dc20   95-48200
CIP

FIRST EDITION

10 9 8 7 6 5 4 3 2 1

Unless otherwise indicated, all artwork and photographs are from the Walt Disney Archives, Walt Disney Animation Research Library, Walt Disney Photo Library, and Walt Disney Imagineering Photo Library.

Book design by Holly McNeely

For Joe Grant,
who continues to inspire us all

Joe Grant, head of the Disney Character Model Department, at work on a Fantasia *hippo in 1938.*

Albert Hurter's graphite visions for the 1934 Silly Symphony
Peculiar Penguins *and an early 1930s version of a pirate for the feature*
Peter Pan, *finally released in 1953.*

Contents

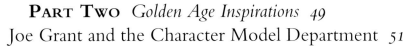

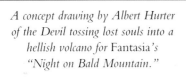

A concept drawing by Albert Hurter of the Devil tossing lost souls into a hellish volcano for Fantasia's "Night on Bald Mountain."

Deems Taylor (left), Walt Disney, and Leopold Stokowski discuss Robert Sterner's inspirational sketches for the "Rite of Spring" section of Fantasia (1940).

Introduction

Pegleg Pete orders Mickey Mouse around atop a skyscraper-to-be in an Albert Hurter idea sketch for the 1933 short Building a Building.

At the beginning of the labor-intensive processes involved in making a Walt Disney animated film—between writing a script and preparing storyboards, and long before animators turn out thousands of sequential sketches that need to be retraced, inbetweened, broken down, cleaned up, repegged, tested, inked, painted, matched to backgrounds, and photographed frame-by-frame; and prior to all the tedious, stress-filled, spirit-draining, bone-crunching assembly-line procedures that are absolutely necessary to make cartoons come alive on the silver screen—a special group of artists profoundly influence the look and content of the final film.

The "inspirational sketch" or "visual development" artists, designers, and stylists create conceptual artwork that explores the visual possibilities in a literary property. Through daydreams and doodles they attempt to "find" the film: the appearance of the characters and their relationships, the action's locale, a sequence's mood and color, costume and set designs, suggestions for the staging of scenes, gags, and a production's overall style.

Inspirational sketch artists are allowed to work with rare and unprecedented creative freedom in the assembly-line factory that is an animation studio—in a sort of "toon" version of the Eternal Dreamtime, the mythical past of aboriginal folklore that determined the conditions of life and its details. Godlike, Disney conceptualizers are encouraged to let their imaginations soar in order to conjure worlds and beings never seen before. Thoughts and words are translated into pictures so beautiful, charming and/or powerful they become inspirational fodder for the entire animation production team.

Many a hilarious sight gag in the Mickey Mouse shorts, many a lyric moment in the Silly Symphonies was born in the investigative explorations of the visual development artists. Ideas for the physical characteristics of the cast of *Snow White and the Seven Dwarfs* (1937) and their behavior originated in drawings by concept artists Albert Hurter and Ferdinand Horvath; Gustaf Tenggren's rococo detailing for settings and atmosphere found its way into *Pinocchio* (1940); preliminary art by Kay Nielsen, Sylvia Holland, Bianca Majolie, and James Bodrero defined fantasy worlds in *Fantasia* (1940), as did Mary Blair's colors and shapes for the cast and settings in *Cinderella* (1950), *Alice in Wonderland* (1951), and *Peter Pan* (1953). Tyrus Wong created an impressionistic forest for *Bambi* (1942), and, armed with a pen instead of a gun, Ken Anderson explored *The Jungle Book* (1967). Hans Bacher suggested an intimidating interior of a monster's castle in *Beauty and the Beast* (1991); and for *The Lion King* (1994), Andy Gaskill staged a ferocious battle and Chris Sanders conjured a lion's ghost.

Animation concept artists are similar to live-action production designers or art directors, as exemplified by the pioneers Walter Hall, Anton Grot, and William Cameron Menzies, on whose drawing boards were born the visual splendors of *Intolerance* (1916), *A Midsummer Night's Dream* (1935), and

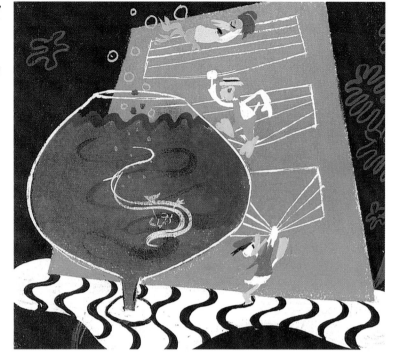

A colorful gouache by Mary Blair of Donald Duck and his South American buddies (Jose Carioca and Aracuan) for the "Blame It on the Samba" section of Melody Time *(1948).*

BELOW *Lee and Mary Blair paint Sugar Loaf Mountain in Rio de Janeiro from a balcony at the Hotel Gloria in August 1941.*

The Thief of Bagdad (1924), respectively. In 1929, Menzies offered a definition of the ideal art director that (despite the period's sexist emphasis) applies equally as well to the ideal Disney stylist (historically one of the few *creative* positions that were open to women in the male-dominated animation industry's hierarchy):

> He must have a knowledge of architecture of all periods and nationalities. He must be able to picturize and make interesting a tenement or a prison. He must be a cartoonist, a costumer, a marine painter, a designer of ships, an interior decorator, a landscape painter, a dramatist, an inventor, a historical and now acoustical expert.[1]

Disney conceptualizers also have much in common with live-action movie directors who delineate their dreams and visions in drawings on paper before committing them to film; as seen, for example, in the direct and simple doodles of Al-

An early (c. 1940) watercolor exploration by Mary Blair of a Siamese cat duo for a film project that eventually (in 1955) became Lady and the Tramp.

fred Hitchcock, Orson Welles, and Martin Scorsese, or the more decorous and accomplished designs of Akira Kurosawa, Federico Fellini, and Terry Gilliam.[2] Animation designers, however, are not limited by the realities of live-action film-making. As Bela Balazs once observed in regards to Felix the Cat: "In the world of creatures consisting only of lines the only impossible things are those which cannot be drawn."[3]

In other words, should Disney artists draw elaborate impressions of the convulsive beginnings of life on earth (as they did in *Fantasia*), or a breathtaking escape on a flying carpet through a lava-filled labyrinth (as in *Aladdin,* 1993), those images can be brought directly to the screen without compromising detail or concern about mundane things, such as costs, set and costume construction, the safety of actors and crew, natural laws, or other elements limiting the live-action designer. Anything goes in animation, and should a vision fail to garner the right response, the costs of crumbling up paper drawings and starting over are considerably less than disas-

sembling and destroying real sets and costumes, constructing new ones, firing and hiring actors, and so on.

Within the disciplines of the animation production processes, inspirational sketch artists enjoy an unusual amount of creative freedom. They are "not supposed to concern themselves with the details of making the picture," note veteran animators Frank Thomas and Ollie Johnston, the better to "create a way of visualizing the whole concept so that it would be attractive and fresh and establish an integrity of design for both characters and locales."[4]

Using soft pastel or charcoal, gouache, watercolor or oil paint, pen or colored pencil, and marking any size, shape, or type of surface that is comfortable, they create new worlds, new characters, and new entertainment possibilities *in their own individualistic graphic styles.* By contrast, animators enter late in the production process and must conform their drawings (rendered only in pencil) to approved character designs and layouts. They sacrifice their personal drawing styles so that the

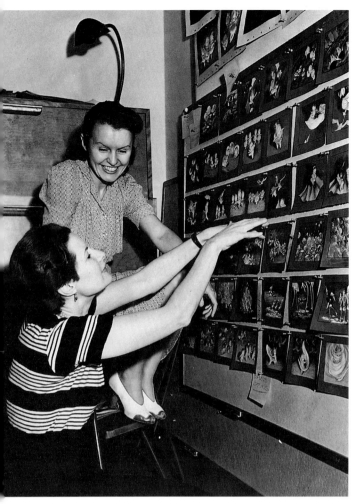

Sylvia Holland gesticulates to the delight of her assistant, Ethel Kulsar, in 1940 before a storyboard of their sketches for "Baby Ballet," a proposed section for a future version of Fantasia.

RIGHT *Famed children's book illustrator Kay Nielsen's painting of Disney's version of the "Rite of Spring." Mike Glad Collection.*

work of many hands appears to be that of one.

While concept drawings can be pure improvisational flights of fancy, many are based on extensive research into (and borrowing from) all kinds of specialized areas and disciplines, including the fine and applied arts, history, architecture, science, photography, cinema, dance, and mechanics, among others. "Now it is all very easy to talk casually about armor and preparations to enter a tourney; but when one puts armor and tourneys upon the screen, he must know exactly what these things are and just how it feels to be enshrouded in cumbersome hardware," wrote Harvard art professor Robert D. Feild in an early scholarly study of Disney production methods. "If he is ever to throw one down, Mickey [Mouse] must know what a gauntlet looks like, and if he is to rescue Minnie from a battlemented keep, he must understand portcullises and draw bridges lest he find himself

at a disadvantage. Somebody must find all this out for him."[5] Who those "somebodies" were and are is the concern of this book, which covers over sixty years of Disney conceptual art and artists, starting in the early 1930s with Albert Hurter up to the present group, imagining and sketching present and future Disney.

Over the years, public attention has rightly focused on Disney's animators, those extraordinary "actors with a pencil" who redefined personality animation as an art form.[6] But celebration and study of the unsung visual development artists and their work is long overdue. Like Yin and Yang, or dyadic parents who share and combine differing functions,[7] conceptualizers and animators are *both* creators who need each other—one to conceive ideas that the other brings to vital life.

The inspirational sketch artists provide a direct interface between the animated film and the graphic arts; historically, most arrived at Disney with academic training in painting and drawing, or with established reputations in periodical and book illustration, or gallery exhibition credentials. In the 1930s, their ability to draw whatever they could dream up, no matter how complex, was a major reason why Disney's animated films achieved such a high degree of visual/narrative richness and sophistication in less than a decade.

Carefully preserved at the Walt Disney Archives and the Walt Disney Feature Animation Research Library in Los Angeles, and in private collections around the world, are thousands of art works that were never meant to be seen by the general public. They were intended only as graphic sparkplugs to ignite the imaginations of Disney storytellers, directors, and animators, and most important, Walt Disney himself. (Herein and throughout, in order to distinguish the man from the studio and the corporate entity, Mr. Disney will be referred to by his first name.)

Walt and his artists, duly inspired, ran with the ideas contained in the concept drawings, altered and fleshed them out, and guided them toward their ultimate destination on the silver screen. Concept sketches—like mayflies who are born, mate, and die in a single day—are a necessary but disposable element in a voracious creative process. However, a great deal of these profoundly functional pieces stand on their own as art and are worthy of a lengthy look.

To gain deeper understanding of the how and why of Disney animated film masterworks (and Disney style itself), it is revealing to know the artists who created it in the context of the Disney organization. Intelligent, often fiercely individualistic and highly creative, their compelling stories bring a human face to an often anonymous process and product. How fascinating and informative it would be if we could know the individual artisans and artists who contributed to the making of Chartres or the pyramids, or were part of Renaissance workshops, or other group efforts that produced great art.

Many arrived at Disney in need of work during the Depression; some looked down on the medium of animation, or found it difficult to be part of a group, or hated to see their ideas changed. The tenure of some was brief, while others thrived happily at the studio for decades and saw animation as the most significant art form of the century. Some succumbed to personal problems or office politics; others survived despite

Charles Christadoro sculpts a maquette of Stromboli, the evil puppet master in Pinocchio.

them. Three women artists profiled were pioneers in a male-dominated industry, and all three struggled against perceptions of (and resentments against) working women. Today's new generation of conceptualizers are supported both by the work of the past and by a computer technology that promises to make anything they can dream come true. Still, the challenge of visualization and the raw creative process itself—to come up with, as one artist terms it, "an idea drawing"[8]—is common to all the artists, past and present. Despite differing attitudes and approaches to working at Disney, each made valuable contributions to the films and all created extraordinary drawings.

And revealed in the drawings are the complex layers of eclectic stylistic influences found in the Disney films—from European fine art and turn-of-the-century illustrated picture books, to twentieth-century illustration art, as well as elements of abstraction, surrealism, and live-action cinema. Ironically, this modernist hodgepodge of visual influences from an international array of high and low art sources melds into a style that is recognizable around the world as an icon of American culture.

Ultimately, the lives of the inspirational sketch artists and the art they produced act as a prism through which one may gain a better understanding of the enigmatic Walt Disney, his special genius and essential role in the scheme of things.

TOADY
EMOTES,

The Squire of Toad Hall (from the 1949 feature The Adventures of Ichabod and Mr. Toad) *hams it up in lively drawings by James Bodrero.*

PART ONE
Early Inspirations

The entire staff of the Walt Disney Studio in the summer of 1932 assembles on the Hyperion Avenue studio lawn in Hollywood to celebrate the fourth birthday of Mickey Mouse. Roy Disney is to the left of the Mickey Mouse doll, Walt to the right.

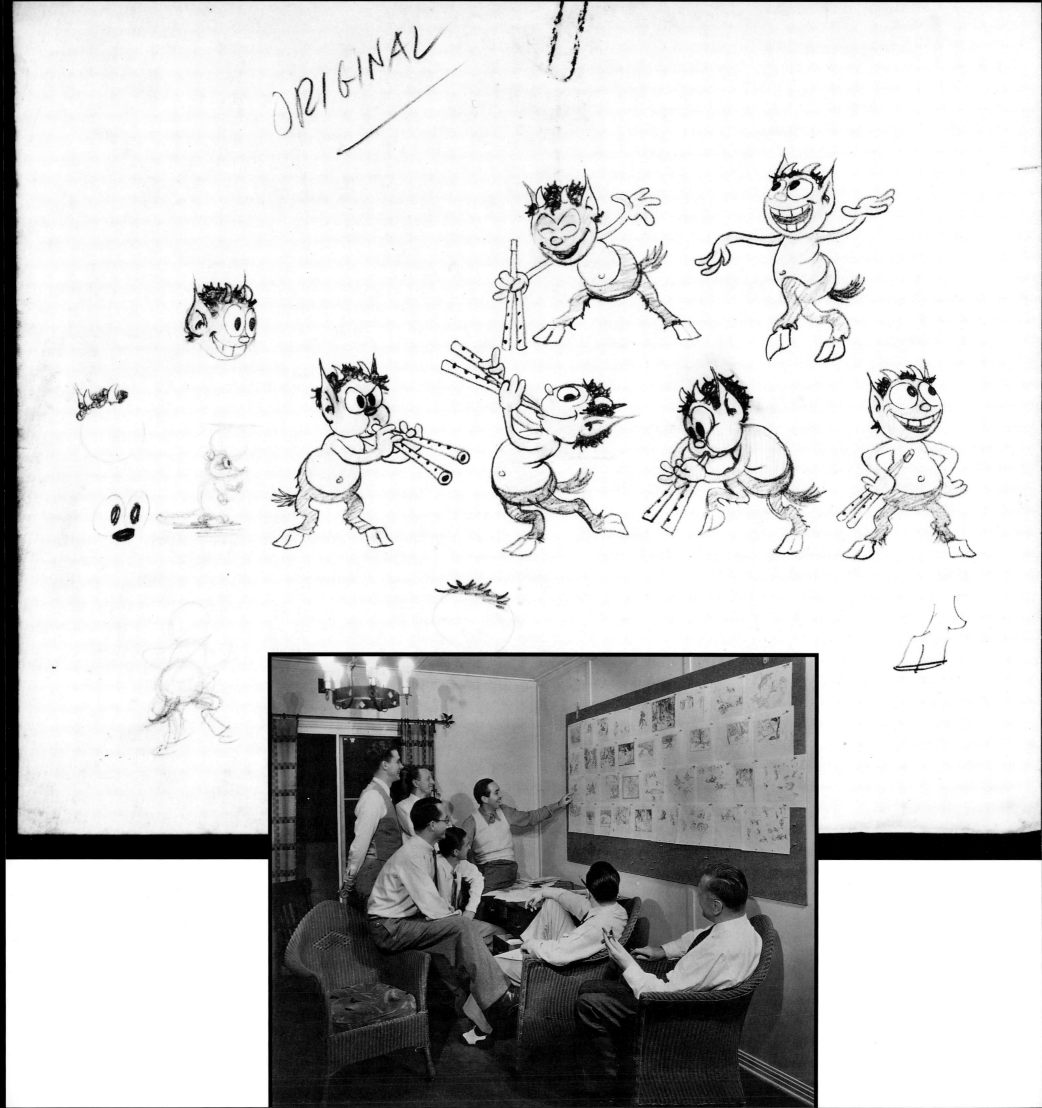

CHAPTER 1

Seeking Inspiration

In 1931, the Walt Disney Studio was on the cusp of unprecedented physical and creative expansion. Only three years before, a clever cartoon with an innovative soundtrack called *Steamboat Willie* (1928) put both Walt and Mickey Mouse on the map. International demand for the wildly popular mouse quickly swelled Disney's staff from half a dozen to about 120. In 1931, twelve Mickey Mouse shorts were produced, as well as ten Silly Symphonies, a series Walt began in 1929 to further distinguish his product line from competitors, and to experiment with music, design, animation, and technology. *Flowers and Trees,* for example, a Silly Symphony released in 1932, was the first cartoon to use three-toned Technicolor and to win an Academy Award.

Walt's vision of animation crystallized during this time and he became increasingly ambitious. "Disney had shaped his aesthetics in vague, unintended, and even ambiguous ways," writes Steven Watts in a forthcoming book *The Magic Kingdom: Walt Disney and Modern American Culture.* "An enormously gifted entertainer in search of laughs, innovations, and sales, he stumbled into the arena of modernist art by the 1930s and became an experimenter with its forms and techniques.

A model sheet for the 1930 Silly Symphony Playful Pan *displays the limitations in draftsmanship and expressiveness of the "rubber hose and circle" school of cartoon animation. Courtesy Christie's East.*

INSET *A late-night story conference in 1933 with Walt pointing out and admiring a drawing for* Grasshopper and the Ants *(1934) by Albert Hurter, seated far right.*

His true artistic heart, however, continued to beat to an internal rhythm of nineteenth-century sentimental realism."

According to Watts:

Modernist impulses flowered everywhere in Disney's world of fantasy as his animation constantly blurred the line between imagination and reality to produce a wondrous universe where animals spoke, plants and trees acted consciously, and inanimate objects felt emotion. A preoccupation with the dream state in Disney's early films likewise triggered a fusion of intellect and emotion, superego and id as warm fairy tales often encapsulated dark, nightmarish visions. And throughout the films there occurred a consistent blending of "high" and "low" cultural forms, a process that produced a vibrant artistic whole. This engagement of modernism may have developed unintendedly, even unconsciously, but it became an important part of the Disney appeal.[1]

He wanted a "caricature of realism," according to animators Frank Thomas and Ollie Johnston. "He could be endlessly innovative, exploring all facets of the entertainment world, as long as he remembered always to captivate the audience by making it all believable—by making it real."[2]

In the early 1920s when Walt lived in Kansas City, he was merely "a talented craftsman working safely within the

3

prescribed limits of comic animation defined by others," a filmmaker who exhibited "not so much a struggle for artistic expression as . . . a fight for commercial stability," note film historians J. B. Kaufman and Russell Merritt.[3] After moving to Hollywood in 1923 and producing two series (Alice Comedies and Oswald the Lucky Rabbit), he wanted (and needed) to make his films different from the competition. Personality animation, he decided, was the way: "I want the characters to be somebody," he demanded of his animators in 1927, a year before Mickey Mouse's debut. "I don't want them to be just a drawing."

How to make a cartoon real? At first, he brought characters *literally* closer to audiences. Piet Mondrian attached paintings atop, rather than within, the frame in order to make the experience of the painting more immediate and "real" to the viewer. Walt Disney, hoping to provide an intimate and real experience, swung or sprung spiders and skeletons from the distance to in-your-face close-ups, and various body parts (udders, groins, and buttocks) loomed up and overtook moviegoers. Audiences often held the driver's point of view in a car speeding crazily down a street or an out-of-control aircraft headed toward earth the hard way.

For the Oswald series, Disney and his staff made a "conscious decision to move towards the stylistic conventions of live-action films."[4] Through intense study of Buster Keaton, Charlie Chaplin, Harold Lloyd, Laurel and Hardy, Lon Chaney, and Douglas Fairbanks, Sr., they learned a *live-action* (rather than a cartoon) way to cross-cut and stage scenes clearly, to time and build gags, or use shadows for expressionistic effect. Gags now originated in a character's personality, so humor became situational rather than scattershot.

Personality animation was successfully explored years before by the great Winsor McCay (1867–1934) in *Gertie the Dinosaur,* a 1914 film cartoon whose believability was greatly aided by solid, detailed draftsmanship, and whose naturalistic timing, "closed forms and trompe l'oeil illusionism,"[5] and personality animation predicted the mature work of the Disney Studio twenty years in the future. McCay made a limited number of films and the studio cartoonists who followed him (including Walt's) did not possess McCay's skillful draftsmanship. Their drawing ability was limited to simple circles for heads and bodies and "rubber hoses" for limbs, as personified by the most popular toon star of the 1920s, Felix the Cat. Basically, ear shapes distinguished one round character from another; remove pointed ears and add two oblong ones and Felix became a Rabbit named Oswald; substitute two round circles, and Oswald begat a mouse named Mickey.

Walt knew instinctively that the tyranny of the circle and rubber-hose template must be replaced by expressive and complex drawings in order to caricature reality. Most of the experienced animators he was recruiting from the east and newcomers he hired in Los Angeles were clever but limited cartoonists, untrained in academic art. There were, however, exceptional talents even among the untrained: Fred Moore, for example, a California kid who showed up one day at the studio with charming drawings on butcher's paper, and Norman Ferguson, a former New York accountant. While both lacked formal artistic training, each had a natural gift for animation—Moore's insouciant drawings were full of visual appeal and rhythm, and Ferguson's characters' pantomimic actions implied they had a cartoon brain. "Through their innovative work," notes Steven Watts, "these two young artists became aesthetic trailblazers for the Disney Studio during this intensely creative age."[6]

For most of the new Disney employees, though, education was the key. As early as 1929 Walt made a deal with Mrs. Nelbert Chouinard, founder of the Chouinard Art Institute in Los Angeles, to accept his animators into night classes. The "youngsters," as Walt (who was all of twenty-eight himself) called them, "didn't have cars to get down. I'd leave [the studio to drive them] and come back and work at the studio myself. And then I'd go down and pick 'em up and bring 'em home. Distribute 'em." "For most of the school year 1931 to 32," said Chouinard instructor Donald Graham, "I worked one night a week with about fifteen Disney men in my regular class. Walt, of course, picked up the tab." Eventually, Walt hired Graham away from Chouinard to head a night art school on the Disney studio premises from 1932 to 1941.[7] In the mid-thirties when *Snow White* was gearing up, Graham began to recruit skilled draftsmen with college and art school backgrounds from all over the country.

More expressive drawings helped to create believably "real" personalities, which in turn affected the narrative vehicles they appeared in. "One of the important steps was taken in 1931 when [Walt] began the story department." wrote Bob Thomas, Disney's official biographer. "He placed Ted Sears in charge and told him: 'If we're going to get better stories, we'll have to split the responsibilities of the story workers and the artists. From now on, I want you to concentrate on developing stories.' "[8] In the old silent days in New York, film subjects were chosen by the animators: "We all helped. We'd spend an evening talking about it," recalled animator Richard Huemer about working for producers Raoul Barre and Max Fleischer. " 'Let's do a Hawaiian picture.' 'Fine. I'll do the surf stuff, you do the cannibals.' " Each animator was "given a portion of the picture, over a very rough scenario. Very, Very sketchy, no [story]boards like we have today, nothing like that," said Huemer. "The scenario would probably be on a

4

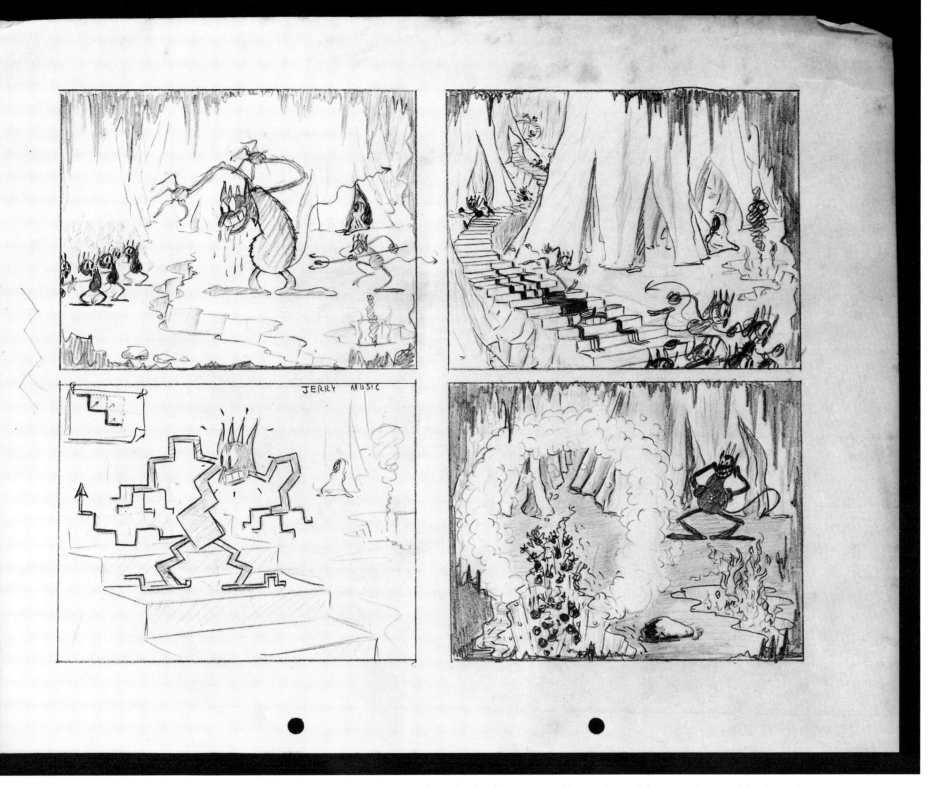

Proto-inspirational sketches from Hell's Bells, *a 1929 Silly Symphony, are rigidly confined within comic strip-like panels—and the artist's drawing ability limits the performance to broad cartoon gags. Courtesy Christie's East.*

single sheet of paper, without any models, sketches, or anything. You made it up as you went along."[9]

Walt reorganized and streamlined his studio's production system by dividing tasks into discrete units and nurturing specialization within them. Productivity increased, as did creativity. The modern storyboard evolved in the Disney story department; prior to that rigid panels similar to comic strips held continuity sketches. By the simple expediency of pinning each drawing sequentially on cork boards (known as "hangin' out the wash"),[10] the narrative flow was seen easily and changes expeditiously made. Ben Sharpsteen, Disney's first production manager, observed that "Walt recognized the value of personality animation and he stressed it in story development."[11]

As to the stories that interested Walt Disney—child of the

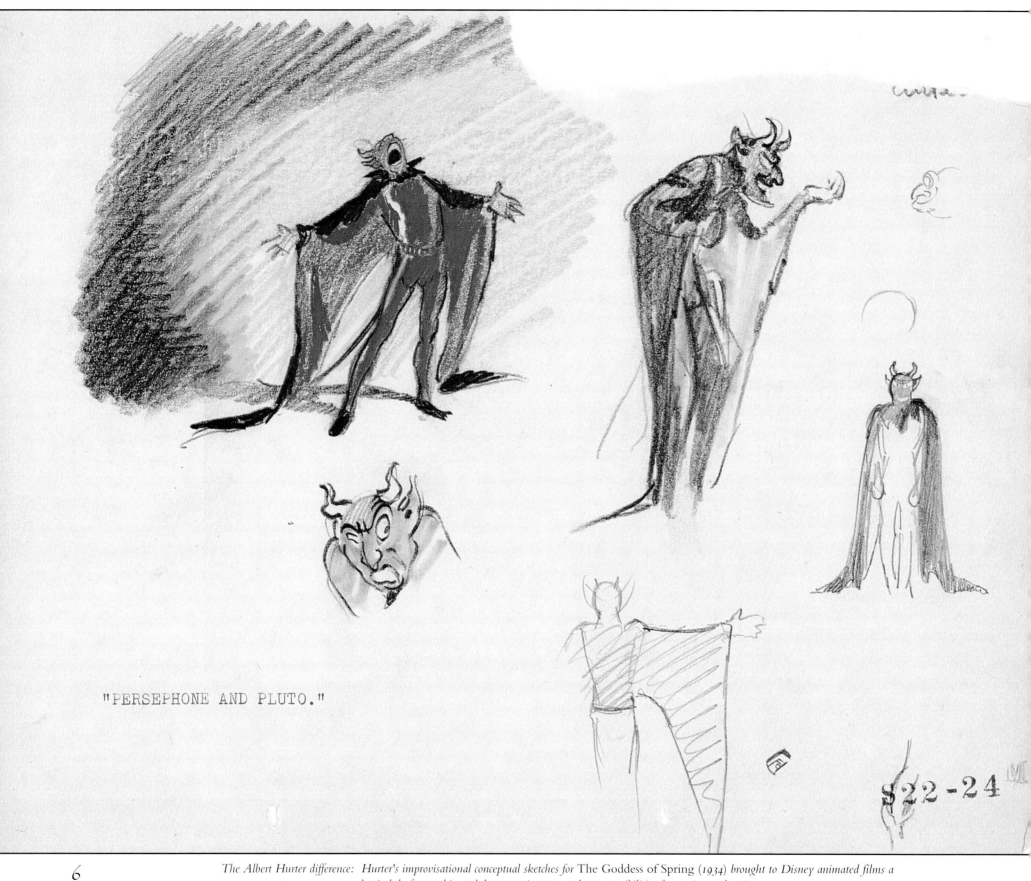

"PERSEPHONE AND PLUTO."

The Albert Hurter difference: Hurter's improvisational conceptual sketches for The Goddess of Spring (1934) *brought to Disney animated films a classical draftsmanship, subtle expressiveness, and new possibilities for staging and acting.*

American Midwest, born in Chicago, Illinois, in 1901 and raised in Marceline and Kansas City, Missouri—those came primarily from Europe. Robin Allan, in his doctoral thesis *Walt Disney and Europe: European Influences on the Animated Fea-* *ture Films of Walt Disney,* explores how Disney "was a master of technological and cultural manipulation, taking stories and characters and style and mood and themes from Europe, and recreating them in animated form."[12]

The importance of Europe, and in particular Germany, as a cultural heritage for the new Americans of the Midwest cannot be overemphasized. At the turn of the century more than twenty-seven percent of Americans were of German stock, with at least one parent born in the old country. They came from all parts of Germany and settled in the Midwest . . . another influx took place in the late twenties and throughout the thirties which in turn affected Disney's work in the late thirties and forties.[13]

Allan notes that the "fairy tale and European folk tale had been used in some of the Mickey Mouse shorts . . . but the exploitation of European sources developed with the *Sillies*" where "references to European popular illustration and entertainment are numerous."[14]

Those illustrative references became major stylistic motifs in the features *Snow White* and *Pinocchio* (both adapted from European literary sources), and can be directly attributed to Albert Hurter, an artist who arrived at the studio in 1931 with "a cigar in his left hand, a magic wand in his right."[15] Walt immediately saw in the academically trained, older artist a conduit for his vision of animation as believable, personality-driven storybook illustrations come to life. Hurter's imagination overflowed with humorous fantasy ideas in gothic, grotesque, and baroque drawings that were designed with "a Black Forest approach . . . a German approach."[16] Hurter's artwork pleased Walt enormously; equally important, it inspired him and the rest of the studio artists, and so had a profound effect on both Disney films and Disney style.

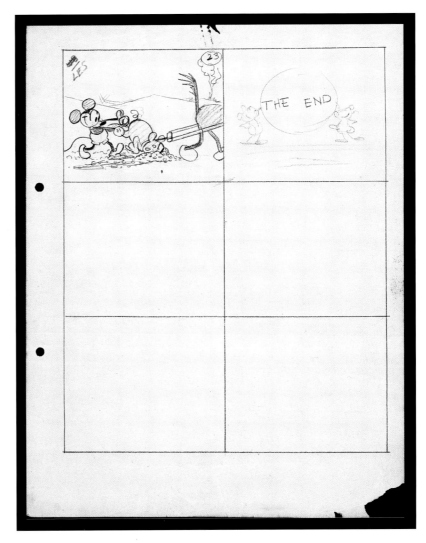

Good-bye to all that: the final panel from the storyboard for the eighth Mickey Mouse short, The Plow Boy *(1929). Albert Hurter's imagination and artistic skills would soon move Disney animation beyond simply drawn crude gags into a new era of creativity. Courtesy Christie's East.*

Albert Hurter

Albert Hurter turned forty-eight two weeks before joining the Walt Disney Studio on June 1, 1931. At the bustling home of Mickey Mouse on Hyperion Avenue in Hollywood, where most of the staff was in their twenties and the boss himself was only twenty-nine, Hurter was considered to be an old man.

He was hired as an animator, although it had been almost fifteen years since he had been the best animator at Barre-Bowers, located in the Fordham section of the Bronx in New York City. That studio, organized in 1913 by Canadian painter Raoul Barre (1874–1932), was the first to produce a *series* of animated shorts. Prior to that, film producer James Stuart Blackton (1895–1941), and two animation geniuses—Emile Cohl (1857–1938) and Winsor McCay—independently experimented with the medium, and each turned out a limited number of films by themselves. Barre hired a staff and devised assembly-line methods to increase the number of films produced; it was the start of animation as an industry. In 1916, the year Hurter joined the studio, Barre formed a partnership

ABOVE *Pinocchio and friend.*
OPPOSITE CLOCKWISE *A hungry* Peter Pan *pirate, circa 1939; a suggestion for a panoramic scene of the Dwarfs' march; Albert Hurter, circa 1934; a Hurter doodle of a glove-about-town; a helpful fire hydrant; a multi-trunk elephant; cavorting imps for* The Goddess of Spring.

with cartoonist Charles Bowers (1889–1946) to produce a series of Mutt & Jeff shorts based on Bud Fisher's popular comic strip.

Animation was becoming a viable and profitable business, although the state of the art was decidedly primitive. As stated, most animators at the time were cartoonists with little (or no) formal art training who learned their craft on the job. Hurter, however, was an excellent draftsman whose skills were honed through years of study and drawing from the live model. A Swiss immigrant, Hurter brought to his animation an extensive background of fine arts training and study in Europe. He was, according to fellow animator I. Klein, Barre-Bower's "only real artist."[1]

Hurter's ability to analyze action led to isolated animation bits—special effects—that astonished his peers. Animator Richard Huemer, who "sat at the same bench in Fordham," once recalled a particularly difficult Hurter assignment: an American flag unfurling in the wind. Instead of taking an easy way out by, say, using three or four drawings crudely flapping repeatedly back and forth, Hurter "looked out a window, saw a flag, and, wonder of wonders, he actually copied the movement. Studied it and copied it! Something which nobody had done before . . . he analyzed the action and its folds . . . And

9

when this scene came out we just thought, 'This is the end! The living end! This is the greatest!' "[2]

"I soon learned to accept Albert as the authority on art," recalled I. Klein. "His description of the vivid colors of Van Gogh's paintings, accompanied by lightning sketches of the compositions, was enlightening. So were such sketches dashed off on the art of the German penman-draftsman Heinrich Kley (1863–1945)," an artist who strongly influenced Hurter's drawing style.[3] Each day Hurter "quietly settled down to the task of turning out his fifty to one hundred drawings . . . in a smooth and methodical manner that Barre and the staff considered nothing short of phenomenal."[4]

The threadbare loft studio had no clock, but employees knew exactly when it was lunch time or quitting time by watching Hurter, who, like a human Swiss timepiece, "would look at his watch, put it back in his vest pocket, reach for his hat and coat and head for the door. Then a scrapping of chairs, shuffling of feet and the studio would be emptied."[5]

Hurter's tenure at Barre-Bower ended in an odd way. In 1918, for a World War I–themed cartoon, Hurter designed and animated the German Kaiser's spies setting up a fake peace conference using dummy figures representing President Wilson, Lloyd George, Clemenceau, and others. When Mutt & Jeff discover the ruse, they knock the fake heads off with large clubs. The realistic design and animation were successful, a feat that only Hurter could have accomplished at that time and place. But some of his co-workers teased the immigrant artist, who spoke with a soft mittel-European accent: "Albert, you might get into great trouble with our government knocking off the heads of all them Allied leaders . . . will you be able to convince the police you are not an enemy German alien?"[6] Hurter became visibly upset ("Go away . . . those were wax dummies I animated . . . not real people. I know you are making jokes with me."). Several days later, "on a work-day at ten in the morning," I. Klein passed through Grand Central Station on a studio errand and was startled to hear Albert Hurter call to him. Surrounded by suitcases, he asked Klein, "Do you know what happened?" as he unfolded an accordionlike string of tickets to the floor. "I am going to California now. I sat up all night thinking should I go or not. I decided I should." The "irreplaceable" Hurter's unexpected departure left his studio boss "thunderstruck," and the staff concluded Hurter "ran scared" because of the teasing he received. "Unpredictable things happen to some people's thinking during war hysteria," Klein concluded.

Hurter wandered into designing "fashions, furniture, stained-glass windows and . . . advertising art,"[7] and traveled toward Mexico and the Southwest. He never married, and in the late 1920s was living in one room in the old Hotel West-minster in a seedy section of downtown Los Angeles, illustrating a printing company's direct mail advertising,[8] and occasionally "turning his hand to bits of animation for Hollywood producers."[9] Ted Sears, head of Disney's fledgling story department, knew Hurter from Barre-Bower and it is likely he brought the tall, gentle man with the graying mustache and owl-like glasses to Disney.

Hurter's animation skills were now considered out-of-fashion. "His animation was all right for Mutt & Jeff, but it wouldn't have done for the then-prevailing style," said Richard Huemer, referring to Disney's primary interest in personality animation, which was never Hurter's forte.[10] What saved Hurter from being relegated to being an "inbetweener" (an animator's assistant who makes drawings between the main poses) or a special effects animator (who draws forces of nature, such as rain, smoke, snow, or flags waving), or, indeed, from being fired, was Walt Disney noticing that Hurter's "outstanding ability lay in humorous exaggeration and the humanizing of objects."[11]

Walt was, as Sears put it, "the first cartoon producer to appreciate the special talents of the individual artist and allow him to concentrate upon the thing he did best." The strange, inventive, often surprising fantasy drawings in Hurter's portfolio delighted Walt, who saw in them entertainment potential. Hurter was assigned to Sear's three-man story department, which included ex-circus clown Lance (Pinto) Colvig and ex-newspaper cartoonist Webb Smith. When each new project was proposed, "Albert was consulted and given free rein to let his imagination wander, creating strange animals, plants, scenery, or costumes that might serve as models for the forthcoming production . . . Disney had found the ideal outlet for Albert's talents."[12]

Thus, in an almost casual way, Hurter became the Disney studio's first inspirational sketch artist. "The word 'inspiration' sums up why he was there," said layout artist A. Kendall O'Connor. "Walt felt he was an inspired artist who could inspire others."[13] Throughout the 1930s, Hurter more than justified Walt's faith in his abilities. His fecund imagination and restless pencil yielded an amazing amount of visual suggestions for Mickey Mouse and Silly Symphony shorts and Disney's earliest features that more often than not ended up in the final films.

Confident in his technique, Hurter would sit quietly all day smoking cigars ("Albert Hurter smoked more than any man I've ever seen," said a colleague. "His ashtrays were always full."),[14] drawing action scenes as well as somber ones, costumes, settings and props, gags, whimsical character designs, and (most important to Walt) personalities.

Three drawings from the many Hurter drew for the 1935

Albert Hurter searches for the hero of Music Land *(1935), a saxophone man.*

Silly Symphony *Music Land* (about a war between jazz and classical music) serve to demonstrate his special gift. On one page he explores both the shape and identity of a saxophone man; in facile, sassy lines, facial features and limbs are placed on the musical instrument's conical bore. What might sax man look like, asks Hurter's drawing, when he is young and fresh, old and lumpy, or giddily inebriated? On another page, Hurter tries a mood sketch of the little sax man plaintively looking toward freedom from behind a barred window inside a metronome-prison; light streams in illuminating a sheet of paper containing blank music staffs on which our hero will literally write a musical note to "orchestrate" his escape. The odd shape of the drawing indicates it served a dual purpose: as inspirational sketch *and* rough camera layout, suggesting to the director how the action might move from window to desk and

lend variety to the staging; in a third *Music Land* drawing, Hurter metamorphoses sax man's habitat into a fanciful musical instrument–shaped apartment house rivaling and predating by decades the heightened identity of ordinary objects by Claes Oldenburg. Hurter, who never wrote or (as far as is known) spoke about his artistic philosophy, would undoubtedly have agreed with a 1966 Oldenburg statement that "[m]anmade things do look like human beings, symmetrical, visagelike, bodylike. Man wants his own image, or simply doesn't know any other way."[15] In only three drawings, Hurter offered valuable ideas for visualizing a personality, a setting, a mood, direction, and camera moves.

During his decade at the Disney Studio, Hurter significantly raised the artistic standards there. His European academic art training and prideful accuracy in rendering details lent

11

his most fanciful and outrageously quirky suggestions a bedrock veracity. Among the hundreds of nightmarish creatures Hurter made believable is a monster dog holding within its muzzle two other dogs (fore and aft), and an elephant with multiple trunks fitted with grasping hands.

Familiar with—and in the great tradition of—the anthropomorphic fantasies of Heinrich Kley and Jean-Ignace-Isadore Grandville (1803–1847), Hurter made perfectly plausible a fire hydrant using its own hose to happily douse a blaze; or flora that became functional instruments in the hands of a bug orchestra (originally considered and rejected for *Fantasia*). Antic Arctic penguins—anatomically correct yet full of a cartoony consciousness—slip, dive, slide and, in one sketch, boogie together as if auditioning for roles in the 1934 Silly Symphony *Peculiar Penguins*.

Hurter's work on the feature *Snow White and the Seven Dwarfs* surpassed his imaginative explorations for the short films. His mark is on every major sequence, from the comic to the melodramatic: from the dwarfs marching home after work—drawings that dynamically relate the little men to their

Jailed inside a metronome prison, saxophone man contemplates freedom. Jeff Lotman Collection.

A pre-Oldenburgian habitat by Albert Hurter—a place where saxophone folk might reside in Music Land.

12

ALBERT

A typical Hurter sketchbook page, full of ferocious imaginings, including multiple mutts within the maw of a single mongrel.

A Hurter meditation: graphic suggestions on how to prevent the Dwarf Sneezy's nasal explosions.

13

*Ideas for the Dwarfs'
ride to rescue Snow
White includes a
couple of brave
rabbits.*

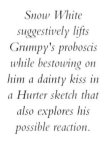

*Snow White
suggestively lifts
Grumpy's proboscis
while bestowing on
him a dainty kiss in
a Hurter sketch that
also explores his
possible reaction.*

14

natural surroundings—to a page suggesting how to tie Sneezy's beard to prevent further nasal explosions; from dwarfs awkwardly riding deer to Snow White's rescue to Snow White daintily (and suggestively) repositioning Grumpy's long proboscis while planting a kiss on him.

One sequence in the film became a breakthrough in the art of personality animation: the seven dwarfs grieving around Snow White's bier. It was Walt's hope (and gamble) that audiences would accept as sincere and believable the emotions expressed by cartoon characters mourning the "death" of another toon. But what if, instead of crying, audiences laughed? Hurter's relentless search in his drawings for the right poses, expressions, and staging helped lead the right animator (Frank Thomas) to success. By placing more than one character on a single sheet of paper, Hurter finds spatial, size, and emotional relationships. In the drawing of the dwarfs weeping over Snow White's body, the mood reads immediately. A funereal feeling is expressed in shadows that surround and threaten to overtake the light, and in contrasting a horizontal, inert princess, with vertical, alive dwarfs, each of whom are experiencing the classic stages of shock: denial, anger, disbelief, and resignation.

It is reasonable to assume that Hurter's encyclopedic knowledge of art and artists came to his aid. Perhaps, in this case, he thought of Giotto, whose expressions of human emotions in his paintings had a believability never seen before in Western art—as in *The Lamentation* (c.1306–13), a work whose composition, mood, and cluster of figures expressing grief Hurter would have found useful.

Hurter gives physical objects in his drawings a symbolic relationship to the characters: a solid and rough-hewn dwarf seems part of the dark wooden column he weeps against, almost a physical component of the cottage he and the others built; light emanates from candles above Snow White's head, but also from the deceased young woman, herself a radiant vessel whose fragile, lovely flame was snuffed too soon.

This one inspiring drawing offers an animation director, a story sketch person, a layout artist, and an animator a host of ideas for emotional cinematic scenes. Among the possibilities: shall we open with a wide-shot, as Hurter has drawn it, then slowly move the camera in on Snow White? Or what if we start on the flickering candles, pan down to take in Snow White and finally the dwarfs surrounding her? How long do we stay with this shot before cutting to a series of close-ups of the mourning dwarfs? And how should *they* look?

Hurter anticipated the last question by sketching nearly a dozen drawings of the little men in various sad poses and attitudes. He must have asked himself, What is the most effective way for the dwarfs to express sensitive emotions? Is it

better to show one of them in three-quarter view covering his eyes? Is that the strongest statement of "sad"? Or does a straight-on shot with tears flowing look convincing? Or is it (heaven forbid) funny? Maybe it's best if one dwarf places his hand on another for support. Does that say "vulnerable" enough?

Animator Frank Thomas, whose superb timing and dramatic sensibility brought the sequence to life on the screen, acknowledged the support of the inspirational sketches: "Of course you always have help. Someone in story-sketch will make a lot of drawings . . . getting the essence of the character. If it was sad, he'd make twelve drawings of a sad guy. You'd only use one in your scene, but you're 90 percent there."[16] As more than one of his co-workers said of Hurter, there was "Nobody like him, ever, *nobody!*"[17]

But who was Albert Hurter? "He never talked about the past," said designer Joe Grant, who once shared an office with Hurter at Disney, but found "questioning him [about his private life] was out of the question."[18] "He was a totally un-Disneylike person. He was a big shambling Swiss. A very difficult man to know. I think he was always an outsider at the studio," said designer Martin Provensen.[19]

Anecdotes abound about Hurter's eccentricities: his methodical work habits, his extreme punctuality, his solitary weekend drives to the California desert and neighboring states, his constant cigars, his aloneness, his stamp collecting, his candid assessments of colleagues' work offered with "an honesty so naive that it was often mistaken for lack of tact." The latter is best illustrated by the story of a young artist who asked Hurter to critique a much-labored-over perspective drawing: "Don't spare my feelings. Just tell me if there's anything wrong with this," said the youngster, to which Hurter solemnly remarked, "Nothing is right with this."[20]

Some, like Thomas, thought Hurter "a pompous talker" who'd "talk an arm off of you. You ask him what time it is and you end up learning how to build a watch or a cuckoo clock!"[21] Others, such as O'Connor, found Hurter "solemn, despite his witty imagination for grotesque gags . . . I never heard him burst into laughter."[22] Sequence director William Cottrell saw him as "very much a loner . . . I think he was quite a lonely person." Cottrell is not sure that even Walt Disney "knew how to handle Albert."[23] Walt implied as much years after Hurter's death, speaking about "[t]hat impenetrable mind of his [that] was never easily figured out, but he was a most lovable character when you knew him."[24]

But no one *really* knew Hurter; his privateness was a wall that few attempted to scale. Disney employment records do not even have his birth date or date of death

15

OPPOSITE *Albert Hurter's emotionally evocative inspirational sketch of the Dwarfs grieving over Snow White found its way almost intact into the final film.*

ABOVE *Examples of Hurter's relentless visual explorations of an individual Dwarf's grief and sorrow upon the death of Snow White.*

LEFT *Hungry vultures hover as the Seven Dwarfs watch the wicked Queen fall to her death.*

17

and burial. In researching this book, however, new information has surfaced regarding Hurter's background that sheds light on this unique animation artist's background, personality, and "eccentricities."[25]

Albert Hurter was born on May 11, 1883, in Zurich, Switzerland. Nine months before, on August 8, 1882, his Swiss father, Albert, a thirty-year old mechanic, married Maria Schmid, a German woman seven years his junior. Two more boys eventually completed the family: Hugo born in 1884, and Ernst in 1890.

In 1889, the family moved from Zurich's working-class industrial quarter, known as Kreis 5 (Chreis Chaib), to the quieter Unterstrass just the other side of the river Limmat. They moved twice more in the same area before finally, in 1894, buying a small two-story row house at Gallusgasse ("alley street") 23. By this time, Albert Sr. had a new profession: Zeichenlehrer, a drawing teacher of mechanical engineering at the Berufsschule, a Zurich professional school. There students learned to become mechanics by working four days a week on the job and going to school one day. Albert Sr. also wrote and illustrated two technical books for use in his classes.

He influenced his three sons' interest in art and mechanics: both Albert Jr. and Hugo became Zeichners ("drawers/artists") and Ernst became an electrical engineer. Albert Jr. studied architecture in Zurich for three years, then on April 6, 1903, he left, at age nineteen, for seven years of art studies in Berlin.

Three years before leaving for Germany, however, teenaged Albert Jr. was diagnosed with rheumatic heart disease, an ailment that would eventually take his life. As a child, he must have been infected with the bacteria that causes strep throat, which led to recurrent battles with rheumatic fever and resulted in traumatizing and damaging the mitral valve in his heart.[26] Today, comments Dr. Kenneth Hirsch, "Rheumatic fever is treated by monthly shots of penicillin, but when Hurter was a child that miracle drug was not even invented." By the time he was diagnosed with valvular disease at age seventeen, he probably had suffered numerous relapses and periods of illness. Damage to the left side of the heart, which pumps blood to the rest of the body, may cause the patient to exhibit weakness, shortness of breath on exertion, and other symptoms.

It is possible to hypothesize that some (if not all) of Hurter's odd behavior and solitary lifestyle can be attributed to medical problems. Given the stage medicine was at in that era, "take it easy" and "avoid strenuous activity" were the only viable "treatments" available, and such admonishments from his parents and possibly his physician could have turned Hurter into a "cardiac cripple." His parents may have been extremely protective, and he was "undoubtedly subjected to prolonged periods of being confined to home and bed rest. There were probably times when he was too physically sick to run around and lead a normal child's life."[27]

It is known that he began collecting stamps as a child,[28] a solitary hobby that became a life-long pursuit. "To collect stamps is a typically Swiss thing," says Swiss film historian and writer Peter Hossli. "Switzerland has a tradition of printing beautiful stamps, which gain in value."[29] Hurter claimed collecting stamps "teaches one a great deal about art and engraving and paper making and history and geography and . . . and . . . you know, stamp collectors."[30] The monetary value of rare stamps was not lost on Hurter who scooped up several large collections that went on the block during the Depression. "He was known to dealers and philatelists everywhere because of his integrity in trading and his keen sense of values," recalled Ted Sears. "He rejected everything but the finest specimens and handled these with meticulous care." Once, on an infrequent visit to the movies, he was shocked at seeing a newsreel in which F.D.R. held a rare stamp with his fingers, instead of tweezers. "To Albert," said Sears with tongue fully in cheek, "this innocent action constituted a form of vandalism, and his faith in the New Deal was considerably shaken."[31]

Another nonstrenuous, solo hobby that filled long hours of recuperation during his childhood was, of course, drawing. Perhaps thoughts of dying and of being different from other kids had an impact on Hurter's morbidly fanciful imagery. The stream-of-consciousness grotesques in his sketches surely originated in a sickly boy's attempt to control his nightmares by making them visible.

"Even a person with a physically mild heart ailment can suffer extreme psychological damage."[32] It is possible that Hurter's almost-comically precise and methodical habits as an adult stemmed from an abhorrence of disruptions, a need to create a life with no surprises, of keeping to a schedule that avoided stressing his heart. Hurter's all-too-mortal heart may also have affected his romantic heart, that is, his attitude toward sex and marriage. Whether he was homo- or heterosexual, he may have feared the exertion of sex. If he thought he might die at an early age, he may not have wished to marry and have children. Then again, Hurter came from a family of bachelors: Neither of his brothers married and there is even less information on their lives than there is on Albert. "The brothers didn't marry," said Hossli, "and there were no (at least officially) children. Another indication that they didn't have children is their vanished [sic] house . . . It is very unusual that a family house is . . . sold and . . . torn down if there are still relatives around. So, I believe, the Hurter [family] died out."[33]

There are only two anecdotes regarding Hurter and the opposite sex, one from animator Ward Kimball, who recalled that "an older girl" from the Disney ink and paint department, believing a rumor that Hurter had a lot of money hidden away, tried to "seduce" him by joining him for lunch in his car. "He didn't pay any attention to her. And it took a lot of nerve on her part because she was sensitive to cigar smoke."[34] Hazel George, the Disney Studio nurse, considered Hurter a typical male chauvinist who had "a European notion that no woman is worth more than two dollars."[35]

Hurter's heart condition obviously did not incapacitate him. Human beings are complex, and the will to fight against limitations rather than give in often yields unexpected results. Fragile Albert was the only one of his brothers to travel outside his home country, first to Germany, finally to America. Perhaps he tired of the overprotectedness of home and needed to try surviving on his own. It cannot yet be confirmed if he taught art or traveled to other European capitals. Because "Albert was a fragile child," opined Peter Hossli:

> maybe this was also a reason he traveled. Switzerland was still a[n] industrial country. And Albert was not able to take a very strenuous job. Maybe he was hoping [to enter] the arts abroad. He studied art and maybe architecture in Berlin. His two brothers never left Switzerland officially. They might have traveled for fun. But they never went abroad to work. They also stayed with their mother at *Gallusgasse* after Albert Sr. passed away.[36]

What is certain is that after seven years of art studies in Berlin he returned home in March 1910. Two years later, his father died at age 60. Did he return to Zurich because his father was ill? One document indicates that in 1912, the year of his father's death, Hurter came to America.[37] If true, perhaps he felt a need to strike out on his own again, knowing his mother would live out her remaining years on her husband's pension (she died in 1925), and that his younger brothers were both employed and living at home. However, a biographical sketch in a 1939 in-house Disney newspaper, the *Bulletin,* contradicts that: "Albert, who was in Paris in 1914, decided to come to America to keep out of the mess," referring to France's involvement in World War I. The official Zurich papers do not indicate that Hurter went to Paris, only that he went away. In any case, by 1916 we know he is in New York and working in animation.

After his abrupt departure from the Barre-Bower studio, Hurter apparently meandered with little energy or ambition for over a dozen years. Was this another manifestation of

Three years before his death in 1942, Albert Hurter contributed to the visual sumptuousness of Pinocchio (1940).

being careful with himself because of health problems? Was he laying low because of a paranoiac fear of deportation?

In the late twenties in Los Angeles, Hurter is the personification of an eccentric straight out of Nathaniel West: living alone in one-room in a "dump"[38] of a hotel in genteel poverty, while owning a valuable stamp collection; walking with a pronounced limp because of the cash he habitually carried in his shoe ("I do not trust some of the neighborhood people").[39] Although "always scrupulously clean in his appearance . . . his clothes had been darned, mended, and patched times beyond mention."[40] His principal support for years was drawing freelance layouts and illustrations for a printing company's direct mail ads, hardly the best use of his art training and knowledge.

Abruptly, Hurter changed the direction of his life as he had years before in New York. "One day he came in to see me," his main employer, Randolph Van Nostrand, wrote years later to Walt Disney:

> [H]e was resplendent in brand new clothes and the work of a tonsorial artist was also very apparent. He announced that he would not be able to work for me any longer; that he was going to Hollywood to get a job with Disney. I asked him how he could be sure of a job and with that calm confidence which you, too, must have known, he assured me that he would be successful. Then I asked him if he had robbed a bank. Albert confessed that each

Twisted baby
heads and
auto-cannibalism?
Hurter's imaginings
often wandered into
the macabre and
grotesque.

time I had paid him for his work he had been investing in a ticket in the Chinese lottery and that the week before he "caught" a six spot, which had paid off several thousand dollars. That was the last time I saw him.[41]

His return to animation full-time would bring new life to Hurter's heretofore undistinguished career. Finally, in middle age, he would fulfill his artistic potential in a way he never dreamed of, and, in so doing, would play a significant (if unsung) role in Disney animation's Golden Era.

To his joy, Hurter had landed in a veritable "drawing factory,"[42] where hundreds of drawings, all *kinds* of drawings were made each day. Since drawing was what he most enjoyed, he devoted himself to his new duties with intensity and seriousness of purpose. At his age and with his health condition, he must have felt there was little time to waste in order to make his mark. "Hurter was always a working fool," recalled a coworker, "interested in what the damn job was and smoking a cigar. Very conscientious, worked hard all the time."[43] Soon his "sketches were eagerly sought by the animators, model designers, gagmen, and writers. They circulated freely about the

studio, with the result that few were returned to the files. This never disturbed Albert, for he derived all of his pleasure from drawing. As soon as the creative process was over, he seemed to have little interest in the finished result."[44]

Five days a week, he arrived at his desk exactly at 8 A.M., and except for a short lunch break, sat drawing all day until 5 P.M. (On Saturdays, work ended at noon.) Bob Jones, a night-shift cameraman on *Snow White* and later a puppet maker for the Character Model Department, recalled running into Hurter sometimes at 4 A.M.:

> During my long hours on camera I had to go out on the patio at Hyperion to get a break and look at the stars. One morning I saw a cigar light up and here was this older man and he introduces himself . . . We had three months of fifteen minutes a day and we talked and hardly saw each other's faces and the tension went out of me.[45]

Hurter rarely signed his work; neither did most Disney artists, it being understood that Walt preferred it that way. But at the top of most of his drawings appeared a Hurter signature

Hurter explores a delicate fantasy world Water Babies, *a 1935 Silly Symphony.* BELOW *Hurter's gloved one: a handy doodle.*

of sorts. Tiny heads and multiple profiles sputtered out of his pencil repeatedly—a printout of his imaginings, a gearing-up perhaps, a testing of the waters, a rehearsal of the graphic scales before commitment to the *big* drawing in the center of the paper. There, witches and trolls appeared, or a page of devils, fair maidens, water babies, and dragons for the next Mickey or Silly short; or perhaps vivacious vegetables, dancing scarecrows, gory eyeballs ambulating on gloves, and other Hurteresque grotesques that would never appear in *any* film. One gruesome page holds a mechanical baby taking a knife and fork to its own disembodied head, a baby crawling with its head backassward, and a severed bleeding infant's head. (Perhaps Albert drew one-too-many cutesy kids under lily pads for *Water Babies,* 1935, that day.)

But gory oddities were part of the deal: one never knew where a gem of an idea might be found in a Hurter drawing that could inspire a scene, a sequence, perhaps an entire film. "All you'd have to do was say 'Snow White' and Albert would go from there," remembered Joe Grant. "It wasn't necessary to explain anything to him, 'cause it's what he gave to you rather than what you gave to him. The exchange was all on his side."[46]

Hurter's improvisational process brought forth the cast, costumes, and settings for the now-legendary Silly Symphony *Three Little Pigs* (1933), whose song ("Who's Afraid of the Big Bad Wolf?") became a rallying cry for millions of Americans during the Depression. His ideas for the witch and forest in

Babes in the Woods (1932), based on Grimm's *Hansel and Gretel,* and the dwarfs and virginal heroine of *Goddess of Spring* (1934), based on the myth of Persephone, are dry runs for *Snow White.* His sketches for Mickey Mouse shorts invariably contain useful suggestions for solidifying the relationships of characters familiar to audiences and for introducing new ones. Hurter showed a wilder version of the anthropomorphic steam shovel than what ended up in *Building a Building* (1933); but Minnie Mouse is there, in danger and in love as usual (her "baloney and macaroni" box lunch affecting her mouseman's heart as well as his stomach). Construction boss Pete, a burly cat, manipulates (like a mad puppeteer) hapless Minnie in mid-air, while solidly grounded Mickey's lunch is interrupted mid-pie.

Hurter brought to the attention of his Disney colleagues the art of Heinrich Kley, Herman Vogel, Gustave Doré, Franz Stuck, Honoré Daumier, and Wilhelm Busch, among others. By 1934, when he began working on preliminary ideas for *Snow White,* he had become the Studio authority on *how things should look*—from characters and costumes to settings and scenery. ("If you brought him a picture of a soldier, he might say the uniform was not right," recalled William Cottrell. "You gave six buttons, but it should have five. There is a tunic in a museum in Switzerland.")[47] David Hand, the gruff supervising director of *Snow White,* complained that other artists' drawings of rocks "are not at all like he [Walt] sees them. They are not fairyland types of stuff," and referred them to Albert who "knows the character of the picture better than anyone . . . It would be necessary for each layout man to work with Albert . . . He is to control the keying of the character throughout the picture—is that clear?"[48] Ken O'Connor corroborates the story: "Walt made all us layout men submit our drawings to Hurter for his input. His drawing was better than his English. He'd look at my drawings and say, 'Well, rocks don't go like that.' Then he'd draw his idea and it was always good."[49] "When you layout men get the rough [sketches] well built," said Hand at another meeting, "give it to Albert before the animator gets it. Then before it goes to Sam [Armstrong, head background painter], Albert gets it once more . . . Albert can make suggestions if they don't destroy gags. He dresses them up. We take them back and shoot them in for the animators. Before final coloring Albert gets them again. That keeps the key of the picture and the characters."[50]

In 1938, Hurter joined the Character Model Department, an elite group of inspirational sketch artists formed that year. Personally, Hurter's world opened a bit when he bought a Ford Model A and later a Buick. "He loved it. Greatest thing he ever had," said William Cottrell, who advised him on his car purchases. He went for long drives at 5 A.M. before coming to work, and weekends he drove into the desert for private sketching forays; for his vacations, he drove as far as Oregon and Washington. Designer John P. Miller described one Hurter vacation as "a pointless tour. He went to Arizona, and then he went to New Mexico, and then back to Arizona, and up to Nevada, and back to Arizona again. He just talked in a monotone, told me everything he had done and all that he had seen."[51]

For Disney's second feature, *Pinocchio,* Hurter was again involved in all aspects of the film's styling. His early design for the film's protagonist and his costume (including the peaked hat made "from a bit of dough")[52] was based on Attilio Mussino's color illustrations for the famous 1911 book version of the tales: a decidedly homely and definitely wooden child. After weeks of tests, Walt approved a softened design by animator Milt Kahl, and Hurter continued to suggest gag ideas for the character, such as the charming drawing of a cute Pinoke in a feathered Tyrolean hat communing with a squirrel that has taken up residence on his long fir-branched nose (see page 9). An early idea for Jimmy shows the natty insect to be a highly dramatic, even operatic, singer of crickety songs. Hurter's finest contribution was the warmth and charm he wove into the props in Geppetto's workshop: toys, dolls, smoking pipes, vases, puppets, mechanical clocks, and music boxes.

For *Fantasia,* (at first known as *The Concert Feature*), cyclops, pegasus, maenads, centaurs, and "centaurettes" appeared on Hurter's drawing board, as well as dancing elephants, hippos, and alligators. He adapted most of the creatures from Heinrich Kley, whose art he greatly admired. Kley's sheer joy

Minnie's virtue hangs in the balance and interrupts Mickey's lunch in a robust Hurter drawing for Building a Building *(1933).*

in the act of drawing, his technical virtuosity, and the droll and cruel *schadenfreude* his drawings exude inspired Hurter's own creativity. Four sketches of a giant satanic figure reaching into a volcano to pull out tortured human souls for *Fantasia*'s Night on Bald Mountain sequence are modeled after several of Kley's demonic giants.

Hurter worked on Disney films that would not be produced until years after his death. For example, rights to *Peter Pan* were purchased in 1939, but due to the war the film was not put into full production until 1951. Hurter's Peter is a very young, Maude Adams–like androgynal sprite and the pirates are uniformly plug-ugly and gruesome (one dines on eyeballs off his sword), ideas that were considerably altered by the time the film was released in 1953. *Lady and the Tramp* had an earlier origin and a later finish. In 1937 Joe Grant came up with an idea for a dog film based on his family's pet, a cocker spaniel named Lady. When finally released in 1955, the sly, mischievous personalities of a Siamese cat duo, seen in Hurter sketches from a couple of decades before, were retained. The last features Hurter worked on that were released in his lifetime were *Dumbo* (1941) and *The Reluctant Dragon* (1941). As prolific as ever, his pencil wanderings covered atmosphere and props for the former film, and, for the latter, medieval

23

crowd scenes and amusing suggestions for knights getting into metal gear, and a climactic battle with a fire-breathing but reticent monster.

In 1941, in the town of Camarillo in Ventura County, Hurter purchased "the first place he owned": a spacious rustic stone restaurant/tavern in which "he saw the possibilities"[53] of a home with a studio and library. He had barely started renovating when "[o]ne morning he came in," remembered Joe Grant, "his arm dropped to the side. It was more or less paralyzed. Even that arm held a cigar. He said it wasn't anything to worry about. I don't think he realized until it increased in intensity that he had a stroke."[54]

He entered Cedar Lodge Sanitarium in Los Angeles for a year and two months of treatment. Walt, Grant, Sears, and a few other colleagues visited him, but "[b]efore we knew it," said Grant, "he was gone." His death certificate states Albert Hurter died in his 59th year on March 28, 1942, of rheumatic heart disease, but there is no telling how much his addiction to smoking contributed to his demise. He was buried at Forest Lawn Cemetery.

Seven years after his death, *He Drew As He Pleased—A Sketchbook by Albert Hurter* was published with over 700 drawings arranged and captioned by Ted Sears, who also wrote the book's introduction. Walt offered a brief tribute to Hurter as "a master creator of fantasy" who possessed "genuine ability as an artist."

The book has been seen as a magnanimous gesture on the part of Walt and the studio, an elaborate thank-you to a special artist for his important contributions to the Disney oeuvre. But the truth is that Hurter planned and paid for the book himself. In his last will and testament, he requested that his executor[55] "employ Ted Sears . . . to assist in the collection and arrangement of [artistic] material and the writing of said book." In his usual methodical way, Hurter further directed his executor to retain from his estate "the sum of five thousand dollars" to cover "completing the said book and procuring the publication of the same."

Hurter—who rarely signed his work and who (it was thought) cared less than nothing about what happened to his drawings and had no idea of their value—was in reality deeply

One of Hurter's many quaint architectural renderings for Pinocchio.

24

CHARACTER MODEL DEP'T.

O.K. by JG

NUMBER M80-D-

DATE 9-27-38

© Walt Disney Prod.

PEGASUS
FLYING HORSES
FOR
"CYDALISE"
CONCERT FEATURE
F-128

A 1938 model sheet for the flying horse family in Fantasia, made from selective exploratory sketches by Hurter, was approved by Character Model Department head Joe Grant (note "O.K. by J.G."). A showcase of Hurter's drawing mastery and flair for personality touches.

proud of the unique art he made at Disney and was aware of its impact. And he wanted to be remembered for it.

Only in the last decade of his almost sixty years had he found his niche in a new art form of which he was a pioneer; but in his mind the importance of what he did and the intensity of his commitment made the time span seem longer. As noted in his will, he created a memorial in book form "for the purpose of placing before the public some of the artistic work to which I have devoted a large portion of my life."[56]

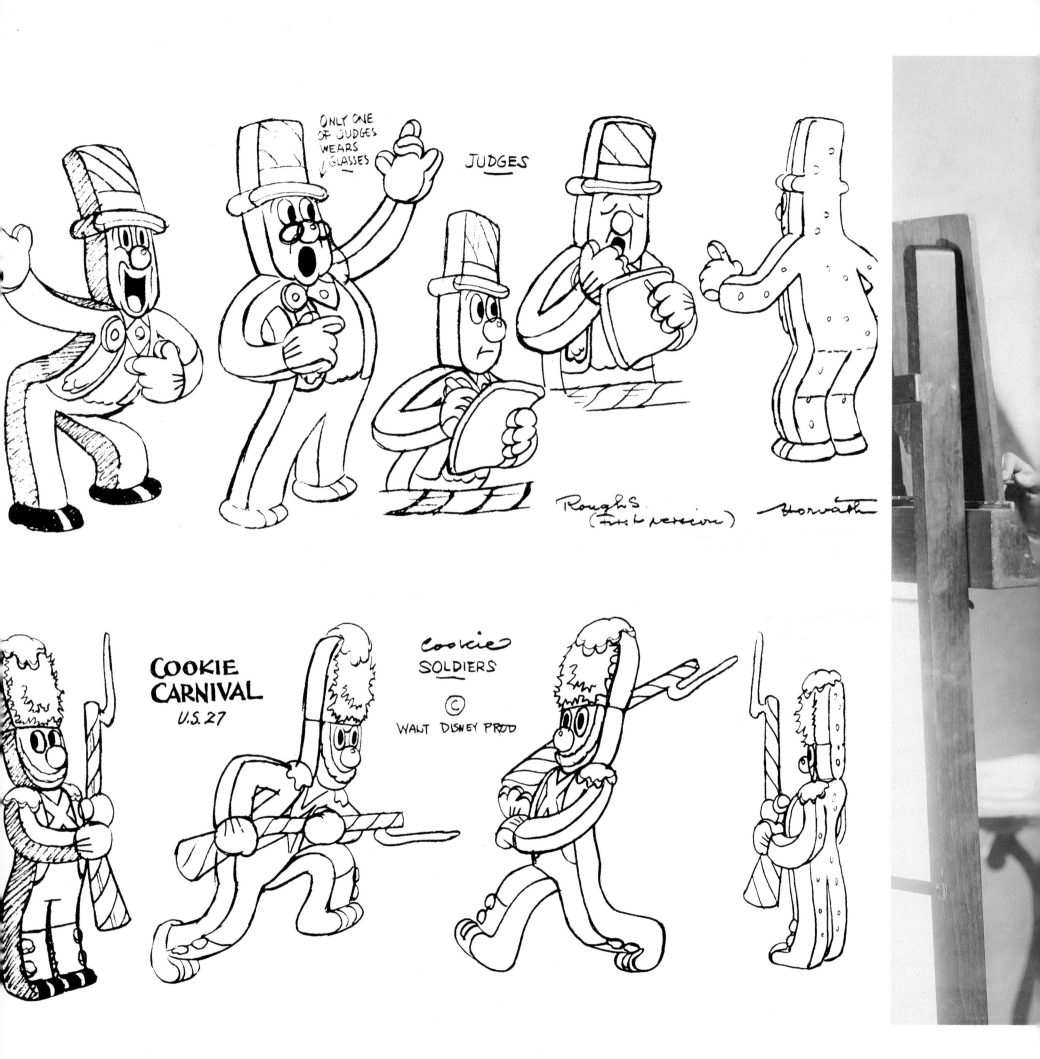

CHAPTER 3

Ferdinand Horvath

"If this is not a crazy house, then I don't know what is. And it is!" complained Ferdinand H. Horvath about the Disney Studio in a letter dated June 1, 1933.[1] Horvath, a Hungarian immigrant and successful New York–based illustrator of books, periodicals, and advertisements, was invited to work at the studio on a six-month trial basis beginning January 7. Five surviving letters from the many he wrote to his wife on the East Coast during his probationary period in "Hulivud" (Hollywood) are fascinating documents. The Depression was at its height and jobs in the commercial art field were scarce. Horvath's letters are frontline reports from the trenches by one of the growing army of artists, illustrators, architects, engineers, art directors, sculptors, and technicians unable to find jobs who flocked to Disney's for employment. "I see how many bankruptcies and mergers take place," he wrote on May 24, 1933. "Not so good. Now it would be difficult to [make a living] out of publishing."

Horvath's letters vividly bring to life the turmoil of a studio in flux and trying to cope with its own success. In the June 1st letter, for example, he grouses about the limited space at the "crazy house" on Hyperion Avenue: "Yesterday morning I moved out from Dave's [David Hand, director] room into an animation room. From 8 A.M. to 2 P.M. only. Then I was ordered to go to [director Wilfred] Jackson's room on the ground floor to do layouts for [the] Pied Piper [a Silly Symphony released in September 1933]. Two movings in one day!" In the same letter he complains about everything from the Cal-

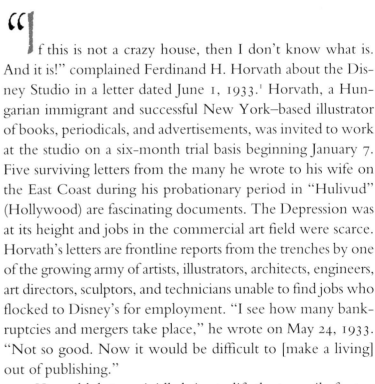

LEFT *Ferdinand Huszti Horvath at the easel, circa 1930. Courtesy Elly Horvath.* OPPOSITE *Cookie soldiers (doughboys?) and doughy judges for a confectionary parade are character design suggestions by Horvath for the 1935 Silly Symphony* The Cookie Carnival.

27

ifornia climate ("Unchangably rotten! No sun, foggy, cold, beginning of June and we have to heat the Studio."),[2] to office politics ("Mr. [Ben] Sharpsteen's [Disney's tough production manager] best tricks were frustrated."). In an earlier letter, he cites the importance of being seen in a favorable light by Walt ("Since he saw personally my work he doesn't listen to the report of others. His attitude toward me is different. At least he is more friendly than before.")[3] In a July 2, 1933 letter, he brags that at a preview of *Old King Cole* (released on July 29, 1933) "the only big laughter came in my scene. You couldn't ask for better than that. Now when we get to discussing my contract, I am in a stronger position with Disney than anytime in the last six months."

Horvath and others in the studio, he wrote, felt the "greatest insecurity" as they waited impatiently for "the new grouping which didn't happen yet [but] it's coming everyday."[4] This refers to studio scuttlebutt that—even as early as May 1933—there was "a very good sign that definitely in the planning [is] the first feature production *Snow White and the Seven Dwarfs*."[5] In July, he writes "Imagine! Disney got *Bambi*, exclusive rights and probably there will be a feature out of it. He is a clever boy. I am very impressed with him."[6] A major

commitment to features was an encouraging sign because it would necessitate Walt regrouping his present artistic staff according to their abilities, and *enlarging* it rather than laying people off. How else could he continue to make Mickey and Silly shorts while simultaneously accommodating the demands of a feature production or two?

Sure enough, Disney's company grew considerably during the Depression. But Horvath, a wily survivor who escaped from a Russian prison camp during World War I, covered himself just in case. During his tryout at Disney (he confided to his wife), he secretly solicited a job at the Warner Brothers animation studio, and would consider taking it "if they pay more than at Disney."[7] Ultimately he did not because as an artist he felt "I have to stick with Disney because . . . within a few years he will outshine all the other studios because it's sure there is not a cartoon that is as good as ours."[8]

Horvath worked nearly four years at Disney, where his versatility and technical virtuosity as a painter and sculptor brought him a variety of assignments. At first he designed advertising and promotional pieces. A letter dated March 2, 1933 indicates he "finished some illustrations and am now working on art for a pop-up book" and (feeling victimized by his versatility) he complains that "every week I have to do something new I haven't done before."[9] He painted backgrounds (for *The Cookie Carnival* (1934) and *The Band Concert* (1935)), he drew layouts (for *Old King Cole,* among others), and constructed a large three-dimensional model of a windmill for *The Old Mill* (1937). He even contributed a one-page critique dated February 22, 1937 suggesting ways to achieve "surprise in gags": "In m.m.o. [my modest opinion], the most effective gags are those that will take the audience by complete surprise. The absurdity of the situation is an important factor."

His attention to detail was fierce; one background layout contains extensive notes to a painter requesting specific effects, like "a *warm* green," an intricate tile floor pattern, and a sampler effect on a wall.

Primarily, though, Disney utilized Horvath as a prolific inspirational sketch artist, like Albert Hurter. Indeed, comic book artist Carl Barks considers Horvath "one of the two finest illustrators to have worked for Disney during the thirties."[10] Horvath suggested character designs and gags for almost sixty Silly Symphonies and Mickey Mouse shorts including such classics as *Father Noah's Ark* (1933), *Old King Cole* (1933), *Mickey's Garden* (1935), *Mickey's Circus* (1936), *Three Mouskteers* (1936), *Thru the Mirror* (1936), *Woodland Cafe* (1936), *Clock Cleaners* (1937), *The Moth and the Flame* (1938), *The Practical Pig* (1939), among others, as well as preliminary concepts for *Snow White.*

Walt and his brother/business partner Roy were no

A spiky thistle man drawn by Horvath for either a Silly Symphony or the "Nutcracker Suite" in Fantasia.

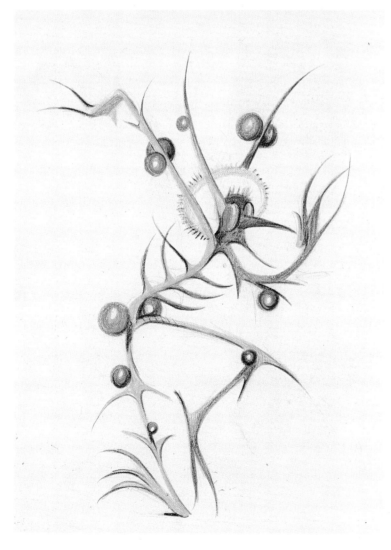

doubt impressed by Horvath's illustrations for fantasy books, magazines, and dust jackets, such as first editions of Dashiell Hammet's *The Maltese Falcon, The Dain Curse,* and *The Glass Key.*[11] Unlike Hurter, Horvath was self-taught and came to Disney with a considerable reputation as a successful and well-known commercial illustrator. And as careful, solitary, and dull as Hurter's personal history was, Horvath's was full of upheaval, adventure, and passion.

Ferdinand Huszti Horvath was born Nandor Mahaly Lowenstein on August 28, 1891 in Budapest. His father, Nandor, was a well-to-do merchant of liquor and baked goods and "the Hungarian representative of a well-known New York firm."[12] For unknown reasons, he changed the Jewish family name to Horvath in 1902 and converted to Roman Catholicism. "I heard my mother say that Ferdinand was part-Jewish," said nephew Martin Collins recently. "He very much did not want to be Jewish."

Nandor Sr. insisted his son follow in his footsteps as a merchant. "His plans foundered on my objections," Ferdinand once said, "for I wanted to become an engineer and so I registered at an engineer's preparatory school. Freehand drawing at school had no attraction for me—I turned out such poor work that I nearly failed at each graduation."[13] However, he decided to study art in Paris, which led to more "arguments and appeals and domestic unrest" with his father.

The outbreak of World War I ended the home front "war" when twenty-three-year-old Ferdinand escaped his father's wrath by enlisting as a reserve officer of the Austro-Hungarian army. He distanced himself further from his father by adding "Huszti" to his last name; "Ferdinand" was a German translation of "Nandor" that stuck when Horvath landed in Berlin at the end of his military service. He rose to the rank of First Lieutenant with the Kaiserjaeger Regiment, was wounded in battle, captured by the Russians, and spent two and a half years in various prison camps. He wrote a novel about his adventures, *Captured,* published (with no illustrations) in 1930; its preface set the author's uncompromising and bitter tone:

> No heroes are these—just ordinary men, who know what it is to carry a pack in the mud, and not what it seems like, from the comfortable cars of war corespondents. Just plain, common, muddy infantrymen who dare admit that the first battle is less a glorious feeling than the deadly fright of hissing bullets.
>
> On these pages I want to take you to a place of action, where the war was less machine-made than in the West, where the last gigantic, classical open warfare was staged, where a strategical straightening of the line meant

ABOVE *Mrs. Horvath with Walt Disney before a model constructed by Ferdinand Horvath of the mill in the 1937 Silly Symphony* The Old Mill. *Courtesy Carol Covington.*

LEFT *"Elly" Horvath, circa 1930. Courtesy Elizabeth Leonard.*

29

like shade upon a wall; in a dank cave a shadow figure approaches the raven sitting on a branch that is also a skeletal creature with taloned feet barely hidden in melancholy shadows. The most over-the-top and cartoonlike illustration shows bone-thin arms and long tapered fingers reaching from a steep valley surrounded by a maelstrom stirred by the raven whose flight is conveyed in three sequential poses.

After thirty months in prison, Horvath engineered a dramatic escape. "Money was exchanged [with a Czarist sympathizer] and a horse and sleigh conveyed the artist-prisoner across Siberia's bleak plains to the nearest railroad station," a six-day ride to Petrograd. There the Russian presence was so thick Horvath "was forced to travel about disguised as a Russian peasant in sheepskin coat, high boots and fur cap." Eventually he reached Finland, took a train along the Swedish border and one night leaped from the train to the frozen river. "Shots were fired, but none took effect. The youth reached the Swedish border," where, after checking his story, the Swedes presented him with a ticket to Berlin and home. "Back in Budapest once more, he rejoined the Hungarian army and fought until the close of the war."[16]

The domestic battles with his father resumed when Ferdinand announced his intention to marry Rafaella Francisca Elizabeth Koellesz. Elly, a vivacious 5-foot-3-inch, twenty-year old ballet dancer, was of the minor nobility—an ancestor on her father's side was knighted for killing invading Mongols and awarded a country estate and a Budapest townhouse. "Swept off her feet" by the 6-foot, 150-pound black-haired soldier, she promptly broke off her engagement to a man from a higher social class. A duel, she asserted, was suggested but declined. Indeed, a rough draft exists of a polite but firm letter from Ferdinand to his rival, an aristocrat of the landed gentry named Nagykalloi Kallay Elemer:

> Elly is my fiancée and as such is under my protection . . .
> Stop meeting with her . . . I feel [sympathy] for you.
> Without willing it, I caused you pain . . . Her good
> name is at stake. I would like to avoid a loud scandal that
> would give cause for ugly and bad gossip.[17]

For Elly to reject a member of the gentry for a man who was an artist, a Jew, and the son of a mere merchant was considered outrageous by her parents and they promptly disowned her. The elder Horvath disapproved of a bride with no dowry, so when the couple defiantly married in 1920, Ferdinand was disenherited.[18]

For the rest of their lives, the couple was fated never to have much money, but they remained happy with each other through fifty-seven years of marriage. "Anybody would be

so many hundred weary miles of marching in advance or retreat.

The war had a ruder flavor here—though that on the West was undoubtedly more deadly. But we had more of the lice and more of the mud and more of other hardships that were spared to the soldiers of the West.[14]

A photograph taken during captivity shows young Horvath wearing a pince-nez and smoking a cigarette while sculpting a figure of a soldier. He also passed the time by drawing in earnest. "I started work on E. A. Poe's 'The Raven' then," he said of a masterful series of illustrations that were published nearly fifteen years later.[15]

Horvath's remarkable black-and-white charcoal and gouache illustrations perfectly match Poe's feverish romanticism: Dark and elegant, they hold a glamorous morbidity, weird dreaminess, and fascination with decay and death. They could be inspirational sketches for a macabre animated film, so filled are they with anthropomorphism, cartoony expressionism, and metamorphic play. Comic satanic shadow creatures grin and dance in a fireplace's glow; the "bird of ill omen" perched "on the pallid bust of Pallas" throws a skull-

Two of the nineteen charcoal illustrations made by Horvath in 1930 for "The Raven" by Edgar Allan Poe. Carol Covington Collection.

crazy about Elly," recalled Marge Champion, the famous dancer whose career began as the model for Snow White, and who first met the couple at Disney's in the early 1930s. "She was the most outgoing, upbeat [person]. Freddy was a very quiet, withdrawn, negative person. And he was married to this absolutely smashing ex-dancer. He was very withdrawn [and] . . . such a bear of a man [but] he was so in love with this woman."[19] Frank Thomas concurs: "Horvath was a big guy with a little stoop and thick glasses, who didn't really see the world. He moved around in a kind of determined stupor.[20] He had a keen wife, a lovely blond lady, witty and smart, very much the socialite. The two of them went every place. Talk to her and you'd have a whee of a time. Charm, charm, charm! She outdid Eva Gabor. Full of life!"[21]

After struggling to sell his paintings and drawings in Hungary, the couple decided to seek a new life in America. Because of limited finances, they decided Ferdinand would leave first and send for Elly as soon as he earned enough for her passage. He traveled in steerage on the liner *Aquitania*, arriving in New York on November 11, 1921.[22] He was thirty years old, with only forty-five dollars to his name and a collection of ivory miniatures he had sculpted and hoped to sell. The

money went quickly for food and a tiny room with a cot and shared bathroom on Manhattan Avenue, and the ivories didn't sell. To survive he painted window frames on Avenue C, then "graduated," as he put it, to painting a coal barge on the Hudson River, then accepted "all the odd jobs that go with the education of a greenhorn."[23] For two months, he "painted fat little cupids for revolving mica-disks" for a stage lighting company, was fired, then painted doll's heads for several months. "With envy I must think what a fine, slim waistline I had at that time," he mused years later.[24]

Eventually, Horvath found "six years permanency with a movie concern making animated cartoons" at Paul Terry's Aesop's Fables studio. In 1927, he became an American citizen, as did Elly the following year. Also in 1928, Disney's success with sound cartoons affected the entire animation industry, and Horvath stated that "the talkies put me on the street once more."[25] He decided to freelance as an illustrator and success quickly followed. After "two weeks of strenuous walking I sold some jazzed-up fox hunting pictures to *Harper's Bazaar* and contributed since many others." That fall, he received considerable attention in the press for his first art exhibition of watercolors, pen-and-ink drawings and miniatures,

31

which was held at the Waldorf-Astoria Hotel. Some newspapers used Horvath's parental problems and personal struggles as a human interest hook; for example, "Artist Spurns Riches for Love; Has Triumph" (*New York American,* November 26, 1928), and "War, Exile to Siberia, Disinheritance for Love, Preventing All Study, Fail to Bar Artist from his Chosen Career" (The *Brooklyn Daily Eagle,* December 2, 1928). His artwork was reviewed favorably by all.

The *Morning Telegraph* (November 28, 1928) found his "variety of theme . . . mood, style and technique . . . exhilarating," and singled out *The Alchemist,* a brooding dark Doré-like drawing:

> [It] demonstrates Huszti-Horvath's ability to develop a theme logically. The retorts, kilns, weights and measures are all of the fifteenth century and must have involved research. The alchemist is huddled in a chair in his laboratory . . . waiting for the auspicious moment.

Horvath's near-death experiences during the war affected his art, and several drawings in the exhibition predict his later moody, death-laden concepts for Disney's *Snow White.* One example from his series of Snow White escaping through a dark forest is particularly eerie. Amid huge twisted and rotting trees, the tiny figure of Snow White flees a giant ghostly wolf that has metamorphosed out of trees. To further enhance the haunting menace, Horvath airbrushed a sickly green aura around the wolf.

The five books he illustrated in three years surely would have appealed to Walt Disney. *The Sons O'Cormac* (1929)[26] contains *Snow White* elements: a fairy tale hero and heroine, dwarfs, witch, and stylized densely detailed forests. *Ole Man Swordfish* (1931)[27], featuring anthropomorphic fish folk, is an imaginative Silly Symphony–like showcase of Horvath's visual drollery.

Walt must have felt he had discovered another Hurter. In a way he had: Both men were idea machines capable of pouring out reams of drawings in the European fairy tale mode Walt loved. But there were differences. Hurter's drawings, including the detailed ones, retain an unfinished quality, and even the most grotesque have a certain gemütlich or folksy, warm accessibility. The humor in the art is often cozy and cute. Also, Hurter's drawings appear to be "Disney" even in their works-in-progress stage, with characters needing only minor adjustments to bring them "on model."

Horvath is less improvisational, his art more finished, almost slick. There is in his work a cool delicacy, an art deco stylishness, a sly droll humor. Horvath's stylized characters and ideas needed complete overhauling to bring them in line with the softer, friendlier Disney style. For the feature, comments film historian Tom Andrae, "his stuff was so eccentric, weird, his gags so wildly imaginative that it didn't fit the mold. Walt kept him around because he was inspirational, but he didn't produce a lot that got used."[28] Horvath's interiors of the queen's castle are cold and dank operalike sets; in one, skeletons illuminate the queen's walk down countless Piranesi stairs past skull-columns. His model for the witch has a gherkin-nose, facial hair, and bird's claws for hands. In other sketches, the witch floods a state-of-the-art torture chamber and his runty dwarfs resemble nothing-so-much as bearded, costumed potatoes.

Horvath's art also had a delightfully whimsical side, seen in sketches of anthropomorphic flowers prepared for an un-

AN APPLE A DAY
WILL TAKE YOU AWAY.

produced Silly Symphony that found their way into research files for *Fantasia*'s Nutcracker Suite.

A practiced professional, Horvath proudly and defiantly signed his name to almost everything he drew, while Hurter did not. But Hurter's name appears in the screen credits of *Snow White* (albeit as a "character designer," which barely hints at the significance of his contribution). Horvath, however, never received any screen credit for his conceptual work

33

Horvath's suggestions for a state-of-the-art torture chamber for Snow White's Prince.

on *Snow White,* nor was he *ever* mentioned in studio publicity, as was Hurter. He also never received screen credit for his considerable contributions to the short cartoons (nor did Hurter); until union contracts forced a change, only Walt's name shone on title cards giving the impression he did it all.

How frustrating it must have been for an artist who signed his name to everything to be denied screen credit. It may have been a major reason why he left the studio in October 1937, two months before *Snow White* premiered. There was also his isolation from most of the crew at the studio, a condition partly inherent in the nature of the job of the in-

spirational sketch artist. Some in the story department realized and appreciated Horvath's worth, but he was far removed from the animators. Many never heard of him, and when they noticed him at all, they saw a rather taciturn, withdrawn foreigner. "An absentminded professor, if you ever saw one. Just completely living in a dream world," observed Frank Thomas.[29]

Horvath's Hungarian accent, and odd middle name made him a figure of jest to others. "I thought Huszti was a funny name," said animator Ward Kimball. "And he looked like he might have been a cousin of Dracula."[30] "He was the butt of

ABOVE *The Queen gazes at her image in the Magic Mirror: one of a dozen of Horvath concept drawings for this particular scene in* Snow White *that suggests decor, architecture, costumes, and placement of figures within the space.*
RIGHT *The Dwarf designs of both Horvath and Albert Hurter were changed and made more "appealing" by two of* Snow White's *supervising animators, Vladimir Tytla and Fred Moore.*

DOPEY.

GRUMPY.

another version of DOPEY.

HAPPY

SLEEPY

DOPEY

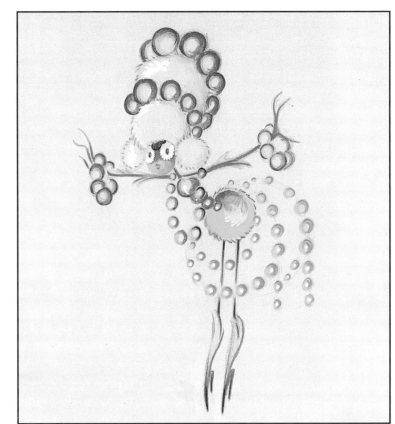

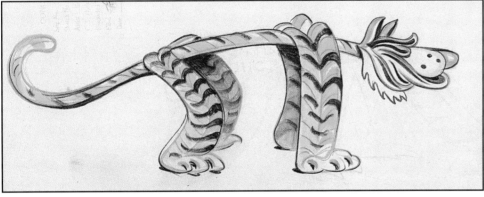

UPPER LEFT *A Horvath sketch, signed and dated September 23, 1936, suggesting color-coded bird labor for the Dwarfs' mining camp. Delightful anthropomorphic flowers from Horvath's fertile imagination include a "tiger-lily" (*LOWER LEFT*), a Ziegfeld Follies seed-girl (*UPPER RIGHT*), a "thistle donkey" (*LOWER RIGHT*), and two ballroom adagio dancers (*OPPOSITE LEFT*).*

a lot of jokes and gags," said Joe Grant. "Bill Cottrell said he eats nothing but red meat, and we always thought of him as a Dracula character. 'Cause he came from Rumania or somewhere in the Balkans. He was a very strange, very quiet, intense-looking man, black around the eyes. Bill used to do a lot of caricatures of him."[31] William Cottrell in fact wrote a story and Albert Hurter drew sketches for an unproduced film titled *Hootsie the Owl*.

After leaving Disney, Horvath worked briefly (1938–1939) designing models and layouts for Scrappy, Krazy Kat, and Color Rhapsodies shorts for Columbia/Screen Gems. In 1940 he sculpted puppets for George Pal's Puppetoons (distributed by Paramount Pictures) and, on the side, made and sold porcelain dogs, ducks, "and little colored boys,"[32] as well as Christmas figures and chess pieces from the back of his rented house off of Sunset Boulevard. "Elly had women working for her," said Marge Champion. "They made molds from

some of the little figures that Freddy would sculpt. She was trying to get the business off the ground where he would be independent of the studios."[33] Horvath never returned to magazine or book illustration.

When America entered World War II, he "went to North American Aviation and later to Howard Hughes in a technical capacity to work on confidential designs." After the war, he and Elly "had a little workshop in Hollywood where he made wooden toys, birdhouses and feeders, and fishing lures," which they marketed by mail order, according to their nephew Martin Collins.[34] In the fifties, the couple moved to Westminster West, Vermont, to live with Elly's brother and

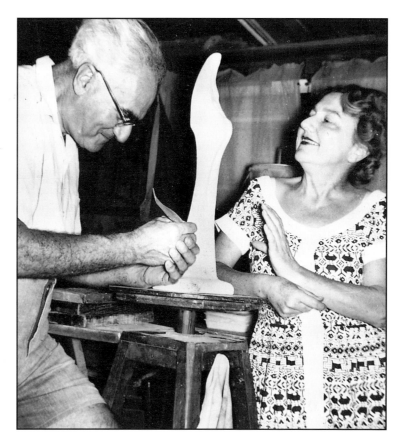

his wife, and their mail order business (called The Little Workshop) continued. "They never had an awful lot," recalled Collins, "They were very frugal. They lived in a former storage shed and instead of paying somebody for insulation, my uncle insulated it with wood shavings and newspapers. It was very effective and warm." "Elly knew how to stretch a chicken for three or four days. One little chicken," recalled Ms. Champion.[35]

The Vermont winters were harsh, and friction developed between Elly and her brother's wife, so the Horvaths moved back to California. For a time they were homesteaders in the Palomar Mountains, and then moved into a "dreary little house" in Hemet, a small town near Palm Springs. "You can't believe what a shack it was and how she pasted it together," said Ms. Champion, a loyal friend who has contributed to the Horvath's finances through the years. "Elly was very re-

sourceful. She gardened, spoke five languages, so she was a translator for the local hospital. There was hardly a time when they could get to Los Angeles. Just the cost of the gas was too much." Ferdinand's health declined and on November 11, 1973, he died of a stroke at age eighty-two. He and Elly never had children, but a few years before his death, the couple themselves were "adopted" by Elizabeth Leonard, a respiratory therapist and sociologist who "just got caught in their charm." She continues to look after Elly, who, at this writing in the fall of 1995, has reached her ninety-ninth birthday.

"In their younger days," remembered Marge Champion, "they were the envy of everybody because they were such a happy couple. She's the one who made it work. I think that was something everybody envied because it doesn't come to many people to have a great love affair that continues throughout one's life."

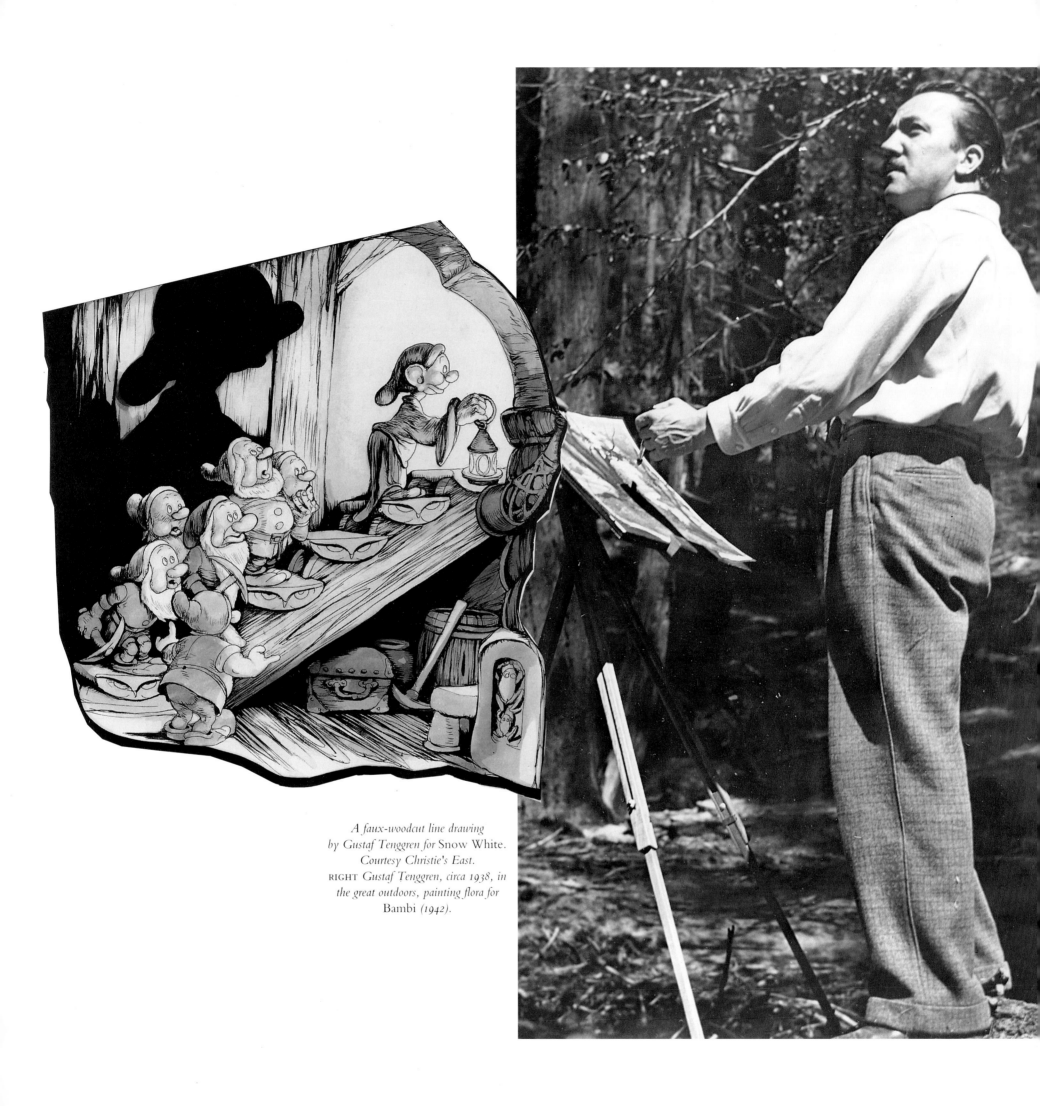

*A faux-woodcut line drawing
by Gustaf Tenggren for* Snow White.
Courtesy Christie's East.
RIGHT *Gustaf Tenggren, circa 1938, in
the great outdoors, painting flora for*
Bambi *(1942).*

Gustaf Tenggren

"Some of those little books which I brought back with me from Europe," said Walt Disney in a memorandum dated 23 December 1935, "have very fascinating illustrations of little peoples, bees, and small insects who live in mushrooms, pumpkins, etc. This quaint atmosphere fascinates me." For eleven weeks in the spring and early summer of 1935, Walt and Roy and their wives vacationed in England, France, Italy, Holland, and Switzerland. It was hoped the trip would relieve Walt's mounting work-related stress and avert a nervous collapse similar to one he suffered in 1931.

Walt did relax, but not totally; he couldn't help but see film potential in the illustrated storybooks he bought in each country. "There are many stories which I think could be developed into very good symphonies," he said. In addition to the large number of books he brought back with him in July, "the [studio] library received a further consignment . . . with 90 titles from France, 81 from England, 149 from Germany and 15 from Italy."[1] Fantasy stories about Mother Goose; Little Boy Blue; Wynken, Blynken, and Nod; Puss in Boots; Punch and Judy; the Emperor's Invisible Clothes; Reynard the Fox; among others, illustrated with charming realistic/romantic drawings, reinforced Walt's interest in the European artistic heritage that so influenced his films.

On staff, the Europeans Albert Hurter and Ferdinand Horvath produced well-drawn imaginative fantasy art for the shorts and the upcoming feature that stimulated the imaginations of the rest of the crew. Walt wanted more of their ilk,

and demanded that Ted Sears find people for the story department "who can not only think up ideas but who can carry them through and sell them to the people who have to do with the completion of the thing . . . [people with] a feeling for situation gags, for personality gags and who have a little showmanship in their system."[2]

Enter, in the spring of 1936, Gustaf Tenggren—at age forty a "name" children's book illustrator who melded "Swedish and American visual traditions into a distinctive personal style."[3]

His biographer, Mary T. Swanson, describes Tenggren as "one of the most successful immigrant artists, merging a visually rich past with contemporary styles and subjects in illustrations that show a nearly seamless synthesis of old and new cultures. The results can only be called 'American.' "[4] Tenggren spent only three years as a Disney inspirational sketch artist,[5] but his beautiful paintings influenced the rich appearance of *Snow White* and especially *Pinocchio,* in which "elements of his Swedish past emerged in this Americanized version of an Italian tale."[6]

Tenggren was born on November 3, 1896, in the rural parish of Magda on Sweden's western coast. His father, a decorative painter of home interiors, immigrated to America leaving Gustaf in the care of his grandfather Teng, a decorative painter and woodcarver who became the boy's surrogate father. Young Tenggren loved the "supernatural forests" of Magra and watched his grandfather restoring several area

churches, which included the addition of sculpted dwarf figures to pulpits and altars. Teng taught his grandson how to paint and carve, and at age seventeen the boy won a scholarship to study painting (from 1913 to 1916) at Valand, a famous art school in Gothenburg, Sweden's largest west coast city.

From 1917 through 1926 he illustrated a popular annual of Swedish folklore and fairy tales called *Bland Tomar och Troll (Among Elves and Trolls)*. His use of silhouetted figures against flattened spaces was influenced by John Bauer, the Swedish painter who preceded him on the publication. Mary T. Swanson finds both Bauer and Tenggren painted similar trolls—"benevolent creatures whose noses consumed their faces"[7]—and she traces their source to the macabre and fantastic illustrative art of English illustrator Arthur Rackham (1867–1939). Rackham's drawings were also a particular favorite of Walt Disney, whom it is said, attempted (unsuccessfully) to hire the artist to work at the studio.

Tenggren was also influenced by nineteenth-century German and Norwegian folk tale illustrators, and was "heir to the Nordic predilection for subjects steeped in fantasy . . . a tradition reinvigorated late in the nineteenth century by an in-

fusion of French symbolism . . . which emphasized emotional reactions to images and scenes."[8]

In 1920 he migrated to Cleveland bringing with him Swedish fine and folk art influences. Within two years, he had his first art exhibit and moved to New York City to begin a successful career as an illustrator. There, he cleverly assimilated his ethnic imagery with mainstream American commercial illustration in twenty-two books between 1923 and 1939 (including *Heidi, Mother Goose,* and *Andersen's Fairy Tales*), product advertisements, and romantic scenes for articles in *Good Housekeeping, Cosmopolitan, Redbook,* and *Ladies Home Journal.* In 1926 he married Malin ("Mollie") Froberg, a nurse who became his protective, loyal, and "relentless"[9] business manager.

In New York, Tenggren was part of a group of writers and artists who gathered in clubs on Greenwich Village's MacDougal Street for drinking, smoking, and highly opinionated conversations. "Gustaf was always somewhat vocal within that group, then always independent enough to go off by himself," according to Mary T. Swanson.[10] He was a moody man, "a very dramatic man," said Mary Anderson, one of several nieces.[11] "His hair was long, he wore a camel hair coat with a sash and suede shoes. He was a true artist. He saw things differently." His aloofness, which would not endear him to co-workers at Disney, was "very much in keeping with the Swedish character," said Mary T. Swanson. Like Garbo, the most famous Swede of all, it was a "quality of aloneness, which is often seen as aloofness. There is the joke about Swedes, Norwegians, and Finns stranded on an island: a year later the Finns have set up a lumber industry, the Norwegians a fishing industry, and the Swedes are looking at each other waiting to be introduced. That gives you a feeling."

"During the Depression, things got very slow," said Mary Anderson.[12] "So, like a lot of artists, he went out there and worked for Disney." Tenggren, a borrower of artistic styles from classical to contemporary, subtly adapted to whatever assignment was at hand. In Tenggren's depiction of Snow White's fearsome flight through the forest, for example, where spindly hands of anthropomorphic trees reach and grab for the girl, there is a debt to both Doré and Rackham, but Bauer is also present, and the years of fantasy drawings for *Bland Tomtar och Troll,* as well as the artist's memories of Magra's magical forests.

Tenggren was "a meticulous researcher and kept files and cuttings"[13] on Hollywood movie scenes containing unusual camera angles, favorite American painters, such as Thomas Hart Benton, Grant Wood, and Edward Hopper, and photos and sketches of European locales. In *Pinocchio,* Albert Hurter met Grandfather Teng; or as Robin Allan put it, "Germany and Sweden come together in the three-dimensionalizing of Geppetto's workshop interior." For the film's street scenes of quaint buildings, cobblestone roads, and details such as lamps, banners, and weathervanes, Dr. Allan has identified the town that Tenggren studied for his inspirational paintings as "Rothenburg ob der Tauber, a medieval town in Bavaria, popular with tourists . . . The backgrounds in the film are generalised, though Geppetto's house and surroundings bear a close resemblance to Tenggren's Rothenburg sketches."[14]

A cinematic influence is seen in the high angle that peers over gabled roofs and down the street below where Pinocchio and the fox and cat dance. Mary Swanson finds such "exaggerated aerial perspective and sharp-edged forms of figures, houses, and landscape . . . show connections to the immaculate edges and heightened perspectives of American regionalist painters of the 1930s."[15] There is also a rounded "fish-eye" lens appearance to several of the ground-level paintings that gives a sweeping "movement" to static scenes.

Between features, Tenggren was kept busy styling the backgrounds and atmosphere for shorts such as *Little Hiawatha* (1937), *The Ugly Duckling* (1939), and *The Old Mill* (1937). The latter short—about a storm's effect on animals living in an abandoned wreck of a building—represents a leap in animation technology. It was a test vehicle for the multiplane camera, which lends an illusion of depth to flat artwork and was used extensively in *Snow White.* More significant is the artistic development found in *The Old Mill* in every department, from special effects animation and layout, to design and direction. Tenggren's continuity paintings of the forces of nature inspired the pictorial beauty of the film. Endlessly inventive, his miniature paintings (some two-and-a-half by three inches) show possible ways to visualize bats flying from the mill at sunset—as shadows cross the ground, in close-up through wooden beams, or seen from a distance—or how moonlight, a driving rain, and sunset can be effectively staged for drama and beauty. One tiny sketch of lightning resembles an Arthur Dove abstraction.

Tenggren "worked by himself and kept to himself," according to Carl Fallberg, storyman on *Bambi* and *Fantasia.*[16] "He was cooperative, but wouldn't socialize." The animators in particular felt "he was avoiding us," according to Frank Thomas. "He was arrogant. Part of him was into being a big shot, the most talented. He wouldn't be interested in anything that was only halfway there. He didn't like team effort. He didn't like to be part of a group that was trying to style something. You want style? Come to him, he'll style it for you."[17] His last assignment at the studio was the feature *Bambi,* for which Thomas conceded "he did do some amazing pictures. They were different than anything anyone else was doing. And they were impossible to use." Tenggren's forest scenes, full of detail, took three days each to paint. "You'd never get the movie made!" said Thomas. Walt agreed, and the styling of *Bambi* (released in 1942) went a completely different direction into minimally detailed impressionism, inspired by paintings of the Chinese-American artist Tyrus Wong.

Tenggren left Disney in January 1939, a year *before Pinoc-*

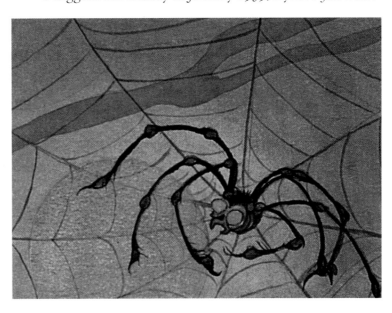

A Tenggren spider for The Old Mill *(1937).*

41

42

OPPOSITE AND BELOW *Tiny
(2 1⁄2 x 3-inch) paintings by
Tenggren explore possible imagery for
the 1937 Silly Symphony*
The Old Mill.

chio was released. There is speculation that his departure had to do with not receiving screen credit on *Snow White* and (more incredibly) *Pinocchio*. He may have been disgruntled over his low salary. "Do not give your art work away," he once told one of his nieces. "If you can't sell it, burn it! Because if you give them something, nobody respects it."[18] Perhaps his leaving was tied with feelings that his work was not respected or wanted *enough* at Disney.

There was also a mini-scandal involving the artist and an underage female that may have hastened his departure from the studio. "He was a womanizer, a chaser who liked the younger gals," recalled Frank Thomas. Seems a teenaged relative ("bubbling with vitality, youth, and innocence") of top animator Milt Kahl, got a summer job at the studio. "Milt introduced her around and the next thing we knew Tenggren had taken her up to Yosemite to camp while he did paintings of the woods [for *Bambi*], photographed the birds, and you can only imagine what else went on!" Kahl, possessor of a short fuse to begin with, "hit the ceiling!"

Tenggren's judgment may have been clouded by his heavy drinking, which he indulged in "on and off at times," according to William Bradford, a relative.[19] "He did enjoy his schnapps," concurred Carl Fallberg. On certain Saturday evenings, so Joe Grant was told, Tenggren and some men from the newly formed Character Model Department and "others around the studio" would "have a nude model up at the house, and they'd all draw and drink . . . Quite a party. It was, I don't know, both esoteric and erotic. I heard stories that are not publishable."[20]

Karen Hoyle, curator of the Kerlan Collection of children's literature research and a friend of Mollie Tenggren, said "Tenggren was an alcoholic, certainly at some point in his life. He would go into these stupors . . . [Mollie] would nurse him back. She was [a health] food fanatic."[21] He painted nudes of his wife, some of his nieces, and other women, and "at least one neighbor was involved with him romantically."[22] His drinking and womanizing was "certainly his pattern, including some kind of affair with a young niece." Part of the pattern was the mopping up and forgiveness of his "very nurturing" and constant wife.

Tenggren left his stamp on the Disney studio style, but in turn Disney strongly influenced Tenggren's style for the rest of his career. This is evident in the twenty-eight books he illustrated for Golden Books between 1942 and 1962. The classics *The Poky Little Puppy* (1942) and *Tawny Scrawny Lion* (1952), for example, have cute, childlike cartoon characters with minimal shading, frolicking against limbo space or flat colors; *Tawny* has a family of cuddly bunnies straight out of a Silly Symphony or *Bambi*. Martin Provensen of Disney's Char-

acter Model Department, once described "Disney tricks in drawing" which he felt he and his wife, Alice, had to "get rid of" when *they* illustrated books: "A certain facility toward expression; a too-facile approach toward gesture, toward expression, toward posture and so on."[23]

In *Tenggren's Story Book* (1944) the stories alternate between Tenggren's old style and his adaptation of Disney style and look like different artists illustrated them. What is consistent, however, is a motif of phallicism that is startling to come upon in a children's book. In over a dozen not-very-subtle paintings, Tenggren overlays male crotches with strategically placed knives, poles, rifles, guns, and hands. Tom Sawyer has a large tree limb angling out of his groin, Rip Van Winkle sleeps with his rifle barrel between his legs pointed and ready for action, and, most blatant, Robin Hood approaches Maid Marian with a large plucked goose whose fleshy neck and feathered head extends between Robin's legs to the ground. "Now come, ye lasses, and eke, ye dames, And buy your meat from me," states the caption, putting a fine point on things. Was this oversexed uncle Gus's private little joke, or something totally unconscious, or perhaps a consciousness affected by alcohol? Was it a cynical comment on the blandly innocent market that primarily bought his art? His serious

Gustaf Tenggren contributed visual ideas to every major sequence in Pinocchio, *as further demonstrated by three never-before-published paintings: Pinocchio trapped inside a birdcage, the Blue Fairy watching as Pinocchio succumbs to the temptations of Fox and Cat, and sequential poses of Geppetto searching for his "little wooden boy" in a raging rainstorm.*

noncommercial paintings and prints were, according to Swanson "not as good as his illustrations [which are] the real beauties because they're like illuminated manuscripts."[24]

In 1944, the Tenggren's made their first trip to Maine "in search of solitude, a place for uninterrupted work."[25] The next year they moved to Dogfish Head, Maine, to a century-old large house on Ebenecock Harbor accessible in winter only by jeep, which they furnished in Swedish folk antiques. "Mrs. Tenggren and I are quite in love with all this," he told a visitor, "Maine is like Sweden, you know. Its firs and pine suggest Sweden."[26]

Tenggren continued illustrating children's books and exhibiting his illustrations and other paintings up until his death on April 9, 1970. Surrounded by reminders of his beloved native land in his house and in the surrounding scenery, the immigrant painter "who carried the burden of the divided heart"[27] was, in a way, still in Magda, although his art had traveled far and become part of American culture.

Tenggren left the Disney Studio in 1939 to return to illustrating children's books. In 1956, he had a last Disney fling when he painted Walt and his characters for a Saturday Evening Post cover. OPPOSITE *Zeus, tiring of tossing thunder bolts at earth, retires in the Olympian clouds: an inspirational pastel by Kay Nielsen. John Canemaker Collection.*

The Saturday Evening

POST

November 17, 1956 — *15¢*

AT LAST
the intimate story
of America's
best-loved, least-
known genius,
told by his
daughter . . .

MY DAD WALT DISNEY

By DIANE DISNEY MILLER

The remarkable
private life of the man
who gave the world
Mickey Mouse, Donald Duck
and Snow White

48

PART TWO

Golden Age
Inspirations

CHAPTER 5

Joe Grant and the Character Model Department

"Walt met me in the hall after *Snow White* was already becoming big stuff," recalled Joe Grant recently. "He said, 'What are we going to do for an encore, Joe?'"[1] Walt's casual remark in early 1938 turned out to be a cryptic order to Grant to form a "think tank" made up of inspirational sketch artists.[2] "It was his idea to get a development department going," said Grant. "It was a wonderful opportunity."

Grant was personally "discovered" by Walt in 1933. After seeing his amusing caricatures in the *Los Angeles Record* newspaper ("Five a week on the Saturday page").[3] Walt phoned and hired the twenty-five-year-old cartoonist to design caricatures of Hollywood stars for the short *Mickey's Gala Premiere* (1933). Soon, Grant was invited to work full-time in Disney's story department.

OPPOSITE INSET *Most of the staff of Disney's Character Model Department gather under Kay Nielsen's drawings for "Night on Bald Mountain" to celebrate Joe Grant's thirty-first birthday in 1939. Standing (left to right): James Bodrero, Earl Hurd, unknown, Bill Jones, unknown, Duke Russell, Martin Provensen, Jack Miller, Helen Nervobig, unknown, John Walbridge, and Bill Wallett; seated (left to right): Campbell Grant (in blackface as Joe Grant's politically incorrect "slave"), Joe Grant, Albert Hurter, and Kay Nielsen. Courtesy Joe Grant.*
OPPOSITE *A Martin Provensen suggestion for the sorcerer in* Fantasia's *"Sorcerer's Apprentice" section.*
ABOVE *A maquette of a* Fantasia *"Dance of the Hours" alligator was made by the Character Model Department as a guide for animators: "a three-dimensional standard for the look of a character which allowed animators to better represent the figure in two dimensions."*

Grant's gags and ideas for the shorts, and his design of the witch in *Snow White* validated Walt's judgment of his talents. Walt, an unread and unsophisticated man with formidable entertainment and storytelling instincts, was impressed by Grant's intelligence, taste, creativity, and knowledge of art, music, and literature. "Grant brought articulate erudition and visual sophistication to the studio," according to Disney authority Robin Allan:

> He was familiar with the work of Busch, Daumier, Doré and other artists and illustrators. He liked reading and knew the work of popular classical writers like Carroll, Dickens and Jane Austen. He was aware of the astringent literary tradition of New York epitomized by *The New Yorker* and he knew the cartoons in *Punch* and the German *Simplicissimus*.[4]

Increasingly, Walt came to trust and rely on Grant's opinions. Often, at the end of a long day, the two men would discuss studio productions, politics, and personnel over sherry in Walt's office.[5] "Wherever we went, we talked story," said Grant recently about Walt's workaholic focus even on social occasions, adding with quiet pride, "He realized I had something."[6]

When first asked to work at Disney, however, Grant was ambivalent because his artwork was "on the brink of getting

Pastels by Joe Grant (c. 1936) of the Witch and the Queen in Snow White.

52

PRODUCTION FI
"SNOW WHITE"
WITCH MODELS
© 1937
W.D.P.
FEB. 25. 1937

SHEET 3

syndication with the *Chicago Daily News"* and other newspapers. But a visit to the studio left him "terribly impressed." He recalled hearing music for a film in production about three pigs and a big bad wolf reverberating through the halls, and thought, "This was the opportunity for me. Music, color, drawing. It was everything. The atmosphere was relaxed but exciting. And there were lots of former newspaper people."[7]

Grant came from a newspaper family. His father was art director for William Randolph Hearst's *New York Journal,* and at one time, Grant Sr. and the press lord were very close; but, predicting Grant Jr.'s future relationship with Walt the animation lord, "it sort of deteriorated." Born in New York in 1908, Grant was the son of second-generation Russian and Polish Jews. His grandparents, he said, "were Jewish but non-Jewish. When they came here some generations ago, there was the problem of race shame because of the prejudice around. So they didn't remain religious in any way."

Joe's father was "an extremely talented and precocious artist on his own" but there was "domestic strife" because he "became addicted to alcohol." Every time there was a problem at home, "my grandfather, who was quite well off, would send for my mother to come [to Los Angeles]." For Joe and his sister, "it was sort of a mobile existence."

He was two when his father became art director on the

53

SUGGESTED MODELS FOR
UNCLE REMUS
1080

CHARACTER MODEL DEP'T.
O.K. by JG DATE 6-24-39
NUMBER MR-2A JM CG
MODEL SHEETS SUBJECT TO RECALL
WITHOUT NOTICE
© Walt Disney Productions

A charming model sheet of critters by Jack Miller and Campbell Grant for the "Uncle Remus" film that became Song of the South *(1946). Courtesy Sotheby's.*

Los Angeles Examiner and the family moved to the beach in the Venice section of Los Angeles where "when the tide was high it would come all around the house." For a year, Joe was a child contract player making $35 a week in Fox Films, such as *Jack and the Beanstalk,* directed by Sidney Franklin near Chatsworth. He attended high school in Venice and, later, art classes downtown at Chouinard, but his main art training came from accompanying his father to the newspaper and "observing."

He loved the "clownish" atmosphere of the art department where a "wild, fun bunch of hard-drinking characters" would ring cowbells under their desks if a pretty woman walked by, or teased newcomers (like the teenaged Grant) by sending them on a fool's errand for a bucket of "vanishing

points" or a "paper stretcher." In between jokes, he learned how to retouch photos and the craft of printing. Through his father, he got a job as an assistant to the political cartoonist on the *Los Angeles Record* at $10 a week. Eventually, he was asked to draw caricatures for the drama page, which led to the fateful phone call from Walt.

At the Hyperion Avenue studio, Grant felt immediately at home among several former newspaper men, such as layout artists Charles E. Philippi and Hugh Hennesy, storyman Webb Smith, and former high school chum and animator Dick Lundy. Grant happily found the studio's atmosphere as clownish and filled with odd personalities as the newspaper art departments he had known and loved. There was, for example, storyman Pinto Colvig, the voice of Goofy (and later

54

55

*Ted Sears,
Otto Englander, and
Webb Smith (left to
right) examine a board
of Character Model
Department suggestions
for* Pinocchio.

Grumpy and Sleepy), who played a trombone attached to a chain around his neck because "I almost swallowed one of these things." Grant recalled that Ted Sears, "a real brain . . . had an enormous head, almost hydrocephalus. He'd sit looking at problem storyboards, his head resting on his hand, then doze off. When his finger hit his hairline, he'd wake up with the answer. It was magical!"[8]

Grant sat in an office between two dedicated cigar smokers, Albert Hurter and Bob Kuwahara, and noted "It's a wonder I didn't get lung cancer in there."[9] Grant worked with "Ted and the boys" in story developing *Grasshopper and the Ants* (1934), *Gulliver Mickey* (1934), *Water Babies* (1935), and other shorts. He was ambitious: At home he made inspirational drawings in colored pastel to give body to ideas and brought them to the studio. Walt noticed and soon others began coloring their story sketches. "Your whole focus was appealing to Walt to stimulate him," said Grant. "And also to raise yourself in his esteem."

He formed "an intellectual bond" with William Cottrell, a former newspaper sportswriter and cartoonist who had written continuity for a couple of George Herriman's Krazy Kat comic strips. Both young men were well-read and knowledgeable about music and art, and as story partners their sophistication was reflected in sparkling visual and story touches in *Pluto's Judgement Day* (1935), *Three Orphan Kittens* (1935) (which won the studio its fourth Academy Award), *Three Little Wolves* (1936), and particularly *Who Killed Cock Robin* (1935).

"We got into the more high-class stuff," said Grant with pride. He found Cottrell "an inspiration" who was "very intelligent in his approach to things." For example, in *Cock Robin,* Cottrell suggested that a jury of birds sing choruses à la Gilbert and Sullivan; he also thought up clever scene transitions, as when a cop's truncheon pounding on a prisoner's head smoothly cross-dissolves into a trial judge's gavel pounding on a desk. One of Grant's inspired ideas for the film was to create Miss Jenny Wren as a caricature of Mae West.

"We worked well together because I could picture what he had in mind and also ideas of my own." The young pair's eagerness and energy was felt by Walt: In a 1935 memo to Ted Sears he noted that Cottrell and Grant "are very anxious to do the story of Wynken, Blynken and Nod . . ." and are "quite enthused over this Hollywood idea where all the personalities of Hollywood are gathered together in bird and animal form in the big wood called The Hollywoods."

The team was assigned to *Snow White* to develop sequences involving the Queen as beauty and as hag, and Grant's pastel sketches of both characters were turned into model sheets for the animators. (Grant and Albert Hurter share screen credit as the film's character designers; Cottrell is listed as a sequence director.)

The fruitful partnership ended when Walt asked Grant to form the Character Model Department. "He [Walt] didn't include Bill in it. He just decided I was the one to take over, so that was it. But it was typical of him to divide and conquer."[10] Walt jealously guarded his power and often felt the need to reassert control. He "had something within him," said Grant, "that if we got too chummy, too close, and maybe too successful, he'd break it up."[11]

Snow White and the Seven Dwarfs was a major popular and financial success. Walt had, at that time, extraordinary confidence in the future of animated features and it led to a period of unprecedented (and expensive) creative activity at the studio. *Pinocchio* was in story, a "concert feature" (later titled *Fantasia*) was in the pipeline as were other long-form films, such as *Bambi, Peter Pan,* and *Alice in Wonderland.* With his staff edging toward 1,000 employees and the Hyperion studio bulging at the seams, Walt also planned construction of an expensive new superstudio in the San Fernando Valley.

Grant saw his new department as a golden opportunity to play a major creative role not only in the extraordinary expansion of Disney's dreams, but the art of animation itself. "I was enthusiastic as hell about [animated films]," he said. "I thought it was the greatest thing. I couldn't think of anything beyond it. All of the great art of the past, all the achievement, there couldn't have been anything like this. I imagine the people who did tapestries in the seventeenth century felt the same thing, you know, 'Look what I'm making.' "[12]

The Character Model Department began in a single room on the second floor in the northeast corner of the animation building at the Hyperion studio. Grant quickly assembled a first-rate team of graphic artists, who at one time or another included John P. (Jack) Miller, Bob Jones, Martin Provensen, Campbell Grant (no relation), John Walbridge, Fini Rudiger, Tom Codrick, Mary Blair, Aurelius Battaglia, James Bodrero, Kay Nielsen, and Albert Hurter, among others.

At first, they literally drew models of characters, props, tools, toys, and so on for *Pinocchio,* for use as drawing guides by the layout artists and animators. "Drawing was everywhere," recalled Martin Provensen:

The walls were plastered with drawings. You walked into the drawing when you went into the studio . . . I

Mlle. Upanova, the graceful ostrich ballerina from "Dance of the Hours," in pastel parodies of Degas by Campbell Grant. Courtesy Pierre Lambert.

57

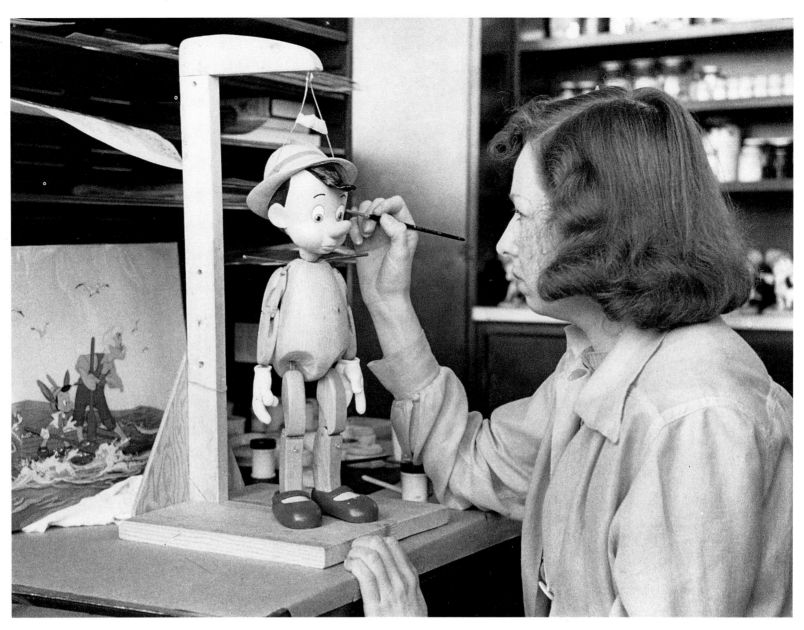

was plunged into this sea of drawing. You really waded up to your neck in it . . . And you developed a certain attitude toward drawing. You saw drawing as a way of talking and a way of feeling. Instead of regarding an individual drawing as a sacred thing, it was waste paper.[13]

Bob Jones remembered Grant's rapid analysis of the drawings and his ability to express to the artists what refinements were necessary. "When the design was finalized, I would spread the drawings on a table for Joe's inspection. He would indicate key poses and review the construction notes. These were mounted on a sheet of cardboard . . . copies [were] made and distributed."[14] "No model sheet of characters was official until it bore the seal, 'OK, J.G.,'" wrote animators Thomas and Johnston. For Joe Grant was "the studio's authority on the design and appearance of nearly everything that moved on the screen, and his taste and judgment were largely responsible for the pleasing style that identified the Disney product."[15]

An expansion of the Character Model Department was triggered by another of Walt's cryptic remarks: "The model sheets establish what the character looks like, but something else is needed." To give animators more of a "feel" for new characters, Bob Jones, a puppeteer, suggested a sculptor be hired to model small figures. Subsequently, Grant hired Charles Cristodoro, Ted Kline, Lorna (Shirley) Soderstrom, and Duke Russell to produce sculpted character models, and Helen Nerbovig and several women from the ink and paint department to paint them. Bob and Bill Jones managed this special area, which also built three-dimensional props, such as cuckoo clocks, a gypsy wagon, fully articulated marionettes and a whale for *Pinocchio,* planets, volcanoes, and a miniature earthquake set for *Fantasia.* The character model department also supervised the costumes and makeup for the live-action cinematography of actors and dancers used to guide the animators.

It was Grant who moved the model department into the

Martin Provensen, who became a well-known children's book illustrator, creates a turtle character for an unknown project.

In May 1940, members of the Associated American Artists looked over a table full of Character Model Department maquettes: (left to right) George Biddle, A.A.A. director Reeves Lewenthal, Thomas Hart Benton, Ernest Fiene, Grant Wood, and George Schreiber.

59

area of story. "Walt gave it the title Character Model Department," said Grant. "But we weren't just making sculptures, we were doing ideas. He used us like a brain trust. We'd have a board full of ideas. He'd pick something, enlarge on it. Come back two or three times a day to discuss it. Things that came out of that would be *Pinocchio,* some of *Dumbo,* some of *Fantasia."* In fact, many shorts and animated features released through 1955 (up to and including *Lady and the Tramp*) either originated in or were developed before the war in the Character Model Department. There were lists of projects that never went beyond exploratory sketches, such as classic fairy tales by Hans Christian Andersen, including *The Little Fir Tree, The Emperor's New Clothes,* and *Through the Picture Frame,* and witty stories by Joe Grant, such as *Roland the 13th* (a W.W. I pigeon spy), *Lorenzo the Magnificent* (a pampered cat's tail that takes on a life of its own), and *The Square World* (about conformism and totalitarianism), among many others.[16]

"We would just sort of bat ideas around one to the other," said Campbell Grant. "Some days we would be really hot and we could think of all kinds of ideas. Other days we would just be given a standard job to do a model sheet of a certain character, which had been roughly conceived but had not been put into final form. But always there was time on our hands when we just enjoyed drawing stuff not related to the [current] studio work at all."

"Joe would cook up a story line," said Martin Provensen, "and improvise . . . He was very good at inventing peripheral characters." Jiminy Cricket (nameless and murdered early on in Collodi's original story) developed over a period of months in character model with the input of key animators (particularly Ward Kimball) and became a star. "Joe was a remarkable man," said Campbell Grant, "and Disney never really knew how to use him very well because he wasn't in the mainstream of the Disney cartoon point of view. He was more European, more—well, avant garde isn't really the word, but he was interested in peripheral aspects of drawing."

Joe Grant's early pastel sketches for the old wizard in *Fantasia*'s Sorcerer's Apprentice, which already have the basic dour countenance of the beetle-browed elderly magician, play with hair and beard shapes and color. Hovering over a glowing-eyed skull, the sorcerer looks to be a first cousin to *Snow White*'s witch. Martin Provensen's red conte crayon explored a full-length version of the character, and both his and Grant's designs influenced the choice of Nigel De Brulier, the silent movie actor who was outfitted with a large beard and wig and photographed in live-action as reference for animator Vladimir Tytla.

"We write graphically," Grant recently said of the task of the inspirational artist.

The character model folk were shielded from all that by their immediate boss, who was "laid back" and "way ahead of his time" in his "cool" demeanor.[20] Grant "had the happy faculty of having Walt's ear and could walk in on Walt at any time and sell him ideas," said Campbell Grant. "Joe was very good, and brash enough to do this and lucky enough to get away with it."[21] There was about the model department an air of privilege, a snobbism, and more than a whiff of condescension regarding the intellectual and artistic sensibilities of the rest of the poor slobs in production, particularly the animators. Grant once admitted as such:

> Dick [Huemer], and myself, and Martin [Provensen], and Jim [Bodrero]—these people had read, they were intelligent, they knew music and literature, and they were good conversationalists. They were universal people in their knowledge. I would admit that we were great snobs, that we looked down upon these guys [animators] as a hundred percent yokel. There was no changing them. We were roundly hated for it.[22]

The first steps are to get the big things. Chaplin's eating of the shoe, start with that. A story grows out of that situation. He's hungry in the Klondike. Maybe there's a music hall girl in it. We try with writers to get a story line strong enough to hang gags and ideas on. That's the principle. We're not always successful, but writers and story artists are absolutely vital to this business.[17]

The Character Model artists thought of their special department as "a little sanctuary, where we were not quite in the mouse factory atmosphere."[18] One artist told of "floating my way through" by drawing all day with none of the pressures the animators faced.[19] The poor animators—grinding out daily footage on tight deadlines and getting tough, direct criticism from Walt and his sequence directors in stuffy, smelly projection booths aptly named sweatboxes. "The Character Model guys felt they were the lucky ones," recalls Frank Thomas. "They didn't have to put up with all the stuff we did. Nobody was looking over their shoulder—'And how many drawings have you got today?'—and setting deadlines and holding you responsible for stuff."

Martin Provensen developed his Sorcerer from a live model, perhaps Nigel De Brulier, the silent movie actor who, outfitted with a beard, was filmed as a visual reference guide for animator Vladimir Tytla.

In truth, most of the top animators, such as Vladimir Tytla, Art Babbitt, Frank Thomas, Ollie Johnston, Marc Davis, Ward Kimball, among others, were as educated regarding art and as intellectually nimble as anyone in Character Model. But removed from the conceptual/story areas of the studio, their role in the process involved a different discipline. "It wasn't like animation where you're producing stuff that came out on the screen," protests Ollie Johnston. The animators did not have the freedom to explore different styles or to spend all day making a single perfect sketch while discussing schools of art. Their noses *were* to the grindstone because it was their acting

performances that were ultimately seen and felt by audiences, and could make or break all the ideas and inspirations that came before.

The pressure and stress in the animation department was intense, and in the Byzantine beehive that was the Disney studio you can bet the animators hated what they perceived as the patronizing attitude of Joe Grant and his "playboy salon" of a department.[23] Several animators were piqued because "he was always drawing stuff that we couldn't do. It was always pastel." Grant and his department often used hard square pastels (not the smudgy kind) because "you can draw fast with them." But pastel's imprecise line was impossible to duplicate in animation, and animators felt he undercut them when he would ask Walt, "Why can't the animators do this?"

"I think he had his personal agenda," says Johnston, voicing an opinion held by many animators of the time. "He had these drawings always ready to show Walt at an opportune moment."[24] Thomas recalls Grant would "wait till Walt was talking about something that wasn't quite coming off. 'Well,

uh, I was working last night, Walt, and, uh . . .' Walt'd say, 'Whatcha got there, Joe?' Out would come a little pastel sketch from his jacket's inside pocket. 'Yah! Hey, guys. Come look at this!' We'd say, 'Well, Walt, ya can't . . .' Well, you didn't say can't or don't or won't to Walt. You'd say with gritted teeth, 'Yeah, that looks pretty good. Heh-heh.' " Certain production managers resented Grant's access to Walt, whom they regarded as a personal Sun King; and there were directors and story people who grudgingly thought Grant a blatant empire builder, a ruthless accumulator and consolidator of power. To Grant, such niggling jealousies did not take into consideration the big picture: "These projects [the Disney films] to me were just precious. Get them going! I didn't care what the hell they said! But it's sort of a period there of a lot of misunderstanding and jealousy."[25]

More than half a century later, Grant expressed to Robin Allan his passionate commitment to the work and to Walt: "I had fallen in love with the studio. I had fallen in love with the *idea,* particularly the idea and then him later because, God, he was—he *was* the idea!"[26]

63

CHAPTER 6

James Bodrero

"The thing I cling to in my memory of the [studio]," Martin Provensen of the Character Model Department once recalled, "is the extraordinary charm and vivacity that the place had prewar, and the extraordinary people that you met and worked with—brilliantly gifted people the world doesn't know—[and] the zany, goofy, wonderful, bizarre, Marx Brothers character of the place."[1]

To illustrate the openness and eclecticism regarding art, graphic style, and personnel that existed in the important department Joe Grant built, let us consider two Character Model artists who were a study in contrasts: James Bodrero and Kay Nielsen.

James Bodrero was a witty eccentric, a raconteur and bohemian bon vivant: a man, say most of his former associates, of tremendous charm. "He could talk endlessly and make you laugh all the way," said Frank Thomas.[2] "He was a storyteller," according to Marc Davis, "a guy nobody could pass by."[3] Grant thought Bodrero "a genius" who was "amazing at concept." His superb and lively drawings were born of a machinelike facility; in one day, it is said, Bodrero could "do a whole sequence, just grind it out, the way a brilliant typist can

ABOVE *A centaur and a centaurette "dance" together in a spirited Bodrero pastel.*
BELOW *In Buenos Aires in 1941 to research Latin American arts and culture for* Saludos Amigos *(1943): (left to right) Argentinian artist Molina Campos, Herb Ryman (in the background), Disney animator and director Norman Ferguson, Character Model artist James Bodrero, Walt Disney, and Disney Studio publicist Janet Martin.*

type a manuscript. [His pencil] would never leave the paper." He had "the ability to draw anything, and simply pour this stuff out, like a spigot."[4]

There was quality in his quantity. In Bodrero's concept drawings for the bacchanal sequence of the Pastoral Symphony section in *Fantasia*, for example, his reveling centaurs and centaurettes have an appropriately lusty sexuality and ribald wit; a Mediterranean ethnicity pervades the swarthy centaurs in their jet black ponytails. Unfortunately, the earthiness of Bodrero's Dionysian celebrators is absent from the character's design in the final film. *Time* magazine complained of "smirkingly brassiered" centaurettes, "calf-eyed centaurs and kewpie-doll cupids" who made "Bacchus's bacchanale look like a nursery lemonade party" and put "diapers on Olympus."[5]

Bodrero's virile, muscular, hirsute males drunkenly chasing and dancing with bare-breasted lithe females were too much for the Hollywood Production Code, so on film they were toned way down. But his beautifully textured pastels on colored paper still burst with boisterous life, and one sees the artist's restless imagination churning as each sketch inspires a further development or a new direction. He brings in Bacchus's teacher, fat drunken Silenus (erroneously identified as Bacchus), for some healthily vulgar visual jokes, such as the old debauchee astride his loyal jackass/unicorn with the animal's horn between his legs in a "Look, ma! I'm Priapus!" pose.

65

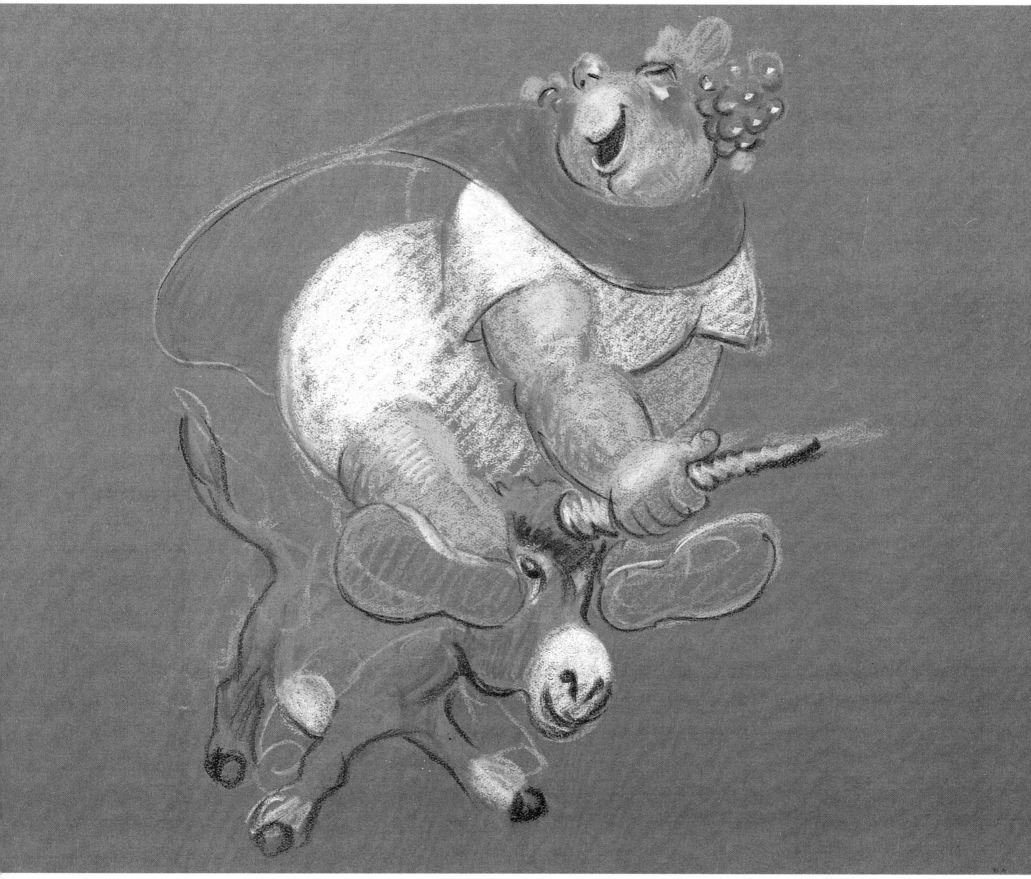

ABOVE *James Bodrero's lusty approach to depicting an anything-goes bacchanal for the Pastoral Symphony section of* Fantasia.

OPPOSITE ABOVE *A Bodrero pastel of Bacchus and a Centaurette for the Pastoral section of* Fantasia. *Jeff Lotman Collection.*

OPPOSITE BELOW *Two stagedoor-Johnny alligators attempt to charm a crocodile ballerina in this amusing Bodrero watercolor. Jeff Lotman Collection.*

Bodrero's first assignment was the Dance of the Hours sequence in *Fantasia*, to which he brought a sly sensuality to balletic alligators and hippopotami. Heinrich Kley's inked beasts were the direct inspiration (ditto for Albert Hurter and Lee Blair, who also created concept art for the sequence). But the slippery and sinister reptiles tossing each other through the air, stepping on each other's tails, and surrounding bovine hippo-ballerinas in a subtly threatening manner (do they want to eat her, make love to her, or both?) are uniquely Bodrero in the robust brush and ink line, agile motion and humor. In another sketch, backstage at the ballet two tuxedoed gators-about-town woo a comely tutu-clad croc as her friends whisper jealously. Bodrero had many friends in the theater and films, and he brings to this charmingly sophisticated sketch and other drawings a knowing quality. Certainly one finds the irresistible humor and charm of James Bodrero in his drawings, and he was, like his jolly centaurs, a man more than a little familiar with the pleasures of both the flesh and the grape.

James Spaulding Pompeo Bodrero was born into privilege on July 6, 1900, in Spa, Belgium, the son of an American socialite mother and an Italian father, who was a career officer in the Italian army and aide to King Victor Emmanuel III.[6] He attended boarding schools in Europe and America, and in summer rode horses (and drew them) with his two brothers and a sister on a sugar plantation owned by his maternal grandparents on the Hawaiian island of Kauai. "His mother," comments Bodrero's daughter Lydia Reed, "bounced him around." He designed, illustrated, and wrote prose and poetry for his high school yearbook, and sold John Held–like drawings to *Life,* the humor magazine, while still a teen. At Pomfret prep school in Connecticut, he divided his time between arts and sports: he played the mandolin, sang in a glee club, performed in a drama club, and was on the hockey, football, and crew teams.

During World War I, seventeen-year-old Bodrero served in France as a corporal in the U.S. Army tank corps; during one battle, his pants were literally shot off him. In Paris, he had a brief reunion with his father, whom he had not seen in a decade. Divorced from James's mother, Bodrero Sr. was now a colonel on his way to becoming a brigadier general. "Wonder who the old wop is with all the hardware," said James to a fellow soldier before the old man covered with medals came up and kissed him on both cheeks. "Jeemy," said his father.

After the war, James returned to school, graduating in 1920. "He was attractive and a very good dancer and led an active social life," according to Mrs. Reed. In 1926, he married the beautiful Eleanor Cole, a commercial artist and granddaughter of the first senator from California. They opened their own studio in Pasadena called ORRO and made batiks, hand-colored textiles, and custom-designed weather vanes. Their daughter was born the next year, and a son five years later. The family moved to Santa Barbara where James freelanced as an artist and his wife as an interior decorator, but because of the Depression they "had difficulty making ends meet." At some point in the mid-thirties he traveled to Mexico with photographer Floyd Crosby (father of David Crosby of the singers Crosby, Stills and Nash) and made brush-and-ink sketches on newsprint paper that was exposed for hours to the sun; the fragile tan sketches matted on white in simple wooden frames sold well at several exhibitions.

Despite the need for "scrabbling about" after freelance art jobs and borrowing money from relatives, the Bodreros socialized with "all sorts of interesting, famous, and colorful people," such as Robert Benchley, Katherine Cornell, Walter Pidgeon, Hoagy Carmichael, Tallulah Bankhead, and Leopold Stokowski, a Santa Barbara neighbor who once brought his girlfriend Greta Garbo to Sunday lunch. James also found time to play polo with Argentineans visiting Los Angeles to compete in the 1932 Olympics, and to have "an affair of six months duration with the actress Miriam Hopkins" that started in Los Angeles and ended in New York.[7] "Typical Jimmy flurries," is how he described his frequent brief affairs to his tolerant wife, meaning they were nothing serious; l'affair Hopkins, however, pushed the envelope and led the Bodreros to talk of divorce.

Like most of the Hollywood crowd they hung with, the Bodreros were heavy social drinkers. Often at parties James would prepare the "Jim Bodrero Special," a potent combination of bottles of gin, Chablis, and soda poured over a cake of ice containing fruit, with a cucumber to "smooth" it. The drink is "so smooth and tastes so good," recalled one imbiber/survivor, "you don't realize what you're drinking until they pick you up off the floor."[8] Although James could hold his considerable intake of liquor and "was more of the same when he drank," his wife (whose family included a number of alcoholics) "had no capacity for alcohol." Occasionally, she would "binge drink" for days at a time and become incoherent.

"We kids loved him," says daughter Lydia of her father. "He was the kind of person who would create a whole fantasy, and you would do it. On Sunday afternoons, we went on picnics a lot because he and my mother were outdoor people. He taught us to ride." A gang of guys from Character Model (including Martin Provensen, Jack Miller, and Campbell Grant) "were like part of the furniture" at the Bodrero home in Santa Barbara, arriving on Friday and staying the weekend. Full of fun and imagination, the four men (including James) were like big kids, sometimes putting on melodra-

mas in the living room for the amusement of the Bodrero children and their friends. "The Monkey's Paw," "a horror story about a curse in which ships sank, people died" was staged in pantomime, the artists silhouetted by a light behind a sheet. The appendage of the title was "a witch's hand they got from the studio."

In 1938, Random House published Bodrero's illustrated book *Bomba,* based on a Sicilian donkey he acquired for his kids. *Bomba* became a best-selling children's book for three years. That same year, Stokowski asked him to come work at Disney's, to which Bodrero replied, "For Christ sake, Stokowski, do you see me making duck's feet move?" "There's something going on there that isn't making duck's feet move," Stokowski answered referring to *Fantasia,* the concert feature he was about to conduct.[9] Bodrero showed galley proofs of his *Bomba* illustrations to Joe Grant and began work on October 3, 1938, commuting to Santa Barbara on weekends.

At age thirty-eight, Bodrero was older than most of the twenty-something artists in the model department, but with his devil-may-care charm and humor he fit right in. "In the Model Department were, even in a society of screwballs, outstanding screwballs. A man like James Bodrero—he was an extraordinary man," said Martin Provensen.[10] His fellow inspirational artists were amused by Bodrero's claims that he knew everyone. "James got around, he was a very social person," says Joe Grant, who saved a caricature of "Bode" (as he was nicknamed) standing in a doorway saying, "I want you to meet a friend of mine," and pointing to Jesus.

In the department's back-and-forth banter about art, Bodrero proclaimed his love for Leonardo, Picasso, and Goya, but not artists "who used a lot of shading to get form," such as Michelangelo who, he claimed, "screwed up art for hundreds of years" and whose "line wasn't pure." His outrageous put-down masked an insecurity about his own work; for despite his facility, Bodrero "was a little self conscious of his drawing," said Marc Davis, who worked closely with him on the wartime feature *Victory through Air Power* (1943). He was "never too sure in using tone, and sometimes would ask me to help him."

But he needed no help with line, as can be seen in the character model sheet dated February 6, 1941, of Toad from *Wind in the Willows* (released in 1949 as *The Adventures of Ich-*

A never-before-published example of pre-production "Leica Reel" drawings (all by James Bodrero) for a Pastoral Symphony sequence. The Leica Reel, according to John Culhane, was "a device for projecting drawings a frame at a time in synchronization with the appropriate musical passage . . . a way to determine if the staging of a scene 'felt' right with the music before spending the time and money necessary to animate the scenes."

abod and Mr. Toad). To animator Ollie Johnston, it is "one of the most expressive model sheets I have ever seen as far as character goes."[11] Polishing a monocle with pinkie akimbo, elegantly declaiming, gesturing, and strutting his dignified stuff, or squatting in the depths of despair tied to a ball and chain,

Toad appears to be a complete character thanks to the strong attitudes in Bodrero's drawings. "They really helped the picture," said Johnston.

Bodrero loved working at Disney, especially as part of the elite Character Model Department. Joe Grant's group was al-

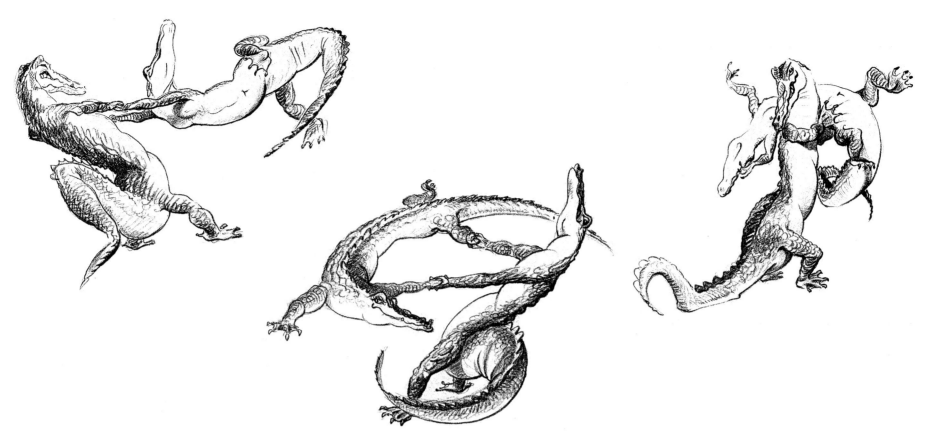

WIND IN THE WILLOWS
"TOAD SUGGESTIONS"
~ 2011 ~

OPPOSITE *A cougar and a centaurette go strutting.*
ABOVE *Inspired by Heinrich Kley's animal drawings, Bodrero brings his own sensual touch to these acrobatic reptiles.*
BELOW *A 1941 model sheet by Bodrero (for the character who starred eight years later in* The Adventures of Ichabod and Mr. Toad) *has been described by master animator Ollie Johnston as "one of the most expressive model sheets I have ever seen …"*

71

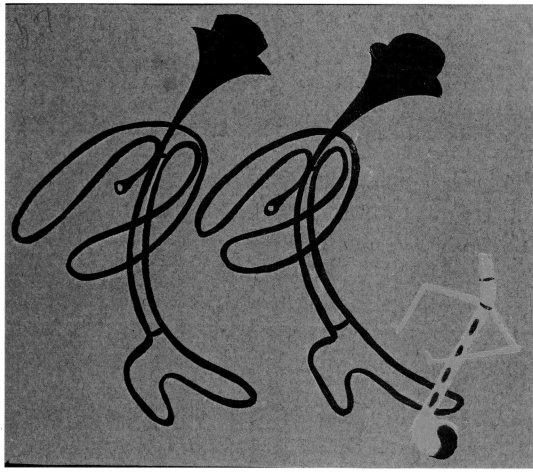

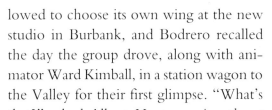

lowed to choose its own wing at the new studio in Burbank, and Bodrero recalled the day the group drove, along with animator Ward Kimball, in a station wagon to the Valley for their first glimpse. "What's that?" asked Albert Hurter spying the studio's huge water tower. "I think," cracked the irrepressible Kimball, "that is young blood."[12]

In 1941, Bodrero was invited by Walt to accompany him and a small group of artists to South America on a trip arranged through Nelson Rockefeller's office of the Coordinator of Inter-American Affairs (CIAA). The visit, part of the U.S.A.'s Good Neighbor Policy, was to research Latin American culture for a series of films. Frank Thomas recalled Bodrero as a "slightly irresponsible but wonderful companion" who tended to oversleep after a night on the town, but could rouse nude and completely dress himself in three minutes flat with a breakfast on the run consisting of two raw eggs in a glass of sherry. Stories of the adventures of Bodrero and El Groupo (as the artists called themselves) became legion at the Studio; two will suffice to demonstrate the *international* popularity of Jimmy Bodrero. In Buenos Aires, for example, his Argentinean polo buddies remembered him fondly; dozens of them, their families and friends ran onto the airfield to greet the arrival of the DC-3 carrying El Groupo, screaming "Jeemy! Jeemy! Jeemy!" and totally ignored Walt Disney.[13] And there was the evening in Rio de Janeiro when Walt attended a performance by opera star Grace Moore and went backstage for an introduction. "In her dressing room, she's in a robe fixing her hair," said Marc Davis. "Walt comes in, meets her, turns,

and as the door begins to close, behind the door *shaving* is Jim Bodrero! Walt said 'I'll be a son of a bitch!' "[14] That Jeemy sure got around.

In 1945, Bodrero volunteered for the U.S.O. and traveled alone to remote war zones in the South Pacific drawing cartoons and caricatures for the troops in field hospitals and on battlefields. His wife kept things going at home through her interior decorating business. Eighteen months later he returned to his family twenty-five pounds lighter and "full of malaria." For years after, he received grateful letters from service men and women whose spirits he had lifted during the war.

He returned to Disney, but was laid off in August 1946 due to postwar cost cutting. "He cried big elephant tears, I remember very well," said Lydia Reed, because "at Disney he was so happy!" He worked briefly as a writer for Hal Roach Studios and painted murals for restaurants up and down the state. His wife died as the result of a fall in 1949. The next year, Bodrero married his wife's best friend, Geraldine Graham McDonald, with whom he'd had a "Jimmy flurry" before his wife's death.

Disney began to rehire laid-off workers, and Bodrero would have been among them. But the new Mrs. Bodrero, a woman of wealth, insisted she could not live in Los Angeles; and so they moved far from the land of Disney to San Fran-

cisco, and built a second home in Spain. The couple led a busy social life among the rich and famous and were hailed in a newspaper society column as "two people who epitomize San Francisco sophistication."[15] Ted Sears sent the article to several Disneyites, ruefully commenting, "Remember when he used to let us lend him money?"[16]

Privately, the Bodrero marriage was full of strife because of alcohol ("When she wasn't drinking, he would drink") exacerbated by "all this guilt—'What we've done to Eleanor?'—that went through the rest of their lives," according to Mrs. Reed. Bodrero now became a binge drinker, often hallucinating and entering hospitals to dry out. He did little art work during his second marriage, but in 1965 managed to write and illustrate *Long Ride to Grenada* (Reynal and Company) about a horseback ride he and friends took in Spain.

When Geraldine died in 1976, Bodrero was "very lost" and in failing health. He died four years later at age eighty in a cheerful apartment he painted bright "Mexican pink" in the El Drisco Hotel in San Francisco.

OPPOSITE AND ABOVE *Five inventive and delightful pastel sketches of personalized musical instruments by Bodrero for an unknown jazz fantasy. Adaptations of his designs found their way into the Benny Goodman Quartet section ("After You've Gone") in* Make Mine Music *(1946).*

73

CHAPTER 7

Kay Nielsen

One day late in 1938, a tall, slightly stooped, dignified fifty-three year old Danish artist applied to the Disney studio for work. Whoever accepted the polite gentleman's portfolio did not recognize the name Kay [pronounced "Kigh"] Nielsen, but Joe Grant did. "I'd known his work from books. I said Jesus, this guy's great!"[1]

Indeed, Nielsen is considered "the third great illustrator of the gift book,"[2] the successor and equal to Arthur Rackham and Edmund Dulac, the top turn-of-the-century "Golden Age" illustrators of deluxe books. "Nielsen's reputation as an illustrator of children's books was based on only four books of fairy tales, two published before World War I," according to author Susan E. Meyer.[3] But what books! His most famous, *East of the Sun and West of the Moon: Old Tales from the North* (published in London in 1914), contains twenty-five stunning colored illustrations. Inspired by the art nouveau excesses of Aubrey Beardsley as well as Japanese and Chinese woodcut artists and watercolorists, Nielsen's art combines sensuous and delicate linework, rich and unusual color choices, and areas of obsessive decoration contrasted with blank spaces surrounding characters. "The great charm of these paintings," wrote Keith Nicholson, "lies in the artist's

power of combining eerie suggestion with beautiful decorative effect."[4]

Nielsen brought his ornamental, flowing and morbidly beautiful designs to Night On Bald Mountain and Ave Maria, the only sections of *Fantasia* possessing high style (or, more accurately, high stylization). "He was born for it," said Joe Grant. "He came at the right time for Bald Mountain. Maybe it's my imagination but everything [in Disney's prewar period] seemed to come together at the right time." In Nielsen's career, however, things were tragically out of sync. By the time he published his first book in 1913, for example, he was already too late for the gift book vogue. "If only he had begun his career five years earlier, he might have surpassed any illustrator of his day," said Susan E. Meyer.

Kay Rasmus Nielsen was born in Copenhagen, Denmark in 1886 into what he once described as "a tense atmosphere of art."[5] His parents were well-to-do, famous theater people: mother Oda was a singer and star of the Royal Theater; father Professor Martinius Nielsen was an actor and manager of the Dagmartheater. It was a privileged and intimidating environment for the child, who was privately tutored in schoolwork. He saw plays, heard concerts, and viewed painting exhibitions, and the Nielsen home was visited by a constant stream of the great playwrights, musicians and actors of the day, including Grieg, Ibsen, Bjornsen, among others. Young Kay was surrounded by art, even in his home's furnishings: "I loved the Chinese drawings and carvings in my mother's

OPPOSITE TOP *A Kay Nielsen pastel of Chernobog, the devil in "Night on Bald Mountain."* Mike Glad Collection.
OPPOSITE BELOW *Kay Nielsen (left) discussing "Night on Bald Mountain" with his Character Model Department artist-assistant Bill Wallett.*

room," he once said, "brought home from China by her father."

Kay drew constantly as a child with his parents' eager encouragement (his nickname was "Little Philosopher of the Pencil"). At first he wanted to follow in the footsteps of his grand uncle, a celebrated physician, perhaps in protest against the arts hothouse he grew up in. When he was seventeen, however, he gave himself over to his parent's ambitions for him and studied art from 1904 to 1912 in Paris.

At the Académie Julian (where Dulac had also studied) and Colarossi's art school, Nielsen received a solid grounding in classical painting and drawing. But he was also attracted by the contemporary art nouveau style made up of delicate sensuous lines, simplification of form, and flat color patterning, as exemplified by Alphonse Mucha and (most interesting to Nielsen) Aubrey Beardsley. Nielsen was also enthralled with Asian art, an influence stemming not only from his mother's

Chinese art back home, but the prints readily available in Paris of Japanese woodcuts by Utamaro, Hiroshige, and Hokusai.

A series of Nielsen drawings titled "The Book of Death" announced his extraordinary talent, and were displayed and favorably reviewed in London in 1912. This success led to his first deluxe book of watercolor fairy-tale illustrations, *Powder and Crinoline* in 1913, followed the next year by *East of the Sun and West of the Moon*. World War I "abruptly interrupted" the twenty-eight-year-old Nielsen's career, wrote Susan E. Meyer. Elaborate fairy storybooks were now out of step with the tastes of a public "far too preoccupied with the travesties of war to indulge in tales of fantasy."

Nielsen returned to Copenhagen and his family's roots in theater. He collaborated with a young actor/producer named Johannes Poulsen and together during the 1920s they produced and designed spectacular stage fantasies, such as *Aladdin, Scaramouche, The Tempest,* and *A Midsummer Night's*

A continuity storyboard made up of sketches by Nielsen and other Character Model Department artists.

Dream. In 1936, Poulsen and Nielsen were invited by the Festival Association of the Hollywood Bowl to come to Los Angeles to stage Max Reinhardt's *Everyman*.

Nielsen's appearance at Disney's door in 1938 resulted from an untimely event: the sudden death of Poulsen. Nielsen's subsequent decision to remain in Hollywood and try his luck in films put the brakes on his stage design career as surely as the first world war had stopped his book illustration career. He sent for his wife, Ulla (whom he had married in 1926) to join him in Hollywood and he looked for work. He arrived at Disney's because, according to Joe Grant, "Kay was fascinated with the medium [of animation]." But as his drawings went through the Disney assembly line, a close friend noted that "he was not well pleased to see his designs altered during the process of animation."[6]

The Character Model Department, thrilled by the opportunity to work with such a gifted and renowned artist, wel-

comed Nielsen warmly. Joe Grant thought him "the most wonderful guy you could ever meet. Sweet and tolerant, extremely talented and quiet. He wasn't one to argue a point particularly, but he could illustrate it so well, he usually won over what was necessary." "Everything that man did was great," said Campbell Grant. "But you couldn't hurry him. He just worked at his own speed, and if the efficiency expert came around and tried to bug him, he just wouldn't talk to him."[7]

In order to maintain a reasonable schedule, Nielsen was supported in front and in back: Albert Hurter would initiate a scene in pencil sketches, for example, of the devil emerging from Bald Mountain, or lost souls from Hades oozing down the devil's giant hand. Nielsen would then create fully rendered color pastel drawings of key scenes based on Hurter's drawings. Graveyards in a medieval village, ghosts, skeletons, the mountain and the devil, mysterious fog, smoke and flames of hell drawn in the inimitable Nielsen style became key mod-

ABOVE LEFT *A pen and ink drawing by German artist Heinrich Kley, whose imagery and graphic style profoundly influenced numerous Disney artists, including Albert Hurter, James Bodrero, and Joe Grant. Kley's gigantic devils inspired* Fantasia's *devil on Bald Mountain; versions of Kley's cavorting elephants, hippos, and crocodiles found their way into the "Dance of the Hours" and echoes of his centaurs are in the Pastoral Symphony section.*

ABOVE RIGHT AND BELOW *Two Albert Hurter drawings of a huge devil crushing tiny human souls in his giant hands and tossing them into hell's fires are based on similar imagery by Heinrich Kley.*

78

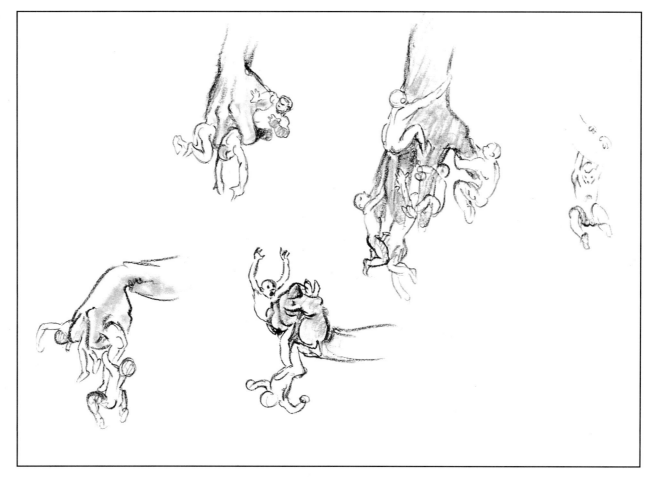

LEFT AND ABOVE
*Hurter's initial sketches
were passed on to Kay
Nielsen, who created
elaborate colored pastel
or black charcoal
drawings in his decorous
style, setting the
"look" of the "Bald
Mountain" sequence.*

els for Bald Mountain's color, characters, and overall design. A young artist named Bill Wallett drew additional pastel styling sketches keying the backgrounds; his dynamic work closely emulates Nielsen, while lacking the master's stylish delicacy. Finally, Campbell Grant drew thumbnail continuity sketches for the sequence to help guide the director and animators.

"Your routine is very foreign to me," Nielsen wrote in a letter to Joe Grant dated May 31, 1939. It was nearly six months after the aging artist joined the studio and three months since a talk with Grant convinced him to "stick it out" until Grant could "be able to see where I could be placed or not placed in the work at Disney's." In the polite and sweetly sad letter, Nielsen shyly asks for more money and a share in the sale of any of his original drawings done at Disney, and pleads

for relief from the "fatiguing" long hours and six days-a-week schedule:

> During my whole life I have worked only for the results not thinking of time, but at Disney's the work is subject to the time element; and in order to be more successful I should need a little more time to myself in which to work out my ideas before I actually try to put them on paper. I also should be less tired and come to the work more refreshed. This subject of hours is open to discussion and suggestions—but Saturdays I must be free, anyhow, as I must have some time in which to rest before the next week starts.

Nielsen also protested attending Don Graham's action analysis evening lectures and classes—"I need my evenings very badly"—and he hoped for the "possibility of carrying out some sections of the work assigned me and already approved of at home."

"Naturally I tried to get some more money for him," said Grant. But the studio was hemorrhaging money on Walt's expensive new feature films and plans for the new Burbank stu-

79

RIGHT *Campbell Grant and Bill Wallett would "fill in" sequential sketches for the storyboards by attempting to emulate Nielsen's style.*
BELOW *A Bill Wallett suggestion for the village surrounding Bald Mountain, painted in the "Nielsen style." Courtesy Howard Lowery Gallery.*

dio, so "[Walt and Roy] were in a tight situation most of the time."[8] Besides, there was a question as to what to do with a unique talent like Nielsen. Hurter, Horvath, and Tenggren all had individual styles, but none was as distinctively stylized or non-Disney as Nielsen. "He didn't quite apply beyond *Fantasia,*" Grant said.[9] Nevertheless, Nielsen was kept busy making pastels of other sections of *Fantasia* and preparing delicate inspirational sketches and storyboards for Hans Christian Andersen's *The Little Mermaid*. When that feature finally saw the light of day in 1989, Nielsen received a posthumous screen credit as a visual developer.

At the end of June 1940, Nielsen was laid off, but three months later he was rehired to create inspirational drawings for *The Ride of the Valkyries* and *Swan of Tuonela,* sections for a proposed second edition of *Fantasia*.[10] Walt, ever the optimistic expansionist, intended *Fantasia* to be the motion picture medium's first "perpetual" entertainment by making "a new version" of the film each year. But when it was released in November 1940, *Fantasia* was a box office disappointment, as was *Pinocchio* released earlier that same year. Both films cost a total of almost $5 million in 1940 dollars and the new studio in Burbank cost $3 million. The healthy profits from *Snow White* were nearly gone, and while money continued to pour out, the war raging in Europe cut off half of the studio's income. Walt found himself "hip-deep in debt ($4,000,000)."[11] Nielsen was released for good on May 23, 1941, one of many layoffs that led six days later to a long and acrimonious employees strike at the studio (in which Nielsen did not participate). "Walt let him go against my wishes," said Grant, "but I had no clout at that time to keep him. The studio wasn't making very much money and *Fantasia* was not a success."

For the next sixteen years Nielsen and his wife lived hand-to-mouth in obscurity. They endured their poverty with dignity and impeccable manners, depending on the kindness of friends and neighbors, who gave them food, a car, even the small cottage they lived in. "People were drawn to them and people delighted to do things for them, not in a spirit of charity but because the donor relished being that much closer to them," wrote their friend and neighbor Hildegarde Flanner. They attempted and failed to alleviate their poverty by raising chickens for income, sold their few art possessions at auction, and even returned to Denmark briefly in a futile search for work. They returned to Los Angeles mainly because of the warm weather. Four commissions came Nielsen's way by sheer luck and helped tide them over for a time. Three were murals, described by Robin Allan as "astonishing, radiant works." Nielsen worked for three years starting in 1942 on a mural of Genesis 1:25 in the library of Central Junior High School. In 1946 he had a year's work on *The Canticle of the*

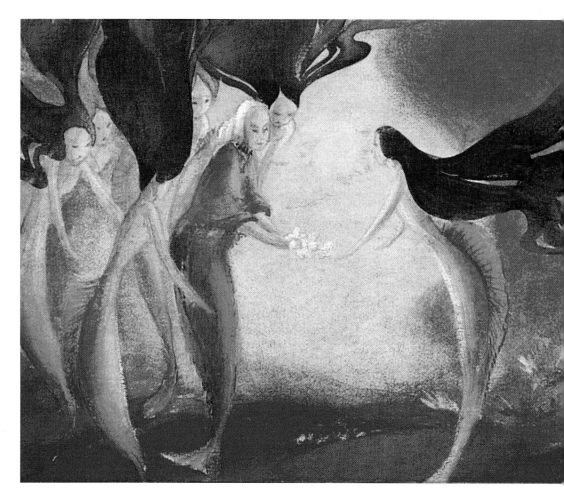

A 1939 Nielsen pastel sketch for Hans Christian Andersen's The Little Mermaid.

Sun, a mural for Emerson Junior High School, and the next year an altar painting for Wong Chapel in the First Congregational Church of Los Angeles. Six years later, he created a wall painting on a pioneer episode for Whitman College in Walla Walla, Washington.

In between murals, there was virtually no work and the couple suffered increasingly failing health. In 1953, Nielsen's presence is noted in story meeting notes at the Disney Studio for a discussion of the feature *Sleeping Beauty,* and it is tantilizing to imagine how he might have styled that medieval fairy tale. Art director Ken Anderson recalled seeing Nielsen's pastels for *Beauty* and thought his style "was just great, but it involved working on black paper, so it had a kind of inherent black mood." Also, his "soft pastel creatures" were not "easy to duplicate in animation where you had outlined characters." Anderson recalled that Walt asked John Hench (who had assisted Dali during *his* brief stay at the studio) to move into the same room with Kay to "interpret" Nielsen's work without losing the charm of the originals by using opaque cel paints.[12] Only one of Nielsen's pastels for the film remains in the Disney Animation Research Library—a subdued and (as Anderson said) dark view of a castle seen from a medieval hamlet, a peasant behind an ox working the land the only sign of life. Eventually, the color styling job for *Sleeping Beauty* went to a young staff artist, Eyvind Earle.[13]

Examples of Kay Nielsen's delicate concept art made in 1939 for The Little Mermaid. *When the film was finally produced fifty years later, Nielsen received a posthumous screen credit as a visual developer.*

Nielsen died destitute in 1957. Ulla, his loyal wife, quietly stopped taking her diabetes insulin and followed Kay the next year. Hildegarde Flanner wrote a touching account of the Nielsen's final years questioning "why an artist of Kay's reputation should find his abilities asking for employment." She concluded "his disadvantage lay in the narrowness of his range in a day that was suspicious of fantasy—unless neurotic or Joycean—that 'the Golden Age of Illustration' . . . had closed, and however vital his skill in decoration he had no ease in self-promotion."[14]

One of many Nielsen pastels for "The Ride of the Valkyries," a proposed section for a second version of Fantasia *in 1941.*

The only example of Nielsen's art made during his brief return to Disney in 1953 to work on Sleeping Beauty (1959).

CHAPTER 8

Fantastic Fantasia

In those heady days before war, financial woes, and a strike changed the tenor of the place forever, Joe Grant's power at the Disney Studio and his influence with Walt was second to none. It increased significantly with *Fantasia,* a project for which he became a story director along with animator/director Richard Huemer. The laid-back, catlike Huemer was intelligent with a gift for story and a love of music; Walt often introduced him: "Meet Dick Huemer; he goes to operas."[1]

Grant and Huemer formed a creative partnership: "I found out he could use a typewriter and we went from there," said Grant. "We got to talking story and began developing. We had a good relationship."[2] At least in the beginning.

The "concert feature" that became *Fantasia* was an oak that grew from the acorn of a Mickey Mouse short animated to Paul Dukas's orchestral scherzo "The Sorcerer's Apprentice." In early 1938, art director Tom Codrick painted a series of utterly engaging (and inspirational) gouache story sketches of the main action. For three weeks that fall, Hue-

ABOVE *Mickey Mouse beckons the universe in a gouache by Tom Codrick. Courtesy Sotheby's.*
BELOW *Leopold Stokowski and Walt Disney sit in front of a row of pastels on black paper for the "Nutcracker Suite" drawn by Elmer Plummer. A James Bodrero Bacchus can be seen peeking from behind Stokowski's left shoulder.*
OPPOSITE *Two evocative Tom Codrick story paintings for "The Sorcerer's Apprentice."*

85

mer, Grant, Walt, Stokowski, and music critic Deems Taylor selected music for the as-yet-unnamed concert feature's program by listening to hundreds of classical recordings. "Day after day playing records until our ears were stopped up with it," recalled Grant.[3]

Eventually, seven large production units of artists, directors, and artisans were formed to produce animation for eight pieces of music, and the number of studio employees headed toward 1,200. *Fantasia* was so unwieldy that Character Model personnel were parceled out to various sequence directors, who also hired their own story and inspirational sketch artists. Grant and Huemer bounced all over the studio keeping track of the development of the different sequences. "It was a very fluid set-up," said Grant. "People were in and out."

Huemer remembered "what fun" it was working on the Nutcracker Suite section: "I had this little group and I'd visit there every day and we'd sit and talk . . . toss around ideas, and you get it worked up and drawn to a point where Walt finally comes in . . . [He] takes it all apart or adds new stuff."[4] Walt "was very susceptible to stimulation" from the inspirational sketches, said Huemer, who likened the process to "bringing logs to the head beaver for him to build his dam."[5]

Walt's gift for storytelling and entertainment-filled continuity should not be underestimated. His creativity in the area of personality-driven narrative is the bedrock upon which his greatest films are built, and he was involved in every scene of the earliest features. He could quickly pinpoint weak areas in a storyboard and often enhanced good ideas, as when he looked at Tom Codrick's colored drawings of Mickey Mouse as the sorcerer's apprentice standing on a promontory conducting the ocean. "Yeah, very lovely pictures," he said, "but that's pretty dull stuff. Why not have him conduct the universe?" *"That's* the kind of enlargement he would bring into it," said Joe Grant admiringly.[6]

The concert feature—which became one of the most experimental mainstream animated films ever attempted (a masterwork that continues to astonish more than half a century later)—generated some of the most eclectic and visually striking inspirational sketch art of any Disney feature. For the Nutcracker Suite, Elmer Plummer, a Chouinard teacher, was brought in as a character designer and made hundreds of drawings on black paper of dancing mushrooms, thistles, and orchids rendered in pastel with a delicate faux Degas touch.

Walt Scott, who later created the comic strip "The Little People," went in another direction and in August 1939 painted charming watercolors resembling lacquered art deco boxes embossed with Chinese mushrooms, slinky Shanghai-lily girls, and mandarin bullfrogs.

Delicate paintings by Jules Engel, current head of exper-

imental animation at the California Institute of the Arts, suggested choreography for dancing snow flakes and ostrich ballerinas.

Nothing is known about Robert Sterner except that he created rooms full of smashing art for the Rite of Spring section depicting the cosmos forming, cataclysmic upheavals during Earth's birth ("Great impressive drawings in pastel where you could feel the heat!"),[7] and the beginnings of life through the age of dinosaurs. Three pastels made in October 1939 showcase Sterner's extraordinary way of placing Mesozoic monsters convincingly within their environments: Two behemoths battle on a rain-swept terrain; a lone raptor, framed by gingko trees, stalks in a steamy jungle; three land-dwelling amphibians stare dumbly at the sky, the sun's partial eclipse reflected blood-red in their eyes.

Air brush expert J. Gordon Legg, more precise and less raw in technique than Sterner, offers a God's-eye view of earth's volcanic birth pangs.

There is no employment record for Faith Rookus, although she appears in a publicity photograph and signed several moody black and white pastels for Ave Maria and a couple of mysterious water maidens and a golden fish dancer for the Nutcracker's Arabian Dance. John Hench (now in his late eighties and continuing to this day as a vice president at Walt Disney Imagineering) made a series of pastels for Ave Maria, extending Kay Nielsen's pilgrim procession through a forest leading to a cathedral with a huge stained-glass window depicting the Virgin and Child. (This finale was cut because of expense and because Walt preferred a secular ending.)

After a false start, the Greek and Roman mythological imagery for Henri Pierne's "Cydalise" was transferred to Beethoven's Sixth Symphony (the Pastoral), and a slew of artists turned out dozens of inspirational watercolors and pastels borrowing from the Symbolists, art deco, and calendar kitsch.

For the Bach Toccata and Fugue in D Minor section, a daring decision to use abstract visuals was made. Oskar Fischinger (1900–1967), master of nonobjective (or "absolute") film, was hired for a brief, troubled time. In 1936, Fischinger and his family fled Germany and the Nazis, who considered his great experimental animated films *entartete Kunst* ("decadent art"). Here was yet another emigré artist, this time a refugee, who found himself (in his wife's words) "strewn on the desert" of Hollywood in desperate need of a job. While still in Berlin, Fischinger had communicated with Stokowski about his dream of creating a long abstract animated film using the Bach, one of the conductor's favorite pieces.[8] They discussed it again when both were working in Hollywood at Paramount Studio. When Toccata and Fugue

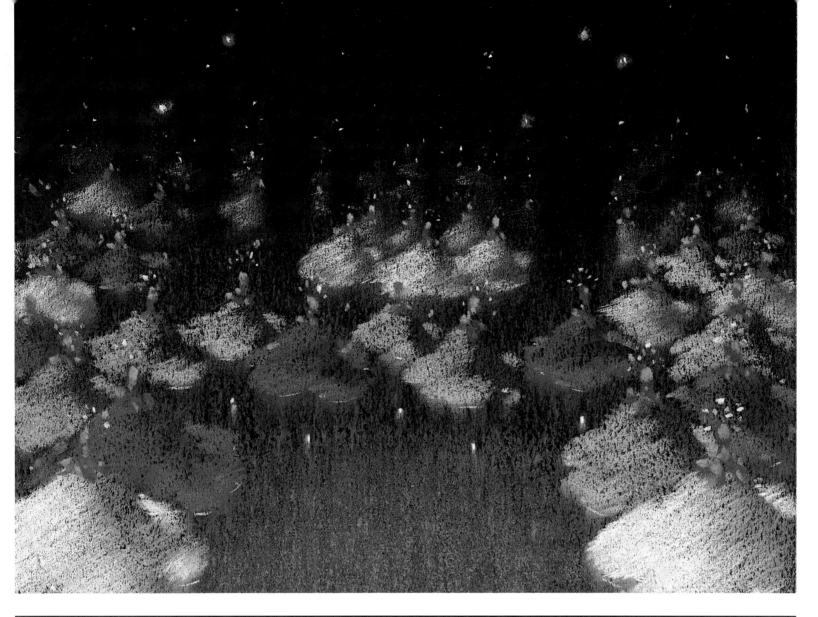

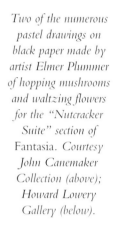

Two of the numerous pastel drawings on black paper made by artist Elmer Plummer of hopping mushrooms and waltzing flowers for the "Nutcracker Suite" section of Fantasia. Courtesy John Canemaker Collection (above); Howard Lowery Gallery (below).

OPPOSITE ABOVE LEFT *One of a series of Walt Scott watercolors depicting randy Mandarin mushrooms chasing Shanghai Lily girls among the bamboo, a concept that never made it into the final version of "Nutcracker Suite."* OPPOSITE BELOW LEFT *Before mushrooms were called upon to play a major role in the Nutcracker's "Chinese Dance," the dance was to be performed by Oriental lizards and a plump frog king, seen here in a watercolor by Walt Scott. Courtesy Sotheby's.* OPPOSITE ABOVE RIGHT AND BELOW RIGHT *Two of the many large-format pastels created by Robert Sterner of prehistoric life for the "Rite of Spring" section.* ABOVE *Snowflake fairies for the Nutcracker finale, delicately rendered by Jules Engel. Courtesy Christie's East.*

was suggested by Stokowski for *Fantasia,* Fischinger's agent was contacted and the artist was hired at $75 a week as a "special effects" animator. The studio, unsure how to approach noncharacter animation, figured the special effect department was the best place for Fischinger, since he was expected to advise on the animation as well as provide inspirational abstract designs.

Fischinger, a fiercely independent film artist, misread the Disney opportunity, seeing it as a chance to fulfill his dream of an all-abstract feature. In the advanced technology at Disney (especially the multiplane camera, which lent an illusion of spatial depth) he saw a means to bring new richness and complexity to "visual music." Instead, he was sorely disappointed to find his ideas misunderstood, ignored, and compromised by committees. "Walt saw the stuff," said Joe Grant, "and that Bauhaus thing didn't mean much to him . . . It wasn't to Walt's understanding." Walt's fear that his mainstream bourgeois audience would be confused and hostile to pure abstractions (which was all too true) lead to a reduction of Fischinger's multiple movements within the frame to a single timid statement per scene, a toning down of the "too gypsy"[9] color, and an orientation of abstract designs within recognizable contexts, so that clouds were placed against a limbo background, and lines became violin bows.

"The film 'Toccata and Fugue by Bach' is really not my work," Fischinger later wrote with bitterness, "though my work may be present at some points; rather it is the most inartistic product of a factory . . . Many people worked on it, and whenever I put out an idea or suggestion for this film, it was immediately cut to pieces or killed, or often it took two, three or more months until a suggestion took hold in the minds of some people connected with it who had their say."[10] "I once bumped into Oskar Fischinger," recalled layout man David Hilberman. "Standing in the hallway [he] almost broke down telling me of Walt's rejection of his artwork. Couldn't understand how he could have hired him because of his body of recognized work and then turn down his interpretation."[11]

Fischinger's films were often screened to inspire various staff members, and diluted versions of his designs inspired semiabstract sequences in the Latin American features *(The Three Caballeros)* and postwar omnibus features, such as *Make Mine Music* (1946). The only pure Fischinger animation to survive from his tenure at Disney was the radiant aura that emanates from the Blue Fairy's wand in *Pinocchio*. In fall 1939, he quit in disgust after only nine months.

After *Fantasia,* and knowing that Walt needed "to do something for a encore each time," and hearing in the back of his mind Walt's oft-repeated comment that "artists are a dime a dozen," Joe Grant protected himself and his department by initiating projects. "I moved right in to *Dumbo, Baby Weems* [from *The Reluctant Dragon*], all that stuff. We got busy in a hurry."[12] Grant and Huemer wrote a detailed script for *Dumbo* and kept Walt's interest by presenting the story to him episode by episode. The boss was distracted by problems with cash flow and labor, so "he didn't have as much to do with [*Dumbo*] as he did with his other pictures."[13]

Toward the end of that production, about a third of Disney's employees went on strike to protest layoffs, low salaries, and nonexistent job security. Walt escaped the turmoil by flying to South America to research a series of "Good Neighbor Policy" films—"At that point I would have gone to China to get away from it all," he said.[14] None of the top echelon animators (with two exceptions: Art Babbitt and Vladimir Tytla) took part in the strike. Strikers attempted to convince Grant to join the line with an idea that he should be running the studio. "That was dangerous stuff," said Grant, "and that obviously got around." He feared it might get to Walt. "That was the last thing I wanted, believe me."

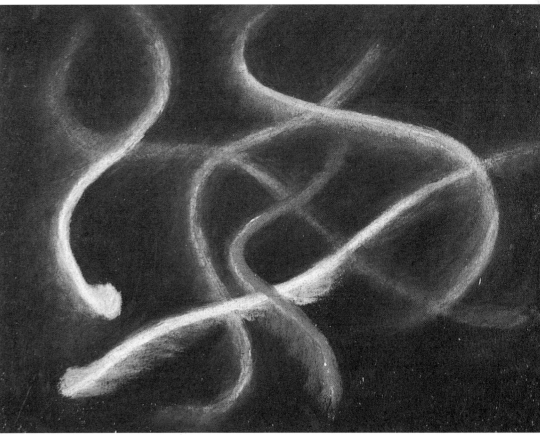

By the time Walt returned in the fall, the strike was settled, but his attitude toward the studio and animation itself was profoundly affected. "It destroyed Walt," said Grant. "It destroyed his whole thrust."[15] Not only did the strike (which Grant likened to "a stroke") cause Disney to lose momentum, it "discouraged him to the point where he lost faith in hu-

ears was completed without Walt, whom *Time* portrayed as an absentee boss. But "moody, sad-eyed Joe Grant" and "his happy-go-lucky partner Dick Huemer" and the "Grant-Huemer script" were given major credit for the "most appealing new character of this year of war."[17] Walt "indicated his displeasure" with the Huemer/Grant publicity in no uncertain terms, and when he heard Grant had called *Saludos Amigos* (1942) "his picture," he "got to hate our little department," recalled Huemer.[18]

World War II was another factor in the disintegration of the Character Model Department. Several artists were drafted or volunteered for the armed services, and the whole production structure changed when the army moved onto the studio lot to occupy buildings. Artists doubled up in rooms, features like *Peter Pan* and *Alice in Wonderland* were shelved, and the main output at Disney became propaganda and training films. Grant traveled back and forth to Washington, D.C., with Walt for production conferences with government officials, and he and Huemer fashioned scripts for two of the most famous wartime shorts (both starring Donald Duck) *The New Spirit* (1942) and *Der Fuehrer's Face* (1943), (which won the studio a tenth Academy Award). "During the war," said Huemer, "Joe Grant and I were finally at odds with Walt and he with us, and we thought we ought to leave."

Grant survived the war years, even if the Model Department and his partnership with Huemer did not. Was the latter another case of Walt splitting up a "too successful" team? Perhaps, but the partners also had a major falling out. For *Make Mine Music* (1946), an omnibus feature using popular music ("kind of a roughneck version of *Fantasia*")[19] Huemer remained in story, but Grant became the film's production supervisor. Now Grant had to "okay everything in back of Walt and not in front." If there was something Grant didn't approve of, he "had to go on Walt's coattails and put him in front of you." Privately, he would discuss production troubles with Walt, who was less tactful and would go directly to sequence directors or story people to say, "Joe doesn't think this is right." In the meantime, Grant "could see the director burning."

Grant felt "sour" and that "something was amiss" during the making of *Make Mine Music*. "I didn't feel the enthusiasm for it. I felt this was secondhand stuff, just putting a bunch of shorts together." On April 13, 1949, he was released from his contract. To this day, he will not discuss the main reason why. "He and Walt probably had some arguments," speculates animator Marc Davis, "and Joe finally said to himself, 'Hell, I don't need this,' and walked out."[20]

Grant has admitted that his departure had partly to do with his strong disagreement with Walt's diversification into

manity. [Walt thought] everybody was a believer, and then he found out that wasn't the case. He no longer had a grip on them like he thought he did. We, the company men, he didn't look at us with any gratitude [because] all people are not trustworthy in a sense."[16]

Walt's suspicions were exacerbated by an article that *Time* magazine ran on *Dumbo* two weeks after Pearl Harbor was bombed. The film about the little elephant with oversized

live-action. To Walt and Roy, the postwar live-action features—those combining animation, such as *Song of the South* (1946), *Fun and Fancy Free* (1947), *So Dear to my Heart* (1949), and those solely live-action, such as *Treasure Island* (1950), *The Story of Robin Hood and His Merrie Men* (1952) and *The Sword and the Rose* (1953)—were a way for the studio to survive. To Grant, who considered animation "the greatest medium in the world," it was "anathema!" Walt, he figured, "just got tired" of waiting two years to see a final version of an animated feature. Animation, an art form that moves so slowly through production "it looks like still water all the time," was "getting in the way of Walt's expansionist ideas. He wanted to move faster. He was in a sense a Henry Ford. Whatever he

was doing he would expand and expand, and if it didn't suit the tempo of his expansion, he'd do something else." Grant also felt that Walt "always wanted to be a live-action producer. That was his secret dream, which was really no secret around the studio."[21]

With his artist wife, Jennie, Grant designed and manu-factured decorative plates and tiles, and later produced sta-tionery. Their mom-and-pop firm became so successful it was bought by a competitor, who made Grant financially inde-pendent. He happily ignored the Disney Studio for years, ex-cept when *Lady and the Tramp* was released in 1955. The film gave no screen credit to Grant for the story's origin, which had developed from his 1939 concept sketches, inspired by the

A goldfish performs a belly dance for the Nutcracker in a pastel by Faith Rookus.

Grant family's cocker spaniel (see page 63), two Siamese cats, and Scotty, the dog next door; the birth in the story was based on the birth of the Grant's first daughter, Carol. "My family has always been up in arms about the *Lady* thing. A real tragedy as far as I'm concerned as far as the credit for it. This I never forgave Walt for. He knew damn well where all this stuff came from."[22]

Grant stayed clear of all things Disney for almost forty years. Then, in 1987, he returned to the studio. This dramatic change of heart has had a profound impact on the latest Disney animated features and will be discussed in the final chapter when we meet the current crop of top Disney inspirational sketch artists.

PART THREE
Inspired Women

Alice is confronted by a talkative Wonderland flower. Gouache by Mary Blair.

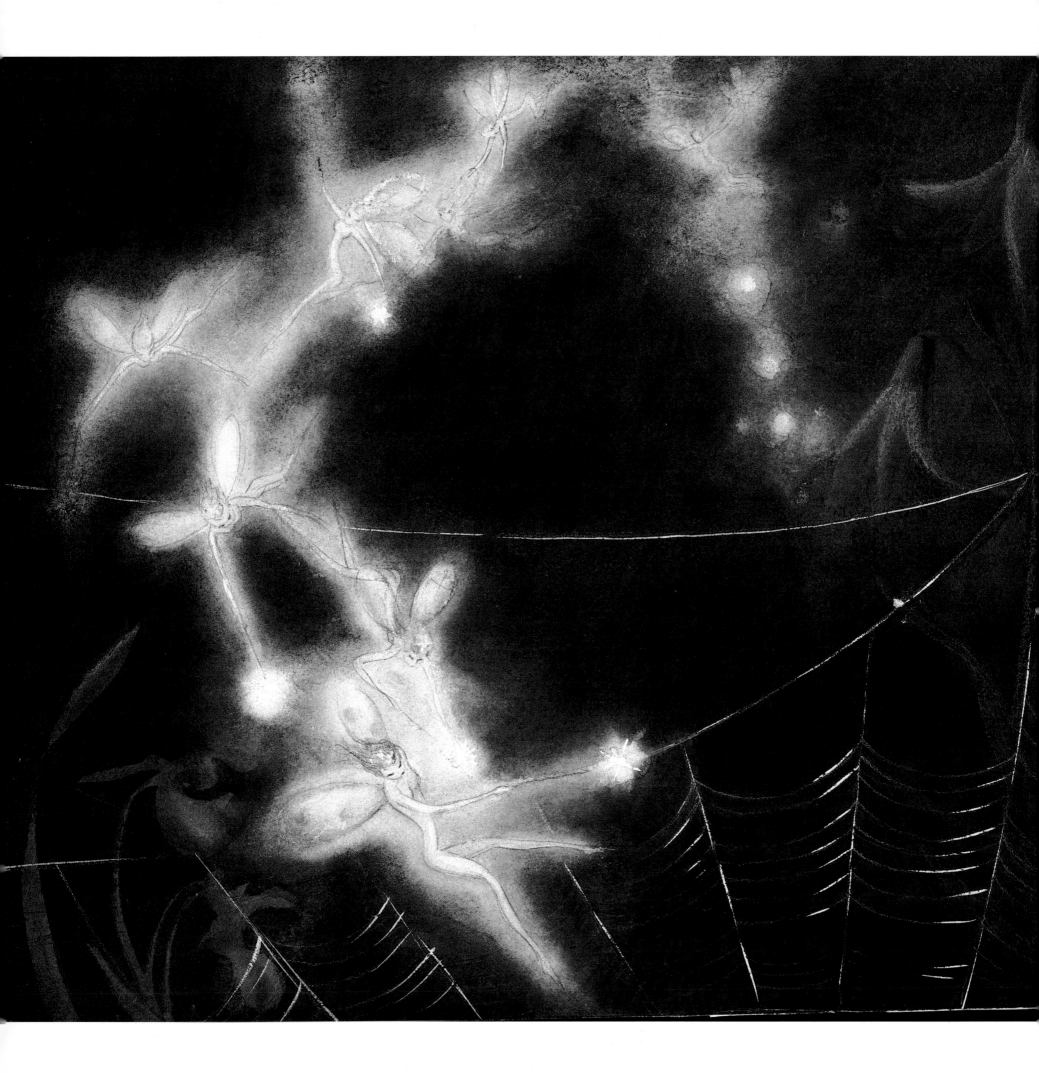

CHAPTER 9

Bianca Majolie

"In the early days of the studio," recalled animator Marc Davis, "it was a combination of a monastery and a nunnery. The ink and paint department was all women and the animation department was all men. They were not encouraged to get close to one another."[1] A 1938 employment policies booklet, *An Introduction to the Walt Disney Studios,* noted that "All inking and painting of celluloids, and all tracing done in the Studio, is performed exclusively by a large staff of girls known as Inkers and Painters. This work, exacting in character, calls for great skill in the handling of pen and brush. This is the only department in the Disney Studio open to women artists."[2]

Tracing animator's drawings onto clear sheets of acetate in pen and ink and painting them on the reverse side is one of the least creative, more tedious parts of the animation production process (one that is today increasingly done by computers). During the Depression, it was a skill that paid the "girls" who did it considerably less than the *manly* tasks of animation, layout, and story. Top animators at Disney in the late 1930s (all males) earned $300 plus per week, while ink and paint salaries ranged from "$18 to $75 per week, [and] would be higher," said a 1941 *Glamour* magazine in classic blame-the-victim style, "if more girls didn't work a couple of years, marry and quit."[3]

As late as 1958, Bob Thomas's book-length tour of the Disney Studio blandly reiterated the sexist bias of the cartoon industry toward women when he described the ink and paint building as "a cool feminine oasis a short distance from the Animation Building. The latter is predominantly masculine." The head of the ink and paint department, "attractive" Grace Bailey, reiterated in Thomas's book the male/female stereotyping by explaining "without a trace of feminine bias . . . why her sex has a monopoly in the department: 'They used men in the early days of the studio, but their work was inclined to be sloppy. Inking and painting is precision work that requires neatness and patience. Women seem to have those qualities, plus a necessary feeling for their work.' "[4]

Today, women hold high-paying positions throughout the animation industry in virtually every area of production, including animation, story, layout, backgrounds, concept development, and the new area of computer-generated imagery. Brenda Chapman, former head of story at Disney, recently broke through the final Hollywood animation glass ceiling by becoming a co-director of the first animated feature produced by DreamWorks SKG.[5]

In February 1935, it was considered "news when a woman artist invaded the strictly masculine stronghold of the Walt Disney Studio" by joining the story department. "Until that time," wrote the *Hollywood Citizen News,* "the only girls in the studio were the few necessary secretaries and the girls

OPPOSITE *Dewdrop fairies tumble over a spider's web in an exquisite inspirational watercolor by Bianca Majolie. John Canemaker Collection.* LEFT *Bianca Majolie in 1938, climbing Mount San Jacinto near Palm Springs.*

97

"Who was this girl?" wrote Bianca Majolie ruefully at the bottom of a copy of the article that anonymously touted her and her story development abilities. Ms. Majolie, it turns out, was a childhood acquaintance of Walt Disney. Born in Rome, Italy, on September 13, 1900, she attended art classes at Chicago's Art Institute and McKinley High School where in 1917 Walt Disney was a lower grade classmate. She did not know him or his friends personally and saw him only once on the day he came back to school dressed in his G.I. uniform to say good-bye.[7] Walt dropped out of McKinley after his freshman year and volunteered in 1918 for the American Ambulance Corps, eventually serving briefly in France after the armistice. Majolie, who graduated at mid-term, handed him her "girl-grad" book, and he drew pictures in it. She would not see him again until seventeen years later when they lunched together at Tam O'Shanter (a restaurant favored by Disney animators) in Los Angeles, where he offered her a job.

Between high school and Hyperion, Majolie went to New York to study figure painting and design under Wayman Adams at Grand Central School of Art, clay sculpture at Art Students League, and "drawing for line continuity" at Leonardo Da Vinci School of Art. Her real name, Bianca Maggioli, was changed by a McKinley High French teacher to "Blanche Majolie" and it was under that name she earned a living as a freelance artist. (Years later, Walt Disney insisted she change her first name back to Bianca, which she did.)

On a fashion assignment for Earnshaw Publications, she traveled in 1929 to Rome, Florence, and Paris. She had a long stretch as art director and brochure designer for J.C. Penney Company in New York until 1934. "Just for the fun of it" she entered a King Features Syndicate comic strip contest that year. Her strip was about a girl named Stella who was trying to find a job during the Depression. "There was always a little twist at the end where she just didn't make it. And neither did my cartoon strip."

Out of work, she was considering taking a trip to the Orient when she thought of Walt and his cartoon studio in Los Angeles. She wrote him a letter to which he replied, and when she got to the West Coast, they met for lunch. Walt was impressed by samples of "Stella," a showcase of Bianca's narrative and draftsmanship abilities. He thought she should try working at the studio, but was unsure if a woman would fit into the story end of the business. Her eagerness won him over, however, and she thanked him for the job offer and "the transition from working for dollars into working for love." She was certainly not laboring for the former—her salary was only $18 a week. She also noted fondly that Walt hadn't "changed, in spite of the terrifying eyebrow uplift, that succeeds only in

who did the inking and painting of the celluloids."[6] Ironically, although the article detailed the female invader's background, her name was never mentioned. Instead, a photo of Walt Disney surrounded by Character Model Department *Pinocchio* sculptures dominates the page, perpetuating woman's invisibility within the industry, while reinforcing male power.

arousing my merriment."[8] Her merry spirits quickly lessened, however, when she began to work with the "charmed circle," as *Hollywood Citizen News* described (without irony) the Disney story department.

The shorts story contingent was populated by mostly rambunctious men intent on supplying as much horseplay and gags in the office as to the storyboards, and included Walt Kelly (who later created the Pogo comic strip), Ted Sears, Harry Reeves, Earl Hurd (an old-timer from the New York silent film days), and bumptious Roy Williams (who decades later gained fame as "The Big Mooseketeer" on television's *Mickey Mouse Club*). Bianca Majolie has been described by a co-worker as a "tiny, very introverted, lovely person. Very sensitive and delicate."[9] It was like throwing a Dresden doll into a monkey cage. She recalled the studio's atmosphere as "crammed and clammy" and that she and the men worked in close quarters in an L-shaped old building with a front parking lot. The only woman in the group "did not enjoy the story conferences which called for action contributions of slapstick comedy gags" and she avoided them whenever possible.

The "boys" didn't know what to do with her, so Majolie was allowed to work alone on an original story of her own devising. Her first effort, submitted in a thirteen-page handwritten and illustrated script, was "Romance of Baby Elephant," which was released in March 1936 as the Silly Symphony *Elmer Elephant*. "Elmer was a story with a moral," she said recently, "meant to teach that usefulness is more important than beauty because none of the animals, though agile and beautiful, who had ridiculed Elmer's clumsiness, were capable of extinguishing the forest fire as Elmer did with his trunk." Obviously transmuting her own feelings into the script, Majolie wove a touching tale about difference, of trying to fit into a group, and how rejection engenders painful feelings of inadequacy. *Elmer* is echoed in the 1941 feature *Dumbo,* the story of another physically challenged pachyderm who (like Elmer and his bothersome trunk) turned a perceived handicap (his oversized ears) into a useful triumph.

In her warm, affecting story, Majolie inadvertently accomplished one of Walt's goals for the story department: to "get ourselves up to the point where we can really get some humor in our stuff, rather than just belly laughs."[10] Frank Thomas and Ollie Johnston cite the importance of Majolie's *Elmer* story: "We could not have made any of the feature films without learning this important lesson: Pathos gives comedy the heart and warmth that keeps it from becoming brittle."[11]

"It really did give me a laugh," responded Majolie recently, "that at this late date someone credited Elmer with teaching Disney artists the value that pathos gives to comedy,

which is an old formula used by Collodi in *Pinocchio.* But the truth is that after Hurd, Williams, and other old-timers had finished with the story sequence, the slapstick comedy brutality left very little room for pathos. I was a greenhorn and my objections counted for very little."[12] By November of 1936 *Elmer* had "taken hold" with merchandising licensees, according to Kay Kamen, Disney's high-octane New York–based salesman, in a "Mickey Mouse Hustlegram to Roy," a copy of which eventually found its way to Majolie. "I think it would be a good idea if we could have another Elmer Elephant picture or maybe more of them," wrote Kamen.[13] A year later Kamen was still asking for another *Elmer* picture because "all Elmer Elephant articles of merchandise have sold well and are still selling."[14]

Elmer Elephant, *a 1936 Silly Symphony short based on an original story by Bianca Majolie, brought pathos to Disney personality animation, and "a glimmer of things to come" in the features, say animators Frank Thomas and Ollie Johnston.*

Despite its success, a *Elmer* sequel was not attempted, and for Majolie there followed "a long period of disinterest in any original new story material that I might contribute."[15] The creative life, she has found, "can hurt one badly because it has no measurable dimensions. The highs and lows that one experiences can shatter the nervous system."[16]

She contributed ideas, drawings, gags, and partial sequences to on-going productions, and sometimes was taken off a picture to do Italian to English translations (for example, for *Pinocchio*) or sent to the San Diego Zoo with a photographer to film the birth of a fawn for *Bambi.* Often she was assigned to the Los Angeles Public Library to research new material, for which she was "grateful to Disney" for allowing her to make inspiring discoveries, such as the works of Henri Fabre, the French entomologist, whose insect world she found "more fantastic than any fantasy man can dream of."

But soon after *Elmer,* she came to the realization that "animated cartooning had very little to do with my own creativ-

ity, [but] it was too late to turn back because we were in the middle of a serious Depression. I stuck to the job." She was assigned to preliminary visual explorations on *Peter Pan,* and created a delightfully feminine Tinker Bell exploring the Darling family's nursery: in one exquisite pastel sketch the slim glowing pixie flirts with a tin soldier and is frightened by a jack-in-the-box; in another, she poses saucily like a half-pint Harlow in front of a mirror, giant pearls draped like a boa around her tiny shoulders. Majolie also drew some of the earliest concepts for *Cinderella,* a fea-

ture that (like *Peter Pan*) was produced over a decade later.

Because she saw little of "the kid I went to school with," except at story meetings, she was surprised when one day Walt personally asked her to research music for the concert feature.

I told him that while I loved symphonies and the great composers, I would not know where to begin on this assignment. "Listen to some of their records," he said, "and bring in what you like." I went into a Los Angeles music

OPPOSITE AND ABOVE *During the late 1930s, Majolie created delicate and gently humorous inspirational pastels for* Peter Pan *(which was finally produced in 1953). Here, saucy Tinker Bell explores the Darling children's playroom.*

shop and asked to hear some recordings by my favorite composers Bach, Beethoven, and Tchaikowsky. And when I told the dealer that I was a Disney employee, he brought in all that I had asked for and many more. I spent the afternoon in an enclosure listening to and enthralled by the musical recordings, some of which I had never heard before. It was an emotional experience and when I stepped into my Oldsmobile with a heavy package of

Victor records, I had no idea how my selection would be met by Disney and his story directors [Grant and Huemer]. But later I was to find out that three of my favorite composers had been chosen, and I was assigned to work on Tchaikowsky's music.[17]

Majolie claimed Tchaikowsky "was responsible for bringing my creative instinct back to life and the paintings I

One of a series of exquisitely conceived and rendered pastel and watercolor visual explorations of the fantasy world of Dewdrop Fairies for Fantasia's "Nutcracker Suite." John Canemaker Collection.

dancing singly or in pairs, or courting: One charming sketch shows a pretty sweet pea and a bumpkin thistle holding stem-hands, reflected in a pool of goldfish, while a gossipy pair of homely blossoms look aghast.

Majolie was partnered on the Sugar Plum Fairy sequence with Al Heath, who, according to a peer, was "an excellent, sensitive artist, good with color."[19] Together, they showed their art at numerous story meetings on the Nutcracker sequence through late 1938 and early 1939. At the January 23, 1939, conference on the overall continuity of the sequence, Walt complained to Majolie in front of a dozen people (including Dick Huemer and Joe Grant) that he didn't "think the continuity is right" in her sequence and he "doesn't approve of what you're doing with [the fairies]. The possibilities are here," he said referring to the beautiful drawings, "but they're not developed yet, Bianca." Soon after, story director Sylvia Holland "came into our room to pick up material Al Heath and I had done for *Fantasia* and [I] don't know what she did with it."[20] Basically, Holland took over the Sugar Plum Fairy sequence and developed it to Walt's satisfaction.[21] "She [Bianca] was so nervous when Walt would take off on these things," recalled Kendall O'Connor, "she would throw up after the meeting each time. Poor thing. Very nervous."[22]

While most of the concept and story artists held a detached attitude toward their work, some like Majolie (and Nielsen and Fischinger) found the constant changes and modifications in their drawings extremely difficult to accept. "Much of the fine art work was deleted from the sequences to make room for Disney's interpretation of the music," she said, "and it would seem that time and effort could have been saved if Walt had interpreted the music himself and given the artists a script to follow."[23] During her last couple of years at Disney, Majolie claimed her "sanity was saved" by taking evening ceramic classes with Glen Lukens at the University of Southern California. "For the first time in many years I was able to complete a work of art without having it changed or torn apart."

Only once (until this book) has the public seen Majolie's superb inventiveness as a fantasist and artist in undiluted form: she was one of several anonymous artists in a 1944 Giant Golden Book, *Walt Disney's Surprise Package,* described as a "joyous preview of stories that have been scheduled for coming Walt Disney motion pictures." The book illustration job was assigned by *Fantasia* story development director Phil Dyke, who assessed Majolie's work, decided "he liked what I did," and put her to work on "Through the Picture Frame," a Hans Christian Andersen story. Here was a fantasy that Majolie could revel in: one with talking paintings, anthropomorphic

did for the Sugar Plum Fairy sequence were my response to the music." She attempted to show "how beautiful what we cannot see clearly at night can be."[18]

Majolie's delicate watercolors and pastels for the Nutcracker Suite section are pure magic. They are delicate realizations of Shakespeare's sprites in *A Midsummer Night's Dream,* who "serve the Fairy Queen, To dew her orbs upon the green . . . And hang a pearl in every cowslip's ear." Her research into Henri Fabre's insects was not wasted; she transformed their minuscule world into that of Mab, the Fairy Queen (from *Romeo and Juliet*) who was "In shape no bigger than an agate stone . . . Drawn with a team of little atomi over men's noses as they lie asleep . . ." Two of Majolie's paintings—one in which firefly dots of light in the distance tumble into view to become glowing nude sprites at the top of a cobweb, and the other of six very busy, winged fairies illuminating the cobweb with dewdrops—are remarkably beautiful hallucinations; the gossamer rendering glows with an ethereal incandescence. In one, a realistic violet flower spattered with jewel-like dewdrops anchors the fantasy and lends a veracity to the whole fantastic scene.

Majolie also contributed numerous colored pencil drawings of flower people (probably for Waltz of the Flowers) furniture and flowers, mermaids, a feisty wooden hobby horse, and a "pleasant fiery dragon." Her disarmingly direct and colorful pastel sketches hold her unique artistic signature and are brimful of personality, fey wit, and charm. *Surprise Package* shows a range in Majolie's work that the studio never fully exploited. "I felt my talents could be used to better advantage," she said years later with great understatement.

After drawing story sketches for *The Ugly Duckling* (1939), Majolie absented herself from Disney's toward the end. "I lost interest," she said. When she returned to the studio on June 1, 1940, after a two-week vacation with her mother, she "ran into someone in the hall who said, 'You know, you're fired.' And my desk was occupied."[24] Jules Engel recalled "all the furniture in her room was changed and a new person was there. They fired her. When you don't have unions this is what happens. She was like porcelain. It was a horrible thing. Difficult to get over."[25] "Somehow," said Majolie, "I felt that I had wasted five years of my time and lost my identity as an artist." On the other hand, she also felt "so happy to break away . . ."[26] I have learned that in life we must bury our losses and count our gains or we cannot move forward."[27]

She worked on private commissions for glass panels and ceramic art sculptures, fused abstract stained-glass windows for three Pasadena churches, and returned to Chicago briefly in 1946 to illustrate *The Children's Treasury* for Consolidated Publishers. She married American artist Carl Heilborn in 1942 and together in the summer of 1953 they opened the Heilborn Studio Gallery. The three-level building with four exhibition rooms and a patio was located on Hyperion Avenue, down the street from where Majolie used to work at the old Disney studio.[28] She displayed her ceramic sculpture and the couple promoted international graphic art and artists. Sadly, the next year Heilborn died of a heart attack.

At this writing, Bianca Majolie-Heilborn nears her ninety-fifth birthday, and, in her feisty opinion, the time she spent at Disney "calls for aid from a psychiatrist." She claims never to have seen *Fantasia,* and now she never will for she has been legally blind for over a decade. Her personality combines tough self-protective cynicism with a sensitive fragility. She once claimed "Life is a big joke. I can't wait until I'm completely blind,"[29] but later claimed her blindness "has made of me an entirely different person—one who has lost

everything and must find an entirely new reason for living."[30]

Attending children's art classes in Los Angeles after she left Disney, she "learned the true meaning of art—that what you see is something deeply related to yourself, and not what the camera can see."[31] Her "dearest possession" is a painting made after the war by a seven-year old Japanese child. "There are no words," she said, "to express how deeply touched I was by this child's depiction of war: harmless birds and animals armed with war weapons. I asked to purchase the painting and was told that if I loved it that much I could have it. And it has had a special meaning for me ever since."[32]

"I don't think that I shall ever be touching paint again, but if it should happen, I shall place my fingers in a paint pot and work like a child. It might be a wonderful experience to start life all over again, as a child."[33]

Some of the earliest visual development sketches for Disney's Cinderella *(1950) were drawn by Bianca Majolie, circa 1939.*

CHAPTER 10

Sylvia Moberly-Holland

One day in the fall of 1938, Walt Disney strode down the hall in the story area and asked out loud to no one in particular, "Is there anybody here who can draw horses?"

"Yes! I can!" answered a tall, dark-haired woman with a British accent. Sylvia Holland proceeded to sketch one as she walked alongside Walt, who "didn't slow down."[1] Mythological horses, such as Pegasus, unicorns and centaurs, were the order of the day for a section of the concert feature originally inspired by the music of Pierne's Cydalise and eventually dropped in favor of Beethoven's "Pastoral" Symphony.

Of course the energetic Mrs. Holland could draw horses. She could draw almost anything required by this marvelous new film and music project, thanks to her extensive art and design education in England, her professional experience as an architect in Canada, and her knowledge of music as a practicing classical guitarist and singer.

At age thirty-eight, Sylvia Holland was a mature and confident woman, full of joy for the work she was assigned at Disney and fired with an ambition to make good. In contrast to Bianca Majolie, she was "more outgoing. She had a physical presence and strength," according to Jules Engel. Walt Disney was immediately impressed by her, and not merely because she could keep pace with him and draw at the same time. Never one to dispense praise easily, he once

wrote glowingly that Holland "contributed immensely to the good taste and beauty of our pictures" and that he personally found her "not only a charming and amiable person but a highly talented artist with a marvelous sense for decoration and color."[2]

Fantasia's music director Edward H. Plumb seconded the boss' opinion, citing particularly Holland's work in the Nutcracker Suite: "She proved to possess a great genius for expression of music in color and design. It is unusual for sight and sound to be combined so successfully." He also noted that "[i]n the many informal discussions with Stokowski and Taylor during the original planning of *Fantasia* subjects she was one of the few people able to 'stay on the beam' with both artists and musicians . . . She has executed all projects from a camera script to a finished painting with equal showmanship and good taste."[3]

According to her 1941 resume, Holland's duties at Disney included "story direction, preparing and illustrating the work from camera script to Leica reels, preliminary timing, and supervising an artist-crew under a production director." This job description indicates that the keenly intelligent and resourceful woman was a leader as well as a creative artist, and came as close as anyone of her sex ever has at the Disney studio to the position of director.[4]

She was born Sylvia Moberly in the tiny village of Ampfield near Winchester, England, on July 20, 1900, one of four children. Her father was an ordained clergyman and a musi-

OPPOSITE ABOVE *A tiny fairy lies at the heart of a maple leaf, gracefully drawn by Sylvia Moberly-Holland. John Canemaker Collection.*
INSET *Sylvia Moberly-Holland at work at Disney, circa 1939.*

107

This early dawn
Sun not yet risen

cian who organized an all-woman string orchestra. "The family traced their lineage through several English generations back to Peter the Great," said Holland's daughter, Theodora Halliday.

His two half-English sons produced hybrids [sic] combining Russian and English strains and there was always a touch of the Russian looks and temperament about Sylvia. And her affinity for Tchaikowsky's music was surely no accident.[5]

Sylvia loved to draw as well as make music. In 1919, she entered Architectural Association School in London, a five-year

college level course with two years postgraduate work as an intern-assistant to British architects. In 1926 she married a Canadian fellow-student, Frank Cuyler Holland, and the couple moved to his home in Victoria, British Columbia. There the Hollands designed houses and Sylvia often proudly claimed she was "Canada's first woman architect." An accomplished pianist, she took up the classical guitar, played and arranged music, and sang with members of the Alpine Club of Victoria.

In 1927, the couple's daughter was born. The next year, Frank Holland died suddenly of a mastoiditis infection, a month before their son, Boris, was born. "The Depression struck, no more architecture," wrote Holland years later. She and her children moved to a farm at Metchosin, which she

ran by herself while raising prize cats and Spitz dogs. Her son was ill with the disease that took his father; antibiotics did not exist at the time, so doctors could only advise Holland to take Boris "to a desert climate or lose him." In 1936 the single-parent family moved to California.

"Mother always had a great interest in the American West, fantasy, drama, and Hollywood," said daughter Halliday. "She didn't collect pictures of the stars, but the idea of entertainment always appealed to her." In 1937, the Universal Studio art department hired her as a sketch artist, including the supervision of stage sets under John Harkrider. She got the job, she said, "because the art director loved cats and I had a drawing of one in my portfolio."

In 1938, she saw Disney's *Snow White* and, according to her daughter, "she made an absolute resolve she had to work for Walt Disney." "When I saw the vulture sequence in the new Disney picture," said Holland remembering the sinister

birds who slowly circle into a chasm where the witch has fallen, "I beat on the doors of Walt Disney Productions." Wisely she decided to gain experience in animation before applying at Disney's, so while at Universal she worked as a cel inker on Walter Lantz cartoon shorts for three months. "She calculated this was the way she would get into the [Disney] studio," said Halliday. Her sample portfolio of animal quicksketches; architectural precision as a draftsman; ability to work in pastels, watercolor, and line; plus her knowledge of music brought her into the Disney fold on September 6, 1938.

Thrilled to be at Disney and with her assignment on the new concert feature, Holland dove into her work.

At story conferences she made numerous cogent suggestions for visual solutions to continuity problems, several of which became part of the final film. For example, for Cydalise (later the Pastoral) she asked, "Couldn't you have the first beautiful centaurettes coming out of the water, so you wouldn't know they weren't girls?" a thought immediately and enthusiastically taken up by Walt: "Yes! And swimming. They look like girls swimming."[6] Holland brought a family perspective and maternal warmth to her extensive written and drawn ideas for the mythical creatures in Cydalise. For example, "Mother teaching little baby centaur to walk"; "Mother and grandmother centaurs collecting fruit, etc. suggesting the preparation of the meal"; "Group of children centaurs making mudpies," among others.

By December, Holland was asked to head the Waltz of the Flowers sequence of the Nutcracker Suite. She attended the continuity meeting in which Walt expressed displeasure with Bianca Majolie's progress with the Sugar Plum Fairies. Soon she was assigned that section as well, and ideas for character designs, continuity, color, rough layouts and suggestions for animation poured from Holland. She related motion with music in subtle ways—"We've depended a lot on the wind in our movement," she noted in one meeting.[7] For months she created fairy characters out of the organic shapes of flowers, until Walt one day suggested, "Let's do leaves instead." Months of leaf dancers followed.

She was assigned an assistant, Ethel Kulsar, a skilled watercolor and airbrush artist who made delicate finished paintings of Holland's ideas. Little is known about Kulsar, although

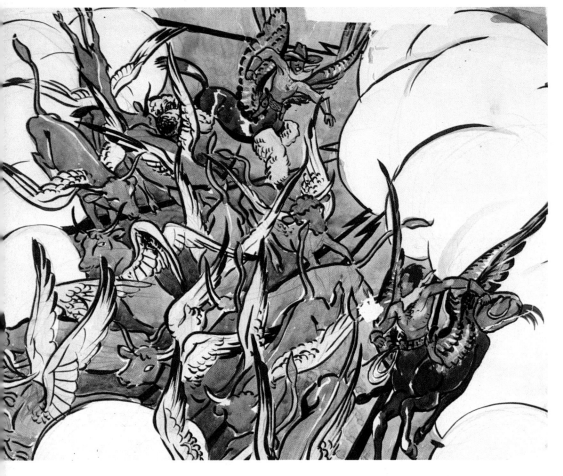

J. Gordon Legg, also a Nutcracker artist, thinks she may have come from "the Buzza-Cardoza greeting card sweatshop" in Los Angeles, where women airbrushed greeting cards using magnetic friskets for stencils and were paid ten cents or less per hundred cards! The company "was a source where the Disney Studios acquired several of its few women (or girl) artists."[8] Disney pay was a step up for the Buzza-Cardoza "girls," and Ms. Kulsar certainly appears delighted to be working with Mrs. Holland in several publicity photos—listening with a broad smile as Sylvia plays the piano or acts out a storyboard. Looking at Holland and Kulsar's many sketches of balletic leaf dancers and atmospheric drawings of seasonal changes, Walt commented to the two women, "These are very effective backgrounds there." To which Sylvia modesty replied, "They are just airbrush and some 'mystery' put in with water."[9]

At a meeting which Walt did not attend, Holland suggested to Stokowski that the Nutcracker music "appears heavy for the material we have," referring to the fairies, and dared ask for "a little more scintillation in the music." The maestro bristled and countered with "a personal reaction": "I don't like the fairies, frankly. That kind of fairy life doesn't seem to me to strike a real note in life today." Stokowski wanted a "remote earth fairy" not "the old idea of sweet little fairies [which] seem to me not to be good for the music, nor for life today." Whatever that meant. Realizing months of work—all of it approved by Walt—was being criticized and perhaps jeopardized, Holland quickly and smoothly moved the conversation into technical matters ("Where theme A begins . . . it jumps a little for what we have. We have willow leaves.") and Stokowski's objection was not heard again.[10]

Although she was "in heaven working on *Fantasia,*" she had problems with a few male artists who (perhaps like Stokowski) "did not like taking orders from a woman," as her daughter put it. Some of the men were victims of rampant homophobia: Working on "fairies" and all that that loaded word evokes led to several artists being "ribbed by the other guys." "That type of fantasy didn't seem to be my style," said one, "so when Otto Englander started story direction on the Pastorale [sic] Symphony I submitted some sketches which Walt liked and I was transferred to that unit."[11] Ironically, as we have seen, James Bodrero's macho centaurs were gelded by the time they left story.

Walt once publicly defended his decision to move

OPPOSITE ABOVE *A vigorous drawing by Moberly-Holland for an unusual concept for the Pastoral Symphony: a rodeo made up of centaur cowboys and Pegasus bulls and steers. Ride 'em, Beethoven! John Canemaker Collection.*
OPPOSITE BELOW *A parade of centaurettes by Sylvia Moberly-Holland.*
RIGHT *Drawings by Sylvia Moberly-Holland and Ethel Kulsar for the Leica Reel of* Fantasia's *"Waltz of the Flowers," a section of the "Nutcracker Suite" whose story development was supervised by Holland.*

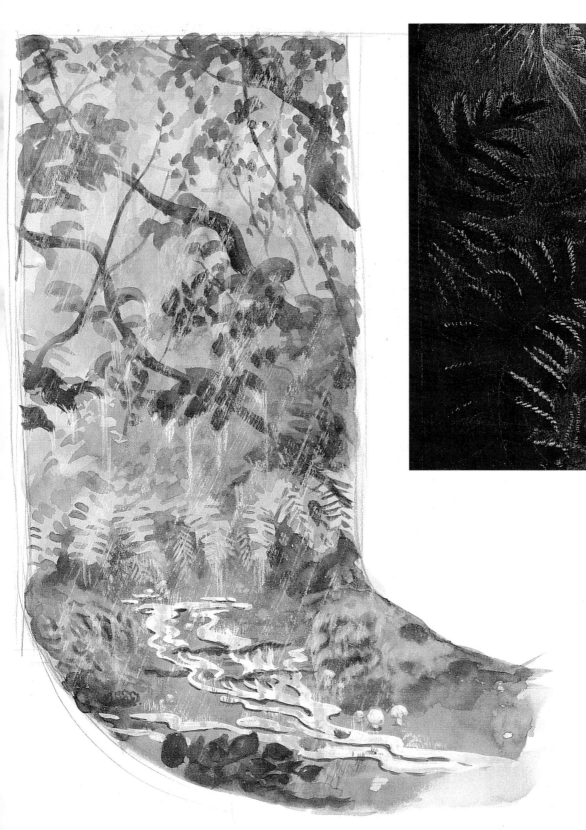

group . . . there are definite prospects, and a good example is to mention the work of Ethel Kulsar and Sylvia Holland on the Nutcracker Suite.[12]

Most of Holland's co-workers enjoyed working with her and "kept coming to her because she knew all the answers, drew pictures and made wonderful suggestions. She knew music backward and forward and could relate to the musicians. Plus she always liked Walt and got along very well with him."[13] In October 1940, a month before *Fantasia*'s premiere, Holland was preparing concept art for a second version of the film. Her suggestions for a view from inside a baby's carriage for "Adventures in a Perambulator" composed by John Alden Carpenter, and lovely pastels for "Swan of Tuonela" by Jean Sibelius, among other music, are remarkably inventive. She also prepared extensive sketches for an unnamed musical film about Greek games and mythological characters, but this new version of *Fantasia* never saw the light of day.

Before she was laid off in the fall of 1941, Holland painted color story suggestions for the raindrop sequence in *Bambi*. Within a year she was rehired to work on war instruction films and the feature *Victory through Air Power*. A Canadian newspaper reported Holland worked eight hours per day, six days a week and averaged sixteen story sketches each day of "sea battle pictures." Her free-form explorations for the "Flight of the Bumblebee" by Rimsky-Korsakov for the second *Fanta-*

women into positions traditionally considered male territory, such as animation, inbetweening, and story, and praised Holland and Kulsar:

> The girl artists have the right to expect the same chances for advancement as men, and I honestly believe that they may eventually contribute something to this business that men never would or could. In the present

sia—sketches of architectural music staffs, notes and aggressive flowers—found their way into the postwar feature *Melody Time* (1948), in a surreal jazz version called "Bumble Boogie." But by its release in 1948, Holland had been away from Disney for a couple of years. She was part of massive layoffs that occurred after the war, when many special talents were let go because the studio had to make do with a smaller staff and discontinued making elaborate films like *Fantasia*.

Holland worked briefly for MGM, did book illustrations with other laid-off Disney artists for Whitman Publishers, created 4,000 drawings for *MacMillan's Readers* and began a long tenure as a Christmas card designer/artist for Chryson Limited Edition. She bought three and a half acres in the west San Fernando Valley, built two houses, and opened a drawing office on Ventura Boulevard.

A remarkable and unusual development in Holland's life after 1950 began as a hobby and stemmed from her love of cats. She achieved an international reputation among cat fanciers when she developed a new breed of Balinese cat. She learned veterinary medicine, guided new breeders, founded the Balinese Breeders and Fanciers Association, and exhibited the line for over twenty years.

In old age, though afflicted with arthritis in both her hands and feet, Holland continued her professional output of greeting cards. She died of a stroke on Easter Sunday in 1974.

113

CHAPTER 11

Mary Blair

Mary Blair's art is flat, antiillusionist, childlike, *faux-naif*. Her color palette is wildly unrealistic, and characters and backgrounds are equal geometric components in the overall design. Her work brings to mind twentieth-century American artists, such as Stuart Davis, Milton Avery, and Adolph Gottlieb, more readily than Arthur Rackham, Edmund Dulac, or Kay Nielsen, the fin-de-siècle Euro-book illustrators so favored by Walt Disney in the 1930s.

If she is to be likened to Europeans, it is to the moderns who found an inner (rather than an outer) reality by playing with form and color: Wassily Kandinsky's early figurative expressionism, the Fauvism of Henri Matisse and Raoul Dufy, the "impish laughter" of Paul Klee.

One would reasonably expect that Walt ran in horror from her work and she lasted at the studio for the same length of time as an ice cube on a July sidewalk. But art is not reasonable and its effect on the human mind and spirit is beyond logic: Walt Disney loved Mary Blair's art. For nearly thirty years he championed it and touted her at the studio, and her stamp is on feature films, such as *Saludos Amigos* (1943), *The Three Caballeros* (1945), *Song of the South* (1946), *Make Mine Music* (1946), *Melody Time* (1948), *So Dear to My Heart* (1949), *The Adventures of Ichabod and Mr. Toad* (1949), *Cinderella* (1950), *Alice in Wonderland* (1951), and *Peter Pan* (1953), special shorts, such as *The Little House* (1952) and *Susie the Little Blue Coupe* (1952), as well as exhibits, murals, and attractions at the theme

parks Disneyland and Walt Disney World, most famously the It's a Small World attraction, originally created for the 1964 New York World's Fair. Of all his artists, this *female* artist was Walt's favorite, and he allowed her to have as significant an impact on postwar Disney style as Albert Hurter had in the 1930s.

Why Blair's conceptual art so appealed to Walt—who demanded a trompe l'oeil illusion of reality and believability in his animated films—is a mystery and a miracle. Unless one keeps in mind that "Walt was constantly growing, constantly reaching out," as Roland Crump, Disney Imagineering artist, explained it. "He always wanted to see things he'd never seen before."[1] Animator and painter Marc Davis said Mary Blair "brought color to Walt in a way that he never conceived [of] color before."[2] Davis also felt "there was a magic that her stuff had that nobody else had, and . . . he [Walt] liked the simplicity of it, too. It wasn't overworked . . . It was very simple, beautiful color, very appealing to the eye."[3] Crump noted that Blair's fresh, childlike art also connected with Walt: "A lot of that childish style of hers and the way she painted—in a lot of ways she was still a little girl. Walt was like that . . . there were times when he was a complete child. He didn't act childish, but he was seeing through the eyes of a child. You could see he could relate to children . . . she was the same way."

Two of Blair's many concept paintings for *Alice in Wonderland* demonstrate her magic: in one, the trial before the Queen of Hearts proceeds in a striking design that owes little to John Tenniel, but much to the shape and color of a deck

LEFT *Mary Blair, a Disney Studio portrait, circa 1941.* OPPOSITE *(clockwise from lower left) Mary Blair's nearly abstract color and camera placement suggestions for the "March of the Cards" in* Alice in Wonderland; *one of many Mary Blair paintings made in South America in 1941; concept art by Mary Blair for* The Little House, *a 1952 short.*

115

of playing cards. Our eye is so excited by the bright bold colors, patterns, and overall composition that at first the tiny participants are barely noticeable. Characters never mattered as much to Blair as the playful juxtaposition of color and form. Slowly, the buxom heart-shaped Queen emerges at center, with a bloblike King to the left, and then down a step in the royal hierarchy we come to the White Rabbit reading accusations from a parchment-scroll next to a dozen heads precariously balanced in a tight jury box. On the opposite side sits a crimson-haired witness in an oversized green hat, the fellow whom Lewis Carroll called merely the Hatter. His chair is so tall it stoops over slightly, a properly "mad" piece of furniture for a truly insane man. Finally, in the decorative row at bottom, we spot the defendant, little Alice, standing with her back to us, book-ended between two armed card-guards. (At this trial, the cards are literally stacked against her.)

Blair may not emphasize personalities, but an emotional "color" is always present in her art to lend a dimensionality beyond the dazzling two-dimensional look. For example, large vertical and horizontal shapes represent a court trial's stiff formality and an overwhelming, inhumane process. Poor Alice looks as small and vulnerable as she must feel, her identity nearly lost among the repetitively shaped cards. A dark black and blue background underscores the seriousness of the litigation against Alice—beheading is, after all, Wonderland's capital punishment of choice. The trial's public exposure and embarrassment is felt in the bright foreground colors that flash and fizz like a tabloid photog's camera bulb.

Feelings are present, too, in a picture of Alice seated between the Gryphon and Mock Turtle on a rock facing the sea. Judging merely by their wonderful silhouetted shapes, we sense a friendship and peacefulness between the odd trio, comfortably sharing a perch together and watching the sun set. Alice has survived another mad Wonderland day, and is now safe and high above the turmoil and dangers of this strange land (represented by jagged boulders in a swirling tide). Who else but Mary Blair would paint the sky mocha, an unusual but perfect color choice for a place where "the slithy toves did gyre and gimble in the wabe." The odd color, falling sun, and forlorn figures hold an appropriately melancholy emotion as they listen to the Turtle's sad song:

> Beautiful Soup, so rich and green,
> Waiting in a hot tureen!
> Who for such dainties would not stoop?
> Soup of the evening, beautiful Soup!

A showcase of Blair's bold, strong compositions, sense of humor, and offbeat color sense is found in her concept sketches

for a sequence considered (and deleted) from *Cinderella*, in which Cinderella dreams she has seven maids to help her do the housework. In these small sketches, Blair's imagination is unflagging as one exciting visualization tumbles into another. There is a theatricality, panache, and painterly joy in her work that one also finds in David Hockney's set and costume designs. In fact, there is a Blair-like playfulness in design and color in Hockney's gouache-on-paper conceptual drawings for Ravel's "L'Enfant et les Sortileges" performed at New York's Met in 1981. Interestingly, Mary and her husband, Lee Blair, collaborated on sets and costume designs for a San Francisco Symphony production of "L'Enfant" in 1974.

Mary Blair's fantasy art is deceptively simple and masks the painter's formidable aesthetic/technical sophistication and range. She was a painter of wide experience: Both she and Lee were part of the California School of Watercolor, a regionalist group of artists who rose to prominence during the Depression. After the stock market crash, America experienced a time of idealism and nationalism, proudly seeking to promote its own culture and values and "free itself from foreign artistic influences."[4] The work of the California watercolorists "reflected the changes that the country underwent as it was transformed from a rural, agrarian society to an industrialized world power." Both Blairs exhibited widely in galleries and exhibitions during the thirties; Lee served two terms (1933–1934) as the president of the California Watercolor Society, and Mary's work was included in the important Texas Centennial Exhibition in 1936 and the International Watercolor Exhibition in Chicago in 1939.

The California Watercolor style of representational art used "a large format, free broad brush strokes, and strong rich colors" and "documented scenes and activities of everyday life on the Pacific coast" by painting them "boldly and directly, with little or no preliminary pencil sketching, while mastering the technique of allowing the white paper to show through as an additional shape or color."[5] The now-familiar "Mary Blair style," with its unique hues and flat fanciful compositions, is not readily apparent in her "se-

Eighteen small concept gouaches by Blair for a Cinderella *dream sequence (later cut) demonstrate her unflagging and unique sense of color and design.*
OPPOSITE ABOVE *Blair's version of Wonderland's trial of the century: Alice, the cards stacked against her, faces the King and Queen of Hearts.* OPPOSITE BELOW *Alice joins her new friends, the Mock Turtle and the Gryphon, in a song about "beautiful soup."*

rious" nonsponsored paintings of the 1930s. However, Susan M. Anderson, curator of "Regionalism: The California View" at the Santa Barbara Museum in 1988, detected aspects of the *other* Mary Blair in "Okie Camp," a 1933 watercolor:

> Unlike the majority of documents addressing the migrant camps that were widespread throughout California during the Depression, Mary Blair's *Okie Camp* makes no direct social commentary. Rather, the painting reflects the artist's unique vision. Instead of approaching her subject with sobriety . . . [she] ironically invoked an animated orchestra of shape and color to describe the camp with touching humanity. Her ability to capture "the slightly cockeyed aspect of everyday happenings" made her one of Disney's favorite artists.[6]

Her early watercolors, though skillfully done, were similar in technique and subject matter to paintings by her husband and numerous other California watercolorists of the period. Where Blair's "unique vision" as a California School watercolorist might have taken her will never be known. Because the "other" Mary Blair—the brilliant commercial stylist—emerged amazingly *full-blown,* like a genie from a lamp, at Disney's and obliterated the "serious" watercolorist. Her imaginative, fey, fantasy art was totally different and hers alone; a personal, stylized approach to subject matter so appealing it brought her success and fame, primarily because of the support of Walt Disney.

It also brought problems. She was always frustrated that her concepts rarely made it to the screen intact. Disney's animators and layout artists claimed that, as undeniably inspirational as her stylizations and colors were, flat two-dimensional art was difficult (if not impossible) to reconcile with Walt's desire to see a three-dimensional world on the screen. Nevertheless, Walt insisted through the years that they put "Mary" on the screen, and this impossible demand, plus her friendship with Walt, generated a palpable jealousy in some of the men she worked with, and even in her husband. "Lee was just doing great at the studio," said Marc Davis. "When Mary came, she just clicked with Walt and he was so fascinated with everything she did that all of a sudden Lee was lost in the deal."[7]

Also, both of the Blairs held a nagging guilt that they—promising fine artists in the Depression years—had sold out. "We are artists, dear, and are in love with art and each other," Mary wrote to Lee soon after they were married in 1934. "We must make these loves coincide and melt into a beautiful, happy, & rich life. That is *our* future and is real. We'll live to be happy and paint to express our happiness."[8] However, in a 1971 newspaper article, she is described as reluctant and "modest to the point of diffidence about her work," and made clear she had little passion for her commercial art: "I just consider it a day's job," she said.[9] Hazel George, one of Mary's best friends at Disney, corroborated the point, noting that "when she's finished with a thing she's through with it. She's interested only in the next."[10]

During an interview with both Blairs in 1976 (two years before Mary died), Lee claimed the jobs they took in animation during the Depression were "way beneath our standards, but we needed to eat." Mary concurred and described juggling the fine and commercial arts—a struggle she gave up but Lee continued—as "a Jekyll-Hyde existence."[11] In fact, the innocent, carefree quality of Mary Blair's art was a "Jekyll" masking heartbreaking "Hyde" aspects of her life, which stemmed primarily from a marriage that tumbled from passion and shared artistic goals, to professional envy and alcoholic codependency.

Mary Browne Robinson was born with a fraternal twin, Augusta, on October 21, 1911, in McAlester, Oklahoma, a town that was originally part of the Choctaw Indian Reservation.[12] Their father, thirty-three year old John Donovan Robinson, was a veteran of the Spanish-American war who became an office bookkeeper, and their twenty-three year old mother, Varda, a homemaker and "excellent seamstress" who took in outside sewing.[13] The family, including first-born daughter, Margaret, lived in a wood-frame house with Varda's mother, Margurite T. Valliant, on the west side of town.[14] Within two years, John sought work in Texas and moved the entire family there; by the early 1920s they had settled in Morgan Hill, about ten miles from San Jose in northern California, preceeding a larger movement of "Okies" from the Dust Bowl region by about a decade.

John became a caretaker of the Friendly Inn in Morgan Hill, and his family lived on the third floor. Money was tight, and so was space in the house—the twins slept in the same bed for years. Varda sewed clothes for the children and robes for the priests at the Episcopal Church the family attended, and "was very active in helping the migrant workers and their families."[15] On Sundays, John made a big pot of "the best" chili using the whole cumin plant.[16] The lessons of the Depression were enduring: Mary's youngest son, Kevin, recalled Varda in old age in the 1950s telling him "more than once to reuse paper towels."[17] Mary graduated from Morgan Hill Elementary School in June 1925 and four years later gave the valediction at her high school graduation (subject: "Self-Destiny").

"The Robinson family was poor during the Depression," said Jeanne Chamberlain, Mary's niece. "They did have struggles financially. I have heard from my mother [Margaret] that

they sometimes did with less food, so that Mary could buy her paints." Mary's artistic gifts attracted media attention early in her career: the April 13, 1931 *San Jose Mercury Herald* newspaper featured a photo of "Miss Mary Robinson, talented young San Jose State college art student," her dark hair pulled back in a chignon, dressed in a long smock seated before a charcoal still life that "she will exhibit at the Fresno convention of the Pacific Arts association" and posed classically with paintbrushes and a palette (not charcoals) in hand. Two months later a headline in the same newspaper breathlessly announced over a photo of "Miss Mary Robinson of Morgan Hill" that she was "On the Road to Fame" having "just won a scholarship at the Chouinard school of art in Los Angeles."

One of Mary's favorite teachers at Chouinard was the well-known illustrator Pruett Carter, a realistic painter who nevertheless admired moderns such as Matisse.[18] Blair's superb color and design sense has often been compared to that of the French master and Carter may have introduced the twenty-year-old woman to his work. Blair told Marc Davis that she found Carter "a major influence, who taught her staging and composition that influenced her tremendously." In turn, Carter "was terribly enamored of her work, the simplicity of what she had, her ability and style. I don't think he ever tried to change her."[19] She was also exposed to the teachings of

Lawrence Murphy, Chouinard's master composition teacher, who had been a personal friend of Albert Pinkham Ryder, and had met Matisse and Picasso "having paid visits to the Steins at 27, rue de Fleurus in Paris before World War I."[20] Murphy held a "cautious respect for the postimpressionists and modernists," and spoke often of the dynamics of Cezanne's compositions.[21]

Mary's family was thrilled by her acceptance at the prestigious art school in the big city "down south." Toward the end of the fall semester, her twin "Gussie" wrote in excited anticipation to say that Mary's holiday visit would be the family's "whole Christmas this year" [because] "ol' man Depression stole Santa's reindeers." Instead of buying gifts, she cheerily added, the family would "concentrate on the 'glad to be alive and eating' idea." Christmas continued to be an important holiday for Mary and her family through the years. "We were always together for Christmas," said Mrs. Chamberlain, "It was an exciting fun time. One year [Varda] made green-colored satin brocade dresses for 'the twins'—they looked great!" Another year "Mary made my mother and dad a huge birdcage to serve as a Christmas tree. It was done in bright orange, complete with an orange bird, some Xmas ball ornaments & tiny white lights. We put presents under it." Both of the twins "had creative talents in writing poetry, but

119

[they] never [shared] the driving ambition that Mary had."[22]

The 1932 Chouinard catalogue acknowledged Mary Robinson's talent by showcasing the emerging two Marys—the commercial stylist and the fine arts painter. On one page is a design for a Cannon Mills bath set that won her $100 that year in a national competition: a stylish white art deco horse leaping on a black field toward the stars, a fresh design full of charm and verve. Already she displays a certain detachment from the world. On a second page is illustrated a competent but mundane oil still life of a potted plant (next to which she proudly wrote "Also mine all mine" on the copy she sent to her parents). It was the "Trojan Horse design" that got Mary Robinson a photo in the *Los Angeles Times* with the headline "Winning Design Gains Girl Fame."[23]

Also attracting attention that year was another Chouinard scholarship pupil who would profoundly affect Mary's life: Lee Everett Blair, a twenty-two-year-old native Californian and dedicated watercolorist whose work had been exhibited widely up and down the west coast for two years. Blair was among a select group of Chouinard students who in 1931 assisted David Alfaro Siqueiros in the completion of a fresco mural in the school's courtyard. But his reputation received a spectacular boost when his watercolor "Rodeo" was awarded a gold medal at the 1932 Olympics in Los Angeles.

It now seems inevitable that these two young Chouinard "stars" would fall in love. Besides sharing artistic ambitions, there was a strong sexual attraction between soft-spoken, shy Mary, who was 5-foot-5, pretty with green eyes, light brown/blond hair, and an aquiline nose that gave her a strikingly elegant profile, and exuberant six-foot tall Lee, with his wide forehead, twinkling blue eyes, auburn hair, and cleft chin, who exuded intelligence and a confident masculinity.

The young couple idealistically vowed to dedicate themselves to a life as fine art watercolorists. Lee, at age twenty-three, was elected president of the California Water-Color Society and he actively arranged for his and Mary's work to be exhibited in numerous exhibitions during the mid- and late 1930s. Mary passively allowed Lee to control her career in tandem with his and once wrote him a note stating her emotional and artistic dependence:

Mary Browne Robinson and Lee Everett Blair on their wedding day March 3, 1934, in Los Altos, California. Courtesy Kevin Blair.

120

My lover—You're always with me and can't leave you, dear. [sic] You're going to help me always—in everything I do—help me to paint & draw and be a success with you—for I adore you and love you so. Mary.[24]

After graduating from Chouinard in 1933, with no jobs in sight, financial reality set in. Mary returned to live with her parents in San Jose, and Lee looked for a commercial art job, which, during the height of the Depression, were scarce. "I didn't know where I was going," he admitted years later, "until one day I found they were hiring people out at Ub Iwerks [Studio] in Beverly Hills as inbetweeners on Flip the Frog," a new series of animated shorts.[25] Iwerks, Disney's Kansas City chum and the designer and first animator of Mickey Mouse, had set up his own animation studio on the thin shoulders of a slimy cartoon amphibian with no charisma. The job paid $25 a week, which "allowed me to get married," said Lee, and so the twenty-two year old couple were wed on March 3, 1934. Mary then went back to her parents and Lee returned to flipping the Frog in Los Angeles.

"All my peer group thought I was prostituting my art," said Blair, "but I had to do that to make a living. I couldn't live on my painting. Once I was in it [animation], I just stayed in it. I led two lives."[26] In a July 1, 1934, letter from Los Angeles–based Lee to Mary in San Jose, he divides their "two lives" into "the animated cartoon situation" and "the Fine Arts situation," and demonstrates the control and dominance he maintained over Mary. He reports that while at Iwerks, he is actively seeking a new job at better pay at Leon Schlesinger's studio (soon to be the producer of Bugs Bunny shorts), and Hugh Harman and Rudolf Ising Productions (two more former Disney/Kansas City animators), where he feels he "should be able to get on at forty a week or more." He also "decided it would be the result of a lazy attitude to get a job at any other studio than Disney's," so he has also made an appointment there.

So much for the animation situation. Lee's letter comes alive with enthusiasm when he reports on the "Fine Arts situation":

Philip Ilsley [a gallery owner] called me on the phone Friday eve. and I went over to his apartment, which by the by is most sumptious [sic], to learn . . . he wants of you, and I, nothing less than an exhibition of both oils and watercolors and to be precise he wants it soon [within two weeks] . . . Saturday I ordered two dozen watercolor frames and three oil frames, which will suffice according to my calculations.

He proceeds to tell Mary the titles of the seventeen paintings (all watercolors) she will show and the fourteen watercolors and ten oil he intends to exhibit. He warns her (like a parent to a child) to "not get the mats dirty because that is a big item in a watercolor show, clean white mats!" and promises to "write you later as to what time I am coming up to get you." He closes with "I think of you a great deal, Mary, and sincerely miss you. Rest assured that I am trying to keep my eyes averted from the coy glances of unattached maidens," the last comment a tease calculated to inflame his lonely wife's jealousy and remind her of his desirability. Five dollars is enclosed "to defray a few expenses and buy a sweet nosegay," and he ends with "I love you."

In order to be near Lee, Mary took a job in Los Angeles as a barmaid at the long-running play *The Drunkard*. Then Lee arranged for her to paint cels at the Iwerks Studio, where they "worked there together until she got tired of the place. And I said, 'Why don't you just quit and go home?' So she did that."[27] Lee maintained Mary "didn't want to have anything more to do with animation, so she went home and started painting seriously."[28] After about a year at Iwerks, Lee got a job as an animator's assistant at Harman-Ising where his experience as a painter led to the position of color director.

Lee's fondness for alcohol is hinted at in a letter postmarked May 19, 1936, to Mary (who had returned to her parents in San Jose for a "rest"). It begins with Lee excitedly describing the "new springtime picture" (released in 1936) he and two others have been given creative control over ("It's going to be one huge splendiferous blast of symphonic music and masterful art"), proceeds to news on his fine art efforts (which he says "hasn't been forsaken completely"), then segues to an expression of loneliness for Mary and plans to take the train to visit her. By the end, the letter has become so incoherent Lee himself calls it "drunken babble."

Lee was hired at Disney as a color supervisor on *Pinocchio* in May 1938 and Mary in effect replaced him at Harman-Ising. Lee often ruefully told the story that Harman and Ising said "Why don't we hire his wife, she's better than he is." Mary agreed to take the job as color director "for a month or two" but she stayed nearly two years.[29] The couple continued to paint "seriously," once driving to Mexico for six weeks to paint "rural life." Mary's work from that trip was shown in a 1938 one-woman show at the Tone Price Gallery in Los Angeles, and that same year she was elected an exhibiting member of the Foundation of Western Art in recognition of her "ability as an artist and her services to Western art," and profiled with a photograph in *Western Woman* magazine.

Lee's versatility, artistic skill, and gung-ho energy impressed Walt. In *Pinocchio,* he color keyed several sequences;

for example, in six studies of Jiminy Cricket running through a burning and desolate Pleasure Island, Blair's quick, deft technique conveys mood through bold washes of color. Next he was assigned to *Bambi,* but that feature's pretentious director (who requested, for example, that Bambi's mother perform like Katherine Cornell) got on Lee's nerves. "He hated it," according to one source. "Said he wanted to go home every night and puke."[30] He went to Warners looking for a job, but Walt personally asked him to stay at Disney and work on *Fantasia*. He enthusiastically created exquisite watercolor story sketches for Dance of the Hours (with James Bodrero), styling the Toccata and Fugue and the animated soundtrack sequence with effects animator Cy Young after Oskar Fischinger left, and planning the color cinematography of Stokowski and the orchestra. For the latter, Blair's many small watercolors of musicians touched with pastel highlights on their instruments and faces are so specific it is small wonder the complex live-action cinematography took only three days to complete.

So improved were the finances of the two working Blairs that they commissioned architect Harwell Hamilton Harris to design a house to fit on a steep slope in North Hollywood. In the small, elegant three-level house, completed in 1939,[31] the couple threw parties for their young friends. Mary was "a very good cook, but surprisingly insecure as a hostess; she was constantly asking 'Is everything all right?' "[32] Both the fine arts crowd and the cartoonists were hard drinkers and the hosts kept up with them. The powerful "Bodrero Punch" was invented in the Blair's kitchen, where James Bodrero once almost electrocuted himself using an electric iron to make space in a block of ice for the punch's fruit. However, *"the* drink was martinis straight up. That's what everybody drank."[33] A number of friends recall Mary's pixilated and oft-repeated joke, "There'll always be a candle in the refrigerator and a martini in the window."

Mary was hired by the Disney story department in April 1940 at Lee's suggestion. "She would come home [from Harman-Ising] all upset," Lee once wrote to a friend, "because Joe Barberra [sic] [later a co-founder of Hanna-Barbera Studio] was making passes at her, so I got her a job over at Disney's."[34] (A third Blair was working at Disney at the time: Preston, Lee's older brother, a superb character animator who made hippos dance and Mickey Mouse tread water in *Fantasia*.) During the little more than a year Mary was at Disney, her traditional watercolor style came into play in numerous charming paintings she did for Joe Grant's dog story *Lady*. For Sylvia Holland, however, a more stylized signature appeared in pastel studies of children in tutus for the never-produced "Baby Ballet" (based on music by Chopin, Mozart, and Brahms), part of a proposed second version of *Fantasia*. These cute but strange infants with hydrocephaloid heads, widely spaced eyes and tiny bodies became a Mary Blair trademark; they first appear on screen in the Christmas Celebration sequence of *The Three Caballeros* (Las Posadas) and variations followed in her children's books in the 1950s, in Disneyland murals and the It's a Small World attraction.

In June 1941, Mary resigned because, according to Lee,

she "didn't like it, so she quit and started painting" again.[35] Less than two months later, on August 11, she was rehired at Disney, and six days later was on a plane headed for South America. When Lee informed Mary that Walt invited *him* to Latin American to paint and do research, she "got all upset because she wasn't going to go along." Her father and mother, who were living with the Blairs in their new house, suggested Mary simply "get yourself all dressed up and make an appointment with Mr. Disney and tell him that you want to go, too." It worked: "Walt thought it was a great idea."[36]

The trip to South America resulted from unrest in a distant part of the world that had begun to have a profound impact at Disney's fantasy factory. The war spreading in Europe had cut off more than half of the studio's revenue at a time when Walt was in debt from building an expensive new studio, and from two costly features, *Pinocchio* and *Fantasia,* which were box office failures. Layoffs inevitably resulted, and fear and rage over the lack of job security, poor salaries, and nonexistent raises led 300 Disney employees (40 percent of the work force) to an acrimonious strike in favor of unionization starting on May 28, 1941.

At the same time, Walt was approached by the United States Office of the Co-ordinator of Inter-American Affairs (CIAA) to make a goodwill tour of South America as part of the U.S. government's "Good Neighbor" policy. The plan was devised by President Franklin D. Roosevelt as a hedge against the spread of Nazi and Fascist sentiment in Latin America, and to foster markets for all kinds of products on both sides of the hemisphere ("a kind of hemispheric partnership in

which no Republic would take undue advantage"). It was an attempt to make North and South Americans familiar with and appreciative of each other's cultures, customs, and products.

Walt saw it as an opportunity to escape from the studio's strike, which threatened to drag on all summer (it ended on September 15 with a screen cartoonist's union firmly in place) and to build new markets for his films and licensed materials. Publicly, his stated purpose was "to make pictures both Americas would like so that in the end they would like one another better." He suggested a working tour with eighteen hand-picked artists and associates (including William Cottrell, Frank Thomas, James Bodrero, Herb Ryman, and the Blairs) to research a series of films that would "utilize properly, in the medium of animation, some of the vast wealth of South American literature, music, and customs."

It is not known if Walt accepted Mary's proposal to be part of the group because he wanted to keep the volatile but valuable Lee happy by bringing his wife along, or because he had noticed Mary's visual development potential, or both. What is certain is that the paintings Mary Blair created in Brazil, Chile, Argentina, Peru, and Mexico during three months in 1941 changed her life.

At first she documented native houses, clothing, and people in notebooks filled with rough pencil sketches on onion skin paper (a photograph taken in Peru shows a delighted Mary kneeling to capture the likeness of a woman and her child), and she made numerous spontaneous watercolor studies. Sunrise on the pampas seems to be the subject of one deft and classically "California Watercolor" experiment: a

broad wash of subdued colors with white paper sparkling through and certain areas "held back" to silhouette objects, such as a little house and a single large haystack. Within the contrasting light and dark portions of the haystack a tiny black rooster and two white chickens are cleverly outlined. The painting is a traditional watercolor of the sort that Lee Blair, Jack Miller, Herb Ryman, and others were tossing off by the dozens.

A 1940 Mary Blair watercolor for Joe Grant's early version of Lady.
BELOW LEFT *Character Model artist Jack Miller's caricature of Mary Blair in South America.*
BELOW RIGHT *Mary Blair sketching a mother and child in Peru. Courtesy Kevin Blair.*
OPPOSITE *Examples of Lee Blair's conceptual artwork: one of a series of watercolors of Pinocchio's Jiminy Cricket roaming an after-hours Pleasure Island, and two samples of his extensive watercolor and pastel studies for* Fantasia *orchestra set-ups.*

Seven examples of the transforming influence of the 1941 Disney Studio visit to South America on Mary Blair's painting style and color palette.

But Mary's research was mere rehearsal for the major works she painted on location that seemed to explode from her palette: paintings with high-key color and a heightened stylization never seen before in her work. One reason for the difference was technical; she eschewed pure watercolor technique for a mixed media approach. Watercolor might be used for a loose sky wash, but main areas and subjects were in gouache (or tempera)—an opaque, more controllable paint offering intense hues and the possibility of layering colors.

Her work is also more subtly cinematic than before, integrating movement into compositions through perspective and by overlaying subject matter—sailboats float from the distance into our laps, veiled women wander past a tropical bandstand from "medium" to "long shot"; the rounded hats of villagers at market are "overlays" for middle ground subjects that finally lead our eyes to llamas and smaller figures in the distance.

As to why her strong stylization appeared so fully realized, Roland Crump, Mary's colleague at Walt Disney Imagineering years later, theorized: "When they went on that trip to South America in a lot of ways it was something Walt hadn't done before. It was one step beyond. There was some discussion that we've got to capture the flair of South America. Deep down inside Mary had her own style, but she never brought it forth. She did that one little train with the black background. That's the first time she stepped out of what she'd been doing and said this is fun! That was it from then on."[37]

Crump's reference is to a *Three Caballeros* sequence in which a colorful toy train (with one square wheel) rhythmically bounces on its rails across a black background studded with Day-Glo tropical plants and flowers. The stunning de-

sign is quintessential Mary Blair—she even painted the key production backgrounds. "Only on the little train sequence," she wrote years later to film historian Ross Care, "did I feel that it was really my own artwork and my style."[38] That is not quite true: *Saludos Amigos* and *The Three Caballeros,* for example, are veritable showcases of Mary Blair's art: Las Posadas in *Caballeros* is a series of her paintings of children, and many of her original on-location art works are seen as narrative linking devices throughout both films. "It's an example of what still drawings can do, how entertaining they can be if they have that rare design that she was able to get," said one of *Caballero's* animators, Ollie Johnston.[39] But Mary was correct in that her paintings *in motion* never made it to the screen intact.

She also claimed that nothing "specific from the trip inspired those designs other than the fact that Brazil is really a very colorful country. The jungle colors, and, as they say down there, 'The Black North' has lots of colorful qualities. The costumes and native folk art are really bright and happy like the same things in a country such as Guatemala."[40]

But something special did happen on the South American trip, a once-in-a-lifetime experience that couldn't help but affect the artists and their work. There was the danger of it: "The travelers realized the closeness of the war when the plane landed at British islands during nighttime; the cabin's curtains had to be drawn, and the runways were unlighted. Luggage was carefully examined at each airport."[41] Aboard a

Pan Am DC-3, the passengers continually sniffed oxygen from tubes; Bill Cottrell recalled "wherever we stopped they had a big truck that came out with a big hose . . . that pumped cold air in. And that had to last until you got a mile high where it was cooler. Then when you started down the [airplane] heated up like an oven."[42]

There was the sensual excitement of it: the beauty of the people and the land, the beaches, the jungles, the heat, the rhythms, the music. The Disney visitors, who called themselves "El Groupo," were thrown headlong into a different world; eagerly, with openness, they welcomed new experiences with sounds (musical and otherwise), colors, art, designs, foods, drinks, smells, and tastes. Everywhere they went they were welcomed, lionized, and feted; Walt's fame and the popularity of his films and characters (especially *pato* Donald) preceded them, opening doors that would otherwise have remained closed.

In Rio and São Paulo, they met composers both classical and pop (from Heitor Villa-Lobos to Ary Barroso), heard singers and poets; met painters and viewed their work; attended concerts, nightclubs and festivals; went to zoos, farms, and beaches; and learned to dance the samba. In Buenos Aires, they attended barbecues and watched gauchos rope and break horses. They took balsa boat trips on Lake Titicaca, watched bullfights in Lima, rode llamas in La Paz. Everywhere they drew, painted, and animated their impressions, and compared notes and artwork at makeshift studios in hotels. With the inundation of new sensations, inhibitions fell away, friendships solidified, and group members became (and would remain) close. Even Walt loosened up and enjoyed himself so much he literally stood on his head on stage in front of 2,000 school

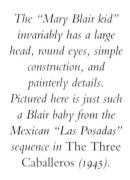

The "Mary Blair kid" invariably has a large head, round eyes, simple construction, and painterly details. Pictured here is just such a Blair baby from the Mexican "Las Posadas" sequence in The Three Caballeros *(1945).*

children at a special showing of Disney shorts at a theater in Mendoza, Chile.[43]

Mary Blair was affected by the South American experience more than she ever put into words. In her paintings, she went inside herself to find how it *felt*, rather than how it looked. To paraphrase Kandinsky, she took ten looks at the canvas, one at the palette, and half a look at nature. Mary Blair's South American art detonated rather than evolved. Suddenly, there it was—spectacularly rich and special, full of gaiety and color, and a delight to Walt Disney's eye. As an art supervisor of the South American films, Mary's color styling sketches inspired and keyed most of the sequences. "She had a lot to do with making that picture [*The Three Caballeros*] as memorable as it is," said Ollie Johnston.[44] South American material found its way even into the postwar feature *Melody Time* in 1948: the Blame It on the Samba segment was inspired by Blair's hallucinogenic colors against black setting off Donald Duck and friends grappling with music staffs and a giant brandy

snifter; pop organist Ethel Smith is a surreal "eye" (a large hat) and her keyboard a "smile" in a portrait of her giddy music.

During the South American trip, Lee Blair proved himself as versatile as ever; he painted dozens of watercolors of local scenes, and, for *Saludos,* the 16mm movie footage he shot of the locals and of Walt and the artists at work and play, along with additional footage taken by Walt himself, was used to connect the cartoons in the final film. But it was Mary's art that captured Walt's attention, and many think he was mesmerized by her colors. Kandinsky wrote of the "purely physical effect of color," of "perfumed colors" and "the sound of colors" which the eye receives "like a gourmet savoring a delicacy;" and of the psychological effect of color as "a spiritual vibration" that directly influences the soul:

> Color is the keyboard, the eyes are the hammers, the soul is the piano with many strings. The artist is the hand that plays, touching one key or another purposively, to cause vibrations in the soul.[45]

"Walt said that I knew about colors he had never heard of before," Mary once shyly admitted.[46] Walt told Mary's niece "that he would see all these wild and beautiful colors of Mary's—then he'd go outside and see all these colors in the sunset."[47] Marc Davis feels "her color was better than Matisse."[48] Ironically, Mary had poor vision: "She always had a purse full of eyeglasses," recalled Alice Davis. "Sometimes she would have two pairs of glasses plus contact lenses to see something. I said to her, 'My God, Mary, that's why you're so great with color! We have to stand back and squint to see how colors work together and you have that naturally.' We always giggled about it."[49]

The envy some felt toward Mary's work and Walt's unabashed admiration of same seeped into print in *Three Caballeros* publicity: "Mary Blair has a nickname around the Disney studios," said one article. "Sometimes they call her Marijuana Blair, because of the ideas she dreams up."[50] But Mary needed no help from pot to aid her imagination; she smoked only regular cigarettes in alternating white and black cigarette holders, part of an elegant fashion sense that blossomed during the war years that was as individual as her concept art.

"In my business, we'd say she was tailored with class," said costume designer Alice Davis. "She was always a sharp dresser. There was an almost mannish tailoring with a lot of feminine flair. She had that and very good taste in scarves and jewelry." Later in New York, her clothes and hats were custom-made. She once brought Roland Crump along to a chic fashion salon in a Manhattan brownstone, where she

A 1944 watercolor painted on location in the Atlanta, Georgia, area for Song of the South *(1946).*

sipped wine as fabrics were fitted on her. "She dressed beautifully and very originally," said A. Kendall O'Connor. "Mixed black and yellow and orange. She was not necessarily a beauty but striking, especially when she put her own color schemes up." A publicity photo for *The Three Caballeros* contradicts part of O'Connor's assessment: In a simple wide-necked white peasant blouse, with shoulder-length auburn hair framing her long elegant face and intense eyes, Mary Blair appears quite beautiful and sexy to boot.

A year after Pearl Harbor was bombed, Lee joined the Navy and served for four years (1942–1946), attaining the rank of lieutenant commander as supervisor of production of classified projects used in the instruction of military personnel. Mary joined her husband near the U.S. Naval Air Station at Anacostia, D.C., and they lived in a small house with a grape arbor at Galesville, Maryland. She flew to the Disney Studio to attend important conferences or to present artwork, a "frequent flyer" pattern she continued for over twenty years.

Her best friends at the studio during the 1940s were two women who, like Mary, adored Walt Disney: Hazel George, the studio nurse, and Retta Scott, Disney's first female animator, who animated the vicious hunter's dogs in *Bambi*. George, who had an earthy sense of humor that both Walt and

Mary loved, thought some male studio artists were jealous of Mary because "they felt she was taking unfair advantage of Walt, because she was a woman. But that's the usual attitude toward women artists."[51] She described animator Scott as "a wild one," and claimed to have never understood the close relationship between the two because "Mary was a cut above her in refinement."[52] "Mary was my best friend," Scott told Robin Allen in 1989. "Our friendship went over all those years. She came to France to see me when I was there and everywhere we'd get together . . . I said let's go up to Canada, so we took a motor trip to Vancouver and the islands." During the war, Scott married an Army man and she lived with Mary when Lee was stationed on the East Coast. "I was renting a house not far away but she said [she was] going down to Georgia to do *Song of the South* there . . . so I stayed right there for several weeks."[53]

In October of 1944, Mary was in Atlanta, Georgia, on assignment for Disney at ten days of conferences and field trips with a local artist and historian "to collect historical and scenic background" for the live-action/animation feature *Song of the South,* based on the folk tales about Brer Rabbit by Joel Chandler Harris. She told a reporter she was "brought up on Uncle Remus stories" by her Maryland-born father, and that Walt

127

"expected her to bring back to Hollywood many watercolors of the Georgia countryside . . . I want to know what a Georgia cotton field looks like and all about the brier patch . . . I want to find out about the weather and the terrain and to get the feel of Georgia for myself."[54] In one of her research paintings, five African-Americans accompany a mule and wagon down a road next to a cotton field, and one almost feels the heat at the end of a long summer day in the wet "sweating" sky and hot red dusty trail.

An unusual postwar assignment was two large paintings of Baia scenes for Carmen Miranda's new Beverly Hills home. Miranda, whose sister Aurora starred in *The Three Caballeros,* commissioned the watercolors from Walt. Mary's colorful artworks were set within adjoining turquoise walls that also held books in the living room, behind an art deco table and a leopard skin couch.[55]

After the war, Walt wrote Lee Blair to ask him to rejoin the studio:

> With your past experience here and your present experience gained in the Navy, plus your talents, I know you are bound to fit very well into our organization . . . I also know there is a place in our setup that will be entirely worth your while—just what that is, I do not know at the moment, but there are many spots where you can play an important part . . . there's no doubt in my mind that when better cartoons are made, you know where they'll be made![56]

But Lee declined the offer and instead moved with Mary to the East Coast. In February 1946, he and a Navy buddy, Bernie Rubin, established Film Graphics, Inc. for the "production of animated motion pictures, educational training films, technical industrial films, slide films, and diagramatical [sic] animation."[57] Later, the firm became known as TV Graphics when Leon Levy, an opticals specialist, became a partner and the company focused on lucrative television commercials. Animator Lou Garnier, their first employee, remembered "the studio was over a movie theater in the Corona section of Queens on Long Island and later moved to Manhattan. I never could understand why Lee, a golden boy of California, came East. Except maybe he was wise enough to know TV was coming in."[58] As Lee explained it to art historian Nancy Moure, he sensed the future was in television and it would happen in New York. "There was no sense coming back to California because Long Island is closer to New York. TV was just starting. The rents were a lot less back there."[59] Also, "Lee wanted to grow on his own. Be his own boss," opined Lee's friend Neil Grauer.

Alice Davis, however, believes that Lee's "jealousy of Mary's talent and closeness to Walt,"[60] played a part in his decision to "remove" both of them from Los Angeles. "It must have been unhappy for him," concurs Marc Davis. "Here his wife comes and she's the prize of the studio."[61] In any case, Lee's business took off and soon he was, as he put it, "rolling in dough . . . making films and TV spots."[62] He also served as president of the New York Film Producers Association and set up a section of the mayor's office to deal with film, radio, and television. In 1947, at the age of thirty-six, Mary gave birth to Donovan Valliant, and three years later to their second son and final child, Kevin Lee; both babies were delivered by Caesarian section. The Blairs exchanged their house in Los Angeles with a couple who had a garden apartment at 9 East 61st Street off Fifth Avenue; a German nurse took care of the kids when Mary was in California at Disney. Said Lee of nurse Steigmuller: "She ran us like Hitler ran Germany."[63]

Soon the Blairs built a house less than an hour outside Manhattan in Great Neck, Long Island, at that time a small rural town which had a population (in 1950) of about 8,000.[64] Their home, designed by architect Frank Nemney, was a modern glass structure surrounded by large trees on several acres of land, with eight-foot ceilings and a fireplace in the center of the living room. A separate studio with large windows for Mary was connected by a thirty-foot enclosed glass walkway at the end of which "was a circular wall with a staircase up to the studio . . . elevated on stilts."[65] At the new house, the Blairs entertained clients, new friends and old ones visiting from the West Coast; Walt and his wife Lillian once dropped by to see Mary's *Cinderella* concept sketches.[66]

"I had three jobs," Mary once told an interviewer. "Raising children, keeping house, and doing my art work."[67] Despite juggling her 1950s obligations as wife and mother with (rare for the time) a professional career, the quality of her concept art reached a particularly rich peak in the late forties to mid-fifties. For the live-action/animation feature *So Dear to My Heart,* she created a series of colorful concepts of turn-of-the-century rural America brimful of nostalgia redolent of Grandma Moses.

Tantalizing are conceptual sketches for a sequence cut from Johnny Appleseed in *Melody Time,* the last of Disney's omnibus pop music *Fantasia*-like features. Blair brings great color excitement to depicting Indians and the burning of settler's cabins: brash reds; yellows and fuchsia; sensuous fluid shapes for flames, trees, and shadows; and marvelous light and dark contrasts.

Her bottomless well of inventiveness and supremely satisfying implementation of pattern and color is showcased in sixteen paintings for the short film *The Little House,* based

One of many charming and imaginative Mary Blair concepts for the short The Little House.

on the beloved children's book by Virginia Lee Burton.

Blair led the way in color and styling contributions to Disney's postwar return to full fledged animated features *Cinderella, Alice in Wonderland*, and *Peter Pan*. Suggestions for settings, costumes, character relationships, mood, props, and, most of all, color poured effortlessly from Mary Blair's brush. She was, as was once said of Ravel and music, the bed of a stream through which paint flowed. Like Braque, she accomplished herself each day by making paintings and, like him, probably thought it was "very bad when one notices that one is a painter."[68]

But as Frank Thomas observed, "As strongly as she influenced Walt and the design of the characters, the colors, the *whole concept* of the thing—it didn't take."[69] Meaning that the people who followed after made significant compromises in Blair's artwork in order to make it "Disney." There was a great resistance to Mary's designs, partly because of a distaste for the new and the modern. But mostly because Walt had placed his artists in an untenable position: While he loved the visual excitement of Mary Blair's style and color, he could not articu-

late how to integrate her two-dimensional flatness into the familiar rounded/dimensional/realistic Disney style.

Animator Ollie Johnston expressed his frustration with *Johnny Appleseed* this way: "Walt told us he wanted us to get Mary Blair's stuff on the screen, but it was impossible. Her stuff is very flat!"[70] Walt himself didn't know how it could be done. Nor did he give permission to the layout artists, the directors, and the animators to go in a completely different, fully modern way.

Several participants in the Disney strike did go all the way when they formed a studio called UPA (United Productions of America) and won kudos for "daring" modern art designs in shorts, such as the Academy Award-winning *Gerald McBoing Boing* (1950). Later, John Hubley, a Disney striker and UPA art director, formed a creative partnership with his wife Faith, and produced animated films based in principles of character/personality animation but wildly free-form and painterly in design, such as the Academy Award-winning *Moonbird* (1959).

There is no knowing where Walt Disney might have

taken character animation in terms of style and content if war, the strike, and overwhelming economic problems had not rerouted his energies and interest. Mary Blair seems to have been oddly oblivious of and unaffected by the political, economic, and artistic forces affecting Disney. "The strike had no influence on the design of the films," she once claimed. "Expenses didn't enter into the change either, but a desire for something new probably did tend towards a more modern and less baroque look." As for UPA, she did not think their style "had any influence on the [Disney S]tudio's design style at the time." But even as late as 1977, she was apparently unaware of UPA and its films: "Frankly, I had to ask Lee 'What is UPA?' "[71]

Walt was reaching for something different in Disney film design in the postwar years, but, at the same time, feared losing the believability that his mass audience expected. Still, he hoped something new might evolve (perhaps by osmosis) from the creative chaos. In January 1946, he went so far as to hire Salvador Dali to create inspirational sketches for a short

titled *Destino.* John Hench worked for three months as Dali's assistant, filling storyboards with continuity drawings between the master's surreal concept sketches. Ultimately Dali style totally overwhelmed Disney style and sensibilities; in sketches allegedly depicting a "love story" on a typical Daliesque landscape, Dali added a baseball game, an apt surreal touch representing (according to Dali) "the regard of the universe." That literally threw an already-puzzled Walt a curve ball. "Jesus Christ! $70,000 down the drain," he said, and the film bit the dust.[72] Surrealist touches, however, appear in the 1940s features (including *Dumbo*) through to *Alice in Wonderland* in 1951.

The tense standoff between old and new Disney style gives the postwar omnibus features a fascinating *searching* quality. Walt's interest in Mary Blair's difference opened doors for similar stylings by Dick Kelsey, a Disney staffer who decoratively sketched in pastel a musical note amusement park (which was never used) for *Melody Time.* For a musicalized version of the sappy poem "Trees" in the same film, Kelsey was luckier:

His color-filled designs of stylized flora and fauna were transferred to the screen with minimal changes, probably because the segment was mostly special effects (snow and leaves, rainstorms, sunsets) with no personality animation. The delightful anthropomorphized musical instruments in the surreal "After You've Gone" segment from *Make Mine Music* (featuring jazz by Benny Goodman's quartet) were also required merely to move, not emote. The stylish (unsigned) designs of dancing clarinets, muted trumpets, drums, and piano may have been drawn for an "Instrumental Ballet" by James Bodrero, who said in a 1977 interview with animator Milton Gray, "We started trying very hard to get into abstraction. I did a whole storyboard . . . on a thing with Benny Goodman . . . That was a little too far ahead of its time."[73]

When it came to putting Mary Blair's art on the screen, a compromised mix of styles usually resulted: a selection of certain elements from Blair—a color, prop, character, or composition—were uncomfortably blended into a dominant fully-dimensional traditional style. Movement, it was said, was the big problem. Art director Ken Anderson, who admired Mary's work, said "If you moved Mary Blair's things the question is whether it would be as wonderful as it is static."[74]

As noted, Mary herself thought the "little train" sequence in *The Three Caballeros* was the one and only time pure Blair made it from concept to screen in movement. However, *Melody Time* contains segments that come close: Johnny Appleseed, for example, has whole scenes whose colors, layout, and design are directly transferred from Blair's concepts, such as the tiny figure of Johnny, kettle-hat firmly on his head and Bible in hand, dashing over rocks below three waterfalls and a menacing red sky. But in many other scenes (and always those that required "acting") rounded human and animal characters are incongruously placed against flat color fields or stylized backgrounds.

"Once Upon a Wintertime," another section of *Melody Time,* is more coherent in design. Perhaps because Blair found a champion in layout artist A. Kendall O'Connor, who felt she "could put colors together like the devil" and had "a great satisfying sense of design." At first, O'Connor drew the layouts "in the old-fashioned way. I said 'Damn! This is no good compared to the way she has styled it.' I told my assistant Don Griffith we're going to reclean this up the way Mary started in a contemporary manner." He spoke with the segment's director Hamilton Luske, who agreed to ask the animators to work "in a decorative, not completely natural way, a designy way." O'Connor said one particular animator "didn't think much of me, but he did it. And it worked very well." Next, O'Connor found "a sympathetic background painter in Art Riley who "carried out the flat contemporary design like

ABOVE *Artist Dick Kelsey's suggestion for the title to the 1948 omnibus feature* Melody Time. RIGHT *"Once Upon a Wintertime," a section of the compilation feature* Melody Time, *was one of the few times Mary Blair's stylization reached the screen unaltered.*

Mary started it." O'Connor said the reason he was "so brave was [because] Walt was in Europe. Too late to change it. Maybe he liked it."

"Walt thought a great deal of her work," said production manager Ben Sharpsteen in a 1974 interview. "Walt always hoped that he would somehow bring Mary closer to the animation problems."[75] "This woman was an extraordinary artist who spent most of her life being misunderstood," said Marc Davis. "All the men that were there, their design was based on perspective. Mary did things on marvelous flat planes. Walt appreciated this and wanted to see this, but he, not being an artist himself, was never able to instruct the men on how to use this. It gives me a warm feeling toward Walt because he was [at least] aware of that and he wasn't trained as an artist. And it was tragic because she did things that were so marvelous and never got on the screen."[76]

Mary branched into illustrating children's books and advertisements in the 1950s. *The New York Times Book Review* of February 12, 1950, favorably reviewed kid's books illustrated by two former Disney inspirational sketch artists—Martin Provensen (*Funny Bunny* and *The Color Kittens*, artwork by both he and his wife Alice), and Gustaf Tenggren (*The Little Trapper* and *The Big Brown Bear*)—and one who remained at Disney: Mary Blair's *Baby's House*, which "catches the young child's satisfaction in everyday objects as Baby marches through his house, making a joyful inventory of those things which are important in the first years of life."[77]

Blair resigned from Disney in February 1953, a few days before the release of *Peter Pan*. It was an amicable parting; there was not much on the immediate horizon for her at Disney. Besides, not traveling back and forth to the West Coast allowed her more time for the children, now ages six and three. Her duties as a wife and mother, plus commercial art assignments for books, advertising (Pall Mall cigarettes, Johnson

Mary Blair's color styling and concepts dominated Disney features from the forties to the mid-1950s. In two examples from Cinderella, the pomposity of Cinderella's stepmother and stepsisters is emphasized in their grandly over-the-top home decor and furnishings; in contrast, Cinderella is depicted in the dark and dank stairwell between her humble upstairs garret and the lavish downstairs life of her cruel relatives. Mark Mitchell Collection (right).

Blair's Alice attends a mad tea party and cries a pool of tears. Mark Mitchell Collection (above).

baby products, Baker's Instant Cocoa, Blue Bell children's clothes, Nabisco, Pepsodent, among others), and American Artists greeting card designs kept her busy. She also designed sets for Christmas and Easter stage shows at Radio City Music Hall.

"A Mary Blair horse, though quite unlike a horse, is yet a horse," said a profile in a 1958 *American Artist* magazine. "The same tenuous reference to human beings is seen in her delightfully impossible girls with moon faces, pipelike necks, and

legs which dangle helplessly without bone or muscle even when skipping in a field of daisies."[78] As for her fine art ambitions, they had gone a-glimmering long ago.

"Lee always maintained that he continued his work in fine art. He never gave it up," said Neil Grauer. "Mary didn't pursue it, went into commercial art. Walt may have wanted Lee back, but he had a greater hold on Mary."[79] "Funny thing about her," mused her brother-in-law Preston Blair. "She started drawing somewhat of the same type of thing as Lee— big watercolor splashes. One thing she told me: 'I don't think I could draw another watercolor if I wanted to.' She'd become so accustomed to the design, and she was so successful at it. It just wasn't her cup of tea anymore. She was very successful at being liked as an artist."[80]

Countless children have certainly "liked" Mary Blair's charming book illustrations through the years. Her most famous book *I Can Fly* was first published in 1951 and remains in print. (First Lady Jackie Kennedy wrote the artist on White House stationery to say *I Can Fly* was her daughter Caroline's favorite book.) Blair's children's book art is gentle, cute, and carefree; but there is also a bland sameness in the illustrations that is less interesting than her animation concepts—an overdone concern with cheerful patterning and a lack of drama in the activities of floating circle-headed tots and fuzzy animals. One also feels an almost claustrophobic insularity and self-protectiveness in this careful and controlled world created for children and (one imagines) for herself.

For in the real world, both she and Lee must have felt they had lost their moorings. By the 1950s, both were addicted to alcohol. Mary was a quiet imbiber, "part of that forties group that drank martinis," said Roland Crump, who worked with her in the 1960s. "We would go out to lunch and Mary would have three or four gin martinis straight up. If we went out to dinner she'd have three or four more. So there was never a time when she'd have less than two or three martinis at lunch or dinner. But I never saw Mary tipsy. She could handle it."[81] Mary drank, according to Crump, "because of an unhappy marriage. Lee was always screwing around and she knew it."[82] Lee was, according to Lou Garnier, "a nasty drunk. Used nasty language and was mean."[83] (Ironically, Lee was related on his mother's side to the saloon-shattering Carrie Nation.) Debbie Rubin, the wife of one of Lee's partners, described Lee during the 1950s in one word: "Drunk." Asked why she thought he drank so much, Mrs. Rubin offered, "The same reason everybody drinks. He liked it. It was fun. Those were great days. We were the yuppies of that time."[84] But there was more to it than that. For all his success as a top New York TV commercial producer, Lee was deeply frustrated and angry.

Alice pauses on her way to Wonderland.

For Peter Pan, *Blair visualized the flight to Neverland, Captain Hook's rendezvous at Skull Rock, and the love triangle between Peter, Wendy, and Tinker Bell.*

His successful business now consumed most of his time and he painted fine art watercolors infrequently. The bright promise of the Olympic Award–winning painter had faded. Years later in an interview with Nancy Moure, Lee admitted to being "a Sunday painter" during his New York years. When queried about how many watercolors he had actually produced per year since coming to New York, he defensively answered: "My wife was flying back and forth to Disney, and we were raising our children. Spent our summers up in Cape Cod. We led perfectly normal American lives. We weren't 'artists.' "[85] A more brutal reminder of their youthful ambitions came in December 1955 with the news that Pruett Carter, one of the Blair's favorite and most influential teachers at Chouinard, shot and killed his wife and handicapped son before taking his own life.[86]

Neil Grauer met the Blair family in 1960 when he was a teenager and schoolmate of their oldest son. "Lee was great in the morning but by noon he was smashed," he recalled. "He was multitalented. Mary was a fabulous painter, but Lee could do *anything*. He had a phenomenal range of disciplines. As a kid he built award-winning kites. He knew aerodynamics, he knew physics. He built the last sailboat he had. He could sail a 27-foot Triton drunk by himself. I've seen him do it. And at the same time barbecue a steak in back."[87] Besides his diminished output as a serious artist, another of the gregarious Lee's frustrations was, according to Grauer, his two sons: the elder a gifted artist but "slow academically," and the younger a mathematics whiz, but a shy stutterer with poor vision, like his mother. Lee withdrew emotionally from them—Kevin Blair said his father told him he loved him only on his deathbed.[88] (Lee died in Santa Cruz, California, on June 19, 1993.) Or he removed himself physically by ignoring them or passing out drunk in front of them. Roland Crump witnessed a dinner in which Lee fell head first into the salad; after Mary wiped him off and put him to bed, Crump distracted the boys with magic tricks. Later, in another room he found Mary weeping: "You have spent more time with my two sons in the last two hours than Lee has with them in five years."[89] In private, Lee's "mean" streak often turned into physical abuse. "His drinking was hard to control," said Kevin Blair. "He would get violent. He'd hit me and mom. She did not want to be married to him. I have scars on my head from one fight at dinner when I refused to eat my salad."[90]

Then there was the Mary/Disney thing. "There was an intense, probably unstated professional rivalry between Lee and Mary, exacerbated by the fact that Mary clearly was a favorite of Walt's," noted Neil Grauer.[91] "I'm sure Lee loved her very much," said Alice Davis. "But the conflict of the profession with the love got terribly mixed up and eventually started destroying it."[92] Like an old wound, their "rivalry" reopened when Walt personally asked Mary to design the It's a Small World attraction for the 1964 New York World's Fair.

In 1955, Walt had opened his first theme park, Disneyland. It proved to be an enormous popular success, though he considered it a work-in-progress and (as always) sought to top himself by continuously seeking projects "to stretch the creative muscles of his Imagineers." He saw an opportunity in the World's Fair to use outside sponsor's money (Ford, General Electric, and others) to develop attractions that, after public testing and exposure, he would own and transfer to Disneyland. It's a Small World, proposed by Pepsi Cola to benefit UNICEF, was such a project.

After a decade of non-Disney activity, Mary leaped at the opportunity and flew to Glendale to meet with Walt and his WED (later Walt Disney Imagineering) team, which included Roland Crump, and Marc and Alice Davis. "There were very simple meetings," remembered Crump. "The concept for the project came from Walt himself who said, 'We're going to do this little boat ride, Mary, and we need you to do some stylings, concepts, and set pieces on children around the world.' She went home [to Great Neck] and this stuff started pouring in. Just wonderful! It was the largest single project that was ever given to her and she was able to just go nuts!" Her creative "explosion" was due to a combination of Walt personally asking her to return to the Disney fold; a grateful Mary wanting to please him because of his trust and loyalty; a project involving children that was tailor-made for her design talents; and best of all, a three-dimensionalizing of her art, but (unlike an animated film) without compromising her designs. "It was like she'd died and gone to heaven."

"This is the most interesting job I've ever had," she enthusiastically told a reporter from the *Herald Tribune* after the fair opened.

It took 1,500 people to put it together and the results are more delightful than anything I've tried before. I guess you could call it theater-in-the-round, but it's really much more. The audience travels right through it in small boats, seeing its five main areas unfold as the boat floats along a serpentine canal. The audience moves, the performers move, and everyone—especially the children—seem to have a grand time.[93]

The article discussed the exhibit in general and Mary's color choices in particular:

Color is one of her best-cultivated senses: in the five geographic regions presented in It's a Small World, she presents Asia in warm colors, Africa with a blue and green background, South America and Central America in pink, orange, and other vivid hues, and Europe in a variety of colors representing its many mixed nationalities. In the finale, where all the world's children are shown together, she made white the dominant color because it strikes her as festive.

In designing backgrounds for the hundreds of dolls in the show, she whipped up a Taj Mahal for Asia, plaid mountains for Scotland, a leaning tower for Southern Europe, Chinese kites and curving roof-lines for the Far East, and shimmering cellophane strips for a realistic rainstorm.

All the dolls dance, gyrate, wink, sing in ten different languages (but not in close proximity to one another), beat drums and have a whale of a lively time. Tapes and other automatic controls keep everything in perfect synchronization.[94]

According to Ben Sharpsteen, this was the climax of "all the years that Walt spent trying to bring Mary Blair's influence into his productions."[95] Crump feels the project "was a crescendo for her because I'd never seen anything as powerful in her work as the conceptual collages she did for Small World. She just whipped the stuff out. I think it hit her at the right time." Personally, it removed her temporarily from her domestic troubles; she spent two months in Los Angeles in the winter of 1963, and her son, Kevin, said her frequent flights to and from the West Coast made her "a TWA million mile club winner."[96]

Mary now wore her hair in a blond pageboy and at age fifty-two was still attractive, svelte, and sartorially chic. Imagineering artist Crump, long an admirer of her art, was excited to meet her and work with her on Small World. "I have gods and goddesses in art," said Crump. "Over the years I've been in love with certain art: Lautrec, Eames. Mary Blair was one of my goddesses. We were very close. I was in love with her, but as a goddess, not as a woman. I was so thrilled to be with her. She never fooled around, ever. There was this little girl quality about her." Platonic as the relationship was, Mary no doubt found the attentions of the handsome thirty-three year old artist flattering. It was an emotional oasis from the turmoil back east, as was her renewed friendship with Marc and Alice Davis, with whom she often stayed. "She called our house her home away from home," said Mrs. Davis. "We'd always fix a drink and have a toast: 'Welcome home, Mary.' "

Sometimes she joined Crump, his wife and children for dinner and would relate idyllic stories about "her boys, their beautiful home, her husband. She said they went sailing into the bay, would take a barbecue, take some wine, then dive overboard and ride an inner tube on a rope. In winter they skated on the mill pond on their property. The way she described it was like a little girl talking. But what she was telling me was like she's Alice in Wonderland. I found out it was not

Mary Blair in 1966 designing a 1,000-square-foot mural in the reception area of the Children's Wing of the Jules Stein Eye Institute at the University of California at Los Angeles.

138

true," said Crump. "It might have been that way once a long time ago when she and Lee first went to New York."

On a couple of occasions, Lee accompanied Mary to California. "I think Mary was aware that Lee was jealous of her and Small World," said Crump. "He was open speaking [in front of Walt] 'Well, I could have done this. This is what I do, too.' I think she held herself in. He was jealous because of Walt. He didn't pay attention to Lee like he did Mary. Mary grew within the company." Lee also expressed jealousy about Mary's friendship with the muscular Crump. "We were all in a restaurant one night and he got real drunk and said, 'Well, I've got muscles, too, you know.' " Lee titled a caricature of Crump "Sorta-swing" and gave it to Mary.

It's a Small World was an immediate success and eventually was moved to Disneyland in Anaheim, California, and has been duplicated at The Magic Kingdom at Walt Disney World near Orlando, Florida, Tokyo Disneyland, and Disneyland Paris. Before it was finished Walt lined up projects for Mary that would extend through the next seven years, including ceramic tile murals for the Tomorrowland section of Disneyland (*The Spirit of Creative Energy Among Children*); a large ceramic mural (*The Small World of Children*) for the Children's Wing of the Jules Stein Eye Institute at UCLA's Medical Center; and her largest project: a 90-foot-high mural consisting of 18,000 hand-painted ceramic tiles in the Contemporary Resort Hotel at Walt Disney World (*The Grand Canyon Concourse*) completed in 1971. "I had seen the finished tiles laid out on large tables in sections as Interpace finished firing the final work," she once recalled of her monumental mural. "When I eventually went to the opening of Disney World in Florida and walked into that giant concourse my reaction was 'Oh, wow!' "[97] She also painted the large entry wall mural and show scenes for the It's a Small World attraction, the show backgrounds for the Mickey Mouse Review and interior wall treatments for a proposed Small World restaurant. She designed a mural and carpet pattern for the Polynesian Hotel and forty pieces of furniture; working with Marc Davis, she developed twenty color studies for a Western River Ride that was never built.

Mary was the color designer for the live-action musical film *How to Succeed in Business Without Really Trying* (1967),[98] a project which had a Disney connection in David Swift, the film's producer/director. As a former Disney animator and the director of Disney's *Pollyanna* (1960) and *The Parent Trap* (1961), Swift was familiar with Mary's reputation as a colorist.

Walt Disney never saw any of the above projects completed for he died on December 15, 1966. "When he died Mary was destroyed," said Gyo Fujikawa, famed children's book illustrator and the designer of the 1940 *Fantasia* theater

brochure. "So sad and unhappy. She wept."[99] In a 1971 interview Mary remembered Walt warmly as "one of the most wonderful men in the world. He was a family man, and he was willing to go along with all my commuting expense . . . Walt had a great deal of courage in starting new projects and in encouraging talent. He knew talent when he found it."[100] In 1977, she said simply of their relationship: "All I know is that he liked what I did. I got along with him all right."[101]

An observation made by WED imagineer Rudy Lord that when Walt died "Mary Blair lost her most enthusiastic patron" proved all too true.[102] For when the projects initiated and designated by Walt for Mary were completed, she was offered no new work by either WED management nor the Disney feature animation producers and directors. "There was a lot of jealousy in respect to this marvelous woman," said Marc Davis. "A lot of things she did have been taken out of Disneyland, Disney World. Beautiful things replaced." The tile murals for Tomorrowland, for example: "They chipped them all up and threw them away."[103]

Professional jealousy may have been one reason for Mary's final withdrawal from Disney, but mounting personal problems also began to take a toll on her work. Alice Davis was the first to notice. "Mary was working on the first sketches of the tower in the Contemporary Hotel in Florida. I looked at her drawings and said to Marc that night something terrible has happened to Mary. Her color's gone to mud. She doesn't have the color." When Mary came to dinner at the Davises that evening, Alice gently said, " 'Mary, excuse me. I happen to love you very much. And I think something terrible has happened in your life. Could you share it with me? Would it help you to get it off your chest?' She started crying."[104]

She told Mrs. Davis that her eldest son had had an extremely negative reaction to an experimentation with drugs while at college. Kevin Blair recalled his brother was subsequently "in and out of hospitals" that "cost a lot financially and emotionally."[105] By 1970, the Blair family had sold their Long Island house and moved back to California to the northern town of Soquel. Before leaving Great Neck, Mary managed to design a mural for a neighborhood children's wading pool.[106]

Lee sold his portion of TV Graphics because, according

to his partner's wife, he was "just disenchanted with the advertising business. They were a very big success, but then everybody who worked for them decided to go into competition."[107] Kevin Blair recalled that "there was not a lot of work for either Lee or Mary" in the San Francisco area. Lee, in fact, was unavailable for work because he promptly spent over a year in the Santa Cruz County Jail for drunk driving offenses. Mary "put a portfolio together and went to San Francisco" where she was devastated because, as Alice Davis described it, "some young snothead at a top agency looked at her work and told her she was a has-been and had no style." Mary told Neil Grauer, "I can't sell my work anymore. I'm too old." Grauer responded, "'That's ridiculous. You can't tell your age by your art work. It's as young and lively as it ever was.' But she was very depressed by that. I think San Francisco broke her heart."

Lee joined Alcoholics Anonymous, eventually dried out and was clean for the remaining nearly quarter-century of his life. Mary, unfortunately, went in the opposite direction. "A few years before she died," recalled Grauer, "I'd go out to Soquel, and Mary was constantly drunk. Lee would shrug, 'I went to AA. I can't talk her into going. She's going to have to work this out on her own.' He was right. She had to come to grips with the problem herself. But I always thought then and now that's pretty cold."[108]

Some thought Lee exacerbated the problem. At a benefit for the Disney-funded California Institute of the Arts—Disney Artists for Cal Arts (DAFCA)—held at the home of Mr. and Mrs. William Lund (Walt Disney's daughter Sharon), artwork by Mary and two other Disney artists (Al Dempster and Blaine Gibson) was for sale. One guest told Roland Crump he witnessed Lee fill a water glass with gin, which he gave to Mary. "Oh, she'll just sip it," he said. She quickly drained it. "And then he went back and got another half a glass. He practically carried her out of there and put her in the car. For him to go clean and not try to get her to go clean. Why?"[109]

Why indeed. Perhaps it was an unconscious (or conscious) attempt to keep Mary as dependent on him as she was in the early years of their marriage—before Disney, before she found her artistic voice, before her subsequent independent successes. If that is true, it worked. In her final years, Lee totally controlled Mary, as in the old days. Because of her passive inebriation, Mary's interviews with reporters or animation historians in the last five years of her life were *always* given in tandem with Lee; by default he would dominate the interview and *his* accomplishments were invariably emphasized. As he had in the 1930s, the newly sober Lee continued to paint broad brush "California Watercolors" and to exhibit his work locally. One of Mary's last commis-

sions was a collaboration with Lee on illustrations for slides that accompanied concerts by the San Francisco Symphony Orchestra (conducted by Seiji Ozawa) of Ravel's "L'Enfant et Les Sortileges" on December 18 to 20, 1974.

Marc and Alice Davis last saw Mary at another DAFCA fund-raiser which Lee did not attend; Mary came with Retta Scott Worcester. It was the only time they ever saw her visibly intoxicated: "We were in shock," said Mrs. Davis. "We couldn't believe what we saw. Mary had changed so and looked so terrible. Frumpy and haggard. Everybody was shying away from her, which was terrible, too. I found her a number of times. She was standing by herself, just kind of turning in circles."

In 1977, the Blairs were befriended by a Soquel teenager with artistic aspirations named Fred Cline, who is currently a visual development artist at Warner Bros. Feature Animation. Coincidentally, Cline's father was the Blair's podiatrist, and the couple often met with the youngster to gently critique his artwork. "During the year that I knew her," said Cline recently,

Mary was having a little difficulty walking and talking—certain words would not come easily and she would get frustrated. She was always full of encouraging words for me, and would playfully debate with Lee as to whether Walt Disney was a genius or an asshole—she maintained that Walt was a genius.[110]

During the last year of her life, Mary "was going senile," according to son Kevin. "She was starting to relive her childhood." After slipping in the bathroom, she injured her leg and a resultant blood clot slowly worked its way to her brain. "One day as I was getting ready to leave their home," recalled Fred Cline, "Mary walked up to me and gave me a long, tight hug. She had never done this before. Not too many days after that, she passed away." On Wednesday, July 26, 1978, Mary Blair died of a cerebral hemorrhage, three months shy of her sixty-seventh birthday.

Services were held at St. John the Baptist Episcopal Church of Capitola and, according to Cline, "there were very few people in attendance. Lee handed out sets of copied material at the funeral—some press material about Mary's career and photographs of Mary and her family."

Lee sailed his boat out to sea and scattered Mary's ashes in the Pacific. He kept "his eye on the plastic bag that had contained them, watching it bob up and down as he came about and sailed back to shore."[111] Lee told Neil Grauer of "a lost period" after Mary died. "He moved to San Francisco and got some animation work," and lived in a seedy hotel "in a not very nice section of town. That was his way of running away from it, [to] be by himself."[112] He later returned to their house in Soquel.

On October 22, 1991, the Disney Company posthumously recognized the creative contributions of Mary Blair by awarding her a Disney Legend Award—a bronze sculpture and a bronze plaque embedded in the concrete in front of the theater at the Disney Studios in Burbank. On stage for the presentation were Mickey Mouse, Michael Eisner, and Roy E. Disney, who accepted for the Blair family, none of whom attended. Apparently, the old Lee/Mary professional "rivalry" flared up because of the honor. Neil Grauer expressed "shock" when Lee phoned him to ask bluntly, "Why are they giving it to Mary? She's dead!" He refused to go to Los Angeles to pick up the award and later wrote Grauer to reiterate, "I'm alive. I'm here."[113]

In her last years, Mary Blair created private artworks that are barely recognizable as hers: a series of garishly colored, partly dimensional paintings mixing innocence with eroticism. They have an *art brut* feel, like the art of the self-taught, the insane, or the recluse. In one, a man in a tux and a woman in a white dress and flowered hat are served wine by a waiter under a striped umbrella on a wooden boat in the middle of a body of water; on the far right side of the deck a nude woman is stretched out on her back, arms above her head. The sky is hot pink and ochre. The couple have fixed smiles and manic eyes: the man stares ahead, she looks toward him in wild anticipation. A phallic pole with dimensional flags separates them from the nude.

In another painting, titled *Le Chat,* a woman with bright red hair sits in a red room on a raspberry-hued bed; she is dressed in a sheer negligee with her breasts and pink nipples exposed and a yellow-orange cat asleep on her lap. The dimensional parts include a paper doily fringe on the negligee, a framed portrait of a cat on the wall, and bits of gold and doily as the woman's choker. The woman's pasty white face has rouged cheeks and a rigidly fixed smile; her right eye is slightly crossed lending her both a frightened and a sad look. Outside a windowsill on which a clock sits, a full moon rises.

Time and movement (and life) seems frozen in both these mysterious works; the prone naked boat-woman with eyes closed and the woman with a sleeping pussy sitting enclosed within a coffinlike bed are isolated from life, perhaps dead. *Le Chat* particularly distressed Lee Blair; he hated the painting because the woman, he said, had "the look of death on her face."[114] Are the violent passionate colors an expression of rage? Does the imagery scream with spiritual and physical longing, sexual frustration, loneliness, perhaps a cry for help?

The works might also be interpreted as courageous state-

ABOVE *Mary Blair working on Pall Mall cigarette advertisements, circa 1970.*
LEFT Le Chat *was one of Mary Blair's last art works.*

141

ments from a tenaciously creative artist. In her final paintings, Blair rejects detached fantasies for an expression of deeply felt emotions in a raw new way. In brave defiance of her circumstances, she displays an honesty in dealing with libidinous emotional needs and feelings that is very moving. Ultimately, the symbolism's true meaning remains the artist's secret.

Secret, too, because of inaccessibility, is the inspirational art Mary Blair created for the Disney studio at the peak of her creative powers. Amazingly prolific, she sustained for over three decades an unflaggingly high level of creativity. Her impact on the postwar features through *Peter Pan* is undeniably there in styling and color; but the promise of more radical experimentation did not endure, contested as it was by her co-

workers mainly because of Walt's inarticulate mixed signals.

Ironically, it is the art deemed "disposable" by a ravenously insatiable animation process, the art that Blair herself thought inferior to her "serious" watercolors that is her legacy to the world. Herein is contained but a glimpse of the brilliant, witty, mesmerizing designs and (especially) colors conjured by a dazzling sorceress of an artist. Mary Blair saw the world in a fresh way, and made us see it, too, like children when everything is new. She brought a special beauty, charm, and gaiety to animation graphics—the "vacation in the country" feeling Paul Klee said art should convey.

One feels good just gazing at Mary Blair's paintings. Like feasting on rainbows.

Mary Blair, a diminutive woman with a great artistic gift, before a wall layout of her ceramic mural designs for the Tomorrowland area of Disneyland. Courtesy Kevin Blair.

PART FOUR

Inspiring
Eclecticism

A Ken Anderson sketch of an alligator disciplining a child for The Rescuers *(1977).*

CHAPTER 12

Tyrus Wong

Wong's brilliantly colored phantoms are kites—large, complex aerodynamic constructions he has designed, built with string, paint, paper and ripstop nylon, and flown since 1978. For the eighty-four-year-old artist, it is less a hobby than a continuation of his indomitable creative spirit. "I got painted out,"[1] he said of his disinterest in the traditional painting arts after a long and varied artistic career as a watercolorist, muralist, lithographer, Warner Brothers film production illustrator (1942–1968), greeting card designer, and Disney inspirational sketch artist (1938–1941). Now, using the sky as his canvas, Wong continues to make art that comes alive when in motion, much as he did when he drew set designs and storyboards for John Wayne, Joan Crawford, and Paul Newman movies or concepts for Disney's *Bambi*.

Although Wong considers his work on *Bambi* to have been "a minor, very small part" of his life, his impact on the film was very large indeed. "He set the color schemes along with the appearance of the forest in painting after painting, hundreds of them, depicting Bambi's world in an unforgettable way," acknowledged Ollie Johnston and Frank Thomas in their book on the making of the cartoon feature.[2] "Here at last was the beauty of [Felix] Salten's writing, created not in a script or with character development, but in paintings that captured the poetic feeling that had eluded us for so long . . . The remarkable paintings of Ty Wong not only inspired the other visual artists, but created a standard that was met by musicians and special effects, too."[3]

Twenty-eight-year-old Tyrus Wong in a 1938 Disney employee photo.
OPPOSITE *A dynamic inspirational pastel for* Bambi *by Tyrus Wong.*

145

The conditions must be just right: a bright sun to banish all traces of fog, a wind blowing between eight and ten miles an hour, and a generous stretch of beach without trees or telephone poles. When those conditions are met on certain golden afternoons at certain Santa Monica or Venice oceanfronts, Tyrus Wong launches his amazing visions: a 124-foot centipede with more than 150 segments, a flock of swallows with 40-inch wingspans, giant butterflies, white doves and black swallows, and even a gaggle of angels swoop and glide, dart and hover in the California sky.

"The influence Ty had on this film *made* the film!"[4] concurs Marc Davis, whose subtly expressive animal designs for *Bambi* were also a major aesthetic breakthrough for the animators.[5] Wong's art was a mix of occidental and oriental influences, combining the broad brush, spontaneous California Watercolor style with the contemplative balance of composition, limitation of details, and restraint of traditional Chinese painting. "The Chinese," wrote E. H. Gombrich, "consider it childish to look for details in pictures and then to compare them with the real world. They want, rather, to find in them the visible traces of the artist's enthusiasm."[6]

Tyrus Wong's enthusiasm for art stemmed from his father, who loved calligraphy. Wong Sr. was a strict parent who encouraged his son's artistic explorations and instilled in him an appreciation for the self-discipline and control needed to master any art. For instance, he forbade his son to play baseball, lecturing him, "Suppose you break one finger? You ruin your whole life. [sic]" Each evening, he made young Tyrus practice Chinese writing by dipping a brush in plain water and making wet impressions on pages of old newspapers. "We can't afford ink or rice paper. But he made me do it with water. That's a good training," says Wong.

Father and son came to the "Gold Mountain" that was America from Canton, China, in 1919 when Tyrus was nine years old. Mrs. Wong agreed that she and her daughter should stay behind, and the family never was reunited. "Oh, gee, I was sad," said Tyrus recently of his lifelong separation from his mother and sister. "I am sure my father would love to be with his wife again. But in China it was hard to make a living. They [sic] always thinking about America. They say think about the future. My mother probably encouraged him. The son in China had no opportunity. Take him to America."

The Wongs encountered their first bit of Gold Mountain racism when two weeks passed before they were allowed to clear the Angel Island immigration center in San Francisco Bay. "Man from England come in, no trouble," said Tyrus speaking a broken English that embarrasses him to this day and into which he liberally sprinkles Americanisms such as "golly" and "gee." "But being Chinese, you have to go through all kinds of questions and so forth." Mr. Wong and son lived in a Chinese community center in an alleyway in Sacramento; after about two years, Wong Sr. went to Los Angeles to find work, leaving his son alone. "I was scared to death," admitted Tyrus. "I had a tiny room and three other men stayed there in separate rooms. To wash your face you had to go down to the basement. I hate the basement! Very dank and *eeeyew*! I hate it."

His father sent him money, but young Tyrus was basically self-supporting. He cooked for himself ("Chinese kids have to learn to cook rice"), found work in a grocery store ("I got my meals there, too") and attended public grammar school. But he was an indifferent student, poor in the three Rs ("I have to take off my shoes to count to twenty"). Drawing was another matter. "I *love* to draw!" he says dreamily, with an emphasis on the word "love." The unsupervised boy played hooky from grammar school for days at a time, and when his report card was sent to his father in Los Angeles, his concerned teacher wept. "She's Caucasian lady," recalled Wong. "She try her best to teach me. She said, 'You make me very sad, Ty. You're a real bright boy. I can't understand why you're absent so much. I'm sorry but I can't promote you.'"

After Tyrus's father had the report card translated, he immediately sent train fare to his son and ordered him to come to Los Angeles. When fourteen-year-old Tyrus arrived, his father gave him a special greeting. "Before I get a chance to say hello: *whack! whack! whack!* 'Just because I'm not in Sacramento to watch, you play hooky!' My little suitcase fly open and socks and things. He was really fuming." Mr. Wong, who (according to his son) found only occasional menial employment "helping out in stores" during his lifetime, felt his errant son was wasting his American opportunity.

He arranged for Tyrus to attend Benjamin Franklin Junior High in nearby Pasadena, and to live in a dormitory in a Chinese Methodist Church with six young men who were going to school or working as houseboys, waiters, and store managers in downtown Los Angeles. But again, says Tyrus, "the only thing that interested me was painting and drawing." One of his teachers and the principal noticed the posters he made (for Fire Prevention Week and such), and arranged for a summer scholarship to the Otis Art Institute, a Los Angeles art school slightly older than Chouinard.

The summer went by too fast for Tyrus, who refused to return to junior high. "I said I don't wanna go back there! This is what I wanna do. This is it!" He asked his father to help him raise the $95 necessary for tuition ("which is a lot of money in the thirties"). Mr. Wong borrowed the money from several people, and in order for Tyrus to pay back the loan, he lived with his father in Los Angeles's Chinatown. He also got a job at Otis as a janitor. Because he had no car, he walked several miles to school each day through MacArthur Park. "For a young kid, no trouble walking. And in those days, you don't worry about mugging." Sometimes after a late class drawing from the model, he threw a smock over the model stand and slept there overnight. He moved into a job as a busboy in the school cafeteria, where an elderly waitress who was "like a mother" fed him lots of leftovers. " 'Help yourself, Ty,' she say. 'Won't be good tomorrow.' I got plenty to eat."

He attended Otis for five years, four of them on schol-

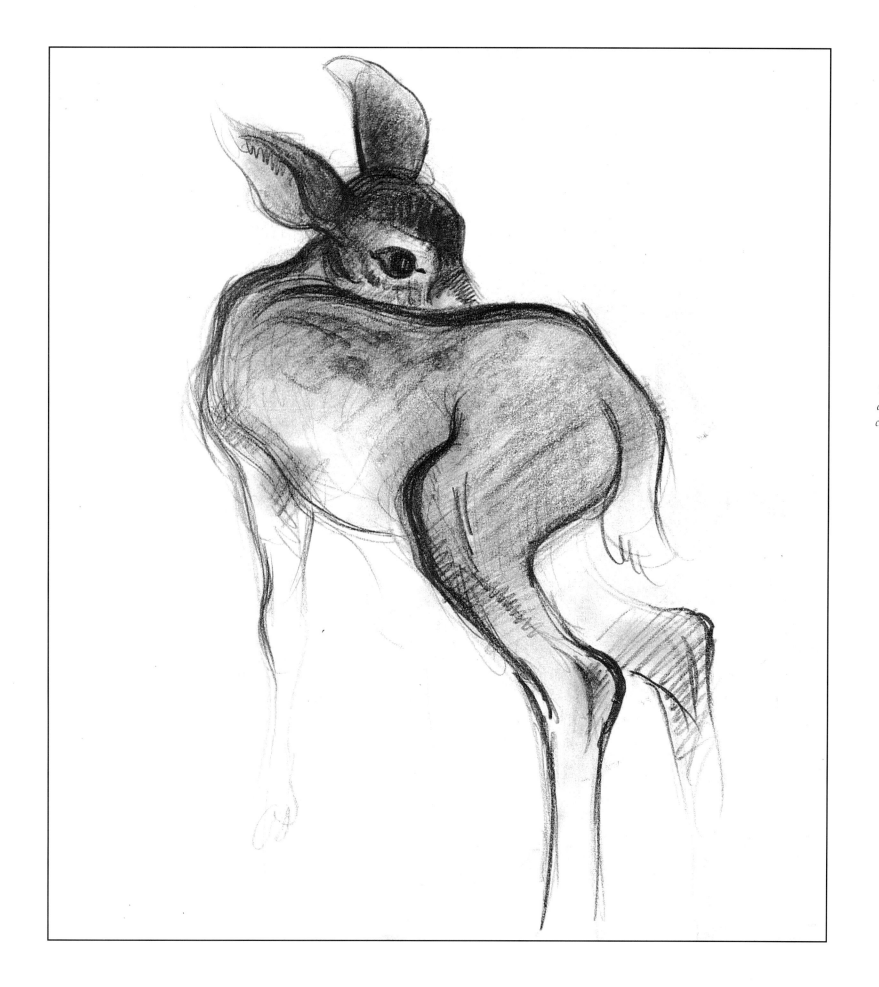

This sketch of a deer demonstrates Wong's classical and confident draftsmanship.

147

arship. The school recognized his special talent for drawing and knowing his financial situation gave him paints and canvases left by students who had graduated. When recently asked which artist he most admired when a student, Wong immediately answered "Michelangelo! He's not a bad fellow to be influenced by." Wong's early nude studies have a bold and muscular draftsmanship that surprises if one is familiar only with his impressionistic *Bambi* concepts. In contrast, he was also attracted to James McNeill Whistler's rapturous *Nocturnes,* a series of delicate paintings that may have influenced Monet. In Asian art, Wong particularly favored the Sung and Yung dynasty because "already the Ming beginning to get a little too fancy for me, too much detail, too glittery. Sung dynasty artists are really powerful painters."

Wong tells a comical story about the school getting him

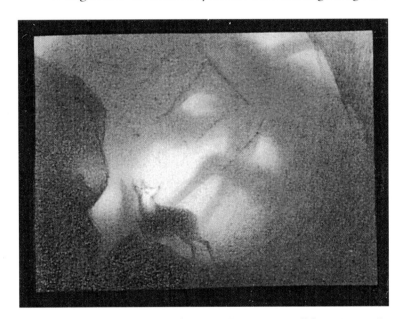

a job designing a sign to advertise "Her Secret" brassieres: "I really didn't know what a brassiere is. I didn't know a woman wears it. So the manufacturer asked his fully clothed secretary, an older woman near fifty, to put one on over her dress. So on the way home, I think Caucasian women wear that just to keep chest warm? I didn't know till after I got married. Chinese philosophy don't tell kid about sex. When they're old enough, they know enough. Anyway, I made the sketches and they paid me $25, darn good money." When Tyrus's father saw the bra sign, he expressed to his son how proud he was. The elder Wong never saw his son's later artistic accomplishments; he died before his son graduated from Otis in 1935.

After graduation, the young man continued (with permission) to return to the school to draw from the live model. He began to exhibit his watercolors, but the work was not steady. A W.P.A. project turned up ("Thank God for the Roosevelt administration! It kept lots of artists from going hungry"), for which Wong submitted two paintings each

month (and was paid $95 in turn) for exhibition in public libraries and government buildings. Wong also decorated the walls of a former curio shop that a friend turned into a restaurant called the Dragon's Den and worked there as a waiter. "That's how I met my wife. She was a Chinese girl from Bakersfield, Ruth Kim, going to UCLA. She worked as a waitress and we split the tips." Soon a romance blossomed and they were married. The couple raised three daughters and shared sixty years of marriage until Ruth's death in January 1995.

In searching for their first apartment, the Chinese newlyweds were often rejected by bigots. "They say, 'Oh, I'm sorry. We already rented it. My husband forgot to take the sign down.' Two weeks after, the sign was still there." Eventually, they bought a roomy house on a hillside with dense trees in the Sunland section of Los Angeles, where Wong has lived for

over half a century. "After we got married and were expecting the first daughter, I say I need a job. So I went over to Disney. I was established as a landscape painter. Exhibited in the New York World's Fair, the L.A. County Museum. But I couldn't make a living selling my work."

He also felt the studio was "more related to art and more famous" than any other cartoon studio. *Pinocchio* was in production in March of 1938, but Wong was hired as an inbetweener (despite his obvious gifts as a painter) on Mickey Mouse shorts at $35 a week. "Inbetweening" was (and is) the tedious craft of making drawings between the "main pose" sequential drawings made by higher echelon animators and was the obligatory starting position for artists new to animation. It was overseen in classes and on the job by a martinet named George Drake, described by Richard Huemer as "a Torquemada. He was a very stupid guy and thoroughly hated by all the kids."[7] "I hated it," said Wong, echoing the sentiment. "Flipping all these drawings over a light table all day. When

148

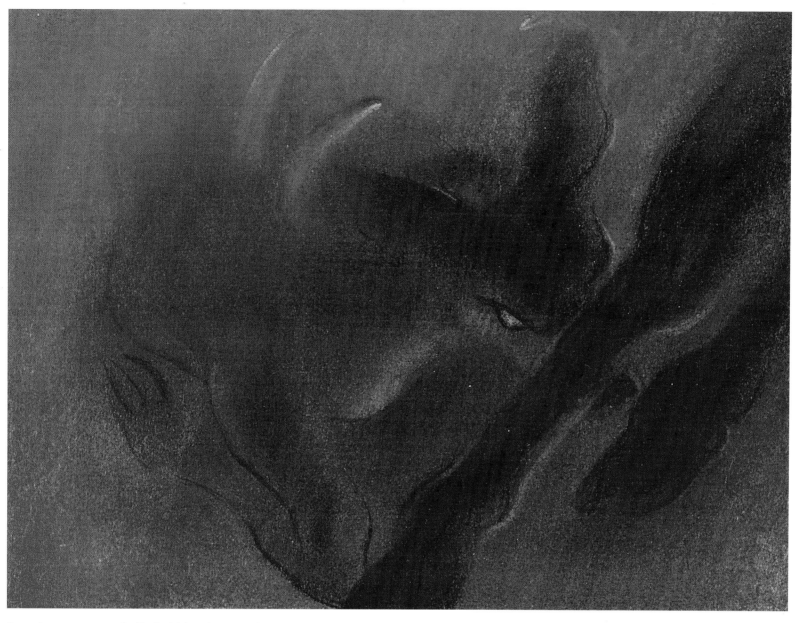

LEFT AND OPPOSITE
*Wong's sensitive
studies set the visual
style for* Bambi.

I get home my eyeballs feel like they ready to drop out. I told my wife my eyes are killing me."

After hearing that *Bambi* was in preliminary production, Wong prepared landscape paintings at home "and put Bambi in them." He showed them to Tom Codrick, the film's top art director, who showed them to Walt, who immediately appreciated their mysterious quality. "Looks like we put you in the wrong department," said Codrick, who offered Wong the opportunity to "key the whole picture from beginning to end, to make a painting that sets the mood. So that's how I got the job. I say, Gee, that's kinda fun. I loved it. This is right up my alley." He noted that "Gus Tenggren did drawings that were praised but his style fit in more with *Snow White* type of thing, like Arthur Rackham. But Walt wanted something different for *Bambi*."

Wong worked in paint and pastel on small, even tiny, drawing fields. It is amazing how much visual information—mood and action suggestions—Wong packs into spaces no bigger than 2-by-2 1/2-inches. And how beautiful and visually appealing he makes it all. Observe his stag fight, in which Wong creates a world in remarkably small spaces filled with dynamic action, strong compositions, and dramatic lighting. One silvery sketch of the deer Faline in a pool of light framed by boulders and the shadows of stags battling on a large rock wall behind her contains drama and an extraordinary delicacy reminiscent of Whistler's description of his *Nocturnes* as being "like the breath on the surface of a pane of glass."

Animators Johnston and Thomas wrote:

In contrast to the paintings that showed every detail of tiny flowers, broken branches, and fallen logs, Ty had a different approach and certainly one that had never been seen in an animated film before. He explained, "Too much detail! I tried to keep the thing very, very simple and create the atmosphere, the feeling of the forest." His grasses were a shadowy refuge with just a few streaks of

149

the actual blades; his thickets were soft suggestions of deep woods and patches of light that brought out the rich detail in the trunk of a tree or a log. Groups of delicate trees were shown in silhouette against mists of early morning rising from the meadow. Every time of day and each mood of the forest was portrayed in a breathtaking manner. An ethereal quality was there. Best of all, Walt was enthusiastic. "I like that indefinite effect in the background—it's effective. I like it better than a bunch of junk behind them."[8]

Wong never spoke to nor received direct praise from Walt, whom he saw only in story conferences. As an inspirational artist, he was, as usual, isolated from the animators, including (oddly) the only other Asian-American then at the studio, special effects animator Cy Young. There was jealousy and the whiff of racism on the part of a few layout and background staff members. "You could count on one hand some who had a certain coldness to me, a certain resentment. Everything I do they're against it. 'Why do we have to follow his style?' But most at Disney were very nice, being artists they're very liberal-minded." Codrick was Wong's champion and closest colleague: "He gave me a lot of encouragement when I feel, gee, like the water is coming up to here. 'Don't feel bad, Ty. I know you can do it.' Without him I didn't think I could stay there."

When the Disney employee's strike came along in May 1941, Wong sided with the studio. "I was being a good boy. I say I'm not going to go out. I'm gonna stay. Walt been very, very nice to me. I enjoyed [the work], though Disney didn't pay a hell of a lot. But we lost the strike and some of the strikers don't like me at all. So I guess they put the word around. So I got canned, I got laid off, I got fired.[9] After three and a half years." *Bambi* was released a full year after Wong left the production; and once again, screen credits misrepresent the contributions of a special artist: Tyrus Wong is not acknowl-

edged as the film's most significant stylist or art director; instead his name is listed among nine others under the heading "Backgrounds."

"I don't feel bitter toward Disney at all, except for a few guys who I know to this day kinda resent me. I just tried to forget it. I got a job very quick over at Warner Brothers." What landed him the job was not only his *Bambi* sketches, but two superb storyboards made of tiny sketches he quickly created, one depicting a genie escaping from a magic bottle and another showing an explosive World War II battle. "I love war and action pictures," he declared. "The drama, the tragic." He stayed at Warners for more than a quarter of a century making storyboards and concept sketches that established visual continuity, settings, and camera angles of films starring Frank Sinatra, William Holden, and Richard Burton, among many other stars. He gave live-action directors a taste and feel for the final imagery, for what might work on the screen within a given budget. "The director might say let's cut that part out in production. You save a lot of money that way."

At Warners and after taking early retirement,[10] Wong exhibited and sold watercolors, designed Christmas cards (for Hallmark and California Artists), illustrated magazine covers (for *Reader's Digest* and *Coronet,* among others) and painted ceramics sold through Neiman-Marcus and Marshall Field. Then came the kite constructions to fill a brief (and rare) creative vacuum when Wong felt "painted out."

Recently, Joe Grant asked Wong to rejoin the Disney studio as an inspirational sketch artist on the upcoming animated feature *The Legend of Mulan,* which is set in ancient China. But Wong declined saying his "style had changed so much. I told Joe I couldn't do it like *Bambi*. I wouldn't do it justice." His work in animated films was a long time ago, and, to him, not the most important part of his artistic life.

Today, he prefers to design and build colorful balsa wood and nylon birds, butterflies, and angels, and to send them sailing heavenward. But only when the wind is just right.

151

CHAPTER 13

David Hall

Here is the little that is known about David S. Hall: he was born in Ireland in 1905, and later immigrated to America. His first film work was as a production artist for Cecil B. DeMille's 1927 silent film *The King of Kings*. He was an art director for Twentieth Century-Fox and then MGM, an associate producer for Lester Cowen, and he helped design Freedomland, a now-defunct amusement park in the northeast corner of New York City. Film productions to which he contributed designs include *The Four Horsemen, Solomon and Sheba, National Velvet, Raintree County, Quo Vadis?,* and *The Robe.* Hall was working as a set designer for George Stevens's *The Greatest Story Ever Told* when he died of a heart attack at age fifty-eight in July 1964, leaving a wife and son.[1]

For a little more than a year (from March 1, 1939 through June 1, 1940), Hall worked as a Disney inspirational sketch artist. During that brief time he created beautiful concept art full of invention and vigorous draftsmanship for *Alice in Wonderland, Peter Pan,* and *Bambi.* Hall's drawing style was in sync with the Euro-book illustration stylists who set the tone for prewar Disney film design, such as Gustaf Tenggren, Albert Hurter, and Ferdinand Horvath. There is in Hall's fluid, sure line, narrative detailing, and muted watercolor palette a debt to the great British illustrator Arthur Rackham; Hall's technique of layering transparent color pigments over black ink lines is similar to Rackham's own version of *Alice* published in 1906.

One is also reminded in Hall's work of the charm of Beat-

A heartless Queen of Hearts leads Alice to the guillotine in an elaborately detailed and cinematically dynamic watercolor by David Hall for a 1930s version of Alice in Wonderland.

153

rix Potter's realistically modeled and delicately colored and clothed anthropomorphic animals, as seen in *The Tailors of Gloucester* (1903), *Two Bad Mice* (1904), and, of course, *Peter Rabbit* (1901). Like his predecessors, Hall tells a story in each drawing with confident, insouciant draftsmanship and an eye for particulars in character's expressions, poses, and actions; judging by the amount of artwork he produced—over 400 *Alice* drawings within three months[2]—and the high spirits found in it, Hall also shared with his predecessors a great love of drawing.

His *Alice* sketches faintly echo the beloved (but stilted) line illustrations that John Tenniel drew for Lewis Carroll, but Hall's art is distinguished by a lively cinematic quality: in almost every concept drawing there is an awareness of the possibilities of the motion picture camera and movement as captured on film.

Hall's background as a designer of silent films full of pomp and pageantry comes to the fore in an impressive panorama (or "pan") drawing of a medieval group marching toward the Queen of Hearts's castle. Alice is bowing to the Queen of Hearts amid anthill-like detailing of flying banners, marching armored soldiers, crown-carrying courtiers, black-hooded torturers, pig-chasing jesters, ass-kissing myrmidons,

and kowtowing sycophants. Our camera-eye "pans" from right to left with the parading throng as it moves into a huge and threatening black castle that swallows the multitudes. (Notations at the bottom of the painting indicate animation camera "field" positions and suggest that this painting was shot for a test reel with other Hall sketches for Walt's perusal.)

Inside the gothic castle in an interior setting worthy of a Zefferelli Metropolitan Opera production, Hall concocts a dramatically lit scene as the Hatter and March Hare stir a giant cauldron of soup, whose glories are extolled in song by the Mock Turtle ("Soo-oop of the e-e-evening, Beautiful, beautiful soup!") standing on a high platform as a line of hapless vegetables prepare to sacrifice themselves before a royal audience, including Alice and the Queen, all with soup bowls in hand and at the ready.

Pantomimic actions (à la silent movies) and odd, dramatic camera angles abound in Hall's art: the Lobster-Quadrille is alive with aquatic characters dancing, singing and circling Alice and the Turtle; as Alice floats down the rabbit hole into a vast cavern, red bats swoop and surround her amid huge bubble-encrusted stalagmites; even in a tranquil scene of Alice and her cat lying on the edge of a pond ("All in the golden afternoon/Full leisurely we glide . . .") motion is implied by

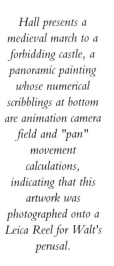

Hall presents a medieval march to a forbidding castle, a panoramic painting whose numerical scribblings at bottom are animation camera field and "pan" movement calculations, indicating that this artwork was photographed onto a Leica Reel for Walt's perusal.

"Down, down, down.
Would the fall never
come to an end?" mused
Alice after tumbling
through the rabbit-hole.
In Hall's painting, he
jazzes up her descent
with huge red bats,
big bubbles, and
skyscraper-like
stalagmites.

155

a family of swans languidly swimming from close-up to mid-distance.

"David Hall's vision of Wonderland is as fresh and as full of imagination and ingenuity as the story it illustrates," wrote film historian Brian Sibley in the afterword of a recent book of Lewis Carroll's masterwork illustrated with Hall's Disney drawings. He "adds an extraordinary dimension to the book, capturing that elusive—often funny, sometimes frightening—atmosphere of dreamland, which so few illustrators of *Alice's Adventures in Wonderland* have succeeded in grasping."[3]

Hall's paintings for *Peter Pan* continue to showcase his flair for visually arresting staging; he delights in showing us Tinker Bell's viewpoint when she is discovered in a bureau drawer by mischievous John and Wendy, and offers, in another drawing, a truer view of her pin-spot size compared to Peter's, as seen from a low angle outside the same bureau. He makes use of expressionistic shadows when Peter Pan's lively shade jumps up and over Mr. and Mrs. Darling, or when Pan is confronted by Captain Hook, whose sword is as threatening as the shadow of his curled hook looming large over the defiant boy's form. Hall also worked on *Bambi* continuity

sketches and "captured in realistic detail the momentum and emotion of the [stag's] charge from the meadow,"[4] among other sequences. Tyrus Wong remembered him vaguely, as "very much a gentleman who always wore a tie. A very nice fellow who got into Disney through his friend Harold Miles," a DeMille live-action sketcher who became a *Snow White* art director and *Bambi* concept artist.[5]

Why Hall didn't last longer at the studio is subject to speculation. Not everyone was enamored with his work. Joe Grant, who had Walt's ear at the time, felt "there was no business in it. They were just straight illustrations. Which to him [Walt] would be useless."[6] Sibley notes that "a legend grew up that Hall had been hired to work on [*Alice*] by a production assistant, who was anxious to impress Disney. Hall, so it was said, worked in secret, behind locked doors, but when Disney found out he was so angry he refused to use the pictures and fired Hall."[7] Sibley feels (and I agree) the story is "hokum."[8] A number of Disney story meeting transcripts note that Hall was in attendance with (not hidden away from) Walt.

When Hall's *Alice* story drawings were individually pho-

"All in the golden afternoon, Full leisurely we glide." David Hall's depiction of Alice lolling near a brook on a hot summer's day is a lovely evocation of Lewis Carroll's English countryside.

tographed onto film and shown in continuity in November 1939, Walt commented, "There's certain things in there that I like very much, and there are other things that I think we ought to tear right out."[9] Walt's dissatisfaction was with the story department's adaptation of Carroll's _Alice_ to the screen, not with Hall's visualizations. _Peter Pan_ suffered similar development pains and was also shelved; like _Alice,_ it was not produced until the early 1950s. _Bambi_ was well into production when Hall was assigned to it and there was little for him to contribute, since the character designs were already developed by the animators (Thomas, Kahl, Johnston, and Davis) and the overall production design was set by Tyrus Wong's impressionistic style.

There was also a shift away from the lavish rococo European storybook illustration style; _Pinocchio_'s box office failure in early 1940 was a factor. Also, the war spreading in Europe was beginning to be felt in Hollywood in terms of revenue, and budgetary belt tightening at Disney affected the look of the films. Horvath and Tenggren were both gone from the studio; Hurter would be dead within two years. The Disney strike, America's entry into the war, and Mary Blair's influence on the design of the South American and postwar features all contributed to the change. Hall came along too late in the game with a style soon to become passé.

Yet, his drawings continue to weave a magic spell on all who view them. The impressive richness, lavish details, grand conceptions, and sheer beauty draws us into a timeless fairy-tale world. How wonderful it would have been to see them come alive on the screen as only Disney could have done in the mid to late-1930s. Today, one looks at these lost masterworks with admiration and a certain sadness for what might have been.

157

CHAPTER 14

Eyvind Earle

In 1951, a thirty-five year old painter and greeting card designer named Eyvind Earle was hired by the Disney Studio at $78 a week as an assistant background painter for one short, *The Little House*. Within two years, he had become the supervising color stylist/inspirational sketch artist for *Sleeping Beauty*, a feature that was (in 1959, the year of its release) Walt's most ambitious and expensive animated feature.

Like Tyrus Wong, Earle had a significant impact on the design of a single feature film; in this case, a Technirama 70, six-channel stereophonic version of the Perrault fairy tale that took over five years and $6 million to make into the "moving illustration" Walt desired. For the film's visual style, Earle created an opulent medieval tapestry based on the paintings of Durer, Van Eyck, Breughel, and fifteenth-century French illuminated manuscripts, particularly the *Tres Riches Heures de Jean, Duc de Berri*. "All my foregrounds were tapestry designs of decorative weeds and flowers and grasses," wrote Earle in his autobiography *Horizon Bound on a Bicycle*:

> And since it is obvious that the Gothic style and detail evolved from the Arabic influence acquired during the Crusades, I found it perfectly permissible to use all the wonderful patterns and details found in Persian miniatures. And since Persian miniatures had a lot in common

Eyvind Earle, circa 1958.
OPPOSITE *An elaborate test background by Eyvind Earle for* Sleeping Beauty. *Animators complained their characters would be lost in the painting's excessive detailing.*

159

with Chinese and Japanese art, I felt it was OK for me to inject quite a bit of Japanese art, especially in the closeup of leaves and overhanging branches.[1]

The self-taught artist considered his nearly half-dozen years on *Sleeping Beauty* akin to putting himself through art school, for at Disney he had access to the finest art books in the world "to browse over, to incorporate into the paintings I made."[2] His eclectic borrowings, in addition to the list above, included the unreal color, decorative landscapes, and delicate beauty of works by Uccello and Botticelli, and the weightlessness, stillness, and naivete of Fra Angelico.

"He captured everybody's imagination," said Ken Anderson, one of the film's layout artists, and "showed a possibility of a very medieval . . . and fairytale-like treatment that Walt had never seen the like of."[3] But whereas Wong's impressionistic settings for *Bambi* were (so to speak) "character friendly"—in that their broad color fields and limited detail did not obscure the animation of the characters placed in front of them—Earle's grandiose, angular, detail-encrusted styling and backgrounds threatened to overwhelm the characters.

Red flags went up among the top animators who argued that the "highly romantic" fairy tale "called for warmth and humor and dramatic moments more than austere design."[4] The layout personnel were also upset: "I didn't like Eyvind's stuff," admitted Ken Anderson, "because to me it was too cold. I had to fight myself to make myself draw that way. It was a constant battle to train myself to work that way, but I learned."[5] He and the others *all* learned because Walt settled the argument in Earle's favor, declaring: "For years and years I have been hiring artists like Mary Blair to design the styling of a feature, and by the time the picture is finished, there is hardly a trace of the original styling left. This time Eyvind Earle is styling *Sleeping Beauty* and that's the way it's going to be!"[6]

Adjustments in the look of the animation and layouts resulted in *Beauty* becoming one of the most consistent design statements by a single concept/color stylist in the Disney feature animation oeuvre. "More than any other Disney feature, *Sleeping Beauty* reflects a single design idea," comments animation historian Charles Solomon. "Earle had a greater impact on the look of the characters and backgrounds than any designer at the studio."[7]

For Earle, it was a grand learning experience: "Walt Disney paid me a good salary [about $400 a week in 1958][8] all the while I unwittingly . . . perfected the style that would stay with me the rest of my life." Eventually his distinctive painting style made him wealthy through gallery sales of his originals and serigraphs. His path to Disney was a long one—he had periodically applied (and was turned down) for work at the studio since 1936. The path to wealth was, however, circular.

He was born into money in 1916, the son of Ferdinand Pinney Earle, who had inherited a million dollars from *his* father. Eyvind has no idea how his grandfather, a one-time U.S. Army general, made his money: "I let everybody leave this earth and never thought of asking."[9] Ferdinand was handsome and multitalented: a painter, poet, writer, and violinist. He was, according to Eyvind, "in the motion picture business in New Jersey long before I was born." At outdoor studios in Fort Lee and at the warehouselike Vitagraph in Brooklyn, Ferdinand used his ultra-realistic painting technique to create "glass shots": a shot obtained through a glass on which part of the scene has been painted. Live actors on partial sets are seen through the clear portion of the glass providing an illusion of a complete setting. With this optical effect, films with even meager budgets could have exotic locations and fantastic buildings without incurring expensive travel or construction costs.

"Then they all moved to Hollywood when I was two," recalled Eyvind. Ferdinand worked for MGM as "the big art director on the first *Ben Hur* [1926], and he produced his own version of *The Rubayat of Omar Khayam,* which was never released. Then he worked with Cecil B. DeMille on *King of Kings* [1927]."

Ferdinand was a troubled man possessed of an "insane uncontrollable maniacal temper that . . . ruined much of [his] life." He beat each of his five wives, numerous girlfriends, and the several children he sired, and never paid alimony or child support. "Oh, he was cruel to everybody," said Eyvind recently. "Had a terrible temper and loved to beat up everybody, mostly little children and his wives."[10]

With the arrogance of a moneyed dilettante, his anger also alienated employers, such as MGM's Louis B. Mayer. Eventually Ferdinand Earle ran through his fortune and died broke at age 73 in 1951. But even when he needed a job, his temper was unmanageable. This was evident at Disney's, where (ironically) the elder Earle found work years before his son. During World War II, Ferdinand Earle "painted clouds with lightning effects" for armed forces training films, recalled Ken O'Connor. "He did a beautiful job. A leonine type, older man, dignified head. He raised hell, made a lot of enemies. Having painted the thing, he followed it down to photography, knew all the technical terms, told them how the hell to do their job. It didn't go over well."[11]

In January 1927, after Ferdinand's fourth wife (Eyvind's mother) divorced him, he kidnapped ten-year old Eyvind and took him from Hollywood to Mexico, Cuba, and ten European countries. "From the very first," wrote Eyvind years later of his three-year ordeal, "as the train headed for Mexico City, my father announced to me that, starting at once, I was to read fifty pages of a book or paint one painting every day."[12] He was forced to do both. The reading began with *Oliver Twist,* a novel the child found "hardly fun or easy reading." Dickens's protagonist suffered harsh discipline and was a young survivor with whom Eyvind identified. In addition to the daily readings, he spent mandatory hours each day painting with his father, struggling to make his rudimentary daubings resemble Ferdinand's academic realism. At age fourteen, he had his first "one-man exhibit" of paintings in a room at a hotel in Ascain, France.

The child was also subjected to daily physical abuse from his father: "I cannot forget the hundreds and hundreds of spankings, whippings, slappings, along with the thousands of hours of punishments . . . [E]verlasting punishments that kept me indoors long, long afternoons writing in my most careful penmanship that I would never again do some God knows what terrible misbehavior at least five hundred times."[13]

While in the south of France in August 1930, Eyvind ran away. Five months later, through the help of a half-brother in Paris, he was reunited with his mother in Los Angeles. The first thing he asked her was, "Do you mind if I never paint again?"

The Depression forced Eyvind to reconsider that request; he also found that within him was a genuine, strong desire to continue painting. For survival, he painted house numbers on street curbs for five cents per house. "I would come home just before dark having earned an average of fifteen cents which bought enough food for my mother and I for supper."[14] Then he landed a job as an assistant sketch artist at United Artist Studio at $20 a week. "Suddenly," he thought, "I was one of the richest persons in the whole world."[15] Ten months later he was laid off. With the financial support of friends, Earle went to Mexico in 1935 for a year of painting, followed by an exhibition of his work in Hollywood. He then applied as a background painter at Disney, where art supervisor Phil Dyke asked for samples for almost a year without offering the twenty-one-year-old a job. Years later a disingenuous Dyke told Earle "I never gave you a job because it would have ruined your style," which Earle thought "a lot of baloney to say to someone in the middle of the Great Depression."[16]

Each day Earle made one or two paintings, often pedaling on his bike fifty or sixty miles to scenic locations, and several times he hitchhiked or rode trains up and down the coast, once as far as Portland, Oregon. In October 1937, loaded with 110 pounds of baggage, he rode his bike across America. "I painted forty-two watercolors in the forty-two days it took me to cross the country and I wrote a ten thousand word diary." In Manhattan, he immediately secured the first of three exhibitions of his art at Charles Morgan Galleries in Manhattan. Although Earle's work sold (and the Metropolitan Museum of Art purchased one painting), "my prices were so low that in a few months I was down to zero again." He could not make a living from his paintings alone, so he diversified into magazine illustration and murals, and producing his own Christmas cards. He was drafted into the Navy, where he met a WAVE who became his first wife. With the birth of their daughter and the end of military service, Earle found himself continually scrambling for commercial art jobs, painting portraits, or the occasional art exhibit. A friend was "disgusted" at the low prices Earle allowed his work to be sold for, but he, said Earle, "didn't have to support a wife and a child and a mother and himself."[17]

His luck began to change in 1947 when he joined American Artist Group where, over the next twenty-five years, he created 580 Christmas cards. The stylized card designs caught the attention of Disney artist John Hench (one of Walt's closest advisors), who arranged for Earle's employment at the studio. "That was the end of my years of poverty," said Earle. "Suddenly, a miracle had happened. I was allowed to paint from 8 A.M. till 5 P.M. plus evenings and Saturdays overtime, and be paid for every minute of it. I no longer had to run all over the place."[18] Adaptable as most self-taught artists are, Earle could sling paint with the best of them in the traditional Disney way. "All I had to do was watch one of the background painters do something I had never seen or heard of before and instantly that was added to my own personal knowledge and technique."[19] On his first day of work at Disney, Earle noticed 100 "exquisite little paintings by Mary Blair. It was her job to do the first original styling for a feature or special short. She was a great artist, a great designer, and a great colorist. In my mind, I said to myself, 'That's the job I want at Disney.' "[20] After proving himself on *The Little House* short, Earle painted over 100 backgrounds for the feature *Peter Pan.*

The more decorative style honed through years of gallery exhibitions and stylized greeting card designs came to the fore when Walt gave animator/director Ward Kimball permission to "try something new" for the three-dimensional short *Melody* (1953) and the CinemaScope® short *Toot, Whistle, Plunk and Boom* (1953). Earle drew attention to his special abilities by painting a series of flat, sharp-edged color styling sketches playful in form and color, in the UPA cartoon studio's modernist manner. "Ward wanted to do a completely contemporary modern art style," recalled Earle. "I came up with about forty little paintings of all kinds of jazz musicians and instruments. I knew the secret of doing color schemes in all different variations, so that the story board as a whole made a very colorful exciting picture by itself."[21]

161

Twenty tiny
(2 x 2 1/2-inch) concept
paintings by Earle for
Lady and the Tramp
showcase the artist's
imaginative use of a
limited palette and his
economical, yet
evocative, stylization.

We can see his "secret" color schemes in twenty 2-by-2 1/2-inch concept paintings for the feature *Lady and the Tramp*. Here, Earle suggests romantic nighttime scenes in and near a small-town park (depicting crickets and cats, owls in a tree, colored lanterns hanging from tree branches, a couple on swings against a starry sky, and a riverboat steamer). Earle shows an imaginative use of shapes and patterns and a facile way with a brush, even within a limited palette.

Eventually, Earle's work caught Walt's eye. "Let's see what Eyvind can do styling *Sleeping Beauty*," he said casually to his staff one day.[22] "They gave me a whole room to myself," recalled Earle, "and I proceeded to fill every wall from floor to ceiling with the most detailed and carefully executed paintings ever attempted by me."[23] "When I first saw his stuff, I almost fainted," says inspirational sketch artist Vance Gerry. "It was just breathtaking."[24] After a number of weeks, Walt viewed the artwork and met with the top story, layout, direction, and animation staffers. He simply told them, "See what you can do to get this in the picture," a typically cryptic statement that served as an approval of Eyvind's efforts and

a command to *get that look* on the screen. Earle learned he was in the big time when Hench dropped by his office to brief him on how to get along with Walt, what to expect, and how to understand him. "It was apparent to me that it was Walt himself who was really telling me those things," said Earle.[25] Earle felt the "whole project fit me like a glove," and claimed he always "knew I was going to style *Sleeping Beauty* as well as paint all the key backgrounds, and all I had to do was to do it in my own style. How utterly simple it was going to be for me."[26]

How utterly wrong he was. He told Ken O'Connor, "My old man fell out with everybody here and I'm certainly not going to make that mistake." But, said O'Connor, "in about two weeks he did the same thing."[27] "It seemed to me the painter should make his own layout!" said Earle.[28] "He wasn't too successful in his public relations," remarked layout veteran O'Connor dryly.

Then there were the animators, who worried about surrendering warmth and "audience involvement to this strong style" which they saw as "cold and ponderous, but startling."[29] The design of the characters would need to be "altered to fit the overall design of the backgrounds" and the angularity and two-dimensional patterning "was calling for a new type of drawing in the animation," drawings that ultimately took four and five hours to complete. The last straw was Earle insisting that he alone choose colors for all the characters:

The old time animators, who were revered as gods at the Disney Studios, were in the habit of telling the directors of each sequence what colors they wanted their characters to be and working directly with the ink and paint department. Whereas, I saw the job as designing a complete stage setting, where every detail from A to Z was considered and harmonized to make a total picture that could only be done by letting one single artist create the color schemes in the first place.[30]

The meeting in which Walt sided strongly with Earle's vision supposedly decided the issue of design, but there were still certain compromises in that vision. For example, the princess, prince, and evil fairy are as angular and grayed down as the backgrounds, but the three good fairies are rounded, traditionally designed Disney characters and dressed in bright pastel hues. Also, the obsessive detailing and muted color of the final backgrounds is less stylized than Earle's original stunning concept paintings. Compare the simple, direct presentation of large areas of color with limited detailing found in the sketch of a fairy's wand lighting a gargoyle visage, or one of the evil Malificent atop her castle tower silhouetted against gathering clouds, with an ornate elaborate test background of a cottage in the wood. In the styling sketches, we are in "Mary Blair country" and that must have driven the animators wild with anticipatory anxiety.

"He got suckered into it. He won't admit it," said art director Gordon Legg of Earle's move toward a more "acceptable," subtler stylization. Legg notes that the early concepts had "very stagy, very dramatic setups where most of it would be just a flat color, and then there'd be this one streak of light in there, and in there, there'd be this intricate detail. The stuff was just terrific. But, as you know, when the backgrounds finally came out, it was just solid embroidery. There was not a quiet place [in the paintings]."[31]

Part of the reason for such compromises was that Walt's attention during this period was, to put it mildly, divided. In the mid-1950s he was mainly involved with launching Disneyland and two television series, as well as continuing to initiate, monitor, and approve each and every short and long film (live and animated) his studio turned out. *Beauty* took so long to complete and the story was so weak because Walt's time, energy, and gift for entertaining storytelling were not fully engaged on the project. When the film was released, it found itself more than $1 million in the red, "the only time that unfashionable color had appeared in the Disney ledgers since 1949."[32] It wasn't until the 1979 and 1986 reissues that *Sleeping Beauty* found its audience among "the students and young adults of the fantasy audience" (the *Star Wars/Star Trek/Lord of the Rings* fans) for whom the film offered "a cinematic vision of a heroic world unlikely to be equalled."[33]

Even two of the animators who objected to the film's design conceded that the:

pageantry of the Middle Ages was captured with a magnificence that never will be duplicated again in this form; and when viewed on the wide screen required by the 70mm film used for this one production, it is extremely impressive . . . we have not made a comparable feature

with so much beauty in both appearance and color and such consistent treatment from start to finish—which is just what Walt wanted for the picture.[34]

Earle left the Studio in March 1958, almost a year before the film was released. His duties as *Beauty*'s art director and main background painter were completed, and his elaborate, overpowering style was too special for the features planned and a couple of short film projects ("a Christmas story and a cowboy story") he designed storyboards for. Ostensibly, they were turned down because of the diminishing theatrical shorts mar-

ket, but Earle described the proposed projects as "not Walt Disney. It was 100 percent me," which certainly would not have advanced his cause at the studio.

Instead, Earle concentrated on his own artwork, whose gallery sale profits have "never stopped going up from 1948 on." In Earle's large paintings and serigraphs, bold shapes, jewel-like color, an intricate patterning (particularly on trees) dominate dramatic landscapes. Gallery owner Victor J. Hammer described them as "at once mysterious, primitive, disciplined, moody and nostalgic . . . His landscapes are remarkable for their suggestion of distances, land masses and weather

164

moods."[35] The work is also strangely cold and sensuous at the same time, realistically detailed at first glance but ultimately highly artificial. Across this rigid, pristine fantasy environment, with it's crème brûlée surface gloss, no human figures traverse, only the occasional tiny stylized cow. No warmth or sense of humor is evident; the artist's emotions are not be- trayed. Earle has, predictably, a bitter hostility toward painters who ignore precise technique for the expression of their emo- tions. He dismisses art by the New York abstract expression- ists in particular as "insane trash" and "way-out avant-garde rubbish,"[36] and rails against contemporary art critics, blaming them, Magoo-like, for the mess the art world is in:

"How to paint a tree." Earle demonstrates (for the Disney background department) his method of layering details one upon the other. Courtesy Howard Lowery Gallery.

The greatest sin of all as far as they are concerned is for the public to really like the work. To the critics, that is proof that the work isn't worth taking notice of . . . I'm a million times more concerned with the taste of a million people than I am with some weird critic who happens to have a job on a certain newspaper.[37]

The facile and perfunctory quality of his serial paintings reminds one of the forced conditions by which the artist first came to art: mechanically turning out one painting a day to please daddy. Now he turns them out one after the other to please the buying public. "Galleries all over the United States carry them," he says proudly, "and my biggest of all buyers are in Japan."

Earle may not be a critic's darling, but his stuff sells. For this Depression era artist/survivor, that is what counts; he considers the recent lawsuit he endured from a former art dealer as a yardstick of his success. "The verdict against me was $10 million, 900 thousand, which the judge reduced to $3 million: $1 million in art, the rest in cash. My insurance paid one and a half, so it wasn't that bad." Not bad, indeed, for one who used to charge his fellow Navy gobs five bucks a head for a painted portrait. Currently, Earle lives with his second wife in northern California and continues to paint; four employees in a plant in Monterey make prints from his originals.

Said the indefatigable seventy-nine year old artist recently, "You might say I'm just getting started."

Ken Anderson

W alt Disney once introduced Ken Anderson to a gathering as his "jack-of-all-trades,"[1] an apt description for one of his studio's most versatile and gifted artists and a company man par excellence. During his forty-four years at Disney, Anderson dabbled in animation, majored in scene layout, and mastered character design and art direction for films and the theme parks.

Anderson's inspirational sketches and concepts dominate the art direction of post-*Sleeping Beauty* animated features, such as *101 Dalmatians* (1961), *The Sword in the Stone* (1963), *Jungle Book* (1967), *The Aristocats* (1970), *Robin Hood* (1973), and *The Rescuers* (1977). A grounding in architecture ("He wanted to be the world's greatest architect")[2] and a brief stint as a movie set "sketch artist" lent precision to Anderson's natural drawing abilities and honed his talent for technical details. It was Anderson who agreeably took on technically complex assignments—animating a moving background in the Silly Symphony *Three Orphan Kittens* (1935), devising and photographing a miniature set of the dwarf's cottage for *Snow White,* designing the seamless combination of live action and animation in *The Three Caballeros* and *Song of the South,* and bringing the animator's original pencil lines to features via Xerography in *101 Dalmatians.*

In addition, Anderson "always had a feeling for characters from the very beginning."[3] "Ken was big almost from the start," recalled Frank Thomas, who was in the same Disney training class as Anderson in 1934. "Way back he was recog-

nized as a special talent. If he drew a character he'd nearly always put them in a situation either with another character or with a background so you could see how the thing was going to look. He'd draw the whole thing like a storybook. He never had the flair of design that Mary [Blair] did, he never had the color, but he was maybe as inventive as [Albert] Hurter."[4]

Anderson's invention and evocative placement of characters within environments is seen in a large *Jungle Book* concept sketch of the domain of a monkey king. Languidly sprawling on a throne at the foot of a giant tree, the royal orangutan holds forth to a few simian subjects amid the ruins of an ancient man-made city. Anderson admired British cartoonist Ronald Searle, who once advised him to use a Mont Blanc pen and India ink for a line similar to his; Anderson's nervous, scribbled Searle-like line imparts a goodly amount of detail about the locale and characters—their sizes, attitudes toward each other, and so on. Broad strokes of colored felt-tip pens of green and orange-yellow evoke the jungle and the scattered gold treasure, both of which the monkeys take equally for granted.

In an inspirational drawing for *Sword in the Stone,* Anderson brings us inside the cramped thatched cottage of Madam Mim, who is seated at center—short, stout, and totally engrossed in a hand of solitaire. Through the room's detailing we learn some things about Mim herself; for example, the sock dangling from a ceiling beam, food bits strewn on the floor, and (most tellingly) cobwebs on a broom indicate the

Medusa's "pets" capture a child and her doll. Anderson's drawings offer ideas for staging this dramatic action, color, and character relationships.
OPPOSITE LEFT *Ken Anderson, at work on* Song of the South, *circa 1946.*
OPPOSITE RIGHT *An early Anderson concept for Madame Medusa in* The Rescuers *as a Bacall-esque grande dame.*

169

In the lair of the monkey king: Anderson brings a mysterious fantasy world from Jungle Book *alive with humorous touches and an emphasis on characters and their relationship to their setting.*

lady is a slob; a mobile made from bones, containers labeled "bat gizzard" and "eye of newt," a BEST WITCH banner and the partially hidden cauldron impart information of a more sinister nature: Is it possible that the unkempt granny at the table rubs pitchforks with Beelzebub?

Anderson's experience in architecture and set design is apparent in both of these concept sketches. And something more. Topping off his gifts, Anderson brought a joyful exuberance to his work at Disney, as seen in his drawing's lively, gently humorous line. "He had architectural training, lots of

guys did," commented Thomas, "but Ken had enthusiasm as a person."[5] "I absolutely love doing these things," Anderson said on more than one occasion about making animated films, which he considered "one of man's highest forms of expression."[6]

Anderson was born near Seattle in 1909, the son of a lumber man. His story took an exotic turn when his father moved the family to the Philippines when Ken was three. Anderson's most vivid memory of the Pacific archipelago was an operation performed without anesthesia in which his tonsils were

Anderson's nervous Mont Blanc pen and Ronald Searle—like ink lines describe the home environment of Madam Mim in The Sword in the Stone *(1963). By subtle and not-so-subtle visual hints, Anderson leads us to think Mim may be, well, a witch.*

thrown out a window and immediately gobbled up by a stork—a cartoon image worthy of a macabre Silly Symphony.[7]

Seven years later, the story turned tragic in a Dickensean way when Anderson Sr. died of malaria aboard a ship returning the family to the States. Ken, his sister, and mother were penniless and the boy was placed with relatives in Washington who treated him so cruelly he ran away. "I figured life was too damn hard," he told Robin Allan, "so I found a log cabin and caught 127 trout for my dinner and lived there for a month before they found me."[8] His mother reclaimed him, and, at age twelve, he worked at odd jobs to put himself through school, including becoming a printer's "devil." The ambitious young man attended the University of Washington at Seattle, where he studied architecture, "slept above a library, read voraciously and finished his fellow students' assignments

for a fee."[9] He won a scholarship to Europe where he studied at the Ecole des Beaux Arts at Fountainbleau, which "no one had won west of the Mississippi before."[10] In Europe for two and a half years, he also studied at the American Academy of Rome. According to Robin Allan, "he admired art deco and the illustrative tradition of Arthur Rackham and his contemporaries. He drew and painted wherever he went, relishing the warm colors of Southern Europe in general and Spain in particular."[11]

He met his future wife Polly at Washington U. "I was certainly interested in him," she said recently. "You can always tell a good guy by the way he treats his mother and he was always good to his mother."[12] They were married in the summer of 1934, the height of the Depression. A six-week job at MGM sketching sets for Greta Garbo's *The Painted Veil*

171

(1934) and Helen Hayes's *What Every Woman Knows* (1934) was over and the couple "were living on the beach on beans and all sorts of things for about a month. We were having a wonderful time."[13] Or so Anderson said in an interview two years before his death in 1993. Twenty years earlier, in an interview with Bob Thomas, his memory of the early days of his career was closer to the actual events and not so rose-colored: The MGM job was "a most unhappy experience" and his wife was "fed up with our living on credit."[14]

It was Polly who suggested he apply for work at Disney. "We were riding in a car and passed the Mickey Mouse sign [atop the studio on Hyperion Avenue]. I said, 'Why don't you go in there and get a job?' He says, 'I don't do cartoons, I do architecture.' But he went in and got the job."[15] But first he had to endure two weeks of inbetweening classes conducted by the sadistic George Drake, described by Anderson as a "tall skinny guy with big flappy ears," and by animator/director Jack Kinney, as "an irascible son of a bitch with a terrible temper and a short fuse [who] was frustrated, having been relegated to his position of power because he flunked animation. He made it as tough on us as he possibly could."[16] Drake once threatened to fire newcomer Frank Thomas because his smile was crooked, and once decreed anyone who drove a Ford would be dismissed.

From behind a glass cage, the dictatorial Drake observed the aspiring, perspiring talent. "We were drawing Mickey and all of those things, and having drawing tests and so forth. We weren't allowed to talk to anybody . . . one by one, most of these guys were let go." Drake summoned Anderson: "I think you are going to make it here," and offered him a shot of whiskey. "I said, 'Gee, George, I can't take that.' He said, 'Go ahead, you deserve it.' Anderson took the drink with a chaser of sparkling water Drake also offered. "I was smiling and happy looking at him," said Anderson, "and his ears were getting redder and redder. He started jumping up and down like a madman. He said, 'Get off this property and don't you ever come back. That's one damn thing we can't have is drinking on the studio property.' He followed me out the door . . . I went back home to Culver City and told my wife that I got a job all right, but I lost it in ten minutes." Polly encouraged him to go back and a couple of weeks later he did. " 'Anderson, how are you,' Drake said with a big smile, and he put me on staff."[17] At $15 a week.

Polly worked as a painter in Disney's ink and paint department for three years until the first of their three girls was born. "We were married with nothing at all," she recalled. "I got fifty cents more a week than Ken did. Then he went up slowly."

Anderson first worked in a large room "doing various fill-in scenes in various pictures"[18] with other "junior animators," such as Milt Kahl, Ollie Johnston, Frank Thomas, Jack Hannah, and Jim Algar, men who became important, longtime contributors to Disney films. Then, because of his background in architecture, Walt singled Anderson out for a special assignment. "Walt was a great one for using everybody for everything he could think of," said Anderson. "He didn't ask me, he told me . . . that he was counting on me doing this" animation of a moving background in *Three Orphan Kittens.*

The first scene was the kittens in the kitchen running across a tile floor under a kitchen table, past an icebox, coming to a step, jumping up a step and under a grand piano . . . I just did the tile and the perspective as a changing perspective point all the way through the thing and then it even changed on eye level. You jumped up on the step. So getting an underside of the grand piano and getting the kitchen tables and all these things moving was a helluva job, but Walt was delighted.[19]

Anderson, featherless since age ten, saw Walt from the start as a father figure from whom he constantly attempted to win approval and validation. His commitment to Walt and the work of the studio remained constant and unconditional; often in interviews he sounded like the good and loyal son defending an irascible dad. He once told Bob Thomas, "I know that Walt wasn't a man who never did wrong. As a matter of fact, he did things to me that hurt me terribly. But by the same token, if a guy can hurt you that much, he can also make you love him that much."[20]

After *Kittens,* Walt offered Anderson a position in the new layout department headed by Charles Philippi and Hugh Hennesy. Layout artists, said Anderson, "were the artists he was going to rely on to make his pictures really outstanding. They would be graphic artists, but capable of planning a scene so that they had the best angles and the best color and they were responsible for the background . . . [and] the staging and they were to be the art directors of the picture . . . He said 'Use your architectural background with your animation.' "[21] *Snow White* was in the planning stage, and "Walt Disney lit a fire under all of us," recalled Anderson of his boss's charisma during that exciting period. "Every one of us was under his spell."[22]

Anderson dove into the feature like it was a pot of jam. "This studio has always encouraged people to seek their own level, do what they want themselves," he said. "You just make yourself valuable."[23] Anderson made himself *invaluable* by animating scenes in the complex party-in-the-dwarf's-cottage sequence, and also by creating layouts and inspirational sketches for the "Someday My Prince Will Come" dream sequence; his charming and sensitively rendered pencil drawings survive, though the sequence was cut in the storyboard stage, and he proudly signed two of them: One features a round, old-style cartoon sun beaming from behind cumulonimbus clouds, and the other (dated January 23, 1936) pictures a sequential image of Snow apparently entering a reverie and about to burst into song regarding her prince's coming, as the dwarfs sit before her in rapt attention. There is an appealing Hurteresque quality in the details and shading in both sketches. "Ken loved Hurter's work and was definitely influenced by him," according to Disney historian Paul F. Anderson (no relation).[24] (The dated drawing is interesting: considering there was only a year and a half before the film's release, the characters were still "off-model," that is, the designs were not yet finalized.)

On *Snow White,* Anderson also worked with a team that experimented with the multiplane camera, and, according to Frank Thomas, "he was always so pleased Walt picked him to design the inside of the dwarf's house."[25] In fact, Anderson built a model of the house:

> that came apart . . . painted it all white, but . . . everything else . . . outlined like a drawing [on a scale of one inch to the foot] . . . I would have the [live-action] camera pan across the room, past all the various artifacts and things in the dwarf's room, little chairs and everything . . . Then I would go on the stage and I would shoot [the model for Snow White] Marjorie Belcher [later known as Marge Champion] in her dress . . . opening this door, looking in, running across this room and pivoting around and sitting down in this little chair, which was an inch high.[26]

When the two films were composited, a live Snow White

Anderson's sketch for a dream sequence (later cut) for Snow White: *(signed and dated January 23, 1936) that resembles Albert Hurter's style.*

173

appeared to be performing on a three-dimensional "drawing." The experiment was used as a guide for animation as it related to the setting, but Walt may have been searching for a way of actually using it in the film. "He was just so curious and interested in things," said Anderson. "He was trying and trying. Trying to perfect his processes and trying to train people to do a better and better job and get his organization working for him better."[27]

By fall of 1936, Anderson was so well regarded he lectured to the Disney evening art classes, waxing eloquent to studio newcomers about the "spirit of progressiveness, of wanting to explore things, to try new things, that makes good layout men."[28] Walt showed his appreciation of Anderson's gung-ho attitude and his creative gifts by awarding him screen credit—as one of several art directors on *Snow White, Pinocchio* (the complex layout of the opening multiplane shot above the village was Anderson's), and *Fantasia* (the first movement of Beethoven's Pastoral through the storm)—as well as frequent salary raises. On the strength of his art direction for the short *Ferdinand the Bull* (1938) his pay rose from $18.70 to $50 a week, a "real damn big raise for those days." And best of all, remembered Anderson, "he complimented me."[29]

"Ken had a good strong ego," recalled Roland Crump, who worked with Anderson at WED. "Frank [Thomas] and Ollie [Johnston] had incredible egos, but you never saw it. But Ken Anderson felt pretty strong about Ken Anderson. He believed this is the way we're gonna do it." The *Ferdinand* raise was, in fact, the happy outcome of a power tussle between Anderson and the film's background painter Mique Nelson over painting techniques—Anderson wanted to experiment with saturated opaque colors in the backgrounds and Nelson wanted traditional tinted watercolors. "I kept pushing," admitted Anderson, "so Mique wound up washing his hands of the whole thing and he was going to complain to Walt that he had nothing to do with it, really, that he had done the best he could to hold this crazy guy."

Fortunately, Walt liked the result and gave *both* men raises; but Walt was a canny reader of people and he must have sensed within Anderson's transparent ego the emotional child who wanted attention and discipline. Like Judge Hardy lecturing headstrong Andy, Walt issued Anderson a warning:

He said, "Ken, I'm impressed by what you've been doing . . . but . . . I want you to know one thing . . . there's one thing we're selling, just one, and that's the name Walt Disney." And, he said, "If you can buy that and be happy to work under the name Walt Disney, you're my man. But," he said, "if you got any ideas of selling Ken Anderson, it's best for you to forget it right now." And

honestly, I thought nothing could be more honest and fair than that.[30]

Anderson, like his boss, was a perfectionist who, according to J. Gordon Legg, "kept a tight rein on the artists" in his unit:

> Like most people who worked successfully at Disney's, [he] was willing to do a thing over until it was right, by somebody's judgment. I remember working on a background for *Fantasia*. I designed this tree that the Pegasus was sitting in. [Ken] had me redesign one limb . . . about twenty times before he decided it was just right. I appreciated his sense of design, and he appreciated mine, so I didn't mind doing it. He was right . . . It's when you have to do things over that you know are already right, that you don't want to do it . . .[31]

Anderson worked closely with fellow Art Supervisor Mary Blair on *The Three Caballeros*. Observe how he, chameleonlike, adapted Blair's pastel sketch of Aurora Miranda leading a group of men through the streets of Baia and used it as inspiration for his cartoony set designs for the live-action and animation segments.

A posed photo taken on the live-action set for *The Three*

Caballeros alludes to the working process, showing a stylishly dressed Mary drawing a caricature of wide-eyed, all-smiles singer Miranda, while Ken caricatures Mary.

Anderson's challenge on that film (and later on *Song of the South*) was to retain Blair's color and flat styling while devising ways to combine it with live actors and animation. In the days before computers and high technology made cinema magic comparatively easy to accomplish, the processes were "so doggoned involved in every instance."[32] Anderson had to deal with placement of performers, lighting, rear and front projection, traveling mattes, lab processing and color quality, live-action cinematographers (including one who refused to keep a space in the camera field for the "invisible" cartoons that would be added later), animators, and animation directors, who had to be brought in on the planning of action not totally in their control.

It was a plateful even for "an experimenter in layout" and "jack-of-all-trades" like Anderson. And invariably when one problem was solved, Walt would "come in and he'd want to do something different":

> And I thought, "What the hell does he want to do it differently for?" . . . And I didn't realize that he wasn't capable of saying why . . . he just wanted to find better and newer ways of doing everything. In retrospect, I can see

175

Anderson's pastel suggestion for a live-action set of a town square set in Baia (Brazil) for The Three Caballeros. *The graphic style was adapted from Mary Blair's inspirational paintings made in South America.*

all kinds of things that, at the time, had I been more intelligent I would have worked with him a little better . . . I never knew a man who was more inspirational and who, to me, was a genius."[33]

When Walt began to develop Disneyland in the early 1950s, he formed an organization to plan and design the park called WED (the initials of his own name). "Walt was to WED and imagineering in the 1950s and sixties what he was to animation in the 1930s," observed Paul F. Anderson about Walt's true interest and energies during this expansive period. He recruited talent from the animation department, and among the first were the versatile Marc Davis (de-

signer, painter, and one of Disney's legendary "nine old men" of animation) and Ken Anderson. Anderson recalled:

Walt said, "I'm going to take you off payroll. I'm going to pay you out of my own pocket . . . make me drawings that are like Norman Rockwell. Make them big but make them with a sense of humor" . . . So I made twenty-six of them which he loved. While doing that we had to go downtown to pick out the architecture and the various things . . . But, he forgot to pay me. Three weeks went by . . . I was living off my paychecks and I didn't know what I was going to do. But luckily . . . he paid me more than I could ever save in my life."[34]

Anderson designed the Fantasyland "dark rides" (enclosed three-dimensional environments in which the audience drives or flies by scenes from *Snow White, Peter Pan,* or *Mr. Toad*), Storybook Land, and the interior of the Sleeping Beauty castle. "I want to make this come alive," instructed Walt. Anderson was one of the first "imagineers" to work on what would become (after twelve years of development) the Haunted Mansion. "I think Walt recognized he could use Ken anywhere," said Polly Anderson.

But some perceived Anderson's boyish dexterity as overreaching ambition. "Ken was a very talented guy, but he was always in on everything," complained Marc Davis.[35] Sometimes his eagerness to please Walt led to embarrassing faux pas, such as the time he set fire to Walt's mustache with a new cigarette lighter, or sat in Mrs. Disney's chair at a Mexican bullfight (and was told to leave by Walt in no uncertain terms).

"I think there was a lot of Walter Mitty in Ken. He was an extremely emotional man," commented Roland Crump. "His emotions went from here to there. One day, wild and laughing, the next sitting at his desk like he's gonna commit suicide. He's probably one of the most talented men ever to work for Walt Disney. Powerful story man. Maybe that personality made him what he was."[36]

"He was a tremendous talent, but if it was possible for anyone to consistently do something wrong at the right time, it was Ken," said Davis. *101 Dalmatians* was a case of doing something right at the right time; but in his blind enthusiasm, Anderson misread Walt, who ended up displeased with a film that (ironically) saved the animation department from elimination.

"Walt was unhappy with the cost of *Sleeping Beauty,*" explained Anderson, "and it was rumored around that he didn't even intend to make another [animated] picture."[37] "The financial guys had Walt's ear and were trying to get him to dump animation," according to Paul F. Anderson. "They said the parks are making money, the merchandising, the TV shows. *Sleeping Beauty* was a money-loser. The message was get out of animation."[38] If medieval *Beauty* was "too arty and didn't come across real well in warmth and story,"[39] Dodie Smith's juvenile novel *The 101 Dalmatians* was an exciting, fun romp set in contemporary London, full of warm, amusing animal characters. Walt was interested and Anderson tipped the scales in its favor by suggesting there could be substantial cost savings through a new technology.

"I got to fooling around with the cost people," said Anderson, "and it turned out that if we were to eliminate the ink and paint process, we would save over half the cost of the pictures."[40] Instead of dozens of laborers hand-tracing the thousands of animator's drawings in different colored inks onto transparent celluloid (which then tediously had to be painted),

Anderson proposed Xerography. This photographic (or "electrolithic") process, recently adapted by Ub Iwerks, allowed the direct transfer of animator's original pencil lines to cels, thus eliminating the need for inkers. Anderson became excited about the possibilities for saving not only on inking costs, but also on "background painting because I was going to apply the same technique to the whole picture." That is, line drawings of the backgrounds would also be shot onto cels and positioned over swatches of color, and the cells of the characters would be registered over that. For the first time, there would be a true marriage in the design of the characters and backgrounds. In addition, "the original drawing of the animation on the screen couldn't help but have more life than a tracing."

Anderson thought "Gee, that's attractive, and I went to Walt with it." Distracted and preoccupied with Disneyland, TV shows, and traveling, and disenchanted with animation—its slowness, its expense—Walt said, "Ah, yeah, yeah, you can fool around all you want to."[41] Mickey-like, Anderson plunged headlong into *Dalmatians* as the feature's solo production designer. "My idea was it would all be one style . . . there was no attempt to disguise the lines. I knew they were going to be a half-foot across on the big screen, but they were good-looking lines, and [because] they were animator's lines they always had more life than tracings. The animators were high on it."

Inkers and painters were not. When Anderson blithely gave an interview to a trade paper about the financial benefits of the new process, he was "taken to task and I don't mean in a gentle way" by an army of tracers and opaquers. "Their jobs were jeopardized by this new thought," he realized too late. His stress level grew on the few occasions Walt would quickly peek at tests and comment negatively on them. "I realized what a terrific hole I had dug for myself but there was no turning back." When the film, which cost only $3 million, was released in 1961, it was a critical and financial success, grossing $10 million in it's first run and over $200 million worldwide. A tight, witty story adaptation by Bill Peet, brilliant character animation by the "nine old men," and Anderson's smart, superb art direction helped make *101 Dalmatians* one of the studio's most outstanding and popular films; in a 1985 rerelease, it grossed $32.1 million.

But Walt disliked the film. Perhaps remembering *Dumbo,* another film that had become a hit despite his minimal participation, he resented being left out of the creative loop. However, he claimed to be unhappy with *Dalmatian*'s look. "Walt was one who inherently hated lines," said Anderson.

> He hated to see a drawing on a screen. He wanted to
> see them disguised . . . he was the one who really pushed

us into cel-paint ink lines, where the ink line is the same color as the area it is encompassing . . . so he was very upset when he saw what was happening on *Dalmatians.* However, we had gone so far and it was coming off well . . . but I didn't find out he didn't buy it until it was all over. Had it all done. Then I found out that he was extremely displeased with it.[42]

In a meeting with the animators and Anderson on future films, Walt said, "We're never gonna have another one of those goddamned things"[43] referring to *Dalmatians* and its technique, and "Ken's never going to be an art director again."[44] "He really hurt me," recalled Anderson. "This was in front of my friends. It couldn't have been any worse. And he didn't talk to me for about a year."[45] Rejection by his surrogate father–figure was bad enough, but Anderson also had to personally fire a number of artist friends in his unit because of continuing cost cutting at the studio. It proved too much. Stressed out because he thought he had failed Walt on a film that ironically saved animation at the studio, overweight and a smoker, Anderson suffered two strokes in 1962 in one week.

He fought his way back to health through exercise and the help of his wife and family. As part of his recuperation, he and Polly would visit daily the peaceful acres of flowers and trees in Descanso Gardens near their home in the La Canada section of Los Angeles. He called the gardens his "laughing place," after the mythical feel-good locale in *Song of the South.* "Trees mean life to me," Anderson told Robin Allan.[46]

Anderson was eager to return to the studio. Walt, now the "good dad," sent him flowers and encouraged him to "just get better," and assured him he would be welcome. Anderson worked on story and character design for *The Jungle Book*—the last feature Walt was involved in before his death in 1966—and found his creativity undiminished.

Walt relied on him as much as ever: on *The Jungle Book* he turned to Anderson for suggestions for a particular type of tiger for the villainous Shere Khan. After an all-night session working at home, Anderson came up with a suave Basil Rathbone–type (voiced in the film by the equally suave George Sanders) who nearly stole the picture.

Anderson's graphic creativity continued unabated through the rest of his career at Disney. For *The Rescuers,* his pen-and-wash visual development sketches are a tour de force

of inventiveness. In his search for the right Madam Medusa (a bizarre child-hating, pawnshop-boutique owner), he tries her as a Bacallesque grande dame, an overdressed Sadie Thompson–like tart clutching, with phony affection, the little heroine to her ample bosom, a jack-booted, leather-jacketed, whip-wielder, and even a Cruella look-alike modeling a stuffed alligator boa. He also explores Medusa within her surroundings: in one sketch she sleeps in a bed bearing a skull and cross bones on the headboard; in another she and her pet crocodiles wile away the hours in the dank dungeon she calls home. He explores emotionally involving camera angles, staging, costumes, personality, and use of props in one imaginative drawing after another.

Anderson's creativity was always in full throttle. Frank Thomas recalled:

On *Robin Hood,* during lunch he spilled some water on a napkin. He wondered what that would do. Took his pen out and drew on it. That faded the line out, then he got some color, put that on there. Brought that up to his room, got a series of napkins, put water and drew on *them.* He thought maybe [the effect might work in] some

179

Four more idea sketches for Madame Medusa are examples of Anderson's inventiveness and unrelenting search for distinctive personalities.

part of the picture that was misty out in the woods, mysterious, nighttime, or something very romantic. After it dried he drew over it to get actual shapes and contours.

Polly Anderson also attested to his restless creative spirit: "Ken was always working at home. Just always. He would sit in a chair here and be working on something or studying animal books. A person like that was hard to live with, but worthwhile."

Anderson, who thought he would work in Disney animation "all my life," did not go quietly into retirement. He claimed that he and several older animators "were pushed out on our ass, and we didn't like it, any of us."[47] "He didn't have

anything to do like most men do when they retire, the golf and things like that," said his wife. So he and Polly traveled—to Antarctica, to Africa, around the world—and everywhere they went, Anderson filled sketchbooks with line drawings of the people they met and the flora and fauna they saw. He even had a coat designed with extra large pockets so he could draw people surreptitiously.

Anderson finally went to WED and got a job designing for the parks again, and then the animation division asked him to design the lead character for the live and animation feature *Pete's Dragon* (1977) and to advise the younger animation team. Anderson also took jobs outside the studio, for example, as one of several story artists on the Japan-produced feature cartoon *Nemo* (1992). In 1991, he received a Disney Legends Award, along with nine other recipients, including Julie Andrews, Carl Barks, Sterling Holloway, and Fess Parker.

"I think he was satisfied when he worked at Disney," said his wife. "He worked with interesting people, and so forth, but he was very glum the last part of his life. After his strokes, he wasn't all okay." It was another stroke that took his life on December 13, 1993.

In an interview with Michael Barrier in 1990, he spoke of his troubles with *101 Dalmatians* and, sounding like the biblical prodigal Son, about how his relationship with Walt was finally resolved. In 1966, Walt showed up unexpectedly at the studio after receiving cancer treatments in the hospital across the street. "He was supposed to be taken home to die. He'd shrunk way down," recalled Anderson. "I said, 'Gee, it's sure good to see you, Walt.' I met him all alone on the lot. He said, 'Yeah, it's sure good to be here,' and he looked at me penetratingly. I knew that there was a difference in his attitude. He never apologized for anything he'd said, but I got the feeling, very strongly, that he was forgiving me for the fact that I had showed his ink lines. It was okay after all."[48]

Anderson often placed characters within a setting and gave them personality-driven activities. Here, Madame Medusa and her henchman, Snoops, force Penny to search for hidden treasure. Anderson explores the location, props, camera angles, and even possible editing (as in the "cut-aways" to animals observing the humans from behind cover).

PART FIVE
New Age Inspirations

The entire staff of Walt Disney Feature Animation in Burbank, California, 1996.

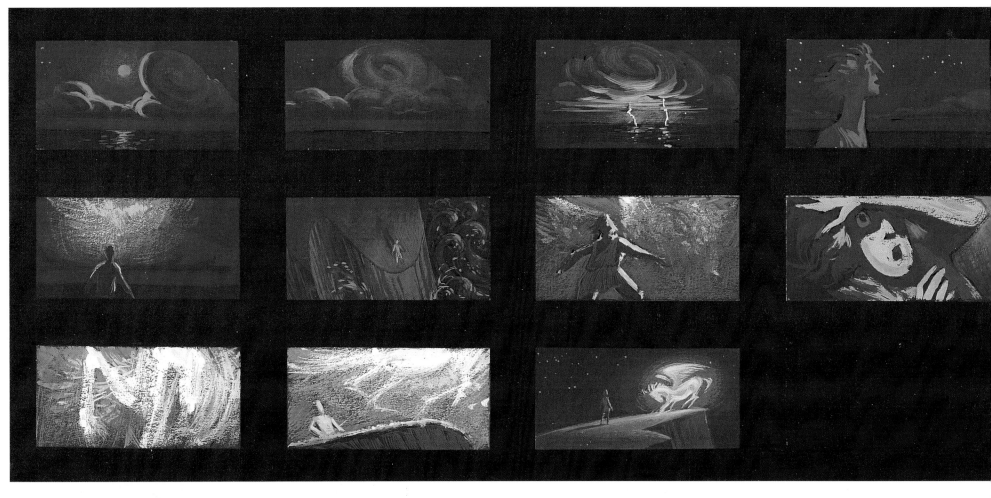

CHAPTER 16

New Age Inspirations

Going sixty on the 134 freeway toward Burbank, between car-exhausted trees whizzing by and smog sitting like a fat brown cat on the San Fernando Valley, one notices the "Mohawk" first—a giant pink and raspberry-striped curved steel ribbon with eighty perforations along the top. Architect Robert A. M. Stern intended this piece of the new Disney Feature Animation building to represent a sprocketed filmstrip, but usually it strikes observers as the hairdo of North American Indians of Iroquoian stock.

Next in sequential view loom fourteen-foot high letters that spell ANIMATION. No mistaking the type of filmmaking going on in the pastel-yellow building beneath. And, after turning off the Buena Vista Street exit onto Riverside Drive, the question of whose animation is vividly answered by an eighty-four-foot-high midnight-blue entrance canopy shaped like the conical sorcerer's hat that Mickey Mouse wore in *Fantasia*, complete with stars and a crescent moon.

This giddy structure is in the great tradition of whimsical "L.A.-crazy" architecture (like the old Brown Derby restaurant, the giant HOLLYWOOD sign, and other ostentatious wonders), and is appropriate for an art form synonymous with fun and imagination. It also announces loud and clear the continuing success and importance of animation to the entire Disney entertainment empire.

Inside, things get down to business and functionality. The sorcerer's hat, for example, serves as the art deco–furnished office of Roy E. Disney, head of Disney Feature Animation.

Housed within three stories is a five acre, self-contained facility for making feature-length animated films; offices of all personnel are within easy, open access, from producers and directors, story and inspirational sketchers, layout artists and animators, to background painters, photography, and postproduction facilitators; the building also has its own cafeteria. Beneath a vaulted blue ceiling studded with starlike bolts and crossed by the obligatory postmodern exposed plumbing and electrical guts, storyboards and concept art for current and future productions line the walls or rest on carpeted floors, awaiting meetings that will decide their fate.

Modern though the house may be, the processes of making animated features at Disney is pretty much the same as in the old Hyperion studio. And like Hyperion, the new facility is bursting at the seams, a victim of its own success: "We could use another 200,000 square feet, the entire building again," said Thomas Schumacher, Senior Vice President of Feature Animation.[1] It is true that computers now assist with various technical problems, including coloring the imagery (yes, the inkers' and opaquers' worst nightmare finally came true—they have been replaced by technology); but character animation is still done by hand, as are layouts, backgrounds and story sketches, and, of course, the inspirational designs.

At Disney, making an animated feature remains a shared creative venture, and the current crop of visual development artists have in common with their predecessors a wealth of imagination and graphic ability. And something more: a

OPPOSITE ABOVE *The magical appearance of Pegasus from the forthcoming* Hercules. *Sequential concept panels by Andy Gaskill.*
OPPOSITE BELOW *A Mike Gabriel conceptual drawing for* Pocahontas *explores locale, color, and characters.*

185

heightened awareness and appreciation of the accomplishments of Disney inspirational artists of the past.

Mike Gabriel, originator and co-director (with Eric Goldberg) of *Pocahontas* (1995), studied Mary Blair's paintings "to figure out why they look so good, why her work is special."[2] Dick Kelsey's pastel drawings for *Hiawatha,* a never-produced feature, proved influential for *Pocahontas.* "His stacks of drawings were a pot of gold," said Gabriel. "His color values and simplicity of shape." Eyvind Earle's limited palette color studies for *Lady and the Tramp* "cracked it for me," said Gabriel. "What a great education those things are. Primary color, secondary color with a complementary accent against a muted complement in the background. When you do that it sings like a million bucks!"

Gabriel's own painting style is "shape-based. Details are secondary. I just look at it like it is a cutout. When you start to draw you tend to concentrate on details—the little eyes, et cetera. The old masters here tell you to pull back shapes, to let the character read against the background."

For *Pocahontas*'s art director, Gabriel chose Michael Giaimo, a distinctive stylist who lists as his "animation muses" Blair, Earle, and "the wonderful unexpected quality" in Kelsey's work. And Giaimo, like Gabriel, "loves the look in the late forties Disney features in which an extremely rich character pulls away from the background." Of his own color-saturated art he has said that he wants to "make color schemes so good you want to eat them." Gabriel and Giaimo, while not exactly joined at the hip, do share similar graphics-oriented painting styles as well as some personal coincidences. Both

186

were born in 1954 in California into large Catholic families (Gabriel is one of eleven kids, Giaimo one of four), and both came to Disney within one year of each other in the late 1970s. But whereas Gabriel was known in his family from age five as "the little artist who wanted to work at Disney's" and struggled for years to reach that goal, Giaimo planned on a career as an art history teacher.

"I thought I'd never make a living as an artist," he said. "That graphically I had nothing to offer."[3] Interestingly, his father is a house painting contractor who "knows color;" the only difference between them, Giaimo jokes, is that his dad paints with a larger brush. Studying works by Picasso, Stuart Davis, Ben Shahn, Matisse, and the pre-Raphaelites Edward Burne-Jones and Dante Gabriel Rossetti, Giaimo began to form his own color theories, implementing them in personal works made with Caran D'Ache oil sticks on bristol board. "I am reductive, minimalist. I don't like clutter. My style is primitive and graphic with unusual color schemes and prehistory Caribbean themes and creatures derived from African/Mexican folk art."

Jobs teaching art were scarce in the mid-seventies, so Giaimo enrolled at the California Institute of the Arts, the Disney-funded university in Valencia, in search of commercial art instruction. He happened onto the newly created character animation department and thus was his future set. At Cal Arts, he was guided by old master animators from the studio, but recalls with particular affection a "tough old bird" unaffiliated with Disney named Bill Moore, who was "one of the greatest design teachers in the world." Moore, a commercial artist, was infamous for burning student projects he didn't

Michael Giaimo. BELOW *A stylized inspirational painting by Michael Giaimo, who set the visual style for* Pocahontas.

ABOVE AND RIGHT
Hercules *inspirational*
artworks by Andy Gaskill,
who seeks to find "the
dramatic meaning of a scene
quickly and the visual
symbols that connect and
explain that."

like, or tearing poorly designed drawings off the wall and stomping on them. "You never resented it," claimed Giaimo, "you were alarmed, but he made you want to learn. You respected him 'cause he spoke the truth. Every day I think about him."

Disney recruited Giaimo upon graduation; he started as an inbetweener, became an assistant animator, animator, then a story man. Somewhere during *Roger Rabbit* he "burned out," left the studio to freelance and create his own art, which excited his peers. As a result, he was invited back to Disney as *Pocahontas*'s inspirational sketch artist/art director.

Mike Gabriel was determined all his young life to get into Disney and wrote to ask for a job starting at age sixteen. He

was rejected for nearly a decade until he could "train the monkey," as he refers to his left hand, his drawing hand, which needed disciplining in the techniques of classical draftsmanship. Self-taught, he painstakingly drew four to six hours a day for years, studying anatomy by Michelangelo, Leonardo, Burne Hogarth, and each and every one of the thousands of Muybridge photos. It wasn't until he captured on his drawing pad live basketball players, surfers, and golfers in all their spontaneous energy and vigor that the Mouse Factory finally gave him the nod. Like Giaimo, he worked in various capacities. Promoted to animator on *The Black Cauldron*, color stylist for *The Great Mouse Detective,* story man and co-director for *The Rescuers Down Under;* he became "known as a design guy" on *The Little Mermaid.*

For *Pocahontas,* Gabriel (learning from the experiences of Mary Blair and Eyvind Earle) formed a block of, as Giaimo called them, "champions"—key studio personnel (like Schumacher and Goldberg) who supported styling the film in a less-than-realistic way, using Giaimo's color-saturated, elegant graphics. "Mike and Eric trusted Mike Giaimo, there was a bond there," said Glen Keane, at age forty, arguably the finest

character animator and designer of his generation. "Had they not all seen this world [of Pocahontas] the same way, I would have fought really hard to go more dimensionally with shadows. I'd have said there's room for me to change that."[4] But the style wars of the past between animators and visual developers did not happen. "Talking about a flat look," said Keane, "there was a time when all kinds of red flags would have gone up." Instead, Keane "took it as a challenge. I'm the guy who has to come around and see it in a different way."

Andy Gaskill is a concept artist who concentrates less on color than on "clear staging and a cinematic approach. Animation people," he says, "tend to focus on characters, rather than how the scene is perceived editorially," that is, through camera angles and movements. "That's an ephemeral thing. It's hard to draw, but I can draw it and define it as a shot." His gift, he feels, is to find in a script "the dramatic meaning of a scene quickly and the visual symbols that connect and explain that." He admires "the whole Lucas/Spielberg/Henson/[Ridley]Scott creative milieu of the eighties," meaning the dynamic, big Hollywood–movie movie approach to fan-

tasy narrative in *Star Wars/Close Encounters/Alien/Blade Runner*. But his life, he claims, "has been a grab bag of people and influences."[5]

Born in 1951 the son of a Japanese mother and an American father, he is a restless soul, easily bored. At Philadelphia's Pennsylvania Academy of Fine Arts he was a sculpture major when he applied for the animation training program at Disney. Accepted in 1973, he stayed five years animating on *The Rescuers, The Fox and the Hound, Pete's Dragon,* and other minor works during an exhausted period in Disney animation's history. "There was a Spielberg/Lucas subculture in Hollywood, a creative force you could feel," he says. "I felt Disney was out of the loop, that interesting things were not happening here."

"Bored," he left the studio to travel, headed toward Asia; soon he "got tired of traveling" and returned to the States and married. For twelve years he worked freelance gaining experience in everything from designing theme park attractions for WED (EPCOT) and Bob Rogers (Canada's EXPO '86)—"I utilized my animation skills—storytelling, staging, some char-

acter stuff"—to working in Tokyo as a director for "two chaotic years" on the ill-fated Japanese-produced feature *Nemo,* then five years as "general art director" on independent animated features, starring the likes of Alvin and the Chipmunks and Tom and Jerry. "I worked in small shops and wore a lot of different hats—storyboard, layouts, even consumer design and packaging. My versatility kept me employed over the years."

He credits four years in Jungian therapy with getting him through this busy but "dark period" by keeping "my hope going." To his surprise, he "brought new ideas to the Chipmunk enterprise that surprised even me, things I pushed to higher levels by extra effort without being cynical or despairing about it." He gained a reputation in the industry as a talented visual problem solver. In the summer of 1992 Roger Allers, another *Nemo* survivor and now co-director of *The Lion King,* asked him to help out on story.

"It was a big deal, took years, to get Andy to come here," said Tom Schumacher of Gaskill's return to Disney. Once he got involved, Gaskill's creative interest in Disney rekindled. As *Lion King* art director, he at last had a project worthy of his creativity, and he enthusiastically defined the film's look in each scene and its action, from the opening Circle of Life to the climactic battle between Simba and Scar. More recently, Gaskill has been "excited" about bringing into focus the staging and production design of Disney's new animated feature *Hercules,* on which he collaborated for a time with Hans Bacher, a designer/painter who considerably influenced the naturalistic yet stylized art direction of *The Lion King.*

Bacher (like Gaskill) finds live-action directors inspirational: "My favorite filmmaker

is Orson Welles. For *Lion King* I used a David Lean look for vast wide areas or then close on characters like Ingmar Bergman."[6] Born in 1948 in Cologne, West-Germany, Bacher earned a degree in graphic design at Folkwangschule, an art school in the Bauhaus tradition, and he taught animation and comic strip art at the University of Essen for fifteen years. At the same time, he freelanced as an advertising illustrator, animation film producer for German television, and a designer for Richard Williams's animation studio in London. He first worked for Disney on *Who Framed Roger Rabbit?* doing character design and storyboarding the Toontown sequence, then contributed dozens of small inspirational paintings for *Beauty and the Beast.* "I felt they wanted a European influence. It was very different, very dark" said Bacher of an early nonmusical version of the film that was later lightened with songs and Americanized. Bacher wanted to "mix several styles together," for example, Eyvind Earle ("but not too elaborate") and the seventeenth-century master Antoine Watteau.

From working under tight deadlines in advertising over the years, Bacher has developed techniques that are quick, easy, and inexpensive, yet yield evocative and often stunning results. One involves felt-tip marker pens and an airbrush. "It's so fast and effective," he says, "I can use over 250 colors one after another without cleaning the air brush, and you could never get the intensity of some of the hues using only gouache." (A colleague calls Bacher "the marker chemist.") Bacher's favorite inspirational sketch artist is Ken Anderson, "the way he builds films' color and style-wise. I studied *101 Dalmatians* by color printing out each scene, and I noticed how one color in each scene goes fluently into the other. He must have thought that out and that is something I have to admire. I want to repeat that quality."

In July 1994, Bacher and his wife moved permanently to Los Angeles to work exclusively for Disney and escape "a gypsy life" bouncing from jobs in London, Duesseldorf, Burbank, and back. At this writing, he is developing the style for Disney's *The Legend of Mulan,* a tale of ancient China. "When I don't like things or something bad appears, I get loud," says the gentlemanly artist. He is preparing a detailed style chart to keep layout artists in line with his vision of restrained Asian art. Referring to a cluttered layout that begs for correction (or destruction), Bacher mutters with quiet contempt, "Looks more Bierstadt than Chinese."

"We pursued Hans for three years to come here," said Tom Schumacher. "He did such beautiful work on *Beauty.* We begged him to work on *Lion King,* which he did long distance. Finally he agreed to move." Schumacher pointed out that at Disney today "each film has its own character model department, rather than an overall one. The staff is widely split

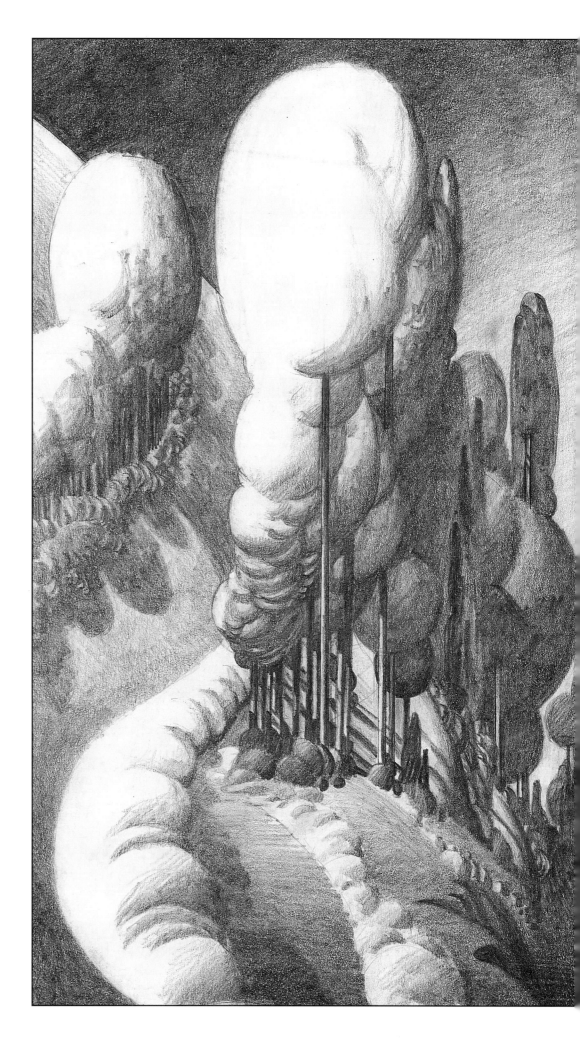

Chris Sanders's early concept for bug-loving Timon of The Lion King. OPPOSITE *Mel Shaw's pastels bring to life a high-speed rhino chase for* The Jungle Book, *and a ghostly litter carrying Belle to an enchanted castle for* Beauty and the Beast.

"the American Indian world, their spirituality, and philosophy about the circularity of life gave me a direction to go with a mostly circular movement. With *Hercules* it was different because Greek art has angularity, so there is a swirl but with an edge."[7]

One of the youngest visual development artists is Chris Sanders, who came to Disney in 1987 at age 25. After graduating from Cal Arts, he worked three years "learning by doing flat-out drawing everyday" at Marvel Productions, producers of the *Muppet Babies* television series. Then came Disney: "I was the first in the new visual development department. Neither they nor I were clear about what the department should be doing." Eventually, Sanders's talent for finding unique visual solutions to problem story points came to the fore. For *The Lion King,* for example, he visualized two quite different dream sequences: one, a rollicking candy-colored childlike musical number, "I Just Can't Wait to Be King;" the other, a mysterious evocation of a lion king's ghost.

"The most powerful attribute an inspirational artist can have is a sense of story," said Sanders. "Lineups of characters are only useful to a point, but a sketch that suggests story—then you've done your job!" Sanders cites as an example one of his early sketches for *The Rescuers Down Under:* a montage sequence of mice wiring a message from Australia to New York. "When I got the globe out for research, I noticed all these little islands inbetween. I did an inspirational sketch of a wreck of an airplane where a little mouse is using old World War II equipment. The directors liked it, it influenced the story and ended up on the screen almost line for line."[8]

Lest one think that visual development at Disney is strictly a pursuit engaged in by the young, there has always been (and continues to be) a healthy sprinkling of "elder statesmen" among the team. Consider Melvin Shaw—born in 1919, and a veteran of the earliest days of the Warner Bros. cartoon studio—who started at Disney on *Fantasia* in the old Hyperion studio and continued to contribute wonderful inspirational pastels until his retirement in 1981. For *Fox and the Hound,* for example, he ran the narrative gamut from gently humorous—a fox startling a cow and a milkmaid, a fox attempting to catch a fish—to harrowing and dramatic—a huge bear on a murderous rampage, a human hunter (also on a murderous rampage) firing a shotgun at two fleeing red foxes. His sketches for *Beauty and the Beast* nod to the dreamy garden ambiance of Jean-Honoré Fragonard. For *The Lion King,* one of his last assignments, Shaw combined humor with action in a drawing of a rhino chasing a hyena who has the tail of a fleeing lion cub in its startled mouth; a small bird atop the hurtling rhino appears to control (or cheerlead) the event.

Vance Gerry, born in 1929, came to Disney in 1955, and

on what's interesting, so I hope the films have a bolder look and the choices do seem stronger." Schumacher and Peter Schneider, president of Walt Disney Feature Animation, attempt to bring to the studio any visually inspirational artist the directors may fancy. Gerald Scarfe, the wonderfully savage British caricaturist, was hired as the main stylist for *Hercules.* "I picked up a phone," said Schumacher, "called London and said, 'Want to play with us?' Easiest thing in the world. I can't think of anyone we couldn't get if they want to work in our medium. It's not about being famous. It's about being fabulous!

"For another project, we tried to get Al Hirschfeld, the great caricaturist, but the film [based on Gershwin's *Rhapsody in Blue*] fell through," said Schumacher. "He said he couldn't take the time to style it but he could do ten pieces of art based on our ideas. So that was one way to skin that cat."

Some of Disney's eclectic visual developers live off-site; one is Bruce Zick, forty-five, who resides outside Portland, Oregon, "with my dogs" and mails his visions to Disney. Zick's big swirling fantasy landscapes (drawn only in black and white because, says Zick, "color is frightening to me") recall the American regionalists Grant Wood and Thomas Hart Benton, as well as the elegance of Rockwell Kent. "I like a certain sense of movement in my work," says Zick, "a rhythmic motion like in Benton's. Depending on the project, I have a geometric quality that relates to art deco." For *Pocahontas,*

Mel Shaw

has been a story and visual development artist since *101 Dalmatians*. Coaxed out of retirement, he works one day a week on the newest projects. Gerry's work has a directness, charm, and the "incredible simplicity" that he admires in drawings by his favorite Disney story artist Jack Miller and the children's book illustrator Edward Ardizzone.

Gerry worked alongside Ken Anderson and the "nine old men" on numerous projects and recalls learning an important lesson in creating characters and stories for animation from Frank Thomas: "He said, 'Don't do continuity. I want to see the big idea, an idea that I can get hold of, all in one drawing like an illustration.' "[9] Gerry praises his former colleagues Anderson and Mel Shaw as "masters of that" and, as an example of a singularly fine inspirational sketch, cites a Shaw *Great Mouse Detective* drawing of two characters fighting on the giant steel hands of Big Ben. "Such a drawing you were really compelled to make a sequence out of. You couldn't leave it out of the picture, whether it fit or not. That one picture gave us a whole sequence!"

Gerry has a relaxed confidence regarding the creative process: "It doesn't take much to get started," he says. "I'd just as soon start with a title of a picture and just start dreaming into it." He finds a script "restricting cause it tells you too much. I'd rather start earlier than that and look for possibili-

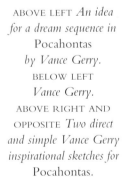

ABOVE LEFT *An idea for a dream sequence in* Pocahontas *by Vance Gerry.*
BELOW LEFT *Vance Gerry.*
ABOVE RIGHT AND OPPOSITE *Two direct and simple Vance Gerry inspirational sketches for* Pocahontas.

ties for animation and entertainment, rather than story elements or structure." He also knows from experience that "a lot of things come quick at first. But once you get really tired of the project and can't stand it anymore, that's the time you're really going to get going on it. All the things that the guys work on so hard for a long time usually come off better."

Gerry worked directly with Walt ("I told him some stories, stood up and survived"), so at the studio today he is a valued creative connective thread. "Walt was everything they said he was," said Gerry. "We all loved him. I thought at first he was a figurehead, but learned that was the least of it." Gerry recalled Walt's power to inspire and challenge. "He always said [of an inspirational drawing], 'What can you do with it?' So the artist would then have to figure out what you could do with this situation, or could you make a situation out of it? Walt played it that way. 'What can you do with it?' Then you'd take it as far as you could. Might end up in a dead end. Well, now we'll try something else. Because you could be tricked into thinking there was something there, and there wouldn't be. Or it wouldn't please him."

If anyone at the studio personifies and embodies the connection to Walt and the creative spirit of the first "Golden Era" of Disney animation, it is Joe Grant, who will be ninety years old in 1998. Yes, working full-time at Disney Feature Animation today is the same Joe Grant whose caricatures caught Walt's eye in 1933, whose sketches and ideas influenced stories and characters in some of the medium's greatest films, including *Snow White, Pinocchio, Fantasia,* and *Dumbo,* the man who started the Character Model Department, which validated and made enduring the process of initiating projects with inspirational sketches, and the same man who had Walt's ear and his confidence for almost two decades until Grant walked away from it all in 1949.

Grant's amazing stamina, undiminished creativity, and continuing excitement for the work is admired by peers, both young and old. "Joe is living history," opines Michael Giaimo, "but the amazing thing is when you work with him the history thing isn't even there. He uses it as a reference point. He's living for today. It's so exciting. He can hardly wait to talk about the next project. All the body of work he's done? That's just stuff he's done, like we have done some stuff. He's incredibly humble that way. I've never seen an artist whose work is as fresh, as exciting, as invigorating as Joe's. It does not look like old-man work. It looks like any person right out of school might have done it."

Thomas Schumacher feels Grant's "drawings are actually creating the cast which is creating the story." He mentions an early sketch for *Pocahontas* that Grant drew of a sawed-off wizened tree with a branch pointing to its rings. "It was to be a narrator looking back in time, and that eventually became Grandmother Willow. The characters change style but he gives an idea of relationships and what the overall story is. Joe's little drawings have a big influence because they feed animation, feed story, characters, and relationships, all the way down the road." "Joe Grant is a magic artist," says Vance Gerry. "He never makes just a drawing. There's always something more than the thing he's drawing. Always something extra."

"The drawings I make are not storyboard drawings. They are inspirational drawings," says Grant definitively.[10] The magic octogenarian sits tall and dignified in a windbreaker, a cumulous cloud of white hair surrounding his broad forehead, a white mustache under the generous nose he and his colleagues have caricatured without mercy for over six decades. Invariably polite and easygoing, Grant's intelligent eyes—under wide glasses—focus intently on the listener as he softly articulates about his art in a disarmingly off-handed way.

"I always like to have an idea in each drawing, so if they look at it they can say that's a possibility, we can build on that. I think that's my function, always has been." An opportunity

for word play presents itself and he goes for it, laughing: "An idea man, not an ideal man." He jokes that his late wife, Jenny, with whom he built a successful design business, "made the decision for me to come back to Disney because of my being around the house for forty years." Actually, it was an accidental meeting with a young Disney executive in 1987 who, upon learning of Grant's credentials, invited him back to Disney. "Why *don't* you go back?" encouraged Jenny Grant. "That's where you belong."

So once again Grant is a full-time Disney artist, coming to the studio every day, sharing an office with Vance Gerry and veteran storyman/director Burny Mattinson, as he once did with Albert Hurter and other visual development artists now long gone. "It is déjà vu," he says. "Nothing is different except size. The same struggle. Much larger scale and considerably more expensive." Once again he is creating characters and enlivening scripts with touches of personality and humor. For *Beauty and the Beast,* he came up with the motherly teapot, Mrs. Potts; for *Aladdin* he developed Abu, Aladdin's pet monkey and suggested expressions and gestures for the flying carpet; in *The Lion King* he worked on the relationships between King Mufasa, the baboon shaman Rafiki, and the bird advisor Zazu. With *Pocahontas,* recalled Grant, "at first they relied so heavily on the script, things were beginning to get sort of pedestrian. It wasn't going anywhere. Then we came in,

195

ABOVE LEFT *Joe Grant in 1996.*
ABOVE AND BELOW RIGHT *"Joe Grant's drawings are actually creating the cast which is creating the story," says Thomas Schumacher, Senior Vice President of Disney Feature Animation. Here are two of Grant's early concepts for* Pocahontas.
BELOW LEFT *Master animator Glen Keane.*

Burny and myself, started adding animals and ideas, rewriting the script with pictures, little details and stuff."

Grant came up with a hummingbird, a talking turkey, and a raccoon, who, said Tom Schumacher, was "totally discarded, thrown out and came back to. The turkey, we thought, had comic potential—he thought he was handsome, a lady's man. When we decided he couldn't talk and, having no hands, he couldn't mime, we figured a raccoon would be better."

Grant does all he can to reinforce his character suggestions, as animator Glen Keane found out. "Joe Grant is fantastic. He would come in with sketches constantly to my room. Joe knew to get an idea sold he would have a lot more success if there was some animation to it. So he'd say, 'Glen, what do you think of this idea?' One day he dropped off a sketch of a raccoon braiding Pocahantas's hair. Cute idea. I fell in love with it and said I'd love to animate it. He said, 'Yeah, I think you should.' " After animating the first tests of

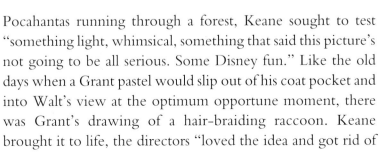

Fist opens face on palm of hand shouts warning you are now entering HADES

ABOVE LEFT AND RIGHT *Grant's suggestions for mythical creatures in* Hercules.
LEFT *In 1987, after almost forty years away from Disney, Grant returned to the Studio and feature animation production to resume his career as "an idea man." In an idea sketch for* The Hunchback of Notre Dame, *back shapes spark an odd friendship.*

Pocahontas running through a forest, Keane sought to test "something light, whimsical, something that said this picture's not going to be all serious. Some Disney fun." Like the old days when a Grant pastel would slip out of his coat pocket and into Walt's view at the optimum opportune moment, there was Grant's drawing of a hair-braiding raccoon. Keane brought it to life, the directors "loved the idea and got rid of the turkey character." Thus Meeko the raccoon (one of the film's most popular characters) was born. "Anything Joe thinks is interesting, I look at. Why argue with success?" says Schumacher.

"My personal belief," said Grant about his seemingly bottomless well of creativity, "is it's not the destination, it's the journey. I'm being curious and competitive, and if I can't

be involved in something, then . . ." His voice trails off, the thought that he could not be involved in his work is so foreign and uncharacteristically negative it leaves him without words. A new thought occurs: "Another thing. I have a vast area to look back on, a resource that's of some value here. But I'm interested not in what happened back there, but what we're doing now and looking forward. The challenge out there now is to fuse ideas and technology and make them work together."

Asked to speculate about how Walt would react to the new technological changes in moviemaking, Grant opined "he would love it. He was the most inventive and curious of all people. A lot of people think he'd be old fogyish about it, but not at all." The major difference at Disney today for Grant is that "you have to subtract Walt from this situation. You don't have the inspiring omnipotence of him. He was everywhere. They're on their own here now." Despite past differences, Grant remains in awe of the phenomenon that was Walt, his quick-silver energy and volatility. "I would say he was a father figure for me. The idea was not to please him but to realize his ideas. He was very changeable. Every time you thought you had him he was on to something else. There was a certain power when he came into a room—electrifying. You knew he was out for bear: 'What have you got for me?' His finger-tapping indicated, 'Man, you haven't got it this time.'"

The digression to the past is brief and Grant is eager to return to his drawing board. He is involved with several major projects, including a "flamingo/yo-yo" ballet for *Fantasia Continued*, character designs for *Hercules, The Hunchback of Notre Dame* (Grant brilliantly suggested a snail as a companion to Quasimodo because their back-shapes would make them simpatico), *The Legend of Mulan*, and "a personal project" he jokingly describes as "a new story that's been around the studio for fifty years": *The Abandoned*, a Paul Gallico tale about a boy who changes into a cat. Grant prefers stories that are "not too realistic. I come from *Dumbo* to *Lion King*, the animal stuff in *Pocahontas*, that's where I live." he explains. "To me, that's the cartoon biz."

Rival studios have dangled job offers before him, and while Grant is flattered to be head-hunted at his advanced age, his "devotion to the Disney ideal" overpowers any temptation to join them. He intends to continue doing "the same" at the Walt Disney studio, never stopping "till I become infirm." And even then, "I'll work at home by fax."

Grant feels that "technology is running ahead of us right now. We've got to catch up with it with some good ideas. The only thing the computer can't do for us is a good story, fortunately."

Speaking with the confident authority of one who knows, Grant concludes that story and inspirational sketch artists "will go on forever. They're immortal."

Notes
Selected Bibliography
Index
Acknowledgments

NOTES

INTRODUCTION

1. William Cameron Menzies, lecture at the University of Southern California, April 1929; reprinted in *The Art of Hollywood* by John Hambley and Patrick Downing (London: Thames Television, 1979), p. 91.
2. *Drawing into Film—Directors' Drawings,* Exhibition catalogue; The Pace Gallery, March 26–April 24, 1993.
3. Bela Balazs, *Theory of the Film* (New York: Dover Publications Inc., 1970), p. 192.
4. Frank Thomas and Ollie Johnston, *The Illusion of Life: Disney Animation* (New York: Hyperion, 1995), p. 191
5. Robert D. Feild, *The Art of Walt Disney* (New York: The Macmillan Company, 1942), pp. 152–153.
6. Museum and galleries showcasing individual Disney animators include: *Disney Animations and Animators* at The Whitney Museum of American Art, June 24–September 6, 1981; *Vladimir Tytla—Master Animator* at the Katonah Museum of Art, September 18–December 31, 1994. Disney's favorite phalanx of animators known as the "nine old men" first gained attention through television appearances on the Disneyland TV show, and subsequent periodical and book references; two of them, Frank Thomas and Ollie Johnston, have written several books on character animation and appear in a documentary film on their lives and careers, *Frank and Ollie* (1995).
7. Arthur D. Colman, M.D. and Libby Lee Coleman, Ph.D., *The Father* (New York: Avon Books, 1993), p. 6.
8. Joe Grant to John Canemaker, July 24, 1995.

Part One: Early Inspirations
SEEKING INSPIRATION

1. Watts, Steven, *The Magic Kingdom: Walt Disney and Modern American Culture* (New York: Basic Books, forthcoming in 1997), ms. p. 4.
2. Frank Thomas and Ollie Johnston, *The Illusion of Life: Disney Animation* (New York: Hyperion, 1995), p. 35.
3. Russell Merritt, J.B. Kaufman, *Walt in Wonderland* (Baltimore: The John Hopkins University Press, 1993), p. 81.
4. *Walt in Wonderland,* p. 28.
5. Crafton, Donald Crafton, *Before Mickey—The Animated Film 1898–1928* (Cambridge, Massachusetts: The MIT Press, 1982), p. 134.
6. *The Magic Kingdom,* p. 78.
7. Perine, Robert, *Chouinard: An Art Vision Betrayed* (Encinitas, CA: Artra Publishing Inc., 1985), p. 25.
8. Thomas, Bob, *The Art of Animation* (New York: Simon and Schuster, 1958), p. 20.
9. Recollections of Richard Huemer. An Oral History of the Motion Picture in America. Interviewed by Joe Adamson (UCLA 1969), p. 42.
10. Jack Kinney, *Walt Disney and Assorted Other Characters* (New York: Harmony, 1988), p. 62.
11. *The Illusion of Life,* p. 35.
12. Allan, Robin, *Walt Disney and Europe: European Influences on the Animated Feature Films of Walt Disney.* (Thesis: University of Exeter, England, 1993), p. 8.
13. *Walt Disney and Europe,* pp. 15–16.
14. *Walt Disney and Europe,* p. 20.
15. Joe Grant to JC, September 6, 1994.
16. A. Kendall O'Connor to JC, September 26, 1994.

ALBERT HURTER

1. Klein, I., "Pioneer Animated Cartoon Producer Charles E. Bowers." *Cartoonist Profiles* (March 1975), p. 56.
2. Huemer/UCLA.
3. "Pioneer Cartoon Producer," p. 56.
4. *He Drew As He Pleased—A Sketchbook by Albert Hurter.* Introduction by Ted Sears (New York: Simon and Schuster, 1948), p. 5.
5. "Pioneer Cartoon Producer," p. 56.
6. "Pioneer Cartoon Producer," p. 56.
7. *The Bulletin,* Vol. 1, #12, 14 February 1939. Disney in-house publication.
8. Randolph Van Nostrand letter to Walt Disney February 26, 1953.
9. *He Drew,* p. 7.
10. Huemer/UCLA.
11. *He Drew,* p. 7.
12. *He Drew,* p. 7.
13. A. Kendall O'Connor to JC.
14. Del Connell to JC, November 29, 1994.
15. Russell, John, "Oldenberg Again: Whimsy and Latent Humanity." *New York Times,* March 6, 1995, pp. C-1 and C-16.
16. Canemaker, John, "Sincerely Yours, Frank Thomas." *Millimeter,* Vol. 3, #1. January 1975, p. 16.
17. Huemer, Richard, *Funnyworld* #21, p. 41.
18. Joe Grant to JC, September 6, 1994.
19. Martin Provensen to Michael Barrier, July 4, 1983.
20. *He Drew,* p. 8.
21. Frank Thomas to JC, October 10, 1994.
22. O'Connor to JC, September 26, 1994.
23. William Cottrell to JC, December 18, 1994.
24. Van Nostrand.
25. For information on Hurter's personal history I am grateful to film historian and entrepreneur Albert Miller for locating Hurter's death certificate and last will, and to film scholar Peter Hossli for researching the Hurter family history in Swiss archives and libraries.
26. I am grateful to Kenneth Hirsch, M.D., FACEP, for his detailed analysis of Hurter's heart ailment, as listed on his Certificate of Death, Los Angeles County Clerk Registrar's #4726, dated March 31, 1942.
27. Hirsch to JC, December 30, 1994.
28. *The Bulletin,* February 14, 1939.
29. Peter Hossli to JC, June 25, 1995.
30. *The Bulletin.*
31. *He Drew,* p. 9.
32. Hirsch.
33. PH to JC.
34. Ward Kimball to JC, December 13, 1994.
35. Hazel George to JC, January 4, 1995.
36. Peter Hossli to JC.
37. Hurter's 1942 death certificate reads that he has been in the United States for "30 years."
38. Huemer, Richard, *Funnyworld,* #21 Fall 1979, p. 38–43.
39. Kinney, p. 73.
40. Van Nostrand.
41. Van Nostrand.
42. Provensen.
43. O'Connor.
44. *He Drew,* p. 10.
45. Bob Jones to Robin Allan, November 1, 1989.
46. Joe Grant to JC, September 6, 1994.
47. William Cottrell to JC, December 18, 1994.
48. *Snow White* story conference notes December 1, 1936.
49. *Snow White* story conference notes December 1, 1936.
50. *Snow White* story conference notes December 25, 1937.

51. John P. Miller to Michael Barrier, October 6, 1991.
52. Collodi, C., *The Adventures of Pinocchio* (New York: Macmillan, 1969), p. 59.
53. William Cottrell to JC, December 18, 1994.
54. Joe Grant to JC, September 6, 1994; November 11, 1994.
55. A Disney executive named Oliver B. Johnston; no relation to animator Ollie Johnston.
56. Hurter's last will and testament, filed April 3, 1942.

FERDINAND HORVATH

1. I am grateful to animator Tissa David for translating the Horvath letters from Hungarian to English.
2. FFH letter June 1, 1933.
3. FFH letter May 24, 1933.
4. FFH letter May 24, 1933.
5. FFH letter May 24, 1933.
6. FFH letter July 2, 1933.
7. FFH letter May 30, 1933.
8. FFH letter May 24, 1933.
9. Tom Andrae to JC, February 12, 1995.
10. Barks, a Disney storyman before gaining fame for illustrating Donald Duck comic books, is quoted in an undated letter from Bruce Hamilton to Russ Cochran.
11. Carol Covington to JC, October 3, 1994.
12. *Brooklyn Daily Eagle,* December 2, 1928.
13. Bertha E. Mahoney, *Contemporary Illustrators of Children's Books* (Horn Books), 1930.
14. Horvath, F.F. Horvath. *Captured!* (New York: Dodd, Mead, 1930.), pp. v. and vi.
15. Poe, Edgar Allan, *The Raven.* Ill. by Ferdin and Huszti Horvath. (New York: Dodd, Mead, 1930).
16. *Brooklyn Eagle.*
17. Letter dated March 17, 1920. Collection Elly Horvath.
18. Carol Covington to JC. The Horvaths were married first in a civil ceremony March 29, 1920, then in a formal Catholic wedding at Krisztina Village Church in Budapest on May 15, 1920. Documents: collection Elly Horvath.
19. Marge Champion to JC, October 26, 1994.
20. Frank Thomas to JC, October 10, 1994.
21. Frank Thomas to JC, January 7, 1995.
22. USA Declaration of Intention, December 13, 1921.
23. *Contemporary Illustrators.*
24. *Contemporary Illustrators.*
25. *Brooklyn Daily Eagle,* December 2, 1928.
26. Aldis Dunbar, *The Sons O'Cormac.* (New York: Dutton, 1929).
27. Maxwell Corwen, *Ole Man Swordfish* (New York: Falcon 1931).
28. Tom Andrae to JC, January 12, 1995.

29. Frank Thomas to JC, January 7, 1995.
30. Ward Kimball to JC, October 13, 1994.
31. Joe Grant to JC, November 11, 1994.
32. Clipping *San Francisco Chronicle,* n.d. 1940.
33. Marge Champion to JC.
34. Martin Collins to JC, October 28, 1994.
35. Marge Champion to JC.

GUSTAF TENGGREN

1. Allan, Robin, "European Influences on Disney," paper for the first International Conference of the Society for Animation Studies, UCLA, October 11, 1989, p. 6.
2. Walt Disney memorandum, December 23, 1935.
3. Swanson, Mary T., *From Swedish Fairy Tales to American Fantasy: Gustaf Tenggren's Illustrations 1920–1970,* exhibition catalogue. (Minneapolis: University Art Museum, University of Minneapolis, 1986), p. 6.
4. *From Swedish Fairy Tales,* p. 14.
5. April 9, 1936 to January 14, 1939.
6. *From Swedish Fairy Tales,* p. 9.
7. *From Swedish Fairy Tales,* p. 8.
8. *From Swedish Fairy Tales,* p. 8.
9. Karen Hoyle to JC, October 18, 1994.
10. Mary Swanson to JC, October 13, 1994.
11. Mary Anderson to JC, January 18, 1995.
12. Mary Anderson to JC, Jan. 18, 1995.
13. "European Influences on Disney," p. 69.
14. "European Influences on Disney", p. 69.
15. *From Swedish Fairy Tales,* p. 11.
16. Carla Fallberg to JC, March 5, 1995.
17. Frank Thomas to JC, October 10, 1994.
18. Mary Anderson to JC, January 18, 1995.
19. William Bradford to JC, January 18, 1995.
20. Joe Grant to JC, September 6, 1934.
21. Karen Hoyle to JC, October 18, 1994
22. Karen Hoyle to JC, October 18, 1994
23. Martin Provenson to Michael Barrier, July 4, 1995.
24. Mary Swanson to JC, October 13, 1994.
25. Maxwell, Florence C., "Codfish and Smorgasbord," *Christian Science Monitor,* November 6, 1948.
26. Hallet, Richard, "Man who Made *Bambi,"* *Portland Sunday Telegram,* 1947.
27. *From Swedish Fairy Tales,* p. 14.

Part Two: Golden Age Inspirations
JOE GRANT AND THE CHARACTER MODEL DEPARTMENT

1. Joe Grant to JC, January 7, 1994.
2. Joe Grant to Michael Barrier, October 14, 1988.
3. Joe Grant to JC, November 11, 1994.
4. Allan, *Walt Disney and Europe: European Influences on the Animated Feature Films of*

Walt Disney, Appendix A.
5. Joe Grant to Michael Barrier, October 14, 1988.
6. Joe Grant to JC, July 24, 1995.
7. Joe Grant to JC, November 11, 1994.
8. Joe Grant to JC, November 11, 1994.
9. Joe Grant to Michael Barrier, October 14, 1988.
10. Joe Grant to JC, September 6, 1994.
11. Joe Grant to JC, November 11, 1994.
12. Robin Allan, "Still is the Story Told," *Storytelling in Animation—The Art of the Animated Image,* Vol. 2, ed. John Canemaker (Los Angeles: American Film Institute, 1988), pp. 83–92.
13. Martin Provensen to Michael Barrier, July 4, 1983.
14. "Walt Disney's Amazing Plaster Models," Bob Jones paper, Walt Disney Archives, May 25, 1989.
15. Frank Thomas and Ollie Johnston, *The Illusion of Life: Disney Animation* (New York: Hyperion, 1995), p. 208.
16. See Charles Solomon, *The Disney That Never Was* (New York: Hyperion, 1996).
17. Joe Grant to JC, July 24, 1995.
18. Campbell Grant to Milton Gray, February 2, 1977.
19. Martin Provensen.
20. Martin Provensen.
21. Campbell Grant.
22. JG to MB, October 14, 1988.
23. Martin Provensen.
24. Ollie Johnston to JC, January 7, 1995.
25. Joe Grant to Michael Barrier.
26. Joe Grant to Robin Allan, August 14, 1986.

JAMES BODRERO

1. Martin Provensen to Michael Barrier, July 4, 1983.
2. Frank Thomas to JC, January 7, 1995.
3. Marc Davis to JC, January 7, 1995.
4. Martin Provensen.
5. *Time,* November 18, 1940. "Disney's Cinesymphony," p. 52.
6. Unless otherwise noted, biographical data is from a c. 1981 written remembrance by Lydia Bodrero Reed of her father and an interview with Mrs. Reed by JC, January 8, 1995.
7. Lydia Reed letter to JC, Jan. 21, 1995.
8. Alice Davis to JC, October 9, 1994.
9. Jim Bodrero to Milton Gray, Jan. 29, 1977.
10. Martin Provensen.
11. Ollie Johnston to JC, January 7, 1995.
12. Jim Bodrero to Milton Gray.
13. Marc Davis to JC, January 7, 1995.
14. Marc Davis to JC, January 7, 1995.
15. *San Francisco Chronicle,* March 2, 1958.
16. Marc Davis to JC, January 7, 1995.

KAY NIELSEN

1. Joe Grant to JC, September 6, 1994 and November 11, 1994.
2. Meyer, Susan E., *A Treasury of the Great Children's Book Illustrators* (New York: Harry N. Abrams, Inc., 1987), p. 195.
3. *Treasury of Children's Book Illustrators,* p. 195.
4. Nicholson, Keith, *Kay Nielsen.* David Larkin, ed. (New York: Bantam, 1975), p. 9.
5. Flanner, Hildegarde, *The Unknown Paintings of Kay Nielsen: An Elegy* (New York: Bantam, 1977).
6. *The Unknown Paintings of Kay Nielsen.*
7. Campbell Grant to Milton Gray, February 2, 1977.
8. Joe Grant to Michael Barrier, October 14, 1988.
9. Joe Grant to JC, September 6, 1994.
10. John Canemaker, "The Fantasia That Never Was." *Print,* January/February 1988, pp. 76–86.
11. *Time,* December 29, 1941, p. 28.
12. Ken Anderson to Milton Gray, December 14, 1976; John Hench confirmed working with Nielsen on *Sleeping Beauty* to the author in a brief meeting at the Disney Studio on July 26, 1995.
13. In his autobiography, *Horizon Bound on a Bicycle,* Earle writes: "Even before *Peter Pan* was finished, Walt hired a Danish artist from Denmark to do the original styling for *Sleeping Beauty.* He must have worked on it for at least a year." No employment records for Kay Nielsen for this period have been found in the Disney Archives.
14. *The Unknown Paintings of Kay Nielsen.*

FANTASTIC *FANTASIA*

1. John Culhane, *Walt Disney's Fantasia* (New York: Abrams, 1983), p. 18.
2. Joe Grant to JC, November 11, 1994.
3. Joe Grant to JC, November 11, 1994.
4. Huemer/UCLA, p. 106.
5. Huemer/UCLA, p. 106.
6. Joe Grant to Michael Barrier, October 14, 1988.
7. Huemer, p. 136.
8. William Moritz, "Fischinger at Disney, or Oskar in the Mousetrap," *Millimeter,* (Vol. 5 #2, February 1977), p. 28.
9. "Fischinger at Disney," p. 66.
10. "Fischinger at Disney," p. 64.
11. David Hilberman letter to JC, October 10, 1994.
12. Joe Grant to Michael Barrier, October 14, 1988.

13. Huemer, p. 154.
14. *Time,* Dec. 29, 1941.
15. Joe Grant to Michael Barrier, October 14, 1988.
16. Joe Grant to JC, November 11, 1994.
17. *Time,* December 29, 1941.
18. Huemer/UCLA, p. 219.
19. Joe Grant to Michael Barrier.
20. Siedman, David, "A Toon Man for the Ages," *Los Angeles Times,* January 19, 1995.
21. Joe Grant to JC, January 7, 1994.
22. Joe Grant to JC, January 7, 1995.

Part Three: Inspired Women
BIANCA MAJOLIE

1. Marc Davis to JC, October 9, 1994.
2. In-house publication, p. 18.
3. *Glamour,* "Girls at Work for Disney," April 1941, p. 50.
4. Thomas, Bob, *The Art of Animation* (New York: Simon and Schuster, 1958), p. 175.
5. In Germany in 1926, however, the independent animation designer/director Lotte Reiniger produced and directed the first full-length animated film using silhouetted figures against multiple background planes, *The Adventures of Prince Achmed,* almost a dozen years before Disney's *Snow White.*
6. *Hollywood Citizen News,* "On the Distaff Side at Walt Disney's." February 23, 1940, p. 14.
7. Bianca Majolie to JC, October 7, 1987. All biographical information is from this letter unless otherwise indicated. All quotes are from telephone interviews between BM and JC as indicated.
8. Walt Disney Archive, BM to WD, February 14, 1935.
9. Jules Engel to JC, February 15, 1988.
10. Frank Thomas and Ollie Johnston, *Too Funny For Words* (New York: Abbeville, 1987), p. 61.
11. *Too Funny for Words,* p. 61.
12. BM to JC, May 3, 1988.
13. KK to Roy Disney, November 24, 1936.
14. KK to RD, November 4, 1937.
15. BM to JC, May 3, 1988.
16. BM to JC, May 3, 1988.
17. BM to JC, May 15, 1988.
18. BM to JC, May 3, 1988.
19. Jules Engel to JC, February 15, 1988.
20. BM to JC, October 7, 1995.
21. *The Bulletin,* in-house Disney publication, November 15, 1940.
22. KO'C to JC, September 26, 1994.
23. BM to JC, April 20, 1988.
24. BM to JC, February 25, 1988.
25. Jules Engel to JC, February 15, 1988.
26. BM to JC, February 25, 1988.

27. BM to JC, September 18, 1987.
28. *Hollywood Magazine,* July 1953.
29. BM to JC, February 25, 1988.
30. BM to JC, May 1, 1991.
31. BM to JC, April 4, 1988.
32. BM to JC, March 24, 1988.
33. BM to JC, November 29, 1987.

SYLVIA MOBERLY-HOLLAND

1. Theo Halliday to JC, December 5, 1987.
2. Walt Disney letter, "To Whom it May Concern" to SM-H, August 11, 1941.
3. Edward H. Plumb letter, "To Whom It May Concern" to SM-H, October 1941.
4. Canemaker, John, "Sylvia Moberly-Holland," animation art catalogue (Burbank: Howard Lowery, 1990), pp. 49–50.
5. "Sylvia Moberly-Holland," pp. 49–50.
6. Story meeting November 22, 1938, Walt Disney Archives.
7. Story conference notes, January 22, 1939—WDA.
8. J. Gordon Legg to JC, April 19, 1989.
9. Story meeting Nov. 25, 1939—WDA.
10. Story meeting July 14, 1939—WDA.
11. J. Gordon Legg to JC.
12. Walt Disney speech to employees February 10, 1941—WDA.
13. "Sylvia Moberly-Holland," p. 50.

MARY BLAIR

1. Roland Crump to JC, January 5, 95.
2. Marc Davis to JC, January 7, 1995.
3. Marc Davis to JC, October 9, 1994.
4. Anderson, Susan M., "California Watercolors 1929–1945," *American Artist* (August 1988), pp. 48–53.
5. Gordon T. McClelland and Jay T. Last, *The California Style* (Beverly Hills: Hilcrest 1985), p. 7 and 9.
6. Anderson, Susan M., pp. 48–53.
7. Marc Davis to JC, January 7, 1995.
8. Note n.d. from MB to LB.
9. Barbara Burklo, "Soquel Artist Proves 'It's A Small World,'" *Santa Cruz Sentinel,* July 25, 1971.
10. Hazel George to JC, January 4, 1995.
11. Pollack, Dale, "They Animated Fantasia," *Santa Cruz Sentinel,* June 20, 1976.
12. Delayed Certificate of Birth, State of Oklahoma June 20, 1942.
13. Jeanne Chamberlain to JC, November 4, 1994.
14. Rudy Lord, "Mary Blair Biographical Sketch," n.d.
15. Jeanne Chamberlain to JC, November 4, 1994.

16. Alice Davis to JC, October 9, 1994.

17. Kevin Blair to JC, August 19, 1994.

18. Robert Perine, *Chouinard: An Art Vision Betrayed,* (Encinitas, CA: Artra, 1985), p. 46.

19. Marc Davis to JC, October 9, 1994.

20. *Chouinard,* p. 45.

21. *Chouinard,* p. 45.

22. Jeanne Chamberlain to JC, November 4, 1994.

23. *Los Angeles Times,* clipping c. 1932.

24. MRB note to LB, n.d., c. 1934.

25. Lee Blair to Nancy Moure, April 13, 1991.

26. Neil Grauer, "An Olympic Work and Its Mysterious Fate," *The Washington Post,* July 29, 1984.

27. Lee Blair to Nancy Moure, April 13, 1991.

28. Mary and Lee Blair to Michael Barrier, October 25, 1976.

29. M and LB to MB, October 25, 1976.

30. Neil Grauer to JC, October 30, 1994.

31. *The Architectural Forum,* March 1940.

32. Neil Grauer to JC, October 30, 1994.

33. Roland Crump to JC, January 5, 1995.

34. Lee Blair to Neil A. Grauer, October 18, 1991.

35. Lee Blair to Nancy Moure, April 13, 1991.

36. Lee Blair to Nancy Moure, April 13, 1991.

37. Roland Crump to JC, January 5, 1995.

38. Mary Blair to Ross Care, February 18, 1977.

39. Ollie Johnston to Michael Lyons, March 20, 1995.

40. Mary Blair to Ross Care, February 18, 1977.

41. Thomas, Bob, *Walt Disney: An American Original* (New York: Simon & Schuster, 1976), p. 173.

42. Bill Cottrell to Bob Thomas, June 6, 1973.

43. Disney Studio/South American itinerary, August 6–October 22, 1941, 28-page document courtesy of Kevin Blair.

44. Ollie Johnston to Michael Lyons.

45. Gaeton Picon, *Modern Painting* (New York: Newsweek Books, 1974), pp. 171–72.

46. Mary Blair to Ross Care, February 18, 1977.

47. Jeanne Chamberlain to JC.

48. Marc Davis to JC, October 9, 1994.

49. Alice Davis to JC, October 9, 1995.

50. *Brooklyn Eagle,* October 22, 1944.

51. Hazel George to JC, January 4, 1995.

52. Hazel George to JC, January 4, 1995.

53. Retta Scott Worcester to Robin Allan, November 1, 1989.

54. *Atlanta Constitution,* October 4, 1944.

55. A small color photo of the artworks within Miranda's living room can be seen in the Brazilian publication *O Cruzeiro,* January 28, 1956.

56. Walt Disney to Lee Blair, December 4, 1945.

57. Bureau of Naval Personnel Annual Qualifications Questionnaire, February 16, 1947.

58. Lou Garnier to JC, September 29, 1994.

59. Lee Blair to Nancy Moure, April 13, 1991.

60. Alice Davis to JC, October 7, 1994.

61. Marc Davis to JC, January 7, 1995.

62. Lee Blair to Nancy Moure, April 13, 1991.

63. Lee Blair to Nancy Moure, April 13, 1991.

64. Kellerman, Vivien, "Country Living 20 Miles From Manhattan," *The New York Times,* May 28, 1995, sec. 9, p. 3.

65. "Mary Blair."

66. Mary Blair to Ross Care, February 18, 1977.

67. *Santa Cruz Sentinel,* June 20, 1976.

68. *Modern Painting,* p. 164.

69. Frank Thomas to JC, January 7, 1995.

70. Ollie Johnston to JC, January 7, 1995.

71. Mary Blair to Ross Care, February 18, 1977.

72. James Bodrero to Milton Gray, January 29, 1977.

73. James Bodrero to Milton Gray, January 29, 1977.

74. Frank Thomas to JC, January 7, 1995.

75. Ben Sharpsteen interview April 26, 1974, Walt Disney Archives.

76. Marc Davis to JC, October 9, 1994.

77. *New York Times Book Review,* February 12, 1950, p. 18.

78. Ernest W. Watson, "Mary Blair," *American Artist* (May 1958, Vol. 22, #5 issue 215), pp. 21–24.

79. Neil Grauer to JC, October 30, 1994.

80. Preston Blair to JC, December 27, 1994.

81. Roland Crump to JC, January 5, 1995.

82. Roland Crump to JC, January 5, 1995.

83. Lou Garnier to JC, September 29, 1994.

84. Debbie Rubin Phillips to JC, January 19, 1995.

85. Lee Blair to Nancy Moure, April 13, 1991.

86. *Chouinard,* p. 142.

87. Neil Grauer to JC, October 30, 1994.

88. Kevin Blair to JC, May 17, 1995.

89. Roland Crump to JC, January 5, 1995.

90. Kevin Blair to JC, August 19, 1994.

91. Neil Grauer to JC, October 30, 1994.

92. Alice Davis to JC, October 9, 1994.

93. Gleason, Gene, "About People—Designer," *New York Herald Tribune,* August 2, 1964.

94. "About People."

95. Ben Sharpsteen interview, WDA, April 26, 1974.

96. Kevin Blair to JC, August 19, 1994.

97. Mary Blair to Ross Care, February 18, 1977.

98. *Variety,* February 15, 1967.

99. Gyo Fujikawa to JC, October 27, 1994.

100. "Soquel Artist Proves 'It's a Small World.' "

101. Mary Blair to Ross Care, February 18, 1977.

102. "Mary Blair Biographical Sketch," n.d.

103. Marc and Alice Davis to JC, October 9, 1994.

104. Alice Davis to JC, October 9, 1994.

105. Kevin Blair to JC, August 19, 1994.

106. *Great Neck Record,* May 29, 1969.

107. Debbie Rubin Phillips to JC, January 19, 1995.

108. Neil Grauer to JC, October 30, 1994.

109. Roland Crump to JC, January 5, 1995.

110. Fred Cline to JC, August 5, 1995.

111. Neil Grauer to JC, October 24, 1990.

112. Neil Grauer to JC, October 30, 1994.

113. Neil Grauer to JC, October 30, 1994.

114. Kevin Blair to JC, May 17, 1995.

Part Four: Inspiring Eclecticism
TYRUS WONG

1. TW to JC, Nov. 12, 1994. All Wong's quotes are from this interview unless otherwise indicated.

2. Frank Thomas and Ollie Johnston, *Bambi: The Story and the Film* (New York: Stewart, Tabori and Chang, 1990), p. 152.

3. *Bambi,* p. 166.

4. *Bambi,* p. 152.

5. *Bambi,* p. 125.

6. E. H. Gombrich, *The Story of Art* (London: Phaidon, 1972), p. 111.

7. Huemer/UCLA, p. 194.

8. *Bambi,* pp. 151–52.

9. Wong was released from Disney on September 12, 1941.

10. Wong retired from Warners on February 23, 1968.

DAVID HALL

1. Obituaries: *Los Angeles Times,* July 26, 1964, *Hollywood Reporter,* July 27, 1964, *Variety,* July 28, 1964.

2. Lewis Carroll, *Alice's Adventures in Wonderland.* Afterword by Brian Sibley. (New York: Little Simon, 1986), p. 153.

3. *Alice's Adventures,* 139.

4. Frank Thomas and Ollie Johnston, *Bambi: The Story and the Film* (New York: Stewart, p. 131.

5. Tyrus Wong to JC, Nov. 12, 1994.

6. JG to JC, September 6, 1994.

7. *Alice's Adventures,* afterword (Tabori and Chang, 1990), p. 154.

8. BS to JC, February 7, 1995.

9. *Alice's Adventures,* afterword, p. 154

EYVIND EARLE

1. Earle, Eyvind,. *Horizon Bound on a Bicycle* (Earle and Bane, Los Angeles, 1990), p. 235.
2. *Horizon,* 236.
3. Ken Anderson to Milton Gray, December 14, 1976.
4. Frank Thomas and Ollie Johnston, *The Illusion of Life: Disney Animation,* p. 512.
5. Ken Anderson to Michael Barrier, December 7, 1990.
6. *Horizon,* p. 239.
7. Charles Solomon to JC, June 27, 1995.
8. EE to JC, June 29, 1995.
9. EE to JC, June 29, 1995.
10. EE to JC, June 29, 1995.
11. KO'C to JC, September 26, 1994.
12. *Horizon,* p. 17.
13. *Horizon,* pp. 254 and 30.
14. *Eyvind Earle—Seventy Five Years.* Exhibition brochure. Tamara Bane Gallery, Los Angeles, April 26, 1991, p. 4.
15. *Horizon,* p. 52.
16. *Horizon,* p. 181.
17. *Horizon,* p. 231.
18. *Horizon,* p. 231.
19. *Horizon,* p. 231.
20. *Horizon,* p. 232.
21. *Horizon,* pp. 233–34.
22. *Horizon,* p. 234.
23. *Horizon,* p. 235.
24. Vance Gerry to JC, July 26, 1995.
25. *Horizon,* p. 234.
26. *Horizon,* p. 234.
27. KO'C to JC, September 26, 1994.
28. Horizon, p. 233.
29. *Disney Animation,* p. 511.
30. *Horizon,* p. 239.
31. J. Gordon Legg to Milton Gray, March 13, 1976.
32. Schickel, Richard, *The Disney Version* (New York: Simon and Schuster, 1968), p. 299.
33. Solomon, Charles, *Enchanted Drawings* (New York: Alfred A. Knopf 1989), p. 200.
34. *Disney Animation,* pp. 511 and 512.
35. Victor J. Hammer, foreword, Hammer Galleries brochure, "Eyvind Earle—Recent Paintings," November 20–December 1, 1979.
36. *Horizon,* p. 268.
37. *Horizon,* p. 307.

KEN ANDERSON

1. Ken Anderson to Milton Gray, December 14, 1976.
2. Paul F. Anderson to JC, July 11, 1995.
3. KA to Michael Barrier, December 7, 1990.
4. Frank Thomas to JC, January 7, 1995.
5. Frank Thomas to JC, January 7, 1995.
6. "Disney Personalities," *Storyboard/The Art of Laughter,* August–September 1992, p. 32.
7. Paul F. Anderson to JC, July 11, 1995.
8. Robin Allan, "In Memory of Ken Anderson: Disney Artist," *Animator,* Spring 1994, p. 2
9. "In Memory of Ken Anderson," p. 2.
10. "In Memory of Ken Anderson," p. 2.
11. "In Memory of Ken Anderson," p. 2.
12. Polly Anderson to JC, January 6, 1995.
13. "An Interview with Ken Anderson," *Storyboard/The Art of Laughter,* August/September 1991, p. 13.
14. KA to Bob Thomas, May 15, 1973.
15. PA to JC, July 11, 1995.
16. Jack Kinney, p. 33.
17. *Storyboard/The Art of Laughter,* p. 13.
18. KA to Milton Gray, December 14, 1976.
19. KA to Milton Gray, December 14, 1976.
20. KA to Bob Thomas, May 15, 1973.
21. KA to Bob Thomas, May 15, 1973.
22. Robin Allan, *Animator,* Spring 1994, p. 2.
23. KA to Milton Gray, December 14, 1976.
24. PFA to JC, July 11, 1995.
25. FT to JC, January 7, 1995.
26. KA to Milton Gray, December 14, 1976.
27. KA to Milton Gray, December 14, 1976.
28. Layout Training Course Notes, November 27, 1936.
29. KA to Bob Thomas, May 15, 1973.
30. KA to Bob Thomas, May 15, 1973.
31. JGL to Milton Gray, March 13, 1976.
32. KA to Milton Gray, December 14, 1976.
33. KA to Bob Thomas, May 15, 1973.
34. "Walt Disney's Haunted House—An Interview with Ken Anderson," *The "E" Ticket,* Summer 1992, p. 4.
35. MD to JC, January 7, 1995.
36. Roland Crump to JC, January 5, 1995.
37. KA to Milton Gray, December 14, 1976.
38. Paul F. Anderson to JC, July 11, 1995.
39. KA to Milton Gray, December 14, 1976.
40. KA to Michael Barrier, December 7, 1990.
41. KA to Michael Barrier, December 7, 1990.
42. KA to Milton Gray, December 14, 1976.
43. KA to Michael Barrier, December 7, 1990.
44. Robin Allan to JC, July 21, 1994.
45. KA to Michael Barrier, December 7, 1990.
46. Robin Allan, *Animator,* Spring 1994, p. 2.
47. KA to Michael Barrier, December 7, 1990.
48. KA to Michael Barrier, December 7, 1990.

Part Five: New Age Inspirations

1. Tom Schumacher to JC, July 25, 1995.
2. Mike Gabriel to JC, July 25, 1995.
3. Michael Giaimo to JC, July 26, 1995.
4. Glen Keane to JC, July 27, 1995.
5. Andy Gaskill to JC, July 24, 1995.
6. Hans Bacher to JC, July 26, 1995.
7. Bruce Zick to JC, July 26, 1995.
8. Chris Sanders, July 26, 1995.
9. Vance Gerry to JC, July 26, 1995.
10. Joe Grant to JC, July 24, 1995

SELECTED BIBLIOGRAPHY

Allan, Robin. "The Artists of Disney." *Manchester Memoirs.* Manchester: The Manchester Literary and Philosophical Society, 128 (1990), 91–106.

———. "Fifty Years of 'Snow White'." *Journal of Popular Film and Television,* 15 (1988), 156–163.

———. "Make Mine Disney." *Animator,* April 19–June 1987, 28–31.

———. "Still Is the Story Told." *Storytelling in Animation: The Art of the Animated Image.* Vol. 2. Ed. John Canemaker. Los Angeles: The American Film Institute, 2 (1988), 83–92.

———. "Time for Melody." *Animator,* August 27, 1990, 9–12.

———. *Walt Disney and Europe: European Influences on the Animated Feature Films of Walt Disney.* University of Exeter thesis. April 1993.

Anderson, Susan M. "California Watercolors 1929–1945," *American Artist* (August 1988), pp. 48–53.

———, and Robert Henning Jr., et al., comps. *Regionalism: The California View. Watercolors 1929–1945.* Santa Barbara: Santa Barbara Museum of Art, 1988.

Belazs, Bela. *Theory of Film.* New York: Dover, 1970.

Bendazzi, Giannalberto. *Cartoons: One Hundred Years of Cinema Animation.* Bloomington and Indianapolis: Indiana University Press, 1994.

Canemaker, John. "The Abstract Films of Oskar Fischinger." *Print,* 37 (March–April 1983), 66–72.

———. *The Animated Raggedy Ann & Andy.* New York: Bobbs-Merrill, 1977.

———. *Dreams in Motion: The Art of Winsor McCay.* Catalogue. Katonah, New York: Katonah Gallery, 1988.

———. "The 'Fantasia' That Never Was." *Print,* 42 (1988), 76–87, 139–140.

———. *Felix: The Twisted Tale of the World's Most Famous Cat.* New York: Pantheon Books, 1991.

———. "Sylvia Moberly-Holland." Catalogue. *Animation Art.* Burbank: Howard Lowery, August 5, 1990, 49–50.

———. *Treasures of Disney Animation Art.* New York: Abbeville, 1982.

———. *Vladimir Tytla: Master Animator.* Catalogue. Katonah, New York: Katonah Museum of Art, 1994.

———. *Winsor McCay: His Life and Art.* New York: Abbeville, 1987.

Cochran, Ross. *Horvath, Ferdinand H.* Catalogue. West Plains, MO: c.1985.

Crafton, Donald. *Before Mickey: The Animated Film 1898–1928.* Cambridge, Massachusetts: MIT Press, 1982.

———. *Emile Cohl, Caricature and Film.* Princeton: Princeton University Press, 1990.

Culhane, John. *Walt Disney's Fantasia.* New York: Abrams, 1983.

Drawing into Film—Director's Drawings. Exhibition catalogue. The Pace Gallery, New York. March 26–April 24, 1993.

Earle, Eyvind. *Horizon Bound on a Bicycle.* (Los Angeles: Earle and Bane, 1990).

Feild, Robert D. *The Art of Walt Disney.* New York: Macmillan, 1942.

Finch, Christopher. *The Art of Walt Disney.* New York: Abrams, 1973.

Flanner, Hildegarde. *The Unknown Paintings of Kay Nielsen.* New York: Bantam, 1977.

Hurter, Albert. *He Drew As He Pleased.* Intr. Ted Sears. New York: Simon and Schuster, 1948.

Kley, Heinrich. *The Drawings of Heinrich Kley.* New York: Dover, 1961.

Kinney, Jack. *Walt Disney and Other Assorted Characters.* New York: Harmony, 1988.

Meyer, Susan E. *A Treasury of the Great Children's Book Illustrators.* New York: Abrams, 1987.

Moritz, William. "The Films of Oskar Fischinger." *Film Culture,* No. 58-59-60 (1974), 37–188.

Perine, Robert. *Chouinard: An Art Vision Betrayed.* Encinitas, CA: Artra, 1985.

Picon, Gaeton. *Modern Painting.* New York: Newsweek Books, 1974.

Smith, David R. "The Sorcerer's Apprentice: Birthplace of 'Fantasia.' " *Millimeter,* 3 (1975), 38–45.

Solomon, Charles. *Enchanted Drawings: The History of Animation.* New York: Knopf, 1989.

———. *The Disney That Never Was.* New York: Hyperion, 1995.

Swanson, Mary. *From Swedish Fairy Tales to American Fantasy: Gustaf Tenggren's Illustrations 1920–1970.* Minneapolis: University of Minnesota Art Museum, 1987.

Thomas, Bob. *Walt Disney: An American Original.* New York: Simon and Schuster, 1976.

———. *The Art of Animation.* New York: Golden Press, 1958.

Thomas, Frank and Ollie Johnston. *Disney Animation: The Illusion of Life.* New York: Abbeville, 1981.

———. *Too Funny for Words.* Abbeville Press, 1987.

———. *Walt Disney's Bambi.* New York: Stewart, Tabori and Chang, 1990.

Watts, Steven. "Walt Disney: Art and Politics in the American Century." *The Journal of American History.* Vol. 82, No. 1 (June 1995), 84–110.

———. *The Magic Kingdom: Walt Disney and Modern American Culture.* New York: Basic Books, forthcoming.

Women and Animation. Ed. Jayne Pilling. London: British Film Institute, 1992.

INDEX

207

ACKNOWLEDGMENTS

During this project, considerable kindness and generous assistance were offered to me, beginning with Kay Salz, current Director of Animation Resources at Warner Bros Feature Animation. In her former capacity as Manager of the Disney Animation Resource Library (ARL), it was Kay who suggested that the subject of Disney inspirational art and artists was worthy of a full-length book and encouraged me to write it.

During my initial research at the ARL, Kay and her associates—Susie Lee, Doug Engalla, Ariel Levin, Teresa Grenot, and especially Lawrence Ishino and Tamara N. Khalaf—helped me wade through a sea of artwork, organizing it in a way that greatly aided my research and preserved my sanity. These high professional standards have continued under Lella Smith, the new ARL Manager, who has also been a delight to work with.

At the Walt Disney Archives, I am particularly thankful to archivist Robert Tieman, an invaluable ally who, with patience and enthusiasm, sought out and put at my disposal many hidden art treasures and considerable data. Also at the archives, I was warmly received and helped by Becky Cline, Collette Espino, and, finally, David R. Smith, Director and Founder of the Disney Archives, whom it has been my pleasure and good fortune to work with on various projects for over two decades. At the Disney Photo Library, Ed Squair offered considerable professional support; Jill Centeno and Randy Webster of Walt Disney Imagineering were also most helpful.

This book would not have been possible without the full cooperation of Walt Disney Feature Animation, and I am grateful for the openness with which I was received at the Studio by Thomas Schumacher, Senior Vice President, Peter Schneider, President, and Roy E. Disney. Daniel Jones organized my interviews with the current Disney concept artists and gathered their artwork with exceptional skill. As always, my friends Howard E. and Amy Green generously gave me their warm support and hospitality, even providing a home away from home during one research trip.

I have been extremely moved by the generosity of fellow animation historians who shared with me their invaluable research; I have benefited from special access to the interviews and insights of Robin Allan, Michael Barrier, Paul F. Anderson, Albert M. Miller, Brian Sibley, William Moritz, Jerry Beck, Neil A. Grauer, Tom Andrae, John Culhane, Pierre Lambert, Peter Hossli, Steven Watts, and Charles Solomon, scholar/author in residence at the Disney Studio.

I am deeply indebted to Carol Covington, Martin Collins, and Elizabeth Leonard for access to material on Ferdinand Horvath, to Lydia Reed for her candid remembrances of her father, James Bodrero, and to Kevin Blair for his candor, generosity, and support in sending me correspondence and documents concerning the art and lives of his parents, Lee and Mary Blair.

For many courtesies, support, and kindness, I am thankful to Harry F. Bliss; Curtice Taylor; Tissa David; Kenneth Hirsch, M.D.; Cynthia Allen; Bob Links of the Color Express; Holly Howland; Beth Howland; Charles Kimbrough; and Maxime La Fantasie of the John Canemaker Animation Collection, Fales Section of the New York University Bobst Library.

For illustrations from private collections, my heartfelt thanks to Howard and Paula Lowery of the Howard Lowery Gallery in Burbank, Michael Glad, Mark Mitchell, Jeff Lotman, Miriam and Stuart Reisbord of Cartoon Carnival Gallery, Theo Halladay, Paul Jenkins, Adrienne and Peter Tytla, Frances M. Ingersoll and Dana Hawkes of Sotheby's New York, Elyse Luray-Marx of Christie's East, and Robert Henning, Jr., of the Santa Barbara Museum of Art.

I wish to express my sincere gratitude to a number of individuals who gave generously of their time, memories, insights, and document collections: Frank Thomas; Ollie Johnston; Marc F. and Alice Davis; Ward Kimball; Roland Crump; David Hilberman; Mary Alice and A. Kendall O'Connor; Marge Champion; Polly Anderson; Bruce Abrams; Del Connell; William Cottrell; Karen Hoyle; Mary T. Swanson; Svea Macek; Mary Anderson; Bianca Majolie Heilborn; Carol Hannaman; Tyrus Wong; Joe Grant; Preston Blair; Lee Blair; Jeanne Chamberlain; Fred Cline; Lou Garnier; Gordon T. McClelland; Robert Perine; Nancy D.W. Moure; Gyo Fujikawa; Rudy Lord; Richard F. Gilman; Hazel George; Polly Anderson; Eyvind Earle; John Hench; Alice Provensen; Faith Hubley; Becky, Carla L., and Carl Fallberg; Art Wood; Nancy Starosky; Ross Care; Tom Sito; Richard Taylor of Gifted Images; Vance Gerry; Hans Bacher; Chris Sanders; Michael Giaimo; Mike Gabriel; Sara Petty; Andy Gaskill; Bruce Zick; Tim O'Day and Wayne Smith of Disney Art Editions; Fabiano Canosa; Ibere de Souza Magnani, Director of the Carmen Miranda Museum; Aurora Miranda; Faye Thompson, Coordinator Special Collections, Margaret Herrick Library; Jere Guldin, UCLA Film and Television Archives; and Sheila Saxby.

As always, I am grateful to my best friend and critic Joseph J. Kennedy for reading the manuscript and offering excellent comments and suggestions.

I gratefully acknowledge the continuing support of my literary agent, Robert Cornfield; and offer a sincere thank you to Holly McNeely, the book's super designer, and to the folks at Hyperion: Robert Miller, David Cashion, Lesley Krauss, Claudyne Bianco Bedell, David Lott, Linda Prather, Audra Zaccaro, and especially my fine editor, Richard P. Kot.

About the

Author

John Canemaker
is an internationally recognized animator and animation historian. He designed and directed animation sequences in the Peabody Award–winning CBS documentary *Break the Silence—Kids Against Child Abuse,* and the Academy Award–winning HBO documentary *You Don't Have to Die.* His award-winning short films include *Confessions of a Stardreamer, Confessions of a Stand-up, Bottom's Dream,* and *John Lennon Sketchbook.*

Canemaker has written over 100 essays, reviews, and articles on animation for periodicals, such as *The New York Times, The Los Angeles Times,* and *Time* and *Print* magazines. His books include *The Animated Raggedy Ann and Andy* (Bobbs-Merrill), *Treasures of Disney Animation Art* (Abbeville), *Winsor McCay—His Art and Life* (Abbeville), and *Felix—The Twisted Tale of the World's Most Famous Cat* (Pantheon). He is a tenured professor and head of the film animation program at New York University Tisch School of the Arts. The John Canemaker Animation Collection, an archival resource on animation history, opened to scholars and students in 1989 as part of the Fales Collection in Bobst Library at New York University. Canemaker has lectured on the art of animation and its artists throughout the United States and in Brazil, Canada, England, France, Italy, Japan, Spain, Slovakia, and Switzerland. He divides his time between Manhattan and Bridgehampton, Long Island.